THE
OWL
KILLERS

Karen Maitland travelled and worked in many parts of the United Kingdom before finally settling in the beautiful medieval city of Lincoln. She is the author of *The White Room*, which was shortlisted for the Authors' Club Best First Novel Award, and *Company of Liars*, which is available as a Penguin paperback.

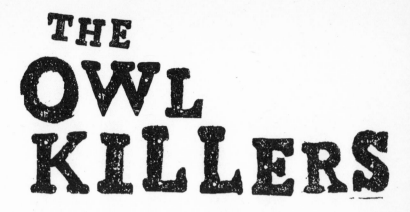

THE OWL KILLERS

KAREN MAITLAND

MICHAEL JOSEPH
an imprint of
PENGUIN BOOKS

MICHAEL JOSEPH

Published by the Penguin Group

Penguin Books Ltd, 80 Strand, London WC2R ORL, England

Penguin Group (USA) Inc., 375 Hudson Street, New York, New York 10014, USA

Penguin Group (Canada), 90 Eglinton Avenue East, Suite 700, Toronto, Ontario, Canada M4P 2Y3
(a division of Pearson Penguin Canada Inc.)

Penguin Ireland, 25 St Stephen's Green, Dublin 2, Ireland (a division of Penguin Books Ltd)

Penguin Group (Australia), 250 Camberwell Road, Camberwell, Victoria 3124, Australia
(a division of Pearson Australia Group Pty Ltd)

Penguin Books India Pvt Ltd, 11 Community Centre, Panchsheel Park, New Delhi – 110 017, India

Penguin Group (NZ), 67 Apollo Drive, Rosedale, North Shore 0632, New Zealand
(a division of Pearson New Zealand Ltd)

Penguin Books (South Africa) (Pty) Ltd, 24 Sturdee Avenue,
Rosebank, Johannesburg 2196, South Africa

Penguin Books Ltd, Registered Offices: 80 Strand, London WC2R ORL, England

www.penguin.com

First published 2009
1

Set in Monotype Garamond
Typeset by Rowland Phototypesetting Ltd, Bury St Edmunds, Suffolk
Printed in England by Clays Ltd, St Ives plc

Hardback: 978–0–718–15320–5
Trade paperback: 978–0–718–15321–2

www.greenpenguin.co.uk

Penguin Books is committed to a sustainable future
for our business, our readers and our planet.
The book in your hands is made from paper
certified by the Forest Stewardship Council.

Tell proud Jove,
Between his power and thine there is no odds.
'Twas only fear first in the world made gods.

Ben Jonson, English dramatist,
Sejanus (1603)

We do not know how strong we are until we
are attacked by the evil of this world.

Mechthild of Magdeburg,
beguine from 1230 to 1270

Cast of Characters

The Beguinage

Servant Martha – Flemish leader of the beguines.
Healing Martha – Elderly physician and **Servant Martha**'s oldest friend.
Merchant Martha – Sharp-tongued trader for the beguinage.
Gate Martha – Dour local beguine.
Kitchen Martha – Flemish cook.
Beatrice – Flemish beguine.
Pega – Local beguine, giantess and ex-prostitute.
Catherine – Teenage local beguine.

The Manor

Agatha/Osmanna – Youngest of **Robert D'Acaster**'s three daughters.
Robert D'Acaster – Lord of the Manor and father of **Agatha** and her twin elder sisters, **Anne** and **Edith**.
Phillip D'Acaster – **Lord Robert**'s nephew and steward.

The Village of Ulewic

Father Ulfrid – Parish priest.
Giles – Villein and his aged mother, **Ellen**.
John – Village blacksmith.
Lettice – Elderly widow and village gossip.
Aldith – Mother to little son **Oliver**.

1st Family

Pisspuddle – Village child.
William – **Pisspuddle**'s tormenting older brother.
Alan – Father of **Pisspuddle** and **William**.

2nd Family

Ralph – Father of **Marion** and her two brothers.
Joan – **Ralph**'s wife.

Outsiders

Old Gwenith – Local healer and cunning-woman.
Gudrun – **Old Gwenith**'s granddaughter.
Andrew – Young female anchorite.
Franciscan friar – Friend and protector to the anchorite, **Andrew**.
Bishop's Commissarius – Envoy from the Bishop of Norwich.
Hilary – Friend of **Father Ulfrid**.

Anno Domini 1321 – Prologue

Giles knew they'd come for him, sooner or later. He didn't know where or when, he didn't know what his punishment would be, but he knew that there would be one. A dead owl had been left in front of his door in the middle of the night. He hadn't heard them leave it, you never did. But at daybreak, when he had left his cottage to work in the Manor's fields, he had found it there, sodden from the night's rain, their sign, their warning.

He had buried the owl quickly, before his mother could see it. He didn't want her to know what was coming. She was too old and frail, had seen too many tragedies in her life to bear the strain of yet another. But from then on he had waited, waited for a hood to be thrown over him from behind as he pissed against a tree, waited for a quarterstaff to crack down on the back of his head as he walked down the track, waited to be dragged from his bed in the night. They might take him from the forest or from the tavern or from the church. They might take him in the early morning or in the evening or in the middle of the day. However much you stayed on your guard, some-where, at some hour, the Owl Masters would find you. All you could do was wait.

He had thought about running, of course he had. He'd come close to doing it more than once. But a villein could not leave without his lord's consent, and even if, by some miracle, he did make it safely to a town where he could lie low for a year until he was declared a free man, he knew they would take revenge on his mother, and if they didn't, Lord D'Acaster surely would.

But it had been weeks now since the dead owl had been left at Giles's door, and when the sun was shining, he was able to convince himself that the Owl Masters wouldn't come after all.

He knew he had been a fool to bed the maid when D'Acaster had given his permission for her to wed another. But the girl was married now and they had not been near each other since. Wasn't their separation punishment enough? He tried to tell himself the Owl Masters would be satisfied with that, but in the long dark hours of night, as he lay awake tensing at every sound, he knew in his guts they would not.

And now, tonight, they were finally here, crowded into the tiny room, their faces hidden behind their feathered owl masks, their clothes concealed beneath long brown cloaks. For an instant he was almost relieved, almost wanted them to get it over with, but then blind fear seized him and it was all he could do to stop himself falling to his knees and howling for mercy.

His mother was standing in front of him trying to shield him, as she had often stood between him and his bellowing father when he was a small boy. Then he had cowered behind her skirts, but now he gently moved her aside. Better he push her away than them. He could do it tenderly; they would not, and he didn't want to hear her old bones crack. Listening to her sobs was bad enough.

'Please, sirs, please don't take him. He's all I've got. I'll starve without him. Merciful heaven have pity ... take me instead. I don't care what you do to me, but don't hurt him, I beg you.' Her swollen, twisted fingers grasped Giles's sleeve as if she could physically wrest him from their grasp.

'Don't fret yourself, old woman. We've just got a small task we want him to perform, something that'll make his dear old mother proud.'

The old woman stared frantically from one to the other of the men towering over her, trying to make out which of them was speaking, but it was impossible to tell for their mouths were hidden by the masks and their voices distorted. With all her strength she tried to force herself between Giles and the Owl Master who was gripping him, but the man lashed out with the back of his hand, catching the old woman across the mouth and sending her crashing against the wattle wall of the cottage.

Giles, twisting himself free, ran to kneel over her, his hand braced against the wall as he tried to shield her with his own body.

'Is this your ancient code of justice,' he demanded, 'beating defenceless women?'

Too late, he glimpsed a flash of metal. A sharp iron talon stabbed into his hand, impaling it to the wall. Giles screamed. Blood streamed down his wrist and dripped into his mother's lap. Four pairs of eyes buried deep within the feathers of the owl masks watched impassively as he writhed and sobbed.

Finally, one of the Owl Masters wrenched the talon out and dragged Giles to his feet. 'Next time, it will be your eyes, boy. And after that you'll not be able to see where we are about to strike.'

Giles, trembling with pain, allowed himself to be led to the low door.

'You'll see your son tomorrow, old woman, at the May Day Fair. In fact, he'll have the place of honour. Now, you go on back to your bed and see you keep your door shut and your mouth too.'

Giles knew his mother did not need to be told to hold her tongue. No one in those parts needed to be told that. As they dragged him out into the darkness, he glanced back at her. She stood in the dim yellow light of the solitary rush candle, tears streaming down her wrinkled cheeks, her hands clenched against her mouth. Even grieving must be done in silence. And as Giles prayed more fervently than he had ever done in his life for a miracle that would save him, a despairing voice inside him told him that miracles did not happen, not for him, not in Ulewic.

✝

May Eve 1321 – First Night of Beltane

First kindling of the Bel-fire, the fire of light. On this night the ancient blue ice goddess, Cailleach Bhear, the old woman of darkness, who reigns from Samhain to Beltane, throws her staff under a holly bush and is turned to stone.

Beatrice

I thought I heard a man dying in the great forest tonight, but now I'm not so certain; maybe what I heard was a corpse rising to life. He was shrieking and pleading, but he wasn't begging for mercy. He'd challenged death to wrestle with him. He'd thrown back his head and demanded to suffer as if he wanted the demons to do their worst and drag him down into the pit of hell. If he was human, then he must have been mad. Staring at the moon can make you run mad, did you know that? And tonight the moon was round as a woman's belly swollen with child. That's when men should fear it most.

I can't ever tell the other women what I saw, not even Pega. How could I explain to them what I was doing out there alone in the forest at midnight? I'm not a lunatic, if that's what you're thinking, not like that madman. Unlike him, I hadn't gone into the woods trying to get myself killed, though I realized the dangers only too well. God alone knows how many deadly creatures slither and prowl through those ancient groves. Venomous adders, wild boar, savaging wolves, even a stag in rut could kill you. And if the beasts are not terrible enough, there are the cutpurses and the outlaws who prey on any stranger wandering into their domain.

Pega, though she's taller than any man alive, won't set foot in the forest after dark. None of the village women will. They say the hungry ghosts, slipping like mist between the trees, will devour you if you should chance to step upon the spot where someone once died. And over the centuries, hundreds of people must have died in the forests and left no mark.

So do you really believe I wasn't afraid to go into those woods that night? I tell you, I'd had to gather up every shard of courage I had, but what else could I do? Jack-in-the-green must be gathered when the moon is fully ripe, for only then does the herb have the strength to bring back a woman's fertility. I dared not ask for any from the infirmary. We are celibate, that is the rule, and why should a celibate woman want to restore her child-bearing years? But I do, I must.

The moon floated yellow and round above the tops of the trees, pouring light down over the branches, petrifying leaf and branch to bleached bone. I started violently at every squeak and cry, forcing myself to keep walking further and further into the trees. I could not turn back empty-handed. Jack-in-the-green is always hard to find by sunlight or moonlight. Devil's Prick, Pega calls it. The herb loves the dark, damp places among the tree roots and its spotted leaves easily conceal themselves.

I knew I must be near the river. I could hear the sound of water thundering over the rocks. I turned away, knowing that the herb would not be growing near the water's edge, preferring the deep shade of the forest. Then I saw it as if the moon herself had parted the bush with her white fingers and revealed the pale sheath. I knelt in the damp mould, and was reaching for my knife to dig at the roots, when I heard a new sound. This was not an animal grunt. It was a man's voice.

My heart thumping, I scrambled up as quietly as I could. With my back pressed against the rough tree trunk for protection and my knife grasped tightly in my hand, I peered round trying to see where the voice was coming from, but I could see no one. Did the hungry ghosts speak before they pounced?

Treading as lightly as I could, I tried to edge away in the opposite direction from where I'd heard the sound. I listened, holding my breath, but there were no footsteps following me. Perhaps the voice had just been in my head. I crept softly on, praying my footfall would not crack a twig and I wouldn't stumble, betraying my presence.

I had come to the edge of a clearing. A lake of quicksilver seemed to spread out at my feet. It lapped around the base of a great hollow oak tree in the centre of the glade. The oak's trunk was so massive that it would have taken half a dozen men or more to encircle it. The hollow inside the oak was as dark as a crypt, for even though it must have been open to the sky above, not a single ray of moonlight appeared to penetrate it.

Suddenly I heard the voice again. It was coming from somewhere in front of me. Instead of escaping from the danger, I had stumbled straight towards it.

The blood of the white stag I pour out to Yandil, lord of the underworld. Let it be as my blood. Drink.

The voice rang out no more than a few yards from me, but the clearing was deserted. Despite the chill of the night, my hands were sticky with sweat and my heart began to pound so violently that I thought it would burst through my chest. I wanted to run, but I was too scared to move in case I was seen.

The flesh of the white stag I lay bare for Taranis, lord of this forest. Let it be as my flesh. Eat.

I clung to the trunk of a tree and stood shaking, knowing that if I let go, my legs would give way beneath me. Then I saw something moving; a black shadow was creeping across the silvered ground towards me, and it wasn't human. A long narrow snout and a pair of branched horns grew out from its chest, and four or five long tails swung from its back. It seemed to be slithering straight towards the place where I stood. It was lengthening and reaching out to me. I shut my eyes tightly, trying not to scream.

The spirit of the white stag I offer up to Rantipole, lord of the air. Let it be as my spirit. Devour it.

I opened my eyes, still not daring to move. The creature was standing facing the open hollow of the tree. It had its back to me and now, as the moonlight fell full upon it, I could make sense of the nightmare I saw. It was no monster. It was a man, tall and powerfully built. Over his shoulder swung the hide of a stag with the horned head still attached. The beast was freshly slaughtered and the heat was still rising from the skin into the cold night air. I could see the blood glistening wetly in the starlight. I could smell it.

I am come to the doorway of the three realms. Give me leave to enter. Ka!

The man pulled off his hood and tossed it aside. Then he lifted the head of the stag and placed it on top of his own head. The blood dripped down over his hair and skin. He caught the two sides of the hide and wrapped the steaming skin around himself, like a cloak. As he raised his head, the antlers reared upwards as if he was challenging the moon.

'Hear me, Taranis, lord of destruction, a great wrong has been done to you and to us your servants. Once your creature, your creation of despair and darkness, ruled this place. This valley was named for him. Your demon brought death to all who defied you in this world and torment in the world beyond. Every man learned to fear him and in their fear they turned to you and to us your servants. But a century ago, on the eve of Samhain, the women came to this doorway. They could not kill your demon, but they sent him into the twilight time, the place of the shadows, where the days pass unnumbered and the years pass unmarked.

'This night I enter the doorway to seek the knowledge that will call the demon forth again. Others have dared to brave the stag's hide before me, but they perished before cockcrow, for they were not strong enough to bear your test and you destroyed them for their weakness.

'This night the hag Cailleach dies. This night Cernunnos, lord of fertility, is born. I have hunted. I have slain. I have taken his sign and his strength. As he is reborn this night, so shall I be.'

The man raised his great arms, fists clenched, and bellowed up at the stars.

'Taranis, lord of the night, grant me the knowledge to summon your creation, the power to call him forth, and the strength to control what is raised from the darkness! *Ka!*'

The man bowed his head and in one swift movement had ducked into the black hollow of the bull oak.

I stared at the place where the man had disappeared, too horrified by what I'd heard to move. Silence flooded back across the clearing. The trees shivered, holding their breath. Suddenly, as panic seized me, my legs started to move. They were trembling too much for me to run and I had only managed to stagger a few paces away when I heard a loud rustling behind me, as if a violent wind had sprung up and was whirling the dry leaves, except that there was no breeze. I couldn't help myself, I had to turn. I had to look back.

The floor of the clearing was still bathed in the ghost light, but it was no longer still and silent. Everywhere I looked the ground was heaving. The leaf mould and newly sprouting plants were being pushed up as if a thousand moles were all trying to burrow their way to the surface at once. The mounds rose higher and higher, until they burst open, and insects began to pour out of them; beetles, worms, centipedes, engorged spiders and great white maggots, all the creatures that feed upon the dead were crawling up from the dirt and into the moonlight.

It was impossible to see the ground for every inch of it was writhing with the bloated insects and all of them were scuttling towards the great bull oak. The wings of the beetles clicked and rattled as they swarmed around the trunk towards the black maw. From inside the hollow I heard the man gasp as creatures began to slither into the oak tree where he lay.

Then, as the vast tide of insects swarmed over the bark and crawled into the hollow, the man's moans gave way to a great cry of defiance and pain.

I give my blood, Yandil, I give you my . . . blood!

And from inside the cavernous hollow, his cry rose to shriek upon shriek of agony as if all the creatures of the grave were feeding on him, stripping his living flesh to the bare bone.

May Day

The second of the three Beltane Fire Days and St Walburga's Day. Walburga was born in the Kingdom of Wessex, England, in the eighth century. She became the abbess in charge of the double monastery of Heidenheim, Germany, ruling over both monks and nuns.

Agatha

Excited barking jerked me awake. Every hound in the Manor was yelping and no wonder, for it sounded as if the hunt in full cry was thundering past our gates. I ran to the casement and looked down. Though it was barely light, the track beyond the Manor was crammed with outlanders jostling into Ulewic for the fair. Carts rumbled over stones. Tiny girls shooed great flocks of hissing geese. Old crones dragged bleating calves on long ropes, tangling them round the legs of the pedlars who struggled under the weight of their bulging packs.

In the long, heavy ox-wagons women squatted among kegs and bales, chattering and singing. Children ran alongside, hitching rides on the back and squealing with laughter when the wagon juddered over ruts. Young men scrambled across the ditches to the banks where the primroses bloomed, tossing handfuls of flowers to the giggling girls in the carts and snatching kisses from them as they hung over the sides. I longed to be in one of those carts, having a boy fill my lap with primroses. But I knew no one would ever try to snatch a kiss from me.

I was dressed hours before the rest of the family and paced impatiently up and down the great hall, desperate to be out there among the crowds. But my mother and sisters insisted on every pleat of their veils being pinned evenly. I think they did it on purpose to keep everyone waiting, knowing the May Fair could not begin without us, for my father, Lord Robert D'Acaster, owned the charter.

And it was my father who finally led the procession of our family and servants through Ulewic towards the Green. He strutted ahead with his fat legs wide apart, like a little boy who'd wet his breeches. Despite the chill of the day his fleshy face was already flushed and sweating with exertion. My mother dragged on his arm, walking with her eyes downcast as if she was afraid of what she might see. My twin sisters, Anne and Edith, followed her, clinging to each other demurely hand in hand. No one would ever think we were related.

I looked like a boy, as my mother was always telling me, too short and too thin and too plain. I'd my mother's brown hair except that mine was curly, and as usual that morning, it refused to stay in its bindings however much the maids tore at it with combs. They grumbled and cursed, for they were sure my mother would blame them, but they needn't have worried, for she always blamed me for everything; why not that as well?

Anne and Edith's hair, of course, lay smooth and obediently bound and coiled round their ears, just where the maids had pinned it. They had inherited my father's sandy hair and the pasty moon-face of my mother. And she guarded their virtue more closely than her own jewels. For my father was determined that they should not so much as raise their eyes to look at a man before they were safely wed.

My father, determined to keep his wealth in the family, had promised one of my sisters to his nephew, Phillip. Which one Phillip picked was immaterial to my father. But so far Phillip had resisted making his choice; he was having too much fun with their maids. At least I wasn't on offer. Though I was only a year younger than the twins, I would never be offered to anyone. As my sweet sisters never failed to remind me, I was born under the demon star and not even old beggar Tom would dare to take me to bed. I suppose I should have been grateful for that.

My cousin Phillip had wandered away from our procession before we even reached the Green. I could see he was already bored and was searching for someone to play with, for he constantly looked around him, winking and leering at any half-passable woman, ignoring the greetings and bobs of all others.

People said Phillip looked exactly like my father when he was young, but there the similarity ended, for my father considered fornication the greatest of all the vices. The servants whispered that it was a wonder he'd ever sired any children, for he had never been seen to touch my mother affectionately and often stared at her as if she repulsed him. He was constantly ordering poor Father Ulfrid to preach that fornicators and adulterers would roast in the hottest pit of hell, even though Father Ulfrid tried to protest this pit was reserved for greater sinners. But if the sermons were intended to curb Phillip's appetites, they had no effect, for he was rarely in church to hear them.

A great shout went up from the crowd. The prize ram, shorn and greased, had been set loose. Young single men, already stripped to the waist, shoved one another as they set off in pursuit, urged on by cheering girls. The ram, as if sensing what its fate would be, easily outmanoeuvred them at first, racing round the Green and through the carefully tended gardens, with the lads whooping after it, dodging the sticks and pots brandished by the shrieking housewives whose herbs they were trampling. But eventually the ram tired and although, when cornered, it made a brave effort to charge its tormentors, the leader of the pack of youths grabbed its horns and wrestled it to the ground.

The beast, garlanded, was led into the churchyard where with one swift slash its throat was cut, and steaming blood gushed out into a basin held beneath. The beaming victor's face and chest were painted scarlet with the blood. Then he mounted a ladder placed against the arch over the church door. Dipping both hands to the wrist in the proffered bowl, he smeared the ram's blood on the gaping pudendum of the naked old woman carved at the top of the arch, the one they call Black Anu.

'Ka!' the villagers yelled, cheering and whistling. And soon the ram was turning on a spit, sending sweet smoke into the damp air.

I turned to watch the tumblers. They had balanced a long pole on their shoulders and a little girl, dressed in scarlet with a tiny pair of wings fastened to her back, was stepping daintily along the pole, as confident as a cat on a wall. She steadied herself, her twiggy arms outstretched. The men began to bounce the pole on

17

their shoulders. She jumped, flipped in a somersault and landed, wobbling but safe, on the pole again. The villagers clapped heartily as she sprang down. Women stroked her golden hair and stuffed sweetmeats into her hands. Men pinched her cheek and tossed her a coin or two like doting uncles. Children gazed at her awestruck, as if she was Queen Mab.

To screeches of raucous laughter, the mummers appeared, led by the fool who tripped over invisible objects with exaggerated tumbles, then feigned indignation at those who laughed at him, striking them with a pig's bladder which made them laugh the more.

The hobby horse pranced and cavorted through the villagers, dodging this way and that as children tried to snatch the cake impaled on the tip of his lance. He teased them, offering it, then sweeping it high out of their grasp. When a lucky child succeeded in grabbing the honey cake, the hobby horse used his lance to lift the skirts of the giggling women or goose anyone foolish enough to turn their back on him.

Moll followed and the crowd roared. She was always a favourite. She was really John the blacksmith, who wore two grossly inflated bladders strapped to his chest under his kirtle. He simpered and minced through the crowd, feigning outrage as the lads tried to pinch his grotesquely padded backside. They'd not have dared that if he was at his forge.

Moll sidled up to my cousin Phillip, winking, waggling her hips and jiggling her massive breasts against his face.

'Here's a riddle for you, master – I am a great gift to women. I am hairy below and I swell up in my bed. A pretty lass pulls me and rubs my red skin. I have no bone, though I squirt white milk for her. I am so strong that I bring tears to her eyes. Tell me, master, what am I?'

Moll winked at the crowd. 'An onion, of course!' She wagged her finger at Phillip's crotch. 'But Moll knows what you were thinking, you naughty boy.'

The crowd screamed with laughter, but Phillip looked far from amused. Even on this day of licence the mummers knew not to push their luck too far and reeled away to find someone less powerful to torment.

The noise and laughter died rapidly. The villagers drew back as St Walburga was led in, a giant figure with a massive conical body topped by the painted wooden head of a crowned woman which lolled from side to side as the figure swayed forward. The withy frame of the body was woven densely with May blossom and ears of last year's wheat and barley, so that no one could glimpse the person underneath the frame. Small children burst into tears, hiding behind their mothers, as the monstrous figure lurched towards them.

Six cloaked men held the ropes which fastened the saint. They pulled her forward and reined her back as if she was a wild bear that might lash out at the crowd. Each of the faces of her brown-cloaked jailers was concealed by the feathered mask of the great horned eagle owl. Their eyes glinted dark and danger-ous, deep within the feathers, and their cruel bronze beaks flashed scythe-sharp in the pale sun. The village women clasped their children tight against their skirts as the Owl Masters went past.

The procession moved on until it reached the foot of the May Tree where the saint was tethered, pinioned by the ropes. The fool danced up to her, but the Owl Masters shooed him away. Urged on by the crowd, he dodged lightly round the Owl Masters to slap the saint resoundingly with his fool's bladder. The Owl Masters drew short swords from under their cloaks. They circled menacingly around the fool who spun in the middle, dodging the blades as they feigned high, then low. The crowd roared, cheering the fool.

Suddenly the flashing swords froze, interlocked in a six-pointed sun above the fool's head. The Owl Masters circled and the metallic sun rotated above the fool as he sank to his knees. The crowd was silent, holding its breath. Only the pleading of the fool rang out, a lone wail across the Green. But the plea for mercy was ignored. The murderous sun descended and locked around his neck. The fool lay dead. The six Owl Masters wordlessly turned, as one, to face the crowd around them, their swords pointing at the hearts of the villagers, their savage owl faces staring them down, challenging anyone else to approach. No one moved. No one dared to move.

Moll pushed her way through the Owl Masters. They let her pass. She bustled about the body on the ground, making great play of holding up his lifeless limbs and letting them flop to the ground. She slapped his cheeks, pulled his jaw open and poured the contents of an empty flagon into his mouth. When that had no effect, she forced one of her massive bladder breasts into his mouth and with that, the fool leaped to his feet and turned a couple of somersaults, just to show he was in the rudest of health.

All the villagers were laughing, that kind of nervous laughter which explodes when tension is shattered. Children rolled on the ground, imitating the fool with exaggerated death-throes, finally reassured that it was only a play. The mummers cavorted about Harrow Green, while the fool kissed Moll and she boxed his ears.

In all the commotion I didn't notice the Owl Masters disappear. Perhaps they simply vanished back into the forest or maybe they took off their masks and brown cloaks and mingled with the crowd. Some villagers looked around nervously as if expecting to see them at their backs. The Owl Masters had no faces and no names. They might be anyone in Ulewic. Who was missing from the crowd when the Owl Masters were here? There are some questions no one is allowed to ask.

The villagers drifted off to stuff themselves and drink and dance and drink some more. St Walburga alone did not move. The great straw frame squatted upon the grass. I knew there had to be someone inside. It couldn't move by itself, even though the village children were convinced it did.

The Green was littered with bones and dung, fragments of pastry and lost ribbons, crushed flowers and broken dishes. The shadows were lengthening fast and, overhead, birds began to wheel towards their night roosts. A cold breeze sprang up out of nowhere. I shivered.

The Owl Masters returned as silently as they had departed. I didn't see where they came from, but when I looked up, there they were as if they had always been there. Those villagers who were still sober enough to stand jerked nervously as they caught sight of them. The Owl Masters had taken up the saint's ropes and now stood motionless in a circle facing us. One by one the laughter and the arguments died away, neighbours nudging neighbours until all attention was fixed upon the six masked figures.

A girl, her hair tumbling loose and her kirtle grass-stained, was shoved and pushed by her friends to the front of the crowd. She made a tipsy curtsy and leaned forward, the tip of her pink kitten-tongue sticking out in an effort of concentration. She tossed the May garland. It caught neatly upon the top of the saint's painted wooden crown. Her attendants, giggling, assured her that her lucky throw meant she would be wed before the year was out. She glanced towards a group of young men. They jeered and pummelled one of their number, who looked as if he'd been praying devoutly she'd miss the throw.

The Owl Masters tugged on the ropes and led the saint as she swayed unsteadily across Harrow Green towards the forest, followed at a safe distance by all the men of Ulewic, at least those who were not already sow-drunk. The women glanced curiously, but made no attempt to follow. We were not welcome in the forest.

My heart began pounding and the palms of my hands were sticky with excitement. For nearly a month I'd been planning what I'd do, but now that it was time, I wasn't sure if I could really do it. Suppose I was seen? Suppose my mother suddenly asked for me and discovered I was missing? But if I didn't try, I'd kick myself later for it would be a whole year before I could try again.

With a long-suffering sigh, my mother signalled it was time for us to depart. She led the way, leaning on the arm of an old and trusted henchman, in the sure and certain knowledge we would all obediently follow her. My sisters dutifully did, but I ducked down behind a cart. In all the bustle of packing up, no one noticed that I was not in the procession following my mother. That's the advantage of being the unwanted child, no one notices when you disappear.

I stayed down until everyone was occupied, then I picked up my skirts and ran, dodging between the cottages, in the direction of the trees. Night was closing in fast. Only the thinnest rind of the sun still glowed orange above the bare black branches. No good girl would be out at this late hour, but as my mother was for ever telling me, I was not a good girl.

Darkness gathered early in the forest. It never really departed, but skulked among the ancient wrinkled trunks all day, waiting to seep out into the meadows again. I couldn't see the path that the men were following, but they lit torches and it was easy to keep pace with the snake of yellow flame as it wound its way through the gloom. The men were too drunk to notice another shadow in the bushes. Ahead I saw the snake of flame begin to coil into a ball of fire. I had no idea where we were for I had never been this far into the forest and certainly never alone, but I knew we must be somewhere near the river for I could hear the sound of rushing water.

The men had gathered in a clearing, near an ancient bull oak, so massive that half a dozen men could shelter in its hollow. They held their blazing torches high, glancing around them. Crouching in the darkness among the trees, I could see without being seen. I couldn't see my father though, or my cousin Phillip, but I knew they must be here somewhere; they came every year.

Women weren't allowed to witness this. They weren't even told what happened here. It was the men's secret – well not any more, because this year I'd finally know. I nearly laughed out loud, thinking how shocked all the men would be if they knew a girl was in their precious forest, just feet away from them.

St Walburga stood alone in the centre of the clearing, faggots of wood piled up around her. She no longer moved. Whoever had animated her must have been released before we arrived. But who had been inside? It was hard to recognize anyone; in the flickering torchlight, every man wore a mask of shadows. The men kept glancing nervously round, peering into the dark mass of the trees. They tried to jostle their way into the centre of the group as if they felt vulnerable on the edges.

I heard a rustle in the bushes behind me and froze. An Owl Master slipped silently out of the shadows no more than a yard from me. My heart began to thump. Suddenly it no longer seemed like a game. What if I was discovered? What would they do to me? What would my father do if he heard that I'd come here? I was a witless numbskull ever to think this was a good idea. I desperately wanted to creep away before I got caught, but I dared not move in case the Owl Master saw me.

Then a second Owl Master appeared a few yards away on the other side of me, and another and another until there were nine of them standing motionless in a circle around the clearing, blending with darkness, only the bronze beaks on their masks glinting in the firelight. The villagers suddenly caught sight of them and edged closer together in the clearing, like sheep circled by dogs.

The saint squatted in her nest of wood. The Owl Masters stood for a moment, then, drawing their swords, strode towards her. The villagers shrank back to let them through. The Owl Masters seized flaming torches from the men standing nearby and raised them high above their heads, turning as one to face the crowd. The wind whined in the branches high above, gusting the flames of the torches and sending shadows gibbering round the men. Outside the flickering circle of light, the darkness had grown thicker, almost solid. No one stirred.

A voice rang out across the silent clearing, deep and distorted beneath the owl mask. It was impossible to see which of the Owl Masters was speaking.

'Taranis will be acknowledged. He will have his due. Those who neglect to give what is owed to him, those who set

23

themselves against the natural order of things, bring down a curse upon all of us. Will we allow that to happen?'

'No!' the crowd roared back at him.

'Will we permit that to happen?'

'No!'

'What must we do?'

'Give him the saint! Give him St Walburga!'

The villagers began to stamp their feet. The Owl Masters slowly circled the wooden saint, crouching low, carnivorous.

'Through blood we renew our strength.'

'Through death we renew our life.'

'Through destruction we renew creation.'

'Through fire we make all things fertile. *Ka!*'

The chanting and stamping of the crowd gathered in strength until the trees themselves seemed to join in. Suddenly one of the Owl Masters sprang forward and plunged his sword into the saint's body. A scream split the darkness. When he drew the sword out, blood glistened wet upon the blade.

Then the Owl Masters threw their torches on to the pyre and the bonfire roared into life. Smoke and flames writhed into the night. Golden sparks exploded above the treetops. St Walburga was squirming; shrieks and howls emanated from her and above the smell of wood smoke drifted the unmistakable stench of burning hair and roasting flesh.

Servant Martha

A restless spirit hovered within our walls. It had prowled around us since the first offices of the day and, with the coming of darkness, it was growing in strength. Roused from their cots for prayer at the midnight hour, the beguines huddled together, edging into the guttering light of the candles away from the shadowy corners of the chapel.

There is a peace that attends those who wait on the Divine Spirit. I always felt it strongest at the first calling of the day. The night might be black as Satan's wings, the wind might shake the wooden shutters, and the rain might beat upon the door, yet inside the little chapel of our beguinage there was always calm.

But not this night; this night there was no peace. It was as if an icy draught had entered with us and I could not shut it out. The women bowed their heads and feigned attention to their prayers, but there was a shiver of unease among them. As horses stir and prick their ears when they sense a beast slinking round their stable, so they were tense, listening for something beyond our walls.

Even the seven other Marthas, who were elected to run the beguinage with me, all mature, sensible women, seemed strangely troubled. Kitchen Martha, Shepherd Martha, even our imperturbable Gate Martha, each of them kept raising their heads and staring towards the shuttered windows as if they too could sense something malevolent outside.

I stood before the kneeling beguines on the steps of the sanctuary, raising my hands to heaven. '*Gloria Patri, et Filio, et Spiritu Sancto. Ame . . .*'

There was a long-drawn-out howl and scratching at the door. Several beguines started and all heads turned towards the sound. Shepherd Martha rose, crossing herself hastily, and made for the door with a mumbled apology. As soon as she had opened it, Leon, her huge shaggy black hound, came rushing in, dodging her outstretched hands and making straight for the furthest corner of the chapel. Even that great brute was nervous.

I was not blind. Like everyone else, I had seen the May Day fires burning on the hilltops since nightfall, twin fires, ruby-bright in the darkness. I too had heard the shrieks and drunken laughter of the villagers staggering to their beds after the day's revelries, but those harsh sounds did not penetrate our chapel walls. And they should not have disturbed our song. Yet the women were disturbed and though I raised my voice until it reverberated off the stone walls of the chapel, I could not command their attention.

'*Sed libera nos a malo.*'

May our blessed Lord indeed deliver us from evil this night.

I looked round, seeking the reassurance of my old friend. Healing Martha was crouching in the shadow of the altar, her back pressed against the wall, her face hidden by her hood. She always prayed in that manner when her back ached. A fall, years ago, on slippery flags, had left her with a limp and pain that chastened her day and night. Some days were worse than others. On bad days she sat, chalk-faced, her lips pressed tightly together as if she feared a cry would escape them. On other days a stranger might detect nothing, but her hand pressed to the small of her back when she thought no one observed her, betrayed the pain she tried so hard to conceal. For all her knowledge of herbs and ointments she could not cure herself. I prayed daily for her healing, but I never told her. I knew she would bid me to save my breath.

'How could I understand the pain of others if I didn't feel the smart of it myself?' she once told me. 'Do you think Kitchen Martha could cook such good dishes for us if she was not constantly hungry?'

'*Pax Domini sit semper vobiscum.*'

The women began to file out. Crossing swiftly to Healing

26

Martha, I helped her to her feet. She pulled heavily on my arm, hauling her body upright, then thrust my hand away, impatient with her own weakness.

I looked down at her. She had always been much shorter than me; most people are for I am too tall for a woman, but Healing Martha was shrinking each year as her stoop became more pronounced. She had seen at least seventy full summers, but though her hair was white and her teeth loose, her hands had lost none of their skill.

Few back in Flanders had been able to match her knowledge of the healing arts. She always taught her assistants generously, holding no secret back, delighting when any displayed a more skilful hand than hers at cutting flesh, or preparing some ointment unknown to her. She had earned an honoured place in the Vineyard in Bruges and not a day had gone by in these past three years that I hadn't reproached myself for bringing her to this desolate corner of England. Not that bringing her here had been my idea.

It had been more than seventy years since the founding of our beguinage in Bruges and life in our community there was comfortable and established. Over a hundred women and their children were living within our walls. And we were not alone; cities of women were springing up all across Flanders and France in Ghent, Antwerp, Leuven, Kortrijk and Lier. Hundreds of women were spurning nunneries and husbands to live in the freedom of the beguinages where they could work for themselves, study and write.

But when Lady Joan de Tatishale bequeathed land to us on the east coast of England, I knew without a breath of doubt that God was calling me to leave the security which others had created and do what those first beguines had done, build the hope of freedom for all women with my own hands from the very dust of the earth. We would be the first beguinage in England and we would blow such a wind that would shake the very roots of that kingdom until every town and village in the land had its own city of women.

The Council of Marthas at Bruges invited any strong, skilled beguines who likewise felt the call to accompany me, but I had not dreamt that Healing Martha might count herself one of them. We all tried to dissuade her from making the arduous sea voyage, arguing that it was not safe for a woman of her age, though not even I dared mention infirmity in her hearing.

But she had fixed each of us in turn with her pale blue eyes. 'Was Abraham younger than me when God called him out to a new land?' she demanded. 'In a new land, a new beguinage, with a new infirmary to build and new beguines to teach, is there anyone among you who can tell me in all truth I am not needed there?'

And that was the end of the matter, although I sometimes wondered if it was the call of God or of friendship that brought her to England.

Healing Martha glanced up at me, her eyes crinkled in amusement despite her fatigue.

'Were you trying to drive out a demon tonight, Servant Martha? I confess I've not heard our blessed Lord praised in such a vehement manner since you gave thanks for this miserable land the day we first laid eyes on it.'

'Was I so forceful back then?'

'The ears of the poor angels are still ringing from it,' she chuckled.

We followed the last of the beguines out of the chapel door and into the cobbled courtyard. The stars seemed unnaturally bright. The vast dark ocean above swarmed with them, as if they were gathering for some great debate.

A small knot of women huddled round the warmth of the brazier, talking in low voices to Gate Martha. Pega, a local beguine, standing head and shoulders above the rest, frowned and shook her head at her close friend, Beatrice. I'd seldom seen Pega look so serious. Usually, she was to be heard telling some bawdy joke or sharing the latest gossip from the village, roaring with laughter at another's expense, but even she seemed subdued.

'What is wrong with the women, Healing Martha?' I asked. 'Most nights they can scarcely keep their eyes open long enough to find their cots.'

'A day of licence, old friend. They've done no work today to make them tired.'

'There's no work done on feast days either, but that doesn't breed this unease. Look at Pega; if I didn't know better I'd say something had frightened her. Yet if you'd asked me yesterday, I'd have sworn nothing on earth could shake her.'

Healing Martha frowned. 'Perhaps it is the fires.'

'The Beltane fires? Nonsense! She's no reason to fear them. The villagers drive their beasts between them to ward off sickness. Even their infants are passed over the flames to keep them from harm. It's a pagan custom and Father Ulfrid should have put a stop to it long ago, as I will make a point of telling him when our paths next cross, but there's no malice in it surely? Pega comes from these parts and was more than likely passed over the fires herself as a child. I cannot believe that she'd be afraid of something so familiar.'

Healing Martha turned, wincing as she did so, and stared in the direction of the forest. For a moment, as the wind gusted, a bright orange glow appeared above the dark mass of trees. Black branches writhed against the flickering light and then the darkness covered it again.

'I think it's not the cleansing fires of the hilltops she fears,' Healing Martha said softly, 'but that one, the fire which burns deep among the trees. That's what keeps Pega and the others from their beds. There is malice and more in that fire, I'll swear, though the villagers will not speak of it to outlanders.'

If truth be told, the villagers barely spoke to us at all these days. Their resentment at our presence in the valley seemed to be increasing. When we went in to Ulewic to take food or physic to the poor or sick, the villagers would pointedly turn their backs on us if we approached them. Those who accepted food did so furtively, whispering their thanks while glancing nervously over their shoulders as if they were terrified to be seen talking to us. Though I knew the Manor hated us and had tried to get rid of us from the first day we arrived, I prayed that in time we might win the villagers over, but if anything, matters were growing worse.

Healing Martha briskly patted my arm. 'If you want a cure for the women's fears I prescribe honest labour and innocent pleasure mixed in equal parts. The birch buds are finally beginning to open after all this bitter weather, and I know Kitchen Martha is longing to make her good birch wine, and I am in great need of birch sap for the infirmary. I think we should start tapping tomorrow. Now go and scold the women to their beds, for I've yet to meet a living soul who is not more afraid of you than any night terrors.'

'I think you are mocking me.'

Healing Martha grinned. 'It keeps you in humility.' She glanced again at the women around the brazier. 'But I'd be grateful if you'd send Pega to me. I'm in need of her strong arm to help me to my cot and her hands to rub some ammoniac and turpentine oils on my poor back to warm it.'

'I'll gladly rub your back for you.'

She threw her hands up in horror. 'Have mercy on a poor old woman! Your fingers would flay the skin from my back; they're rougher than a hog's hide. Pega has the touch and besides, I think she'll not mind sitting with me a while.'

I watched Pega help Healing Martha back to her room. I knew the real reason Healing Martha asked for her. She'd play the helpless old woman for Pega's sake and Pega would confide her fears to her. Healing Martha had that gift. I could not make the women talk to me. I never could, not even in the Vineyard in Bruges, for even there I felt – how did Healing Martha put it? – an outlander.

Father Ulfrid

We separated, rolling away from each other on the bed, and I lay there limply, feeling as if the very life force had been drained out of me. My groin continued to make small involuntary shudders, still thrusting, as if it had a will of its own. The sweat trickled down my chest and between my buttocks. Though the day had not been warm, it felt hot as hell in the room with all the shutters fastened.

It was dark, but I'd not dared to light a candle in case a chink of it should be seen through the cracks. Besides, we did not need light; we knew the shape and contours of each other's bodies only too well. And I did not want to see the look of triumph on Hilary's face. I had sworn it would not happen again. I had given my oath before God. But I could not help myself.

I shifted, suddenly aware of the sticky mess cooling between my thighs. I was overcome with revulsion. Feeling me stir, Hilary's damp hand reached out towards me again, stroking up my leg, the fingers wriggling between my thighs and up to my groin, stroking, touching, coaxing. I felt that urge growing stronger again, making me do what I did not want to. I almost surrendered to those soft fingers, as the all-consuming fire arched up my spine. My legs were trembling, defying me, moving towards the hand, inviting the touch.

'No, stop it.' I pushed Hilary's hand away violently.

'Why? You wanted me to just now. What's wrong with you? Why are you always so irritable afterwards?' I could hear the whining, childish petulance in the voice, which angered me still further.

'I'm tired,' I snapped.

'But I've travelled all this way. You couldn't keep away from me in Norwich and now we hardly get to see each other any more. I've been thinking of nothing else but this for weeks.' Hilary's hand slid coaxingly across my chest, teasing my nipples. 'I know you want me as much as I want you, Ulfrido.'

'I said enough!' I sat up abruptly, pulling away from the prone body beside me. I swung myself off the bed. The rushes were cold and sharp against my bare feet. 'You shouldn't have come. I told you never to come again.'

Hilary laughed. 'It seems to me it is you who have come.'

I leaned across the bed and slapped hard against bare flesh, not sure where I struck and not caring either. My fingers stung from the blow.

There was a gasp, then another laugh in the darkness, shakier this time. 'You want to play that game, do you?'

'Just go. Get out.'

The bed creaked as Hilary rolled over and sat up. 'We can play priest and penitent, if that's what you want. Shall I be the priest or shall you? Shall I punish you? Will that make you feel better? Will that make you clean again? Or will you beat me? Either way it won't make any difference, you know. It won't cure you ... *Father*.' This last word, spat out, intended to wound more deeply than a blow ever could.

'Get out, you little whore,' I shouted. 'Get out and leave me alone. I never want to see you again. I mean it this time.'

'You don't mean it, you know you don't. You've said it a hundred times before and each time you've come crawling back. You can't help yourself. But you want to be careful, Ulfrido. One day you might say it and I'll take you at your word.'

I lunged towards the bed. 'You bitch, you –'

The door handle turned and the door rattled as someone shook it. But it was locked and bolted. There was a loud hammering. I froze, my heart pounding so loudly I was sure it could be heard through the walls.

The banging came again, more urgently this time. 'Father Ulfrid, come quick.'

I recognized the voice at once; it was old Lettice. If she'd seen Hilary come to my door, it would be all round the village before dawn.

The sweat on my body suddenly turned cold. I was horribly conscious that I was naked. I groped frantically about me for my clothes, but I couldn't remember where Hilary had tossed them. I was too frightened to move in case in the dark I blundered into the furniture and knocked something over. Could Lettice have heard me shouting from outside the door?

The hammering came again. 'It's poor Ellen, Father Ulfrid, Giles's mam; she's fair lost her wits. Crying fit to cause the flood, but she'll give no reason. Says she'll only tell you, Father. Giles could calm her right enough, but he'll be in the forest with the rest of the men and I daren't go in there, not tonight of all nights. But you could fetch him, Father ... Father Ulfrid?'

Neither Hilary nor I moved. We waited, hardly daring to breathe. Then finally, after what seemed like an hour, I heard footsteps moving away from the door, then passing the shuttered window, then silence. Even so, I didn't dare move for several minutes, afraid that she would still be standing in the street watching the cottage for signs of life.

'God's blood, where are my clothes? I can't find my fucking clothes. Where did you throw them?' I was on the floor now, groping around blindly in the dark.

I felt my priest's habit thrust silently into my hands.

We both dressed rapidly, fumbling with fastenings and knots in the darkness. The desperate panic to be clothed again served only to increase the heat in the room; sweat was running down my face. My robes stuck to my body as I tried to pull them on. I couldn't find my hose, so I thrust my bare feet into my shoes. Neither of us spoke. I knew Hilary was as terrified of being found here as I was of anyone discovering us together.

I crossed to the door and listened. Nothing. But we couldn't afford to take any chances. I grabbed Hilary by the arm and we stumbled to the rear door leading out to the yard. There was a small wicket gate at the back. The moon shone full on the glistening flagstones. I just prayed that the shadows of the cottages would be enough to conceal Hilary from curious eyes.

As I turned back towards the house, I felt a swift, hot kiss on my lips. Too late I turned, desperate to respond, but Hilary was already at the gate. I felt the loneliness burn more sharply in that one kiss snatched away, than if the kiss had never been given. I knew I would go crawling back. I always did. I couldn't help myself.

'I didn't mean it,' I whispered urgently. 'Forgive me, my angel. Please forgive me. I love you.' But the gate had already closed.

I turned back to the empty room. The night's breeze gusted into the cottage, catching up the smell of us in the room, the acrid sweat, the sweet-salt smell on stained bedclothes, the lingering trace of sandalwood from Hilary's clothes. In the faint owl-light that filled the room from the open door, I thought I saw Hilary lying there still: the soft black curls of hair; the sloe-black eyes dancing with mocking laughter; the full red mouth, open just enough to show the white teeth that bit upon my lip, sometimes gently, sometimes so fiercely I could taste the blood in my mouth.

This time it was me I slapped, hard, hitting my face over and over again to try to stop the awful ache that was stirring and swelling again in my groin, the demon I could not control.

I suddenly hated Hilary, more than any man can hate any-thing, for making me plead, for making me into this creature I loathed and despised. I wished with all my heart that my dark angel had never been created, so that I would never have been tempted, never fallen, never sunk to this. I had never made love to anyone else, but even now, as I stood there at the foot of my empty, ravaged bed I knew that Hilary would soon be lying in the bed of another. I'd known it from the first. I'd known again and again every time we slept together that there were others, and there would always be others. The thought made me sick. I wanted to whip, to beat, to tear, to rape, over and over again, until Hilary screamed and begged me for mercy. And I would grant no mercy. I would go on until there was nothing left except a bloody pulp, but I knew even that would not be enough to kill my love.

Agatha

I ran, but the brambles were clutching at my skirts, dragging me
back. I couldn't find the path. I didn't know if I was running
towards the village or deeper into the forest. Taranis was here,
the demon was here in the forest. I'd felt it. I'd seen the great
black shadow of its wings hovering high above the smoke and
flames. Now I could feel its foul breath hot on the back of my
neck. My eyeballs ached trying to suck in enough light to see
anything. It was so dark. I tried to run faster, but I kept blunder-
ing into trees and stumbling over roots.

Then it came crashing down on me, catching me from
behind, slamming my belly against the trunk of a fallen tree,
forcing me over. My face was pressed into the ground. I
couldn't breathe. Rotting leaves filled my mouth. The stench of
decay was forced into my nostrils. Its hot, naked thighs were
grinding my hip bones bloody against the rough bark. My ribs
were cracking under the millstone of its chest. I grabbed wildly
at earth and air and brambles, not comprehending what I tore,
except that it wasn't its skin, its wings, its eyes.

Wild onion is always in the forest, a sleeping thing, a
harmless thing, but now, crushed and bruised, the stench
choked the air. A sea wind roared inside my skull, but I couldn't
scream. Though every sinew of my body howled and sobbed,
my mouth was silent. My mouth was filled, crammed, stuffed to
overflowing with the corruption of the forest. My lungs were
clawing for breath against my will, because I wanted to die. I
wanted to crawl into the dirt and bury myself among the
worms. But I couldn't. I couldn't move. My body wasn't mine
any more.

The monster wrenched my hair violently back as if it reined
in a mare. It jerked my head back and forth as if it would snap

my neck and make an end of it. But it made no end. Its iron flesh hammered my bones to the tree, again and again and again, until it had pierced me through. And then it was gone and I was alone in the darkness.

May – Rood Een

The third and last of the Beltane Fire Days and the Eve of Rood Day. On this day, byres are covered with honeysuckle and rowan to protect the beasts from witches.

Father Ulfrid

I pounded my fist on the table. 'God's teeth, you've gone too far this time.'

Phillip D'Acaster, by way of response, settled himself more comfortably in my favourite chair, an expression of disdainful amusement on his face.

I tried to keep my temper. 'When I heard you'd taken Giles, I thought you were going to give him a beating, at worst brand him. But you cannot expect me as a priest to countenance murder.'

'You'll countenance whatever I say you will countenance, Father. Have you forgotten who gave you your living and who can have you turned out again just like that?' Phillip suddenly rocked forward, snapping his fingers an inch from my nose.

I did not need reminding. I knew only too well to whom I owed my living. All it would take would be one word from Phillip D'Acaster in his uncle's ear and I'd not only be cast out of the Church, I'd be lucky to escape with my life, though I prayed to God that Phillip didn't realize that.

I felt an iron band tightening around my chest, making it hard to breathe. It seemed to happen more and more often now. I eased myself down on to a stool, trying not to let the pain show.

Phillip leaned forward and casually pulled a pitcher of my best Mass wine towards him, pouring himself such a generous measure that the wine spilled over on the table as he raised the goblet. He tilted it to the candlelight to see the colour, sniffing it cautiously before he took a gulp. It was not yet noon, but I had closed and bolted the shutters and the door of my cottage. This was not a conversation I wanted one of my parishioners to walk in on.

Phillip grinned. 'You know, Father, what you did in Norwich may be a mortal sin, but I don't blame a man for trying, priest or not. In fact I admire you. Rumour has it the wench was a fair beauty. Might have tried it on myself if I'd seen her, but then, of course, I haven't taken a vow of celibacy, not that I hold that against you. Not a natural state for any man.'

He took another slow swig of wine before setting his goblet down. 'But you want to be careful, Father, sowing your oats in another man's field can lead to all kinds of trouble, as Giles could no doubt testify, if he still had a tongue, that is.' He wagged his finger in mock reproof. 'And you should have known better than to pursue a nobleman's wife. That hunt is far too dangerous for a man of the cloth. Husbands are apt to take violent offence at any bucks moving in on their hinds, the more so if the buck happens to be a priest. I trust you've given the quarry up for lost, Father.'

I desperately searched Phillip's face for signs that he was laying a trap, but saw nothing more than amused indifference.

I bowed my head. 'Even a priest is subject to temptation. But I have learned my lesson.'

'I certainly hope so, Father. Were rumours of that kind to reach the Bishop's ears again, I doubt you'd get off with merely being stripped of your post at the Cathedral.'

The crushing pain in my chest intensified as if an executioner had pressed another weight down on it. Had old Lettice seen Hilary leaving my cottage last night and spread the gossip? If she had and he knew, my death warrant was already signed. I could feel the chill of sweat crawling down my face and I had to crush my hands together to keep them from shaking.

Last night I'd thought I could not loathe myself more, but when I learned what the Owl Masters were doing to Giles at the very moment I had been ... vomit rose in my throat. This was all Hilary's fault, that evil witch ... never again, never! Holy Mother of God, I swear I mean it this time.

I saw Phillip studying me curiously and I tried desperately to pull myself together. He lounged back in the chair, holding the goblet delicately in his ringed fingers. He had Robert D'Acaster's flaxen hair and full lips, but his young frame had not yet run to fat. Women seemed to find him handsome enough, not that Phillip ever needed to rely on his looks to woo a woman. Unlike his uncle whose only passions were horses and falcons, Phillip's appetite for women was insatiable and he took his pleasure wherever he wanted without waiting for an invitation, as I knew only too well from the numerous confessions I was forced to endure from the foolish girls whose pleasure Phillip had taken.

I swallowed a mouthful of ale to ease my dry throat, trying to push aside all thoughts of Hilary. If Phillip saw so much as a whisper of fear in my face, he'd seize it like a lurcher taking a hare and not let go till he had shaken out the cause. I tried to stay calm.

'I am grateful for the living, Phillip, most grateful, but you must understand that as a priest I have a duty to God as well as to Robert.' I made a point of emphasizing this last name. Phillip was not yet lord of the Manor, however much he schemed to be.

'I have a responsibility for your soul, Phillip, and murder is a terrible sin to carry upon your conscience. I am only thinking of you and the suffering you would be forced to bear in purgatory if you died with this sin still upon you. But before I can absolve you of that sin, I must, in all conscience, know that you truly repent and are willing to make penance. The penance for such a sin as murder cannot be light.'

'Trying to wring some more gold for the Church coffers out of me? My uncle won't be pleased when he hears about that.' Phillip laughed. 'Anyway, why this talk of sin and penances, Father? There has been no murder.'

My jaw and fists clenched at this blatant lie. 'I went to the place where you burned St Walburga this morning. The ashes are still warm and the place reeks of burnt flesh. Don't try to tell me there were live cats inside her like last year. The stench of roasted human flesh is not a smell I'm ever likely to mistake, not after the burnings I've witnessed, and Giles's mother …'

I saw a spark of anger flash in Phillip's eyes and knew at once I'd said too much.

'What exactly did that foolish old woman tell you?'

'Nothing, I assure you,' I said quickly. I felt myself flushing like a guilty schoolboy. I took another gulp of small ale and coughed violently as it went down the wrong way. I could not afford to make him angry.

'As I was saying,' Phillip resumed softly, 'no murder was committed, so there is no sin to atone for. There was an execution, certainly, but execution, as you well know, Father, is not murder. It is divine justice.'

'Without a trial or a plea?'

He smiled. 'Oh, never fear, Father, there was a trial and by the time we had finished, how shall I put it, *examining* him, there certainly was a plea, many in fact, as I recall. And after he confessed his guilt, there could only be one verdict, as he himself was only too ready to agree.'

He poured himself another draught of wine without waiting to be asked. I watched him warily. Robert D'Acaster had power and a violent temper, but over these last few months I had begun to realize that the nephew might prove more dangerous than his uncle. For what he lacked in power he made up for in cunning, and cunning combined with cruelty is something to be wary of in any man, even one who does not yet have the money or position he craves.

Phillip leaned back in the chair, his hands clasped behind his head. 'Anyway, Father, it's no use complaining to me. You know that I do not lead the Owl Masters. I am merely a humble servant, his most trusted and loyal servant. But it is the Aodh who commands, judges and executes.'

As I thought, Robert D'Acaster was responsible for this. Phillip wouldn't take orders from anyone else. And he certainly had his uncle's trust, though I suspected Phillip's loyalty would last only until he was strong enough to defeat the old stag.

Phillip suddenly swung forward and gripped my wrist hard.

'You'd do well not to oppose the Aodh, Father. One day you may need his help.'

A surge of anger overwhelmed all my resolve to be careful. How dare he threaten me? I was an ordained priest, the voice of God on earth.

'I can assure you, Phillip, nothing would induce me to seek help from him or any of your heathen brotherhood, no matter what the need.' I wrenched my arm from his grasp. 'God's strength is all I will ever trust in.'

'Is that so?' Phillip's eyes narrowed. 'I wouldn't be too hasty in your assurances, Father. You might live to regret them.'

I struggled to contain my fury. I knew it was foolish to provoke him further. The safest course of action was to let the matter of Giles's murder drop. What would be gained by pursuing it? I couldn't undo the deed and there was no chance of the Owl Masters ever being punished for it. No one from the Manor or the village would ever bear witness against them, not even Giles's poor mother. But why should I be burning up with guilt when this bastard sat smirking in my chair, drinking my wine without even a twinge of conscience?

'We are agreed that Giles deserved punishment.' I was struggling hard to keep my tone moderate. 'Fornication is a sin, as your uncle is for ever reminding us, and it is one the Church soundly condemns, but is it justified to kill a man for ...' I hesitated seeing the frown deepen on Phillip's face. 'The point is, Giles died unshriven, and even those condemned to the gallows are entitled to absolution before they die, so that their souls may be saved, even if their bodies are not. And that is something that as your priest I do have the right to insist upon.'

Phillip smiled, but his eyes still smouldered dangerously. 'If that's all that concerns you, Father, next time I will personally see to it that you attend the trial to shrive the condemned. In fact I will insist on it.'

'Next time?'

'Oh yes, there will be a next time, Father, that I can promise you. The Owl Masters reigned in Ulewic long before your whey-faced saints ever trod this land. They have always ruled here. Do not foolishly imagine that, because they have been watching from the shadows, they are weak. They are stronger now than ever before. A fire was kindled last night that will never be extinguished. The new era of the Owl Masters has just begun.'

Servant Martha

The courtyard was filthy, ankle-deep in the mud of winter, slimed with hog and poultry droppings and stinking of piss. It was hard work raking it and I was perspiring despite the biting wind, but it was a good penance for body and soul. The muck would make good nourishment for the soil once it had weathered awhile, though the stench of it turned the stomach. And we would need all we could grow, for last year's harvest had been poor and our stores were dwindling alarmingly fast.

'You want to bind that with reeds and straw, else the next rains will spread it across the yard again,' a voice called out behind me.

I turned to see Merchant Martha scuttling across the yard, her sharp brown eyes darting about as if she was a blackbird on the lookout for worms. I tried not to show my irritation at the unwanted advice. I was always grateful for Merchant Martha's ability to organize, but not when it extended to me.

'Thanks be to God you've returned safely, Merchant Martha. How did you fare at Swaffham market? Did you get a good price for the cloth?'

Her thin lips shrugged, which was the closest they ever came to a smile. 'Tolerable, I suppose, which is as well, since we need every penny we can get.'

That meant better than she expected, for she would not seal any bargain until she was sure she had wrested the last farthing she could from the buyer.

Merchant Martha shook her head dolefully. 'By my reckoning we'll need to buy more grain before the feast of St John. What's in the barn will not see us through to next harvest, not with the food we've given to the beggars this winter. And take it from me, the price of grain won't be falling.'

'But if our stocks are running low, the poor will be in worse straits. We'll doubtless see more coming to our gate before this year is out.'

Merchant Martha scowled. 'The villagers curse us with their left hand whilst holding out their right for any meat we're fool enough to give them. Getting spat at by their lice-ridden brats is all the thanks we get.'

There was no point in contradicting her. Every woman in the beguinage had sensed the growing resentment of the village towards us. I prayed the villagers would stick to spitting and cursing, and their hostility would not boil over into something worse.

I sighed. 'Having to ask for charity breeds bitterness in honest men. God grant us all a better harvest this year than last, so that they have no need to beg.'

'From your lips to God's ears.' Merchant Martha shuffled her feet, impatient to be about her work.

She was a neat, compact woman and though she had a healthy appetite, she was all bones, for she was always restless with a fiery energy that seemed to burn up her flesh. When her husband was alive she had run his wool business single-handed; she'd had to, for when he wasn't drunk, he was off whoring or gaming. It was only her hard work that kept bread on the table of her household and his fortune intact. And even now, as if she still lived in constant fear of ruin, she couldn't bear to be idle for a moment.

'Did you find time to deliver the candles and the book to Andrew, Merchant Martha?'

'I did because you asked it, but I didn't linger there; too many thieves and vagabonds hanging around that church.' She grimaced. 'Andrew attracts the worst sort of rogues.'

'Sinners are in more need of her grace —'

Merchant Martha snorted. 'They may need her grace, but take it from me, that's not what they're seeking.'

'Did she send a message?'

Without warning, Merchant Martha pounced on a hen which

was ambling across the yard and tucking it under her arm, poked expertly at its breast to feel the crop. It squawked indignantly.

'Andrew sent you her blessing.' She glanced at me sideways, hesitating for a moment, before adding, 'You should go and see Andrew yourself. She's ... she's much changed since you last saw her.'

I frowned. 'What do you mean – changed?'

Merchant Martha set the hen down and watched it bustle away, shaking out its feathers. 'Go and see Andrew,' she repeated. 'And do it as soon as you can.' She peered up at me from under her heavy black brows. 'You know I don't hold with what she does, starving herself like that when she could afford to eat, whilst all around there are those that starve because they have no choice. I've no time for such self-indulgent nonsense. But all the same, I feel sorry for the girl and something tells me she may be in urgent need of friends before long.' With that, Merchant Martha strode rapidly away towards the barn before I could ask more.

I stared after her, puzzled. Merchant Martha always had a good instinct for trouble, acquired from years of buying and selling in the seething marketplaces and squalid ports of Flanders, but I couldn't imagine why she would think that Andrew of all women might be in need of friends.

Andrew was an anchorite who lived in a tiny cell attached to the church of St Andrew, never leaving it, receiving all her food through the window on the outside wall and the Blessed Sacrament through the slot that overlooked the altar of the church. A life devoted solely to the perfection of her own soul was not one I could ever countenance, any more than Merchant Martha could, but I envied Andrew all the same. She was so certain that our Lord loved her and approved of what she did. I wished I could feel that kind of certainty, even but once in my life.

She would have been about twenty years of age when I last saw her, though she looked scarcely more than fifteen, with long beechnut hair tumbling loose like a child's. Such a tiny, fragile girl, her pale face with high cheekbones made sharper by her meagre diet of hard bread and herbs, and her skin so transparent that her veins stood out as blue seams in her white marble hands. Even though she was young, she had already gained such mastery over her body that it was no longer polluted by the menses.

Men, particularly her confessor at the church, were fascinated by her and guarded her cage jealously as if she was a rare and beautiful animal, but the priest didn't drive the spectators from her window or silence the cries of the hot food sellers and alewives who spread their wares hard against the walls of her cell. Nor would the crowds of pilgrims have heard him if he had, for they were too intent on bargaining for the tin emblems and snippets of blood-stained cloth which the cleric swore she had worn next to her skin during her visions. As a living cat is sealed up inside the walls of a new manor to keep the dynasty from falling, so she was walled up in the church to keep it wealthy.

I shook myself sternly and picked up my rake, attacking a stubborn patch of compacted mud. A flock of geese wheeled as one, and charged across to the pile of dung, trampling it across the yard again as they squabbled over grubs and worms. A prod from my rake and they scattered, hissing malevolently, and wandered off to find a quieter corner.

The wizened face of Gate Martha appeared at my elbow. 'Kitchen Martha'll not be best pleased if you drive the fat off the birds. There's a lad begs leave to see you at the gate,' she added, before I had time to reply.

'What does he want?'

She shrugged unhelpfully.

'Do you know the boy?'

Gate Martha nodded, but didn't seem to think it necessary to enlighten me. She was a local woman of few words. It was one of the reasons we had appointed her as Gate Martha for she said she was known for keeping her counsel. But there were times when I wondered where discretion stopped and dour began.

I followed her to the gate and there I found a boy of about eleven or twelve years shuffling from one foot to the other, scarlet in the face and sweating. The pony beside him was also in a lather and no wonder, for the boy had been free enough with his whip, judging by the marks on the beast's coat. The boy could scarcely wait for me to reach him before he gabbled out his message.

'My master bids you attend on him at once.'

'Robert D'Acaster,' Gate Martha explained, misinterpreting my frown.

'*Bids* me? Is there sickness in the house?'

The boy shook his head. 'Nay, but if you don't come at once there'll be murder, for the master is in such a rage with his daughter that if I don't fetch you, he'll like as not kill me.'

'Nonsense!' I said. All boys exaggerate wildly. They are incapable of telling the truth simply and plainly, just as they are incapable of standing still without fidgeting.

'Now, child, answer me plainly. What exactly is it that I am *bid* to do? If your master has a quarrel with his daughter, what has that to do with me? I dare say he is quite capable of bringing his own household to order.'

'Please come, mistress. I daren't go back without you.' The boy suddenly looked very frightened.

Gate Martha coughed. 'D'Acaster's a savage temper on him.'

The boy nodded vigorously as if he could testify to that a dozen times over.

I hesitated. I had never spoken with any member of the D'Acaster family, though I'd had several unpleasant disputes with his bailiff, over wood gathering and grazing rights, all of which I'd won. The bailiff had made no secret of the fact that D'Acaster wanted us gone, though as I informed the man, since we owned our land there was nothing his master could do to force us out. He had stormed off in fury, doubtless to inform his master, and I had not had occasion to speak to him since. So why on earth would D'Acaster suddenly send for me in a matter concerning his daughter?

The boy was watching me, his body tense, silently pleading for me to agree.

Curiosity got the better of me. 'Very well then,' I said finally. 'I'll come, if it'll save you from a whipping.'

Relief flooded his face and he beamed, bounding up on to the back of his long-suffering mount.

'But you'll have to wait whilst I fetch my cloak and brush the mud from my kirtle. Gate Martha, would you be so kind as to saddle a horse for me?'

Gate Martha grasped my arm urgently and whispered. 'I'd sooner stick my face in a nest of weasels than trust any up at the Manor. Supposing he means to harm you?'

'Under what law could he do that? I have committed no crime.'

Gate Martha shook her head in disbelief. 'He doesn't need no law; he *is* the law. There's mischief brewing in Ulewic, fires last night were just the start of it. Don't you be riding to meet it.'

'But the fire had nothing to do with D'Acaster, surely? Perhaps he merely wishes to extend the hand of friendship at last.'

'Friendship?' she said incredulously. 'He loathes women, even his own wife. He'd not make peace with the Holy Virgin herself. You keep a tight hold on your knife, Servant Martha.' She stomped off in the direction of the stables.

'Hurry,' the boy begged. 'My master can't abide to be kept waiting.'

'Then,' I said firmly, 'your master will have to be taught the virtue of patience.'

Beatrice

As soon as the wooden gate of the beguinage banged shut behind us, the wind pounced as if it had been lying in wait, a raw wind, whipping across the marshes straight from the sea. But we told each other it would feel warmer once we were in the shelter of the copse. The other beguines ambled ahead of us down the track, laughing and chattering in twos and threes. They wouldn't have been laughing if they'd heard what I had in the forest on May Eve.

You could tell they'd already forgotten all about the Beltane fire now that it was daylight. They were like a pack of little children; when Servant Martha said there was nothing to worry about, they actually believed her. They were gullible enough to believe anything that woman said. They couldn't see through her, like I could. But Pega was still worried about the fire, I could see that, so don't you tell me there was nothing to worry about.

Pega and I threaded our staves through the rope handles of several empty tubs and shouldered them between us. She strode ahead down the muddy track, her rump, as broad as an ox's, swaying as she walked. Little Catherine and I trailed pathetically behind, taking two steps to her one. The wooden staves ground against my shoulders. Pega was a giant, so the full weight of the laden staves was tipping back on me, but I wasn't going to give her the satisfaction of asking her to slow down. She'd tease me for the rest of the day.

The sodden track had been churned to mud by the many hooves and cart wheels that had passed over it for the fair. I slid several times and tried to take small steps, but Pega showed no fear of falling. Nothing and no one could tumble her, unless she'd a mind to let them, which in her younger days she had with a frequency that had earned her a reputation as the most accommodating woman in the village, or so that wicked old gossip, Gate Martha, said.

We were the last to reach the copse. The other beguines were already scattered among the trees, clearing away old undergrowth from around the trunks. The buds were beginning to break and the branches of the birches shivered in their bright green mist. As if the sap was bubbling up inside them too, the young children and some of the women were playing a boisterous game of tag, shrieking and giggling as they chased one another.

Pega smiled. 'Best get started, then we can all join in. Move your arse, lass,' she yelled to Catherine. 'Get those holes bored.'

Poor little Catherine had only just caught up with us, but she obediently scampered off to the nearest tree and tried in vain to screw one of the augers into the bark. She could never tell when Pega was teasing.

Pega, grinning, elbowed her aside. 'Out the way, lass, we'll be here till Lammas at this rate. If my mam had whelped a reckling like you, she'd have drowned it at birth.'

Pega rolled up her grey cloak and flung it to one side. Something fell to the ground from her belt. I picked it up. It was a sprig of woodbine wrapped around a twig of rowan.

'Servant Martha would be furious if she knew you were wearing this.' Our sour-faced leader had expressly forbidden the wearing of the charm during the days of Beltane to keep away witches and evil spirits.

'Aye, but what she doesn't know won't hurt her.' Pega winked, took the twig and stuffed it into her leather scrip. 'A little extra protection never comes amiss and I've a feeling we are going to need all the protection we can get.'

'Because of the fire last night? Gate Martha said it meant trouble for us.' So I was right, Servant Martha didn't know what she was talking about, as usual.

'There was trouble for someone in that fire. It was a warning, make no mistake.' Pega tossed the auger to Catherine and held out her great broad hand for a hollow reed to push into the hole. 'Something's brewing in the village and if the villagers get uneasy, the first people they'll turn on is us. They're suspicious of any outlanders, always have been. I grant you they were quick enough to take the beguines' money while the beguinage was being built, and who can blame them, for you were paying three times what D'Acaster would for labour. But that only made them more wary. They don't understand the notion of a house of women who aren't nuns or whores. For all there's not been a man across the threshold since the building work was finished, it hasn't stopped them gossiping. What they don't know, they'll invent, never fear. Someone should tell Servant Martha to take care.'

'Don't look to me,' I told her. 'You know full well I have no voice. Anyway, Servant Martha won't be dissuaded by anyone, you know that. She treats the word *no* as if it was a gauntlet slapped across her face. The Manor's been trying to get rid of us ever since the day we arrived and she's never taken the slightest notice.'

Pega groped in her scrip for a lump of wax which she kneaded with unnecessary vigour. 'The beguinage may be outside the Manor's rule, but there's those in these parts who have their own rules and they set no limits to them. No one defies them. Those that do live just long enough to regret it.'

'But if they break the law ...' I said.

Pega shook her head impatiently. 'If you were birthed in these parts you'd know there are some forces too powerful to be brought to heel, leastways not by the Law or the Church. They're ancient forces that were worshipped on the mound where St Michael's church stands long afore the parish church was ever built. They're stronger even than D'Acaster or the King himself. Nothing and no one can stand against them, not even Servant Martha.'

'But there is a church there over the place now, as you said, and no one worships in the old way any more. This is a Christian land. It has been for centuries.'

'Not for some, not for the Owl Masters.'

Pega pushed the softened wax around the reed to hold it in place and angled it downwards. Almost at once a thick, cloudy liquid began to drip into the tub beneath.

'The Owl Masters've always been in the valley. They're toadsmen. They've great powers over beasts and men, can stop a runaway stallion in its tracks or get a stubborn one moving. They can see in the dark where normal men'd be blind. And years ago, afore the D'Acasters arrived, the Owl Masters were the law here. Could punish any man as they pleased, even put him to death.

'But when Church and Manor came to the valley, the Owl Masters' reign was over; it was the King's law ruled then. But Ulewic folk still carried on going to Owl Masters in secret to get things sorted out. Quarrels over women and disputes that they were afeared to take to the Manor or Church Courts, 'cause everyone knows you make a complaint to them and you're just as likely to find yourself fined as the man who's wronged you. Besides, D'Acaster and the priest don't understand Ulewic affairs, not if it's to do with rights or grudges going back generations.'

Pega frowned. 'But of late there's been talk of the Owl Masters doing more charming horses or settling fights. Some say they're taking the law back into their own hands and more besides. It's been nigh on a hundred years since they last tried and none in these parts will ever forget what happened then.'

She shuddered and stared back in the direction of the forest. 'You know I hate D'Acaster and his whole tribe of vermin, but I'll tell you this, the powers of any lord in this land are nowt compared to what the Owl Masters can do.'

I followed her gaze. The man who'd worn the stag's hide, had he been one of them? Was it their power he'd being trying to gain that night? If he was, he'd failed. I'd heard his death screams. No one could have survived those creatures. My skin crawled just thinking about them. I longed to tell Pega and ask her what it meant, but how could I? I couldn't explain what I was doing in the forest at night.

'Are the Owl Masters going to kill us?' little Catherine whispered fearfully. She looked as if she was about to burst into tears.

Pega grinned. 'Don't you fret, lass, you've nothing to worry about as long as I'm around. Any man tries to hurt you I'll rip his bollocks off and give them to you to play marbles with them.'

Catherine giggled and blushed furiously, managing to look shocked and delighted at the same time.

Pega had a wicked grin and a mischievous tongue to match, but you couldn't help liking her. I don't think she ever repented her past life, no matter what the Marthas believed. To repent you must regret, but Pega didn't. As a cow is born to give milk, Pega was born to give pleasure. A lecherous gap between her front teeth and her generous breasts that turned men into little suckling pigs at a glance – no virgin could ever be moulded in such a form. She simply practised the trade her body fitted her for. It put bread on the table of her family and more besides. Not from the village lads, she said, they'd think to have a girl for the price of a fairing or for nothing if they could, but merchants and clergy could pay for their comforts and she saw to it they did.

When she came to join us in the beguinage, the Council of Marthas gave her the name Pega, after the blessed virgin saint; new life, new name, her virginity restored. Yet in a way, I think that she never really lost it. Perhaps virginity can only be taken, not given.

Catherine, on the other hand, was from a good family, high-born, and if her mother hadn't died so young I dare say she'd have been kept closeted at home until her wedding night. But after her mother died, her father thought Catherine would stand more chance of keeping her virtue if she came to us till she was of age rather than remain under the same roof as her brothers and their wayward cousins. From what I'd heard of that pack of young devils, there wasn't a maid left in the household worthy of the name. Mind you, if her father had ever met Pega, he might have thought twice about sending her to us to safeguard her innocence.

'Leave the lids – you can fasten them later,' Dairy Martha called over to us. 'All the food will be gone if you don't come and eat.'

Every birch trunk that was thick enough to be tapped now had its own reed dripping with the precious sap and most of the beguines had already settled themselves on heaps of fallen leaves and were tucking into the food with hearty appetites.

Kitchen Martha took no notice of fears of poor harvests; as far as she was concerned, the beginning of wine-making was an excuse for a feast and the great baskets set on the ground seemed bottomless. Out of them came round loaves of bread, pastries as big and broad as Pega's hands, whole chickens with crisp golden skins glazed with honey and spices, tiny brown pigeons wrapped in slices of smoked pork, thick wedges of milky white cheese, dried apricots and figs and great flagons of ale and cider.

Smiles and grins broadened as bellies filled. One of the women pulled out her pipes and began to play and those who weren't too stuffed to move joined in the songs, while the children danced around, mostly out of step with the music, but no one cared.

I leaned back on a trunk. We were sheltered from the worst of the wind among the trees and I was full and sleepy. 'This is almost as good as being back in the Vineyard,' I muttered, yawning.

'Tell me again about Bruges,' Catherine asked eagerly. I'd forgotten she was there. She loved to hear stories about the Vineyard. I sometimes wondered if she thought it was heaven, not the Vineyard, I was describing. Perhaps I was.

'It's beautiful. We have everything you could want there. A cannel comes right inside, bringing water for the latrines and washing right to the door. Our own church, houses, an infirmary, a library for the books, still-rooms for herbs and cordials, and dairies full of butter and cheese. In autumn the air is so heavy with the musts of wine and mead, cider and perry, that it almost sends you to sleep the moment you set foot over the threshold. And every woman who crosses the bridge and enters the gate passes beneath the word *Sauvegarde* – the place of refuge.'

'So why leave such a paradise?' Pega asked with more than a hint of sarcasm in her voice.

God alone knows how many times I'd asked myself that question in the three years we'd been here. I suppose in part, though I could never explain it to Pega, it was that very order and permanence that made me feel ill at ease. I was stepping into another woman's house again. I was reading labels and lists of stores written in someone else's hand. Afraid to change anything that was so neat, so ordered and so settled; having no reason to change it, except to make it mine and it wasn't mine.

My life had always been written in another woman's hand – first my mother's, then his mother's. My mother-in-law's hand was on everything. Her order on the linen in the presses, her pattern in the herb garden, her recipes steeping on the shelves, her words, her virtue, her fecundity hanging over me, like a birch rod above a child. There was no *Sauvegarde* from that.

So when they talked about founding a new beguinage in England, I couldn't wait to volunteer. Among so many in the Vineyard I knew I would remain a beguine, but in the new beguinage I would become a Martha. I'd have a domain of my own. I could arrange things any way I chose. Do you really think that Servant Martha's motives for coming were any more pure than mine? Don't you tell me she was called by God as she wants everyone to believe. Pure ambition, that's all that called her, but at least I'm honest enough to admit what I wanted, and I only wanted some small thing to call my own, not an empire like she's determined to have.

Anyway, we set sail within the year. I'd never been aboard a seagoing ship, but Merchant Martha knew what we were facing.

The sailors swore at her as she followed them round testing every rope and knot holding our stores, but it didn't stop her. You wouldn't believe the stench from the bilges, like a thousand rotten eggs constantly beneath your nose. I felt sick before we'd even left our moorings.

A storm blew up as we left the coast and headed into open sea. The others tried to comfort one another with thoughts of England where cattle lazed in the sweet water meadows and children played in the sun, but all I could think about as the ship juddered and rolled were the tales the sailors told of whirlpools big enough to swallow mountains and leviathans that could break the back of a boat with a single flick of their tails. Icy spray dashed over me, drenching me and leaving me gasping. I clung to the side of the ship and vomited again and again. I thought I'd drown. I prayed to drown, just to end it.

Night shivered into day and day into endless night, but finally one morning I woke to the sound of gulls again. We were drawing into a tiny harbour stinking of decaying salt weed and rotting fish guts. There were no dwellings except for a cluster of fishermen's huts on the slimy boardwalk. The dark green flat of the great salt marsh lay all around, belching and farting its indifference to our presence. Beyond that, a low wooded ridge marked the edge of the solid land. We had arrived in England.

Ulewic itself crouched with its back to the forest, cornered, seeming pushed to the very edge of Christendom. Sullen women watched us as we passed, peering out from the dark doorways of hovels that cattle would have scorned to lie in. Bow-legged children crawled over the rubbish heaps, fighting the pigs and dogs for any filthy scrap they could find in the mud. Even the dirt track from Ulewic went nowhere but to that mud-slimed creek and halted abruptly at the edge as if it had been running away from the village and had thrown itself into the grey waters in despair. And to the west of this midden lay our own benighted plot.

There were just twelve of us, twelve women in a foreign country. Our home was a hillock supporting nothing more than some scrubby bushes and a few moth-eaten goats, a dank wasteland trapped between a dense forest and a rat's nest of a village. Kitchen Martha wept openly when she saw it, tears running down her fat red cheeks and dripping from her chin. The other women stood rigidly, staring as if they might conjure again the cattle and cherub-faced infants of their hopes.

Even Servant Martha, for once, was silent, her head bowed and her face shadowed in her hood. Whether she prayed or despaired I couldn't tell. Gradually all the women turned their faces towards her, an expression of helplessness in their eyes. Servant Martha lifted her head and gazed up for a long time at the great battlements of white cloud swelling up over the flattened land. Then she gave herself a little shake, pushed up her sleeves and patted Kitchen Martha briskly on her plump back.

'Faith, Kitchen Martha, faith and hard work are all we need,' she said with grim cheerfulness. 'Work was ever the master of the demon of despair.'

If she was right, there shouldn't have been a demon left amongst us, for we had worked hard enough since to conquer a legion of them.

Pega prodded me with the end of her staff. All around the women were hastily packing up and making for the track to the beguinage. The wind was whipping through the trees now and a mass of purple clouds was bubbling up behind us, turning the light to a thick, sulphurous yellow. The trees were bending lower and the wind was gathering strength.

Pega nodded towards the tubs slowly filling with sap. 'Best get those lids tied down tight. That storm'll not hold off much longer.'

I held the cords around one of the tubs while Pega's deft fingers bound it tight. Pega's hands always fascinated me, for her right hand was webbed, the fingers bound together with flaps of skin, like a seal's or an otter's. It didn't stop her working though; even with the webs her hands were far more dextrous than mine. Gate Martha's fingers were webbed also. Most of the villagers had the webs on one or both hands, and although they were not identical, Pega said that such webbing was a mark that the bearer came from an ancient village family. I think she was proud of the sign, for it showed she belonged to Ulewic.

'Who's that with Servant Martha?' Catherine was staring up the track.

I turned to look. Two horses were trotting side by side in the direction of the beguinage. There was no mistaking the grey-cloaked figure on the larger of the two beasts. Servant Martha rode with the same grim determination as she walked, spoke or prayed, but I didn't recognize the other.

Pega peered after the riders as they disappeared round the bend in the track. 'Can't tell from here.' She cuffed Catherine lightly over the head. 'Come on, the sooner you get home the sooner you'll find out.'

The first drops of rain hit us as we hurried back towards the beguinage, sharp and stinging. Then it fell in a freezing torrent, heavy enough to knock the breath from you. Our sodden skirts slapped around our ankles. I could hardly see the gate through this curtain of water. My fingers were numb and my kirtle clung to me, twisting round my legs like wet seaweed. Gate Martha was hovering in the open gateway, an upturned bucket on her head to shield her from the rain. She beckoned frantically as if she didn't think we were running fast enough.

'Come in, come in. Kitchen Martha's some warm ale mulling for you. You'll not believe who's come to join us. You're not going to like it, Pega, you're not going to like it at all.'

Servant Martha

D'Acaster's pageboy rode ahead as fast as his little pony would go. Several times he was forced to stop and wait for me to catch up. But I had no intention of allowing my horse to gallop, despite his pleadings. As I told him, such recklessness on a muddy track would inevitably lead to broken bones, ours or our mounts, and nothing could be so urgent as to justify risking that.

A huddle of women and children planting beans in one of the Manor's strips paused to watch us ride past, but I think they stared more as an excuse to straighten their backs than from any real curiosity.

'Please hurry, mistress,' the pageboy begged. 'Look, the Manor's in sight. It's not far now.'

I gazed up to where he pointed. In front of us, on a slight rise, stood a fine imposing gatehouse protected by a huge wooden gate studded with iron bosses and surmounted by sharp spikes. The gate seemed more fitting for a castle under siege than a manor in such a remote corner of England, which no invading army was ever likely to stumble across unless it was hopelessly lost. The gatekeeper sullenly stirred himself to open the gate at the boy's cry, before scuttling back to his smoking brazier.

Beyond the gate, the courtyard was almost deserted. I glimpsed a couple of servants lurking in the dark doorways or slinking about their duties in shadows, but it was strangely quiet. Not even the dogs and chickens rooting about in the mud seemed interested in our arrival. The kitchen, bakehouse and stables were well enough appointed, but the leaking, ill-thatched huts in the corner of the courtyard were evidence that D'Acaster paid better heed to the comfort of his bloodstock than that of his servants.

In contrast, the sturdy grey walls of the Manor were lavishly adorned, though *adorned* hardly seemed the right term for the carved grotesques of men and imps grimacing down as if turned to stone in the very act of shouting, 'Go back!' These human figures were similar to those on the village church, but on the Manor house, between the distorted human heads, were carved the figures of hounds, wolves, lions and birds of prey all captured in the act of killing, doubtless to remind all who saw them that there were some powers on earth they should fear more than those in heaven.

The page raced ahead of me up the stone staircase on the outside of the building and into the great hall. He gabbled something through the open doorway, then fled past me back down the stairs, as if he feared an arrow would come flying after him.

I don't know to whom he made his address, for when I entered the great hall it also appeared to be deserted. The hall was long and narrow. Tapestries of battle and hunting scenes lined the walls, the bloody wounds of man and beast congealed to brown by the smoke of long winters. Wax from the night candles still hung in yellow waterfalls from the spikes and long tables bore the platters and beakers from the last meal, but there were no servants busy clearing up the mess. Only the fire had been repaired and the flames were roaring over the logs as though someone had been poking at them violently and repeatedly.

Something moved in the dark corner on the raised dais at the far end of the hall. A peregrine falcon sat on a perch behind the largest and most ornate chair in the room, the one which Lord D'Acaster would surely occupy at meals. The jesses fastening the bird to the perch were long and it was unhooded. It swivelled its head, watching me, its bright dark eyes ringed with amber. Doubtless it amused Lord D'Acaster to feed the bird during meals, though I had heard some men kept a falcon close by for fear of an assassin's hand. Such creatures can be trained to fly at the face of anyone foolish enough to lunge at their masters.

The bird's wings beat furiously as a man burst out from behind one of the tapestries that I now realized concealed a small door. He strode down the length of the hall towards me. I'd seen him often enough to recognize him as Lord Robert D'Acaster, but I had never before had occasion to waste words with him. Well, let him come to me, I thought, for I would not go running to meet him.

'You took your time, mistress,' he bellowed.

He offered me no courtesies of chair or drink or even greetings. So I stood and waited for him to approach near enough for us to hold a civil conversation. I had no intention of raising my voice.

Though I would not presume to judge the way God designed any man, I couldn't help thinking if there was a design, it was now unrecognizable beneath the weight of loose flesh that sagged upon Lord Robert's bones. He had perhaps been handsome enough in his youth, but what remained of his yellow hair clung to his pate in thinning tufts, like a moulting fowl, and his small eyes had almost disappeared under the florid folds of his puffed face.

He came close and thrust his face into mine, scowling. But if he was hoping I would flinch, he was sadly disappointed. I was a good half a head taller than him. Clearly unused to a woman staring him down, he quickly moved away to pace up and down before me. Height sometimes has its advantages.

'You will take my daughter,' he commanded. 'I want her out of this house this very hour.'

There was a muffled sob behind me. I turned to see a pale, dough-faced woman hunched in a corner of the window seat, her plump, beringed fingers twisting and knotting a handkerchief with such agitation that it appeared her mind did not know what her hands were doing. Her eyes were puffy and her nose was shiny and pink at the tip. She had evidently been crying for some time.

D'Acaster rounded furiously on her. 'I knew that God-cursed whelp of yours would never get a husband. That much was as plain as the prick on a rutting stallion from the day that miserable brat first drew breath, and I would to God she never had. I should have drowned her the moment I laid eyes on her, but no, I'm too tender of heart for that. I raised her, put food in that sour mouth of hers and clothes on her back and this is how she repays me!'

His face ripened to purple as he yelled and his wife shrank back against the walls, as if trying to melt into them. He looked in danger of choking on his own rage. He paused to draw breath, then turned and bellowed as if he was calling a hound to heel, 'Agatha, here, now!'

There was a slight movement in the shadows of the gallery above our heads.

'Yes, you, girl. I know you're there. Get down here at once!'

He paced the floor again, pounding his fist into the palm of his hand until a girl appeared at the foot of a narrow staircase behind me.

'Here!' He clicked his fingers.

The child walked cautiously towards him, her arms wrapped tightly around her ribs, holding herself together. She looked no more than thirteen years of age, but something in her expression suggested she might be older. She was unkempt; her gown, though a rich burgundy, was stained and torn, with dead leaves clinging to it and more tangled in her mop of loose brown hair. She was plainly tense and wary, but for all that she held her head high, her chin jutting out defiantly. She wisely stopped just out of reach of her father's hand. She didn't even glance at me, but stared into mid-space as if trying to shut us all out.

'Look at the little slut,' D'Acaster spat at her, circling around her. 'This is my daughter. This is what I have sheltered at my fireside. This is what I have clothed and fed and nurtured, a shrew and a hellcat. And do you know how she repays my generosity? I'll tell you. She attacks her gentle sisters without provocation. She refuses to master any womanly art. She's stupid, disobedient and wilful. And if that was not enough to

66

make any father rue the day he ever bedded her mother, I find she is nothing but a common village whore.'

The girl stood apparently unmoved by this recitation of her many sins. Much of her face was hidden by her tousled hair, but as the light from the window fell on her, I glimpsed a cut on her cheek made livid by the blue and mauve bruise around it. She didn't look like a demon, but the devil can be at work in many a seemingly innocent form, even a child.

'Look at her; she is so hardened that she does not even weep with shame. Running around the forest all night like a bitch on heat. Crawling back to my gate at dawn.' He rounded on his wife again. 'This is your doing.'

'But I was certain she was in the Manor somewhere,' Lady D'Acaster sobbed. 'I thought she'd returned from the May Fair with her sisters. She's never been out unchaperoned before, I swear it.'

'Swear all you like, I'll not shelter the whore under my roof another night. I'll not suffer her to corrupt her innocent sisters. Nor will her reputation stain theirs. From now on I have only two daughters.'

He scooped three small leather money bags from the table and thrust them at me so hard I grunted from the impact of his fist against my stomach.

'This is all the dowry that comes with her. I'll not waste a penny more on her, so do not ask it.' Dragging the child by the wrist, he slapped her small hand into mine as though he were betrothing us. 'Take the little hellcat and never let me set eyes on her again.'

'And what exactly would you have me do with her?' I asked.

'You may feed her to the ravens for all I care.'

He clicked his fingers at his wife, who obediently rose and followed him down the hall.

As she passed her daughter she muttered, 'Be a good girl, Agatha.' But she did not once look at her child, not even when she reached the door at the far end of the hall.

I felt the small cold hand clench into a fist inside my own, then the door slammed and Agatha pulled her hand out of my grasp. Wrapping her arms around her chest again, she stood glowering at the table. We would have to talk, but that could wait. The important thing now was to remove her from the house as quickly as possible. The girl might well be all that her father described, but I would not have left a mad dog in the care of such a man.

'Will you take your things now,' I asked her, 'or shall I send someone for them later?'

'I want nothing from that . . . that fat toad.'

'Agatha!' I said severely. 'You owe a duty of respect to your father for giving you life.'

She glared at me. 'You heard what my life was worth to him, so much carrion.'

I held up the three weighty bags. 'Most girls in the village would not have a single penny placed upon their lives. See what you are valued at.'

'You hold the value of my father's pride, not my worth. He wouldn't have people say he was too poor to pay a dowry.'

There was such a cold fury in those green eyes that I wondered if her father had been correct in his judgment after all and she was indeed a fiend. Still, even a wildcat may be tamed. It would be a challenge, but I could certainly do no worse than him. God had given Agatha into my hands so that I might bring her into His grace and I was determined to bring her there whatever it took.

Agatha

The small guest room in the beguinage was hot and stifling. My body ached, my head pounded and every joint and muscle was groaning in protest at being made to stand upright. My legs were shaking, but Servant Martha took no notice. She stood erect before the plain table, her hands clasped behind her.

'Now, Agatha, you must understand that beguines make no perpetual vows, but you must be celibate in deed and thought so long as you reside here, and so long as you choose to live here you will obey the rules of this community agreed by the Marthas who are elected by our beguinage to have the running of it.'

I stared at her mouth, watching her lips move over her sharp teeth and the mole on her chin bob up and down. I wanted to shout – *stop talking at me! I can't take any more. I don't care about your stupid rules. If this is a nunnery, just put me in a cell and leave me alone.*

'You're free to come and go as you wish, but you will be expected to attend the Sunday Mass at the church, likewise the daily offices in our chapel. As beguines our purpose is to study, write and teach, to care for the infirm and sick, and work selflessly for our community and for the poor. We put food on our table and clothes on our backs through the labours of our own hands, not from money taken from the people or the Church.'

The room was too warm. I couldn't breathe. Images and faces kept sliding away from me, dissolving before I could grasp them. A fire, roaring up taller than a man; someone screaming; black wings hovering above me. I couldn't move. I was being crushed. His weight was still holding me down and I couldn't break free. It was all I could do to stop myself lashing out. I tried desperately to hold myself together. Concentrate on what she is saying. Don't think about last night. Don't think.

Servant Martha was frowning. Her mouth grew tighter. Her voice snapped like a dog on a chain.

'Your personal belongings, dowry and everything you bring to the beguinage remain yours and you may take these with you if you choose to leave. But if –'

A single phrase caught in my mind. 'I can leave?'

Servant Martha looked startled. 'This is a beguinage, not a nunnery. Did I not say that we make no perpetual vows here?'

'And I can take the money my father gave you?' That didn't make sense. Girls don't own their own dowries. Husbands or Mother Superiors take them.

'We make no vows of poverty. The money is yours, but while you are here you should neither live in luxury nor deny yourself to excess. Both extremes show pride of spirit. Merchant Martha, who is also our Martha of the Common Purse, will keep your money safe for you and you may ask her for it whenever you wish. Who knows, you may yet want it for a dowry.'

'Don't be stupid! You know I won't!'

Everyone in the village knew I could never marry. My sisters had taunted me with this ever since I was born. No one would ever take me and I was glad of it. No, more than glad, I was ecstatic. If anything or anyone ever touched me again, I'd kill them. I swear this time I'd kill them. I closed my eyes tightly, feeling that creature's stinking breath burning my neck. I started gagging. I was going to puke. I bit my fist hard, trying to choke it back.

Servant Martha drew herself even more upright. 'Very well, Agatha, since firm words are all that you will respond to, I will oblige you.'

Her tone was as sharp as a slap, shaking me out of the nightmare. I was almost grateful for that. I took a deep breath and looked up at her as coldly as I could. What firm words? What did she think she could say that I hadn't heard my father say a thousand times before? Whatever it was, I wouldn't let anything hurt me any more.

'Mark this well. If you are sent from here in disgrace, you will leave with only the clothes you stand up in. All else is forfeit.'

I almost laughed. Was that all? I knew it was too good to be true. Whatever she called it, this place was no different from a nunnery. She tried to stare me down, but I wouldn't look away; I met her hard, dark blue eyes without flinching, as she did mine.

Finally Servant Martha stalked over to the door and called out to someone I couldn't see. 'Would you be so kind as to ask Kitchen Martha to attend us here?'

We waited, the silence broken only by the crackle of the fire and the rattling of the shutters in the wind. Finally the door opened, sending gusts of smoke swirling round the room. A small plump woman tumbled in. Despite the bitter wind, her face was flushed and shining from the heat of her fire.

'Kitchen Martha, this is Agatha, she seeks a home with us.'

Kitchen Martha beamed and hurried forward. 'Welcome, child, you are very welcome.'

I had to stifle a scream as she swept me into a great hug, half smothering me in her massive bosom.

'She will be placed in your charge.' Servant Martha hesitated. 'She will need as much guidance as is in your power to give her.'

I scowled at Servant Martha. Her careful words had not fooled me for one minute. What she meant was, 'Watch her, control her and discipline her. She is a hellcat and must be tamed.'

But if I understood the code, Kitchen Martha clearly didn't, for she looked from one to the other of us in bewilderment as if waiting for Servant Martha to say more, but eventually she nodded and began to bustle me towards the door.

Before we reached it, Servant Martha called out, 'One thing more, Agatha, in the chapel on the Sabbath you will receive your new name to mark the beginning of your new life with us.'

I felt a jolt of hope. 'I can choose a new name for myself?'

'Of course not. We do not choose our own names in life; they are given to us. A suitable name will be chosen for you by the Marthas after much prayer and thought. It will be their gift to you.'

The despair came flooding back. It would be no different here than in my father's house.

Holding our skirts out of the infernal mud, we scuttled, heads down, through the driving rain to a long, low building. Kitchen Martha pushed me down on a stool in front of the fire and shook the rain from her cloak before unwrapping a steaming slice of bough cake from her scrip.

'Eat it up, child, while it's hot. I've seen a plucked chicken with more colour in its cheeks. I don't know what Servant Martha was thinking of, talking on like that, when even a blind man could see you were near to fainting. How can anyone attend to anything on an empty belly?'

The smell of the spiced honeyed batter suddenly made me realize how ravenous I was. I bit off a great mouthful of thick sweet batter and soft baked fruits inside and gulped it down greedily.

'Steady, don't burn yourself, child.'

Kitchen Martha turned to poke the fire. Her hands were dimpled like rising dough and scarred with a hundred tiny burns, probably from years of cooking. No one could have called her pretty; her bulbous nose was lumpy and pitted and her cheeks crazed with red veins from the heat of the fires. But she had merry eyes and a mop of greying curls that, like mine, refuse to stay in their bindings.

I gazed around me. We were in a long room. Narrow wooden cots were ranged along the sides and beside each of them stood a simple banded wooden chest. Rough stools were set around a long table in the centre of the room with books and quills neatly stacked upon it. I longed to see what the books were, but I was afraid to pick them up. At the far end of the room several tallow candles were already set for the night around a crucifix. Night! Soon it would be dark again.

I shivered, pulling my cloak tighter around myself. My ribs

and stomach ached. As I shuffled my feet, the smell of thyme rose up from the herb-strewn rushes on the floor. I wanted to fill my body with the sharp cleanness of its smell. They say thyme expels the worm that gnaws at the mind and drives you mad. But nothing could drive that worm out. It was inside me. That demon was inside me and nothing I could do would expel the horror of it from my body. I took another gulp of air, but the scent had dissolved and I could not bring it back.

'And this is where you will sleep, child.' Kitchen Martha was pointing to the cots near the door. How long had she been speaking? What else had she said?

'I think that those four cots are unoccupied. You may choose whichever you wish. That chest has spare kirtles and the grey cloaks. You're sure to find one that fits. You can put your own clothes in that one, though they'll want cleaning before they're stored away.' She came closer and turned my face to catch the light from the door. 'That's a nasty cut. How did you come by it?'

I flinched away from the touch and backed to the other side of the table. 'It isn't anything, just a scratch.'

'Come with me and I'll ask Healing Martha to look at you. She has many ointments that will soothe it.'

'Don't touch me. I'll tend it myself.' I could hear myself shouting, but I couldn't stop. 'Go away and leave me alone!'

Kitchen Martha looked startled. Her hand stretched out awkwardly as if she wanted to soothe me, but she withdrew it. I felt sick and every part of me was burning. I just wanted to hide in some dark corner and never come out.

'The other children will be joining you shortly.' Kitchen Martha waddled to the door. 'Cheer up, you'll soon make friends.'

I waited until the door had closed behind her, then chose the cot in the corner furthest from the occupied ones and lay down, curling up in a ball under my cloak. The straw in the pallet rustled under me. It was harder than the bed I was used to, but at least the cot was too narrow to share.

All day I'd been wandering round stuck in waking nightmare. I hurt so much that I couldn't even think about where I was being taken or what would happen to me. Now, lying in a strange bed, I suddenly realized that for the first time ever, I was alone among strangers, without any idea what to do or what they wanted of me. I began to panic. I'd always longed to escape from my father's house, but now that I had, I wanted to run straight back. At least there I knew what to do. But I couldn't go back; my own father had disowned me and thrown me out into the street as if I was a servant. I had no home and no family. I had nothing but these foreign women.

Servant Martha, Kitchen Martha, Healing Martha – who were they anyway? My father said they were nuns from some wealthy order. He knew that by the way they threw their money about like pig slops. He could always find a reason for docking a hired man's wages and he despised anyone who couldn't.

He knew all about these wealthy orders, he said. Convents made rich by the dowries of highborn women who were too ugly to be married off, so their families hid them away in nunneries where they occupied themselves in needlework and prayer for the souls of their fathers and brothers until they withered up and died quietly. But I knew the first time I saw these women that if they were nuns, they certainly weren't like any I'd ever met before.

The year they arrived was a bad summer, wet and cold. Crops wouldn't ripen. The wind and rain beat them into the mud where they stank and rotted away. The servants at the Manor cursed the foreign women for bringing the evil weather with them.

The first time I saw them close up was at Mass at St Michael's church in the village, standing together in a block, all dressed alike in plain grey kirtles of heavy wool with grey cloaks and hoods drawn about their heads. I couldn't take my eyes off them; they were so still. My two older sisters, Edith and Anne, were praying piously, moving their lips with great exaggeration as we'd been taught, so that everyone could see that they were

74

praying. Everyone else in the church was mumbling away to themselves, like my sisters, but not these women. Their lips didn't move at all. The old priest, the one before Father Ulfrid, was watching them too and he looked angry. The villagers edged away from them. It was dangerous to be different in Ulewic, everyone knew that.

A single bell rang out over the courtyard. Before I could sit up, the door burst open and the wind flung a child into the room. She raced across the floor and threw herself face down on her cot, laughing and panting as other little girls chased in after her.

'I've won, I've won,' she squealed, then sat up as she caught sight of me in the corner. Her playmates followed her gaze. We stared at one another. I knew I should be the one to speak and explain my presence in the room, but the unsmiling faces of the little girls watching me reminded me of the hostile stares of the servants' children who always ceased their games when I approached.

'Are you Agatha? Kitchen Martha said you'd be here,' called a voice from the door. 'I'm Catherine.'

The girl shook the rain from her cloak. She looked five or six years older than the others, about my age, with skinny brown plaits framing a long, melancholy face, making it look even longer. She reminded me of my father's lurcher.

'I thought everyone was called Martha here,' I said peevishly. That wretched little girl was still staring at me.

'Oh no, everyone has a beguine name – not their old name, of course, a gift name, but if a beguine is elected to help run the beguinage she's then called a Martha after the blessed St Martha who worked for our Lord.' Catherine gabbled so eagerly, I could hardly understand what she was saying. 'Servant Martha is the head, then Kitchen Martha runs the kitchen, Shepherd Martha tends sheep –'

'I'm not stupid, I had worked that out for myself.'

She looked as hurt as Kitchen Martha had done and I felt a little prick of guilt, but not enough to make me care.

Catherine bit her lip, 'You come from Ulewic, don't you?'

'What of it?'

Catherine glanced uneasily at the children, but they had already lost interest in me and were huddled round the far end of the table, engrossed in a game of knuckle bones. Catherine came closer and glanced at me shyly. 'I heard some of the beguines talking about the fire in the forest, about the ... Owl Masters. Who are they?'

'No one knows who they are; that's the point. Why else would they wear masks?' I shuddered, desperately trying not to see those feathered masks circling the fire.

'But why owls?'

'I don't know! I suppose because owls bring ill-fortune and death to any house they alight on. That's what the Owl Masters do.'

'Pega says owls eat the souls of dead babies if they die unbaptized,' Catherine whispered.

'So why ask me?' I snapped. 'Ask this Pega. I'm not a villager. Stop asking stupid questions. I don't want to talk about it.'

The bell sounded again and Catherine jumped up. 'Vespers, we mustn't be late.'

Her earnest expression was so irritating that for a moment I almost felt like ignoring her, but Servant Martha's words echoed in my head, *If you are sent from here in disgrace* ... If I was sent away from this place, where would I go? I would have no money and no craft by which to earn a living. What happened to girls like me? I couldn't survive out there alone.

Catherine was jiggling anxiously from foot to foot, her hand on the iron ring of the half-open door. Outside, the rain drummed down on the muddy courtyard. The light was fading fast under the thick canopy of clouds.

If you are sent from here ...

In the deep forest, beyond the safety of the courtyard walls, it would already be dark. The trees would be closing together, their branches blotting out the sky, like the walls of a cave. There was no escape, no way out of that living prison. No way of running from the brambles that dug their claws into my skirts, or the roots that wrapped themselves around my ankles, chaining me down in the suffocating reek of rotting leaves. And somewhere in the forest that creature would be watching for me to step outside the gate. I felt the rush of air from its wings on my face, the cold talons gripping my skin. The demon was waiting somewhere out there in the darkness, waiting for me to come again.

✝

May — Rood Day or Crossmas

St Helen discovered several old crosses. To test which was the true cross she stretched a corpse out on each cross and the one that revived the corpse was pronounced the true cross on which Christ had died.

Pisspuddle

My big brother, William, picked up a fat handful of pig shit and grinned at his friend Henry.

'Watch this. I bet you I can land this right on her nose.'

Henry snorted. 'Even your stupid sister could hit her from there and she's a girl. Dare you to stand behind that post and do it.'

William looked scornful and sauntered back to the post.

Little Marion could see what was coming and she tried to duck her head, but she couldn't move much in the stocks. Thick rivers of snot ran from her nose where she'd been bawling. She wriggled on the narrow strip of wood she was sitting on. It was a thin plank turned on its side and hammered into the Green. She couldn't slide back because of the stocks round her ankles. It was really sharp, that wood. Last time she'd had this big black welt across her backside for days after, from where she'd been sitting on it. Said it hurt worse than a switch.

William took aim and Marion started bawling again.

'Don't, William, that's mean,' I yelled before I could stop myself.

William turned to me, grinning. 'You want me to throw it at you instead, do you, Pisspuddle?' He raised his fist again, this time in my direction.

Henry sniggered. 'Your little sister's got a face like a turd anyway, nobody'd notice the difference.'

'Yeh. Come here, turd-face.'

I started to run across the Green. I knew he'd do it. I kept expecting to feel the wet slap of it on my back.

'Drop that at once, boy.'

I stopped and peered round, with my hands up in front of my face, just in case. Henry was running away, but a tall lady had got hold of William by the wrist and was forcing him to open his hand. The shit plopped on the ground. She pulled William's wrist down until he was bent double. Then she wiped his hand back and front on the grass as if he was a baby still in clouts.

I'd seen the lady before in church. She came from the house of women.

'Outlanders', that's what Mam called them, that's why they dressed so queer. 'It's not natural,' Mam said, 'a group of women living altogether, with no men among them. Only witches or nuns do that.'

I'd seen nuns when they came to the village with the shrivelled lips of St Alphege to collect money. They walked slowly in silence and never ever smiled, as if they always had a headache. But these women were always laughing whenever they came to the village, all except this one; she looked like she'd eaten a sour apple.

The lady let William stand up, but she still had him by the wrist. His face had turned red.

'Now, boy, for whom did you intend that?'

William looked from me to Marion and opened his mouth like a great fat carp, but nothing came out.

'Speak up, boy, I can't hear you.'

She looked like a giant heron, grey cloak, grey hair and grey kirtle. She had a nose as sharp as a beak.

'Her . . . in the stocks,' William muttered.

'Then you should be ashamed of yourself, boy. She's only a little girl. Our blessed Lord teaches us to show compassion for prisoners. Didn't He Himself say let him who is without sin cast the first stone?'

'Wasn't a stone,' William sulked.

'Don't be impudent, boy. Now, get about your business and leave her alone, do you hear me?'

'You can't make me,' William jeered.

'But I warrant I can.' John, the blacksmith, grabbed his ear and twisted hard. William jumped and yelped. He hadn't noticed John walking up behind him. It served him right. John pulled him up by the ear till he was standing on tiptoes. I stuffed my fingers in my mouth, trying hard not to giggle.

'This lad bothering you, mistress?'

'Just mischief, nothing I can't deal with. But tell me, the child in the stocks, what has she done to earn such a punishment?'

'Out gleaning wool before the Terce bell.' John had let go of William's ear, but his thick hairy fingers clutched William's shoulder.

'It's no justice to punish one so young for that,' the lady said. 'The child can be no more than six or seven summers at most.'

'Old enough to know the law. Isn't the first time she's been caught.'

'How long is she to stay in there?'

John shrugged, 'Till the Vespers bell. Maybe longer if her father hasn't paid his fine by then.'

Marion, though she already knew that, began yowling loud enough to be heard right across the Green.

'You can't keep the child in there against her father's debt.' The lady sounded cross.

'It's either her or him and he can't earn the money to pay the fine if he's in there, now can he?' John said.

The lady pulled herself up so tall I thought her head would fall off her neck.

'Then I'll pay the fine, but I want her released now. Her father must be in great want if he sends this little one to glean, and you're only adding to their burden with your fines when you should be giving them charity.'

'Nowt to do with me. D'Acaster's steward gave the orders.' He pointed towards the inn. 'You'll find him supping in the Bull Oak. Phillip's his name, if you've got any complaints.'

'Then I'll speak with him.'

The lady swept off across the Green. She walked so fast that her cloak swirled back behind her as if she was flying like a witch.

'If you ask me,' John called after her, 'you're wasting good money. That family never learn. The brat'll be back in the stocks before the month is out.'

But I don't think the grey lady heard him.

John grabbed the back of William's shirt and gave him a good shake. 'Now, you listen to me, my lad, your father would flay the hide off you if he knew you were messing with those hags. You don't know what goes on behind those walls of theirs; if they got hold of a lad like you, like as not you'd never be seen again.'

'I'm not afraid of them,' William said, but I knew he was, because his face had gone all red and blotchy.

'Well, you should be. All of those women together like that can do things you wouldn't dream of, lad. They can make your nose rot off your face and your cock shrivel up like a worm. So mind you stay well out of their way.'

He gave William another shake and strode off, kicking the stocks as he passed. 'And you can stop your bawling, Marion. You'll not cod Phillip D'Acaster as easily as that daft gammer.'

William stomped furiously towards me.

'What are you laughing at, Pisspuddle?' He tried to clout me one, but I dodged out of his way and that made him madder than ever.

'Nothing,' I said quickly and started to walk home.

William followed me. 'I'll get the old besom back, see if I don't. I'm not afraid of those gammers. What can they do?'

'Cured Cousin Stephen's arm, didn't they?' I reminded him. 'Mam said he'd lose it for sure. Bone came right through the skin, but it healed right up. He was screaming like a scalded pig when he fell off the roof, but they stopped it hurting too. Even the cunning-woman, Old Gwenith, can't do that.'

William snorted and chucked a stone at a fluster of hens, which scattered, squawking.

I walked carefully along the top of a fallen branch lying in the track, putting my hands out to balance myself, but it rolled and I slipped off.

'What are you doing that for?' William eyed me suspiciously.

'No reason.' I stopped at once and started walking fast along the path.

'Yes you are. You did it on the way here too and yesterday.'

'No I didn't.'

A nasty grin began to spread across his face. 'I know what you're doing. You're pretending you're that tumbler's girl, the one walking the pole at the May Fair.'

'I'm not.' I could feel my face going red and tried to run, but William grabbed me from behind by one of my braids.

'Oh yes you are.' He roared with laughter. 'Just wait till I tell Henry, he'll wet himself. Little Pisspuddle thinks she can walk on a pole and have pretty golden curls and have everyone admire her.'

'Let go!' I yelled.

He twisted my arm round and scrubbed my face with the end of my braid. I hated it when he did that. I tried to wriggle free.

'It's not a bad idea, sending you up a pole. With a face like yours everyone would think we've got a performing ferret!'

I yanked my hair out of his hand and ran as fast as I could down the path. I could hear him roaring with laughter behind me. I just wished they'd put him in the stocks. I'd throw all the dung and every rotten vegetable I could find at him. I'd tie a stinking fish right under his nose and I'd drop spiders and worms and beetles down his neck so they'd wriggle inside his shirt. I'd wait until he was really hungry and thirsty, then I'd eat a big juicy apple in front of him. Then I'd put earwigs inside his ears and they'd bite their way right through his brain and plop out of his nose and he'd scream and scream. And then I'd, I'd . . . I'd think of something else to do to him, even worse than that.

Father Ulfrid

'You shouldn't have come, Father.' Ralph pulled the blanket tighter round his shoulders.

Inside the tightly shuttered cottage the air felt chill. Dampness seeped up from the beaten earth floor. The fire in the hearth was banked down with turfs to save fuel and barely any warmth from it oozed out into the one room that served as kitchen, living and sleeping quarters for the family.

I ducked under bunches of dried herbs and onions that hung from the rafters. 'Joan said you were not able to come to Mass because you had the ague. But I'm glad to see you're recovering a little.'

Ralph was sitting hunched in the chair in the furthest corner of the room. I was more than a little surprised to see him out of bed. I'd suffered marsh-ague once myself and I'd not been able to lift my head from the pillow.

'She shouldn't have troubled you,' Ralph muttered angrily. He glared at his wife who stood with her back to the bolted door. I turned to catch her mouthing something at Ralph that evidently I was not intended to hear. There was no obvious sign of fever upon him, but it was hard to see his face clearly by the feeble light of the single rush candle that was burning. Although it was only mid-afternoon, the shutters were tightly fastened.

'And ...' I hesitated. 'I saw your little daughter Marion in the stocks this morning.'

Joan buried her face in her hands. 'There was no call for D'Acaster's steward to put her in the stocks. She's only a bairn. I know she shouldn't have gone out so early. But she's so small it's the only way she can glean anything, otherwise the bigger ones push her aside and take it all. I don't know how we're going to pay the fine … as if I haven't got enough to worry about. What with Ralph being … being sick …' She trailed off with a frightened glance in her husband's direction.

'I believe the fine's been paid,' I told her. 'I heard the leader of the house of women paid it.'

Joan stared at me in disbelief. 'Why?'

'I understand they are women of great charity. She must have taken pity on the child.'

'We don't need charity from the likes of them,' Joan muttered angrily. 'I've told the bairns a dozen times never go near them. It's dangerous to go mixing with outlanders.'

'On this occasion I think you should be grateful, Joan, and I trust you'll not refuse the Church's charity.' I uncovered my basket. 'I've brought you a little mutton, Ralph. I thought Joan might make a broth of it for you, if you couldn't take solid food.'

Joan darted forward to take the meat. 'You're a good man, Father, no matter what they say.'

'And what do they say, Joan?' I asked grimly.

'Nothing, Father,' Joan said hastily. 'Village tattle. Me and Ralph, we take no notice.'

'All the same, I'd like to hear it.'

Joan plucked at her skirt. 'Tongues wag, you know that, Father. I heard tell that your last position was in the Cathedral at Norwich, a good living by all accounts. People have been wondering why you left it … to come to a parish like this.'

'And do they have an answer?' The band was tightening around my chest again.

'They say … well, some say, that you were banished here on account of …' She looked desperately at her husband, but he did not come to her rescue. 'On account of being caught … begging your pardon, Father, in bed with … with a nun, that's what they say.' She caught up the bottom of her sacking apron and covered her face with it, too mortified even to look at me.

My breath came out in a great snort of laughter. They both looked at me in surprise. 'No, no I can assure you I was not caught in bed with a nun or caught anywhere else with a nun, for that matter.'

My chest still ached despite the relief. Once it set in, the pain would take hours to subside. Every day since I'd come to the miserable little village I felt as if I was being stalked by a beast which any moment might pounce on me. Every time I looked into their eyes I wondered if somehow they had found out, if the Bishop's Commissarius had deliberately let it slip. It was the kind of thing he'd relish doing if it served his purpose.

Joan was watching me, evidently waiting for some kind of explanation.

'I was not sent here because of a nun. I came here because, like Christ, I wanted to serve those in need of me. I didn't take holy orders to fawn on the wealthy that come to the Cathedral.'

Joan's tired eyes smiled. 'That's just what Ralph told the neighbours. He said to them, didn't you, Ralph, he said you'd not been sent here as a punishment. Stands to reason, Ralph said, if you'd been caught doing something like that, they'd have flogged you bloody or worse.'

My shoulders jerked and the scars on my back suddenly burned again against the rough cloth.

I tried to force a smile. 'It is good to know I have some friends in Ulewic.'

Ralph seemed so drawn into himself, it was hard to tell if he was even listening. I'd never seen him so miserable. Normally he was such a cheerful man, full of life, no matter what his hardships. I couldn't understand what had brought about this sudden change in him. I looked around for a stool and drew it up close to him, but as I did so, he drew away from me.

Joan's hand darted out as if to pull me back, but she stopped herself. 'You don't want to be getting too close ... in case you fall sick, Father.'

'Christ will protect me,' I assured her.

'Is it true what they say about Giles, Father?' she asked anxiously.

I glanced at Ralph. Was that what was distressing him? I had not thought them to be friends, but it was possible Giles was . . . had been . . . a relative. I had still not managed to unpick the tangled web of who was related to whom in this village.

But I did not need to ask what whispers Joan had heard. The whole village now knew that one of their own neighbours had been tortured, then paraded in the saint's effigy for their entertainment. And the Owl Masters had made quite certain that every man and woman in Ulewic had learned the name of the man who had screamed out his dying agonies in the flames. I shivered. A sour bile rose in my throat. Damn Hilary and damn that bastard, Phillip. It wasn't me who should feel guilty. It was their fault, all of this.

'May they burn in hell!' I blurted out, then, seeing the look of alarm on Joan's face, I tried to control my anger. 'An evil deed was done, a great evil, and the men who did it will pay for it, if not in this life then in the next.'

Joan's brow was creased with anxiety. 'But no one knew that poor lad was inside St Walburga. My brother was there and he swears he didn't know.'

'The Owl Masters knew and no doubt others besides,' I said sternly.

'But you won't . . . You'll not use book and candle against us, will you, Father?'

I studied her carefully for a moment. 'I am prepared to accept that most of the villagers were ignorant of what they did, but you all know now. And which of your neighbours will it be next time? It might even be one of your own family. The villagers must stand together and shun the devilish rites of the Owl Masters.'

Joan glanced uneasily at the door, as if she feared someone might be listening. 'But if the Owl Masters could take a lad just for making love to a maid, then . . .'

'If anyone threatens you, Joan, you must come to me at once. The Church will protect you, I promise you that.' I jerked my head towards the door. 'Leave us now. I need to hear Ralph's confession, if he's to receive the sacraments.'

She nodded and dropped an awkward half-curtsy and, with another anxious glance at her husband, opened the door just wide enough to slip through, before quickly slamming it shut behind herself.

I pulled a fat wax candle from my scrip and lit it with the smoking rush taper, placing it on the corner of the rough table. Beneath it I laid a tiny silver box containing the precious Host. Ralph made his confession in a dull, low voice, his face turned away from me into the shadows. He confessed nothing that he had not confessed before – pride, sloth – I did not really believe him guilty of either, but he judged himself more harshly than most men.

Ego te absolvo a peccatis tuis in nomine Patris et Filii, et Spiritus Sancti, Amen.

I picked up the guttering candle, to move it closer to Ralph as I prepared to place the Host in his mouth, but my sleeve caught on the edge of the table and the candle tipped. A few drops of hot wax splashed down on to Ralph's hand.

'Forgive me, Ralph, did I burn . . .'

I realized he hadn't flinched or moved his hand. Three drops of white wax lay on his skin, but he hadn't felt them fall or burn him. He saw me staring at his hand and looked down. With a belated cry, he swiftly covered it with the blanket.

I lurched backwards. I didn't mean to, but Ralph saw me recoil and the expression on his face changed to one of fear. Now I understood only too well what really ailed the poor man. Christ have mercy on him! In that terrible moment of realization I could do nothing except stand there, the candle trembling in my fingers. Ralph hunched into the shadows, his chin almost touching his chest. Neither of us spoke. There was nothing I could say which could comfort him now.

I gathered my wits and hastily finished what I had come to do. Then I extinguished the candle and returned it to my scrip. I knew he was willing me not to pronounce the dread word and couldn't bring myself to say it. I think we both believed that somehow if the word remained unspoken there was still hope. At the door, I turned and made the sign of the cross.

'*Dominus vobiscum.*'

There was no answering movement or amen, only a desperate pleading in his eyes.

Outside, I leaned heavily against the closed door. Joan was talking to the old widow Lettice, who had perched her massive buttocks on the wall of the well, and had evidently settled down for a good gossip. At the sound of the door closing, Joan's gaze searched my face and her eyes held the same tortured plea as Ralph's.

But before I could say anything, Lettice heaved herself off the wall and came bustling towards me. 'How is he, Father? The poor dear man. I was just saying to dear Joan here, I've got just the thing for the ague, my old mother's recipe, made from the best white poppies. My late husband, God rest his soul, used to swear by it. In the end he drank it whether he was sick or not. He said it was the only cure for his headache. He was a martyr to headaches.

'Mind you, it's a queer time of year to be getting the ague, but then seasons have turned arse up ever since those outlanders came. Outlanders always bring trouble. When I was a lass, some friars came to preach in the village, wild-looking pack. Holy beggars, they called themselves. Owl Masters soon got rid of them, but after they'd gone, a cry went up that three bairns were missing. Whole village searched for them, but we never found so much as a hair. I reckon the outlanders snatched the bairns to sell in London or France or some such wicked place. Those women are from France, aren't they? Shouldn't wonder if they haven't given that husband of yours the evil eye and that's what's ailing him. I'll soon tell you for sure.'

Lettice reached round me to grasp the door latch. I saw the stricken look on Joan's face and grasped Lettice firmly by the arm, pulling her away from the door.

'He's sleeping now. Let him rest. But if you've an hour to spare there's a family that could do with your help.'

Still keeping a firm grip on her plump arm, I began to march her down the street. I might be able to divert Lettice for today, but she'd be back, and I wondered just how long Joan would be able to keep that door shut against Mistress Lettice and the rest of the village.

Agatha

Even behind the closed gates of the beguinage I was scared. Though I was exhausted, I couldn't sleep that first night for I was too afraid of what I would meet in my dreams. I'd lain awake, rigid, listening to every shriek and bark in the valley. I couldn't get the horror out of my head – the flames, the screams, the terror as I tried to fight the monster on top of me, the weight of it pressing me down.

All the next day I was scared even to cross the open courtyard, because I knew that creature was crouching out there in the dark shadows of the forest waiting for me to step outside. Though the foreign beguines were friendly enough, the beguines from the village stared after me coldly wherever I went, as if I was some kind of spy. To them I was D'Acaster's daughter. I felt as if any moment they were going to bundle me out through the gate and offer me like wolf-bait to that monster.

But that evening in the chapel I finally felt safe for the first time since that night in the forest, maybe for the first time ever in my life. Safe because I was in limbo. My old name hovered outside the chapel door. It couldn't follow me in, for the beguines had forbidden it. I was nameless, without a shadow, without a reflection. Without a name that demon couldn't find me. I didn't inhabit the world of the living or the dead. I couldn't be called up to heaven or down to hell without a name. If I died now at that moment, I'd wander formless over the face of the earth. No one would see me. No one would know me. I wanted that, I wanted to stay like that for ever. I wanted to be invisible.

The beguinage chapel was beautiful, small and simple, so different to our parish church of St Michael. The altar of white stone, carved with pomegranates and bees, had a small slab of dark green stone set into the top of it. The green was shot through with flecks of madder as if drops of blood had fallen upon a glossy lily pad.

The paintings on the chapel walls were almost completed. The Blessed Virgin Mary in glory shone down from above the altar, her crown gold-leafed and golden stars circling her raised hand. The other walls of the chapel were decorated with scenes from the life of a woman who had evidently become a beguine for she was depicted in the grey kirtle and cloak.

The service was also like no other that I had ever attended. There was no chaplain or priest. Servant Martha stood by the altar, her hands folded. In the candlelight her face no longer looked stern. Her voice was joyous; her words leapt upwards as if they would spring through the chapel roof. Father Ulfrid always hurried through the service, like a bored schoolboy chanting his Latin declensions, eager to get them over and go out to play. But these prayers were swallows soaring and swooping on the evening air. The words were familiar, but I had not thought they could be spoken like this. A shiver ran down my spine. It felt forbidden, wonderfully forbidden.

Three of the beguines rose and, settling themselves on low stools, took up their instruments. One began the rhythm, beating with a deer horn upon a drum; another much older woman plucked a citole, while a third, waiting until the tune had established itself, ran in and out of it on the pipes like a child between court dancers. The women joined in, singing a hymn of praise, no solemn and mournful chant, but a song that bubbled and cascaded like a stream over stones. The music fell away as softly as it began. A single sob hung in the dancing candlelight, then it too was gone.

Servant Martha beckoned and suddenly the feeling of safety evaporated and I felt the panic rising. I could feel all eyes on me and I wanted to run out of the door, but outside I'd be entirely alone. I shuffled towards her, staring at the floor. My legs still felt shaky. My ribs were still too painful to touch. Why did she have to do this in front of everyone? I watched, as if from a long way off, as Servant Martha sprinkled me with water from a bunch of hyssop. But I didn't feel the drops fall. Then she pronounced my new name, 'Osmanna'.

'Welcome, Osmanna,' echoed back from the belly of the chapel.

I half turned, wondering who they addressed. It wasn't my name. It was borrowed and hung upon me, like the beguine's cloak.

I knew all about Osmanna. She was a princess who fled her parents to live in the forest. A bishop consecrated her as a virgin of Christ, then left her to be raped by the gardener appointed to protect and provide for her. How could they have chosen that name for me? Of all the saints' names, why did they have to choose that one? Did they not realize what had been done to me?

Servant Martha bent down and pinned a small tin emblem to my kirtle. 'The boar, it is the symbol of the blessed Saint. When St Osmanna was living as a hermit in the forest she gave shelter to a hunted boar. She protected the beast with her own body and it did not attack her. When the bishop who was hunting the boar saw how Osmanna miraculously tamed the savage beast, he converted her to Christianity and baptized her. May the symbol of your namesake protect and defend you, Osmanna.'

I wanted to tear the emblem off and grind it into the dust. What use was it now? It was too late. If I'd had Osmanna's power to strike the gardener blind, I would not have prayed for his healing. I would have laughed as he crawled on his hands and knees through thorns and thickets. I would have snatched the food from his hands and dashed the water from his lips. I would have whispered him into swamps and sung him into icy rivers. I would have taunted him through burning deserts and left him silent in the frozen dark lands. I would have made him know what he had done to me. I was not Osmanna.

July – St Everild's Day

Everild, a noblewoman from Wessex who founded a nunnery for eighty women near Ripon in Yorkshire before her death in AD 700.

Pisspuddle

'If you don't get up this instant, you'll get no breakfast,' Mam yelled.

I pushed off the blanket and shivered. It wasn't even light yet, but Mam had flung the shutters and door wide to save lighting a rush candle. William shuffled over to the bench, still yawning and rubbing sleep from his eyes. We both knew she meant it about the breakfast.

The bread was dry, flat and hard. It broke into crumbs as soon as Mam tried to cut it. She stared at it as if she was trying to decide what to do with it. In the end she scraped the crumbs on to a wooden trencher and set it between us. It wasn't proper bread. Mam had pounded up some shrivelled old beans and peas and mixed them with some ground-up bulrush roots, but there were hardly any of those. She turned to the fire to ladle the broth from the big iron pot that swung above it. The broth was thin, mostly sorrel leaves, and it stank.

When he thought she wasn't looking, William pulled a face.

'There's no use you turning up your nose like that, my lad.' Mam could see everything, even when you thought she wasn't looking. 'You'll learn to like it or go hungry, because it's all you'll be getting until the harvest comes in.'

'I bet Father isn't eating this,' William muttered, sniffing the broth in disgust.

'Aye, well, he will be when he gets home, just like the rest of us.' Mam wrapped her hand in her skirt and swung the pot from the fire. 'What he earns at the salterns won't be enough to buy grain this side of Lammas, not with the prices they're charging for it at the minute.'

Mam's mouth was pinched tight. I knew it wasn't Father she was mad at, but the Owl Masters. They'd taken a whole cake of salt in payment for sweeping the burning branch from the mid-summer fire round our cottage to drive out the hungry ghosts. Mam said the salt was worth twice as much as the dried fish and grain they'd taken from others in the road. And the ghosts were still gobbling up our food.

Mam tipped some of the crumbled bread into her own bowl and pressed it down in the broth to soften it. She pointed her spoon at us. 'And don't either of you go taking any bread off Lettice. She's a kind old biddy, give you the last bite from her pot if you asked her, but she makes moon-bread from poppy and hemp seeds, sometimes darnel too when she's nothing else. And I don't want you eating it, hear?'

'Bet it tastes better than this,' William whispered to me behind his hand.

'So it might.' Mam's hearing was as sharp as a cat's. 'But it'll send you mad. There's grown men who've run out into the marsh thinking it solid ground after they'd eaten it and my own mam's cousin threw herself off the church tower saying she could fly. Though she went a touch fey anyway after her man was drowned at sea, it was the moon-bread that turned her, so you take heed.'

She scraped the last of the broth and breadcrumbs into her mouth and set down her bowl. 'Right, my lass, William and I are off to the haymaking. Bailiff wants to start at first light while this dry weather holds. Make sure you fetch the water and wood ready for supper, and put a new rush candle out ready and trimmed for dark, because we'll not be back till light's gone. Then you get yourself out and get to work, do you hear me?'

I didn't want to go purefinding. It wasn't fair. William didn't have to. A day spent in the warm hay meadow was a lot nicer than picking up pieces of dog shit all day in the hot sun.

'Why can't I come haymaking with you?' I wailed.

'You know as well as I do that the bailiff won't pay you, because you're not tall enough to toss hay into the wain. You'd be working for nothing.' Mam was winding a long band of cloth around her hair to keep it from the dust. 'At least working the road you'll earn something, and make sure you only take your pail to the tanner when it's completely full, otherwise he'll find an excuse not to pay you.'

'But Mam . . .'

'You heard! Are you finished, William? Then out the door with you.'

The cottage was silent. As if she knew Mam had gone, a small brown hen came wandering in through the open door and fluttered up on to the table. Bryde, she was my favourite. She had a white flash in her wing where a cat had once clawed out her feathers. When the feathers grew back, they grew back white just like a scar.

Mam said I shouldn't give the hens names because if I did, I'd cry when their necks were wrung. But I wouldn't ever let them wring Bryde's neck. She was special. I brushed some crumbs of pea bread from the wooden trencher into my hand. Bryde stared at my hand sideways, her bright black eye blinked, and then she took a peck at the crumbs. She made a kind of gurgling in her throat, like she always did when she was happy.

I held my hand very still for Bryde in the long thin stream of light that was just starting to creep in through the shutter. My fingers were ugly. I knew they were now. I'd never thought about them much before the tumblers came. The tumbler's girl had long, beautiful fingers that curled around the pole and, when she lifted her arms to balance, her fingers spread out wide in the air, like flowers opening. And her hands were both exactly the same. Mine were different.

The two middle fingers on my right hand were stuck together, webbed, like Mam's and Father's. Nearly everyone in the village had got one hand different from the other. Not the D'Acasters, but Father said they were outlanders generations back, so they didn't count, but most of the villagers had got a web. Father said it was so you could tell your left hand from your right in the dark.

Mam said it showed you belonged to the village. Once she

told me about her uncle who was a sailor. He sailed all the way to France and he was supping in an inn there and this stranger came up to him and said, 'You're from Ulewic. I reckon we're cousins.' He could tell, you see, from my uncle's hand. Mam said, no matter where you went, you never really left Ulewic as long as you'd got the web, for it always drew you back, like a charm.

William's fingers weren't webbed though. It was the only thing he never teased me about. I think he would like to have had webbed fingers, like Henry and his other friends. I sometimes saw him staring at Father's webbed hand, then he'd tuck his own hands under his armpits as if he was ashamed of them. I thought William was lucky. I wished my hands were the same, like the tumbler's girl, then I could run far away and they'd never be able to pull me back by my web.

Great clouds of flies hung over the pail and buzzed round my head. I had to keep my mouth shut tight in case I swallowed one. They crawled over my face, arms and legs, making me itch until I nearly screamed. Most of the dog dung was inside the village, but the lads always tried to beat me to the best bits. Sometimes they grabbed my pail and emptied it into their own. It was no good telling Mam. 'Learn to stand up for yourself,' was all she'd say. So I'd walked by myself as far away from the village as I dared, along the track that led to the house of women.

Mam said I wasn't to go near it, but I couldn't go the other way out of the village along the forest track. Mam said I was never to go there either, not without William to mind me, in case I got lost. I shuddered at the thought. Old Lettice said there was once a terrible monster that hunted in the forest. I knew it was still in there, 'cause sometimes when I was in bed at night, I could hear it shrieking.

'Would you run an errand for me, child?'

I spun round, almost knocking the pail over. One of the grey ladies was standing behind me with a basket in her arms. She was fatter than old Lettice. She smelt of honey, roasted pork fat and spices, like you could eat her.

'Some of the beguines and all of the children are up there haymaking.' She pointed up to one of the meadows on the side of the hill. 'They've onions, bread and cheese with them, but I'm sure it won't be enough. The children will be starving after all that work. So I've made a batch of fresh griddle cakes. Would you be a blessed sweeting and take them up to the meadow? If I went climbing there in this heat, I'd melt like a lump of lard in fire.' She chuckled, and under her heavy grey skirts her belly wobbled up and down. Her face was dripping with sweat as if she'd already started to melt.

I wriggled my toes in the dust. 'Have to fill pail. Mam'll be as mad as a wasp if I don't.'

'How much do you get paid for a pail?'

'Penny.' I was afraid to look at her face. Old Lettice says you must never look a witch in the eye else she'll hex you.

She dug around in a small leather scrip fastened to her waist and held out a coin. 'Here's your penny and if you make yourself useful and help with the hay when you get there, you'll earn another. Now, off you go, and don't eat all the cakes before you get up there.'

I looked up before I remembered not to, but she was still smiling; even her eyes were crinkled up in their own grin. 'I can eat a cake?' My stomach was growling.

She opened the basket and thrust one into my hand. It was still warm and oozing with honey. I licked the honey off my fingers so as not to waste one drop, then took a huge bite.

Mam said to stay away from the house of women, but I hadn't gone inside, had I? I glanced up and down the empty track. If I didn't tell, no one'd ever find out.

Beatrice

'Come on, lass, shift your arse,' Pega bellowed.

Osmanna was gazing down the hill in the direction of the forest and didn't seem to realize Pega was talking to her.

'I swear I'll swing for her,' Pega muttered. 'It'll take two trips to get this hay down to barn and if she doesn't get a move on we'll still be here at midnight.'

'Have patience with the child,' I pleaded. 'She's not used to working the fields.'

'Aye, well, she'd best get used to it quick. Ulewic folk have carried D'Acasters on their backs for generations. About time one of them learned that bread's made from sweat and blisters.'

It was all very well for Pega, she could toss dead sheep on to a hurdle single-handed, but some of us had not been brought up to work the fields.

The oppressive heat was making us all irritable. The air was thick and sultry. Below us the fields striped in emerald and moss-green were shimmering in the heat haze, so that it looked like some great lake of rippling water. Even up on the hill, not a leaf stirred on the shaggy trees, as though they were too sleepy to move. It was not yet midday, but already my clothes were sticking to my back and my arms were aching.

I shouldn't have been working in the fields at all; none of the Marthas were, because they had their own duties. I should have been a Martha myself by now, but Servant Martha had taken against me from the first. She was the one stopping me, I knew that, no matter what the others said. I'll tell you this, Servant Martha might think she ruled the beguinage, but she didn't. We all had a say and I wouldn't be kept down by her. I'd had a lifetime of women like her ordering me about.

A peal of giggles rang out across the meadow. At least the

children were happy, bless them. They loved gathering up the bundles of sweet warm hay, though more got scattered than collected as they tossed it over one another. It wasn't work for them, for they were delighted by any opportunity to abandon their lessons. Only little Margery hung back shyly. She stood behind us, sucking her thumb and staring down the hill towards the river glinting in the pale sun.

'Where does the river come from, Pega?' she asked.

'River comes from a stream and the stream comes from a drindle and the drindle comes from Anu's pool miles away in the great hills. That's where they all begin.'

'What's Anu's pool?' Margery asked.

'It's where Black Anu lives. She gives birth to the river. It runs out from between her legs. Haven't you heard tell of Black Anu?'

Margery shook her head, smiling expectantly.

'She's one of the fay folk; half of her is a woman, but she has the legs of a goat, except no one ever sees those for she hides them under her robes. She sleeps deep in the black pool while it's day, but at witch-light she rises in robes green as pond weed, glowing in the dark with her silver hair trailing behind her. She's so beautiful any man who glimpses her can't take his eyes off her. But that's just her witchery for inside she's really a withered old crone with a heart as black as a marsh pool. If any man should dare to tread near her pool, she lures him to dance with her till he's all tangled up in her hair, then she drags him down into the pool and drowns him. And then ...' Pega stretched out her long arms, grabbed Margery and hissed into her ear, 'she sinks her teeth into him and drinks his blood.' She nipped Margery on the neck and the child ran off screaming in horrified delight.

'Osmanna,' Pega yelled again. 'Bring that hay sledge here – now!'

The poor girl started violently and turned towards us, her hands clenched as if she was about to leap into a fistfight. She always looked wary and guarded. Even when you spoke to her,

her gaze was somewhere else, as if she constantly feared an ambush.

Pega shook her head in disgust as Catherine, always eager to help, ran over to help Osmanna drag the sledge higher up the slope. There was no getting a haywain up to these small meadows on the hillside; you had to use sledges.

I was glad that Catherine had at last found a friend. When Osmanna first arrived, Catherine dragged her round the beguinage introducing her to everyone as if she were presenting her at court. Catherine was so eager to show her every inch of the beguinage. But Osmanna's face wore a perpetually frozen expression as if she was afraid to take pleasure in anything. Poor Catherine did her best. She even tried the story of the well on Osmanna.

'It sprang miraculously from the ground; Servant Martha prayed and then said dig here and the men did, though they didn't believe her, and at once the water came gushing out. The men were so awestruck they fell on their knees in front of her.'

That wasn't quite how I remembered it. Servant Martha was certainly no saint and I couldn't imagine anyone in the village kneeling to any of us, not even if the well had flowed with wine instead of water, but I didn't interrupt Catherine's tale.

'And the water springs up fresh and clear every day. Isn't it the sweetest water you've ever tasted?' Catherine said eagerly.

But Osmanna shuddered and turned away, her arms wrapped tightly round herself, like an abandoned child. I tried to hug her as you would any motherless waif, but she recoiled as if she thought I was going to strike her.

Pega lifted a thick swathe of cut hay and rubbed some of the stalks through her fingers. She grimaced. 'It'll be the devil's own job to get this dry, but we're late haymaking as it is, for it was such a piss-poor spring. We daren't leave it any longer. This heat's near to breaking.'

The sky was hazy, the sun a pale primrose disc, as if a veil of gauze had been drawn over it. You need either a good scorching sun or a stiff breeze for drying; we had neither, just this suffocating steamy wash-tub heat.

'Let's hope it's not a hard winter,' I said. 'If the hay goes mouldy, we'll start to lose beasts this winter, especially if it's a hard one.'

Pega shook her head. 'It'll be wet, not cold, by my reckoning. Wet winters always follow a bad hay crop. But that'll be a blessing, because I reckon it'll be a bad harvest all round again.'

'You think a wet winter's a blessing?' I asked in surprise.

'You'd rather a hard one?' Pega bound a swathe of hay deftly and dropped it ready for Osmanna to collect, before walking on to the next. 'A freeze may be nothing when you're tucked up in some cosy town in Flanders, but you want to try it here with a sea-wind cutting you in half.

'One year when I was a bairn, river froze solid, marshes too, even the edge of the sea. Freeze went on for weeks. We were living forest end of Ulewic then. Wolves came out of the trees right up to the edge of the village. Biting and scratching at the door they were, made your blood run cold to hear them. Mam clattered a stick against some pots to drive them off. Not long after, we heard screams like a girl was being murdered, though none of us dared go out to see. In the morning there was blood and hair all over the snow, with great paw prints trampled all round, and one of Manor's goats gone missing. Wolves had got her.'

'Thanks be to God it was only a goat,' I said, crossing myself.

'You might think that, but my brother was goatherd to the Manor then. He was only a bairn, no match for a pack of wolves.' Pega raised her voice and looked over her shoulder to see if Osmanna was listening, but she didn't look up. 'The bailiff tied my brother to the byre near the forest and gave him a right good thrashing. Then he left him tied there all night, D'Acaster's orders. Next morning I sneaked along as soon as it was light to take him a bite to eat. I found him fainted clear away. He was near dead with the cold and terrified that the wolves might come back. Poor little reckling.'

She glowered at Osmanna as if she held her personally responsible, but Osmanna continued collecting the swathes of hay and refused to look at Pega, though she must have heard her.

I wandered over to Osmanna, saying loudly, 'Pack the swathes well down. If you just toss them on they'll start sliding off as we take them down.' Then I added more softly, 'Take no notice of Pega. She's got a tongue as tart as lemon, but a good heart. She doesn't really blame you.'

Osmanna stared at me, her face expressionless as if she didn't understand what I was saying. After a long pause, she bent and wedged the swathe down in place. 'Like that?' she asked.

I nodded and, defeated, turned away.

'Thank you, Beatrice.' The whisper behind me was so soft I thought I might have imagined it, for when I turned round again, she was stooping over the hay, giving no sign she had spoken at all. I smiled to myself.

Pega took a long deep swig from a skin of ale before handing it to me. Then she picked the big basket of griddle cakes that Kitchen Martha had instructed a scrawny little village child to bring up to us. Grain was running low in our barns, but Kitchen Martha continued to bake undaunted.

'Here.' Pega thrust the basket at Osmanna. 'Make yourself useful, lass, take these to the bairns.'

Catherine and Osmanna wandered off after the children. Pega gazed after them, an expression of disgust on her face.

'Osmanna's her father's daughter all right. You'll not get more than half a dozen words out of her and those as cold as a beggar's arse in winter.'

'Healing Martha says she's shy.'

'Healing Martha wouldn't hear a bad word said about the horned one himself. But I say if a fish is stinking, it does no good to pretend not to smell it, else it'll poison the whole stew. Osmanna's no fool. She deliberately makes a cowpat out of anything she doesn't want to do, so that she's not asked to do it again. Yet, she'll happily sit all day with her books and Servant Martha only encourages her.'

She flashed a look of loathing across at Osmanna. She was well out of earshot, but she was still watching us as if she knew we were discussing her.

'Just look at her,' Pega scowled. 'She looks like she's got the stink of the midden under her nose. Not that she's got any cause to look down on the rest of us. I heard tell that her father turned her out of his gate for whoring. I could almost kiss the little cat, if it was true, but I don't believe it. She'd freeze the cock off any man who tried to bed her.'

Pega had an easy way of talking about the couplings of men and women that I could never match. She'd known all breeds of men. I saw it in her face when she spoke of this man or that, vicious men who hurt her and gentle ones whose memory brought a look of mother softness to her eyes. And then there was the one who even after all these years still brought a sleep-smile to her mouth and a soft escape of breath. Once I asked his name, but she shook her head and turned away. 'They don't have names, nor faces neither.'

A woman who has tasted many men has no more curiosity. But when you have known only one and his bed was cold and cruel, then you wonder constantly if another man might have been kinder to you or if it really was your fault, as your husband constantly told you.

His mother and the priest and the physician, they all blamed me. They all said it was my fault that I was childless; my fault that my husband did not love me; my fault that I made him angry. They all said it so many times that I knew it must be true. The forsaken marriage bed and the empty crib beside it – I only had myself to blame for those things.

Sometimes I looked at men and imagined what it would be like to be loved by them. But even to imagine was a sin; the thought was as wicked as the deed. I'd been taught that with my catechism at my mother's knee. But it was the pain which bound me to the sin, a dull, empty ache that gnawed away inside me. Sometimes it lay so still that I thought it had gone. Then I would see a woman standing just so, her hand rubbing the swelling of her child-ripe belly, or I'd hear the branches of the yew tree in the churchyard rasping together in the wind as if a wailing baby was wombed within its wood. That is when it stirred again and I knew that the desperate longing to hold my own child in my arms would never leave me, not even if I lived to be as old as Abraham and Sarah.

Pega was staring intently over my shoulder at the clump of elms higher up the hill. The rooks, disturbed by something, were wheeling down and out as if trying to drive off a hawk or a cat. Their raucous cries shattered the still air. Pega stood up and shielded her eyes, then quickly crossed herself. I scrambled to my feet too, alarmed by her sign, and followed her gaze.

A young girl was standing motionless under the trees, gazing in our direction. A tangle of flaming red hair tumbled loose about her shoulders. Though she appeared to be about twelve years old, she wore nothing more than a thin dirty shift, ragged and short enough to show that her pale legs were bare.

'It's only a beggar girl,' I reassured Pega.

The children, curious as ever, came wandering up to see what we were looking at. They stood staring warily at the girl, as if she was some strange animal.

Pega spat three times on the backs of her fingers. 'That's no beggar, that's Gudrun.'

'Old Lettice says her mam was a witch.'

I looked down, startled by the small piping voice. The village child who had brought the cakes was standing behind Pega, a fold of Pega's skirt pressed tightly against her face as if she was scared to look at the girl.

'Lettice says her mam could change herself into a grey cat with great yellow eyes. The cat used to slink from byre to byre every night drying up the cows' milk and fluxing the calves. Then one of the villagers caught the grey cat in a trap and cut out her tongue. He was going to hang her, but she scratched him and got away. And the very next day her daughter was born.'

'A wicked thing to say,' I told her sharply.

The child shrugged. 'The woman died giving birth and the grey cat's never been seen again. And Lettice says Gudrun was born dumb, can't make a sound on account of them cutting out her mam's tongue. So that proves she's a witch.'

Pega was still watching Gudrun as if she feared to turn her back on her. The girl stared back at us. She looked so vulnerable and innocent in the torn shift, her skin creamy and soft like a little child's. Threads of gold glinted in the red hair as the leaf-dappled sunlight played over it.

'Poor little thing,' I murmured. 'Who takes care of her now?'

'The grandam, Old Gwenith,' Pega said. 'She has the cunning gift, but unlike her daughter she does no harm with it. She's a good sort. Many in these parts go to her for charms and cures. She can get rid of warts and more besides.'

'Father Ulfrid doesn't mind?' I couldn't imagine a priest tolerating the presence of a cunning-woman in his village.

'I doubt he knows. No villager would tell him, he's an outlander. Old Gwenith lives far up the river, where the valley narrows. No one would ever find the place unless they knew to look. She only comes down to the village when she needs to buy a pot or some such. They say her great-grandam was one of the five cunning-women who rid Ulewic of the monster that was terrorizing the village.'

'What ... what did it do?' Osmanna had stepped forward. She'd suddenly gone very pale. The poor child was not used to heavy work in the heat. Servant Martha had no right to expect it of her.

Pega frowned. 'The old 'uns used to say, though it was years afore they were born, that it swooped down and snatched villagers for its prey, not just bairns, but fully grown men. Ate them alive, tearing the flesh off their limbs while they screamed, and ripping their bellies open to pick at the entrails. And it wasn't just those the monster hunted who suffered. Wherever its shadow touched, disaster followed. Cottages were smitten with leprosy and rotted to dust, crops withered in the fields, wells dried up and byres caught afire without any cause. Only way to appease the monster was to give it cattle. By the end there was scarcely a beast left in Ulewic.'

The children were staring at Pega, their mouths open, their eyes wide with fear. I realized I must look just the same. Was that what the dead man had been talking about in the forest on May Eve? *Your creature, your creation of despair and darkness, who brought death to all who defied you.*

'They say the whole village would have perished, but for the cunning-women. God be praised the beast's not flown since, and God willing it never will again.'

Under the elm trees the girl raised her bare arm and with one finger traced the flight of the rooks in the sky above. The sky over her head was black with them now. They were gathering round her, frenziedly flapping their ragged wings. They wheeled in and out, lower and lower, but they did not touch her and she did not move.

'But Gudrun's no cunning-woman,' Pega said. 'She's the same malice in her as her dam. Dumb she may be, but her bid speaks evil enough for both of them. Look, she has it even now.'

I strained my eyes to see where she pointed. Beneath the red weeds of her hair I glimpsed something large, glossy and black on her shoulder. It was a raven. Its thick beak was so close to her ear, it might have been whispering to her. It was the presence of the raven that was disturbing the rooks, not the child. But like its mistress, the raven showed no fear of the mobbing birds. There was something unnerving about the stillness of girl and bird amid those circling rooks.

Pega jerked her head towards the girl. 'There's something not right. In all these years, I've never known her or her grandam take interest in what other folks are up to. Gudrun'll not come near folks, never mind let herself be seen. We've been here for three years. So why has she taken to watching us now? And more to the point, why's she letting herself be seen doing it?' Pega crossed herself again and with the village child still clinging to her skirts, turned back towards the swathes of hay.

I turned to stare at the trees again. But the girl and her bird had vanished. The place was so empty that but for the wheeling rooks, I would have sworn it had always been so. The sweat on my body felt suddenly cold and clammy. I shivered.

Osmanna

They're in front of me blocking my way. I turn, but they're behind me, all around me, a noose of white faces. Torches clenched in their fists. Flames scorching my face. Choking in the smoke, I shrink, terrified that the flames will catch my hair. My sisters, Edith and Anne, are here among the zodiac. Their sallow moon-faces swim in at me. Their lips curl back, laughing. Bridget the dairymaid, the cook, the chambermaid, the wet nurse who is dead, the crone who begs without a tongue, they're all here.

Edith sweeps the brand across my face. I flinch back, but more torches wait behind me.

'Come now, Agatha, you're not afraid of a little fire, are you? St Agatha will surely protect you from the flames. Were you not named for her? Named for her in every particular.'

They spin around me, laughing. The necklace of eyes glitters in the torchlight.

'Let me go. Please let me go.'

'Why, little Agatha? You're not ashamed of having so fine a name, are you? Are you ashamed, Agatha?' They laugh louder, raucous as the rooks in the elm trees. 'There's no need to hide it. We all know why you were named Agatha. Everyone knows. Can't you see them pointing at you as you pass? Everywhere you go they whisper it, because they all know, Agatha. They all know.'

'You'll die an old maid, Agatha. There isn't enough gold in the kingdom for your dowry.'

They screech with laughter. Edith snatches at the front of my dress. 'Show us, go on, show everyone why they call you Agatha.'

They all grab at me, trying to rip away my robe. 'Show us, Agatha. Show us your name.'

I woke with a cry and found myself fighting to get free from the tangle of blankets. It was a stiflingly hot night, my face was running with perspiration and my body was soaking. For a moment I lay there until my breathing grew calm again.

As I turned over, I was conscious of a wetness between my thighs, and with it a great surge of relief so strong that I almost cried out again. It had finally happened. I had been worrying for nothing. It was going to be all right.

I slipped out of bed as quietly as I could and tiptoed to the door. It creaked as I pulled it open, and Catherine made a little mewling sound in her sleep, but she didn't wake.

The courtyard was flooded with moonlight, a silver sheen glistened on the reed-thatched roofs of the beguinage, but no light shone from any of the shutters on the rooms. No one was awake. I started as a ghost-white shape glided silently over my head, but it was only the barn owl that lived in the threshing barn.

I hurried across to the latrines. The lantern burned there all night, for any who might need it. I crouched against the rough wall and touched my fingers between my legs and held them up to the yellow flame. Nothing stained my fingertips but a faint sheen of perspiration. There had to be, there must be. I tried again and again, but there was no blood. Three moons had gone and still no blood.

Was it growing inside me? I stood up and slowly inched my fingers across my belly. It didn't feel swollen, but when did a woman's belly start to swell with child? I pressed my fists into my belly as hard as I could. If it was in there I had to crush it. I had to kill it. I couldn't have that demon's spawn inside me. It couldn't be happening to me.

I turned and faced the wall, pressing myself against it with my full weight, using it to crush my fists into my belly so hard

I almost cried out. My blood would come, I would make it. The blood would wash that thing out of me.

I mustn't think about it. If I didn't think about it, it couldn't grow. I wouldn't let it live inside me. I wouldn't let it live.

July – St Mary Magdalene's Day

It is said always to rain on this day for Mary Magdalene is washing her clothes ready to go to St James' Fair.

Servant Martha

Father Ulfrid was late. He was normally a rigorously punctual man, but the bell of the parish church of St Michael had long since ceased tolling and the service had still not begun. The church was unusually crowded and the congregation was becoming restless. They always milled about during the service, chattering and laughing, paying little heed to the Mass, but on that day they turned and stared at the door each time it opened, buzzing with excitement as if they expected the arrival of some great dignitary.

The door opened again and Father Ulfrid finally entered, but he was not alone. He was dragging some poor wretch of a man behind him, who was tethered by his wrist to a long length of rope. By the sudden hush, I knew this must be the person the villagers were expecting. The man's face was hidden under a hood. But I now saw why the villagers all drew away as he approached. There could be no mistaking the white patches on the skin of his outstretched arm or the stench of rottenness that clung to his body. Some of the younger beguines drew back too. I frowned at them reprovingly and motioned them to stay still.

On the chancel steps the leper fell to his knees and whispered his confession at the feet of the priest. I was angry. The priest had no need to make a public show of this man's confession. Did Father Ulfrid think God so deaf that he had to borrow a hundred dull ears from men to listen to the suffering of a single soul? One woman was actually cupping her hand to her ear that she might hear better.

'It's well known that sleeping with an adulteress will cause the leprosy,' she said loudly to her neighbour.

'Aye, that or sleeping with a woman in her menses,' her friend replied.

'But what if she be both an adulteress and in her menses?' the woman asked.

'Then he gets pox and leprosy — an itch and no fingers to scratch it with, now there's a torment.' They both cackled with laughter.

The man's confession seemed to go on for ever, as though he feared to stop lest the axe should fall on him. Eventually, Father Ulfrid held up his hands to pronounce the absolution, cutting the penitent off in mid-sentence. He picked up the man's rope and dragged him towards the far corner of the church. Two carpenter's trestles had been placed ready, with a black cloth stretched between them in the semblance of a sepulchre. Father Ulfrid urged the man inside. He pulled back in horror as if it was the mouth of hell, but Father Ulfrid insisted, driving him in as a dog to a kennel. The man crouched under the black cloth, his hood pulled so far over his face that he seemed all shadow.

The Mass continued, but I couldn't attend to it. My spirit was weighted down by the slab of black cloth. I felt the suffocating chillness of the tomb as if the stone still sealed in the stench of Lazarus, and the cry 'Come forth' made but mockery of a soul walled in. The bell rang, the body of Christ was elevated, and the shadow of the man shrank closer to the gravestones beneath him.

When Mass was finished, Father Ulfrid again tugged on the rope and half dragged the man from his cave. Scarcely waiting for him to stagger to his feet, the priest strode from the church, hauling the man behind him. The congregation poured out after them, but at a safe distance. By the time we reached the door, the crowd had already gathered in a wide circle around an open grave.

The wretch stood in the grave, his bowed head scarcely visible above the top. Father Ulfrid waited for his audience to assemble, then he picked up a spade, dug it into a mound of soil and flung the dirt at the man's head. The man staggered sideways, pressing his hands against the top of the grave to balance himself, and the crowd drew back with a gasp as if a corpse was trying to crawl out from a tomb.

Twice more the priest threw earth on the man and then declared, 'Be dead to the world, but live again unto God.'

At the back of the crowd a woman screamed, but no one paid her any heed.

Father Ulfrid tugged again on the rope, indicating that the man was to climb out of the grave. He struggled, but the pit was too deep and the earth continually gave way as he tried to lever himself out. They stood watching him struggling helplessly. I wanted to push every one of them into the pit with him.

I shoved my way forward through the gawping crowd, knocking aside anyone who did not move fast enough from my path. The gravediggers' ladder lay by the priest's feet. I picked it up and slid it into the grave, holding out my hand to the leper. He stretched out his hand instinctively and then, before I could grasp it, withdrew it from me, fearing to touch me.

Summoning all his strength, he climbed the ladder and stood unsteadily on the top. His clothes were smeared with dirt. It had begun to rain. Wet earth oozed down his haggard face but he made no effort to wipe it away. I lifted my arm, intending to wipe his brow on my sleeve, but Father Ulfrid caught me by my arm and tried to pull me away.

'Are you mad, woman?'

'If the blessed Veronica was mad when she wiped our Lord's face, then I embrace that insanity.'

'Our Lord was not corrupted with sin.'

'Our Lord Himself embraced lepers, Father Ulfrid.'

'Do you dare to compare yourself with Christ?'

Without waiting for an answer, Father Ulfrid turned abruptly on his heel and marched off towards the road leading to the forest, the rope jerking in his hands. The leper stumbled blindly in his wake. I followed them. Half turning, I saw the little band of beguines following me.

Father Ulfrid finally halted by the stone on the track which marked the edge of the parish boundary. He turned and faced the leper, letting the rope between them slacken. Father Ulfrid's face was grim. He bowed his head for a moment towards the leper, muttering something too low for me to hear. The man met his eyes briefly, then looked away, staring with leaden eyes back towards the village behind him.

Father Ulfrid stepped back and cleared his throat, declaiming loudly enough for all of us to hear, 'You have been favoured by Christ in as much as you are being punished in this world for your grievous and manifold sins. You must daily give thanks for this great gift of suffering. Do you understand?'

The man continued to gaze at the village as if he would fix it in his mind. Father Ulfrid impatiently tugged on his rope, jerking the man's attention back.

'Now mark this well, for these are the rules you must henceforth live by. You are forbidden to enter a church, a tavern or a bakery, or go into any place where Christian souls meet. You are forbidden to wash in a stream or drink except of that water which has been placed in your cup. You must not touch food, or garments, or well ropes, or anything that Christian souls might touch. You must never go barefoot. When you buy food you must not hand your coin to the merchant, but place it instead in a bowl of vinegar. You must not eat or drink except in the company of others like yourself. You are forbidden to have intercourse with any woman. You are forbidden to come near a child. If you meet any person on the road you must step off it and warn them not to approach you. You must not pass down any narrow street or lane lest you brush against a Christian soul. You shall sound the leper's clapper to warn godly souls of your approach. You must wear at all times the appointed garb so that all men may see at once what you are. When you die you shall be buried outside the parish bounds and may God give you grace to bear your suffering in true humility.'

He gabbled through this list as if he wanted to get the matter finished as soon as possible. Neither man looked at each other. There was a long pause. No one moved or spoke.

'Ralph, you know I didn't ...' Father Ulfrid began. He swallowed hard, staring at the end of the rope. Now that he was no longer reciting the words of others, he seemed to be struggling to find words of his own, but none came.

In the end he simply dropped the rope he was holding, made the sign of the cross over the man and strode back towards St Michael's church without another word. The leper stood bewildered, staring back at the village. He plainly had no idea what to do now or where to go. Rain was pattering on to the leaves and I drew my cloak more tightly about me, but the leper didn't seem to notice the water running down his face.

The beguines and the children were huddled together a little way off, watching me. I knew this day would come sooner or later, just as it had for our sisters in the Low Countries. Some of them knew it too. But I could see the uncertainty in their faces. My next words to them had to sound confident. If I stumbled or gave them time to think, it would only make them more fearful of this dread sickness.

'Healing Martha, return to the beguinage as quickly as you can. Prepare a place in the infirmary for him. Kitchen Martha, you go also and take the children with you. Get your fire stoked for a hearty meal, for I know your hot pottage will do him as much good as any of Healing Martha's herbs. Go on now, hurry. The rest of you remain with me. I have need of you here.'

Beatrice caught my arm. 'But surely you don't mean to bring him with us ... not to the beguinage? You heard what Father Ulfrid said, it's forbidden –'

'The priest may forbid it, but our Lord commands it. And if there is anyone among you who does not know which of them is to be offered the greater obedience, let her not set foot across our threshold this day or any other, for she is not fit to wear the beguine's cloak.'

I saw shocked expressions on their faces and deliberately turned away, willing them to do what I asked. They were not under a vow of obedience to me or to anyone. I could not compel them. I couldn't even enforce my threat if the majority of Marthas opposed me. But if I was unable to hold these disparate women to one common purpose, then everything we had worked for was worthless. The beguinage would fracture and fall apart.

The man stood where the priest had left him, slumped and lifeless, like a hanged man dangling from an invisible noose. The rope still trailed from his wrist. But when I drew his wrist to me, he flinched back as if he feared I was going to strike him.

'Be still, I merely wish to untie you. They call me the Servant Martha. What did Father Ulfrid say your name was?'

He muttered something, but I couldn't make it out.

'Speak up, man, you know your name, surely?'

'His name is Ralph.' Osmanna was standing just behind my elbow.

'I'm sure he is capable of making answer for himself,' I said a trifle sharply, startled to find her so close. 'And I thought I gave instructions that the children were to go on ahead with Kitchen Martha.'

She jerked her chin up. 'I am not a child and you instructed the rest of us to stay.'

I bit back a smile; the girl showed more spirit than the rest of them put together.

I turned back to the leper. 'Ralph, we are taking you to the beguinage. There you will have shelter, a warm bed to sleep in, such ointments as we can provide for your sickness and good food to fill your belly.'

His eyes widened in fear and I almost retreated from him, catching the satyr's look around his mouth, but when I looked again I saw only the misery of an outcast, nothing more. I was annoyed with myself for flinching. To be condemned never again to feel the touch of another human hand; free to roam, yet imprisoned away from all life; to see it, to hear it, but never again to be part of it. It was a sentence beyond bearing. I was determined it should not be so with us.

'Come, Ralph, where else will you go? Driven from hamlet to hamlet, sleeping in ditches, begging scraps that even the pigs refuse. Can any tales you've heard about us be worse than that? At least in the beguinage you'll be close to your home.'

I tried to skirt the village as far as I could. I feared the reaction of the villagers if they saw him returning, but the final stretch of the path took us beside the outlying cottages and there was no avoiding it. I had hoped the rain would keep the cottagers inside, but children do not care about getting wet and there were several playing on the track ahead of us. They ran into the cottages when they saw us coming, their voices raised, giving the alarm. Men and women emerged from doorways, gathering together on the path. There was no other way round. Drawing myself up to my full height, I marched forward, purposefully staring straight ahead, so as to make it quite clear that I would not permit my path to be blocked.

As we approached, the villagers began to jeer and shout. Mouldy vegetables and eggs flew towards us. A rotten egg exploded on my chest. The stench was enough to turn the stomach. Ralph stopped suddenly and the women behind almost fell on top of him. He was trembling. He wouldn't move. I seized him by one arm and tried to pull him forward, snapping at the women to keep walking and stay close together. Then I felt someone pulling Ralph on the other side. Osmanna had locked her small arm tightly through his. I caught her eye and smiled approvingly. She would make a strong beguine one day if only she would take as firm a grip on her own spirit as she had on his arm.

Someone spat at me. The spittle ran down my cheek, but I felt confident they would not dare to lay hands on us for fear of the contagion. I only prayed that they'd stick to throwing eggs and wouldn't pick up any stones. The beguines were cowering under the barrage of filth and dung that was raining down on us from all sides. The villagers were screaming and shouting as we hurried between them, their faces distorted with fear and anger.

The shouting died away. The villagers dropped behind us. Once we were safely away from their cottages, they seemed to lose interest. Only a few children still ran along at a safe distance behind us, jeering and throwing muck, but they were too far away to hit us. At the beguinage gate I risked a brief glance round. There was no one following us. I permitted myself a small sigh of relief and guided Ralph firmly inside. We were safe, but for how long?

Father Ulfrid

I was sitting down to supper when the trouble began. It was already dark outside and quiet. I suppose I should have realized it was too quiet. No sounds of laughter as men made their way home from the tavern, no gangs of young lads hanging around on the corner, shouting and causing trouble. That should have struck me as odd, but I was too hungry and weary to notice.

I'd been later than usual leaving the church after Vespers. Not that there had been many in church to delay me, in fact it had been almost empty, but I had stayed to pray and lost track of the time. I'd much to pray about that day: the business with Ralph, those wretched women who had defied me and brought him back into the village, and above all the longing for Hilary that kept me lying awake through the long empty nights, an accursed aching desire that I dared not confess to any living soul.

The girl who cooked for me had already gone home, leaving my supper laid out on the table next to the unlit candle: the knuckle end of a joint of salt pork, cheese, a little bean bread. The bone seemed to have considerably less meat on it than I recalled from dinner at midday. I'd have to have words with her about that – again.

I was in the act of cutting a slice of pork when the noise exploded so suddenly that I jerked and the knife sliced across my finger. For a moment the pain of the cut blotted out the sound, but as I scrabbled around in search of a cloth to staunch the blood, the sound continued. It was coming from somewhere outside. Wrapping a rag tightly round my finger, I cautiously opened the shutter on the small window and peered out. At once the rumble became louder. It sounded as if a hundred blacksmiths had all started pounding on their anvils at once. At the far end of the street I could see the flames of bobbing torches.

I hastily pulled on my shoes, making a pig's foot of the task as I tried to hold my throbbing finger out of the way. Snatching up my staff, for I wasn't sure what I would encounter, I made my way cautiously down the dark, deserted street.

As I drew nearer, I could make out a crowd of people, mostly men and boys. Some held blazing torches, but most were holding iron pots, tongs, pincers, fire irons and any other bit of metal they could lay their hands on, and were banging them together as vigorously as they could. Children were rattling bird-scarers over their heads.

They were clustered round one of the cottages, trampling over the herbs and vegetables, smashing through the fruit bushes, in an effort to get close to the shuttered windows and door. In all the chaos and darkness, it took me a few minutes to work out whose cottage this was, then I realized. It was Ralph's.

I recognized one of the men standing near me and grabbed his arm.

I had to shout to make myself heard over the din. 'Alan, what's happening?'

He turned reluctantly towards me and bellowed in my ear. 'A little rough music is all, Father. Nothing for you to fret about.'

'Why at this cottage?'

He shook his head, unable to hear the question above the din.

Impatiently I caught his arm and pulled him a little way back down the street. His son, William, trailed after him, still rattling his bird-scarer. I snatched it out of his hand and glared at him. He looked indignantly at his father, clearly expecting him to intervene, but Alan did nothing.

'What's going on, Alan? Ralph's not in there, you know he isn't.'

'His wife and bairns are.'

'And you're terrorizing them. Why? What have they done?'

'It's for their own good, Father.' Alan shuffled his feet. 'It's a warning to them to get out. Got to burn the cottage. Only way to get rid of the sickness.'

'You can't burn the cottage down about their ears.'

'Three nights of rough music to persuade them to leave. If they're not gone by the third night, cottage'll be burned whether they're in it or not. If they've got any sense they'll be long gone by then anyway.'

'They're your neighbours, Alan. You've known Joan all your life. You grew up with her.'

He shrugged and I could see that I was wasting my time.

'At least send the boy home, Alan. He shouldn't be party to this.'

'He's got to learn.'

William, who'd looked aghast at the thought of being sent home, grinned broadly.

'And what about your daughter, Alan, does she also have to learn?'

I pointed to a dark shadow crouching behind the bushes. I'd seen her following them and guessed neither of them knew she was there.

'I told you to stay with your mam,' Alan bellowed. 'You get straight home, lass, and you'd better be abed before I get back or you'll be sorry.'

'Yeh,' William yelled. 'Clear off, Pisspuddle, this is men's work. We don't want you.'

I left Alan and hurried towards the cottage, shoving my way through the crowd until I reached the doorstep. I found an upturned pail and stepped up on it, trying to make myself seen above the crowd. I held up my hands for silence. One or two people at the front stopped banging, but it took some time for the rest to realize I was there. Gradually the noise died away.

'You all heard what I said in church. Ralph was struck down because he was guilty of the sin of lust. He confessed it. God does not smite the innocent. Joan and the children have done no wrong.'

'She's as guilty as her husband,' someone called out from the crowd. 'She hid his sickness, kept him indoors pretending he'd the ague. She let her bairns go on playing with ours, never said a word.'

'That's right,' another shouted. 'If Lettice hadn't managed to slip in one day when Joan was out, we'd never have known. If you ask me, Father, she's lucky a bit of rough music is all she's getting.'

'But I've told you,' I said, 'there's no reason for you to fear Joan or her children. I've examined them myself, there's not a mark on them. You don't need to burn them out.'

Alan had pushed his way to the front of the crowd. 'It's all very well for you, Father, you don't have bairns to worry about. My wife says she won't feel safe until every stick and stone of that cottage is in ashes.'

'And does D'Acaster know about this?' I demanded. 'This is Manor property.'

'You think we'd be daft enough to do it without his say so?'

Someone else yelled out from the back of the crowd, 'Those women brought Ralph back through the village, after you said he was forbidden to set foot in the village again. You going to stand for them defying you like that?'

Young William excitedly tugged on my robe. 'My father said the Owl Masters could get rid of those women soon as look at them, didn't you, Father?'

There was a murmuring among the crowd and several heads nodded in agreement.

I felt my jaw clench. Gossip spreads faster than floodwater in a village. I knew what the men were thinking: if a priest can't even get women to do what they're told, why should we listen to him?

'They are not in defiance of the Church, because the house of women lies outside the village. The women took Ralph in out of Christian charity. It was a kindly act, but an extremely foolish one, and I have no doubt they will come to regret it.'

'So you're saying you can't do anything,' Alan said. 'My lad's right; if you can't, the Owl Masters can.' Everyone began talking and I had to raise my voice still louder to compete with them.

'If Ralph ever sets foot in the village, I will deal with him, but if he keeps to the house of women, then he is out of the village and you need have no fear for your children. But if you care about your families as much as you say you do, you will not turn to the Owl Masters. They are a dangerous and ungodly force, and the sooner decent men like you make it clear there is no place for them in this village, the better. There is no power stronger than the power of God and the Church. If you trusted in that, you would not need the Owl Masters.'

Alan shook his head. 'Aye, well, you being an outlander, Father, you'd not understand.'

'I understand that anyone who does not submit to the authority of Christ and the Church has placed himself under the authority of the Devil. The Owl Masters set themselves against the laws of God.' I looked down sternly at Alan's son. 'And you know what happens to those who consort with the Devil, don't you, William?'

The men looked mutinous and began to mutter furiously among themselves. I could feel their anger rising. It was no use fighting them. If D'Acaster had consented to the cottage being burned or had even ordered the Owl Masters to do it, which he might well have done if he thought Ralph guilty of lust, then I wouldn't be able to prevent it. The best I could do was to make sure that Joan and her children were not inside it when it went up in flames.

'Go home now, all of you. I'll talk to Joan, persuade her to leave without the need for all this. And if I hear of anyone laying hands on this cottage before the family's safely out, he'll have God to answer to.'

The villagers looked at one another, then began to peel off in two and threes and make their way back through the darkened streets. Most were heading in the direction of the Bull Oak Inn.

I walked round the cottage to make quite sure no one was still lurking in the shadows. Even in the darkness I could see the garden was wrecked, everything broken or trampled into the mud. I knocked on the door and stood shivering, listening for sounds on the other side. A chill wind had sprung up and in my haste I had not stopped to throw on a cloak.

'It's Father Ulfrid, Joan, open the door. It's safe, they've all gone.'

There was a long pause, followed by the sound of something heavy being dragged away from the door. Finally it opened a crack.

'I'm alone. Let me in, Joan.'

The door opened just wide enough for me to slip through, then it was slammed and bolted. Joan stood bundled up in her travelling clothes. Her two little sons and her daughter, Marion, were clinging to her skirts, their white frightened faces snotty and tearstained. Joan struggled to lift a heavy pack on to her shoulders.

'You're surely not thinking of setting out on the road tonight, Joan?'

'Been warned, Father, best go tonight before ... there's more trouble.' Like Ralph, she couldn't bear to look me in the eyes.

'I agree it's not safe for you to stay here tonight, but come home with me, have a bite to eat and rest. The children must be famished.'

She shook her head firmly. 'Thank you kindly, Father, but we're going tonight. I've a cousin in Norwich. She'll maybe take us in. It's far enough away for them not to have heard about ...' She trailed off, unable to say the word.

'But that's miles away. A woman can't travel in the dark by herself. There are all kinds of outlaws and madmen out there. God knows what they'd do to a woman alone. What about your brother in the village, won't he take you in?'

'And have his family burned out as well? He's not been near us since word got out and I don't blame him for that. He's his own bairns to think of.'

'Then you must come home with me. No one will dare to

hurt you as long as you're in my house. I promise I'll help you get to Norwich. I'll —'

'Like you helped my husband, Father? Did you keep him safe? Did you?'

The boys cringed at the fury in their mother's voice, clutching her legs and burying their faces in her skirts. Little Marion began to sob.

'Ralph was your friend, Father. He always defended you, no matter what was said about you in the village, he'd not believe it. And you ... you paraded him in front of the whole village like a beast. You tied him up. You forced him to stand there in that grave while you threw earth at him. And you declared him dead, Father. A living man, my husband ... and you said he was dead, in front of his friends, his neighbours, his family ... in front of his own bairns, you told them their father was dead.'

For the first time that evening she looked at me, tears of hatred in her eyes, but she dashed them away angrily.

If she had punched me in the stomach, I could not have felt the words harder. She had no right to blame me after all I'd done to try to protect her and Ralph. I'd known ever since that day I spilled the hot wax on his hand that Ralph had the dread disease. I'd tried to keep it hidden, but when that wretched gossip, Lettice, had barged her way in, there was no hiding it any more. It was all round the village before I could recite a paternoster. If I'd failed to pronounce him dead publicly as the Church insists, the D'Acasters would have reported me to the Bishop. Phillip was just waiting for that chance. And Bishop Salmon had made it only too plain that if I failed in my duty in any way, this time the punishment would be worse, much worse.

'Joan, believe me, I didn't want to do it. But I had no choice. I only did what the law demanded. If I hadn't done it, another would have. The villagers might even have taken matters into their own hands. At least this way he's safe.'

'No thanks to you,' she spat. 'Those women who took him in

may be outlanders, but they were more of a friend to him than you ever were. I'm not learned, Father. I can't read, but I know what mercy is, that's what those women have, no matter what's said about them. That leader of theirs, she's got more charity in her little finger than all you priests put together. Stay in your cottage? I'd rather get my throat cut on the road than sleep one more night in Ulewic.'

She seized the children and pulled them towards the door. On the doorstep she turned. 'You know, Father, I hope that what they say about you and that nun is true after all, because then you'll rot in hell where all priests belong.'

She stepped into the darkness and was gone.

Servant Martha

I loved the dawn hour, the soft pale light on the rim of the world, whispering the start of a new day. The bell for Prime not yet rung, the beguinage hushed, still wrapped in sleep. I knelt on the rushes, gazing up at the wooden crucifix pinned above my cot.

'*Sanctus, sanctus, sanctus, Dominus Deus Sabaoth.* Lord, send the fire of your spirit to rest upon all those who rise cold and hungry –'

There was a rapid knocking on the door of my room. Before I could rise, the door was flung open. Gate Martha burst into the room, breathless and agitated.

'Come quickly, Servant Martha, see what's at the gate.'

'Who is it at this hour? Unless they are urgently in need of Healing Martha's skills, they'll have to wait. It's almost Prime. Put them in the guest hall.'

She shook her head, and tugged my sleeve. 'Please come, Servant Martha, quickly.'

Her fingers were trembling and I started to feel anxious myself. What on earth could have troubled her so? Gate Martha was a local woman, a widow, unable to read or write, but ideally fitted for the task to which God had called her for she was a stolid, practical soul, not easily given to fright. Something dreadful must have happened to alarm her.

I dared not delay to dress, but hastened after her across the empty courtyard clad only in my shift and cloak. She stopped before we reached the gate and pointed. Something was lying on the threshold. I moved closer. Someone had fashioned a hurdle of willow. A dead barn owl lay crucified upon it, its wings stretched out across the frame. A sprig of dark, glossy ivy leaves was fastened in its beak and more were entwined in the wicker frame. The feathers and leaves trembled violently in the morning breeze.

Gate Martha hovered inside the gate as though the abomination might fly up into her face.

'Did you see who left this here?'

She shook her head dumbly, still staring transfixed at the crucified bird.

'But you know?'

She nodded and mouthed so faintly I could scarcely hear her, 'The Owl Masters.'

'Why should they leave such a thing at the gate of the beguinage?'

She turned her face away and stared towards the infirmary. 'You took the leper in. He's dead to the village. No one must give him shelter. That ... that bird is the Owl Masters' curse.' She shuddered and raised her hand against her face as if to shield herself from it.

'The ivy leaf proclaims the Holy Trinity of God. How can that plant work against us who are his servants?'

'The old 'uns say ivy's an evil omen,' she muttered sullenly. 'It kills whatever it embraces.'

'But we do not believe in the old ways, do we, Gate Martha? Now, fetch me a faggot of very dry wood and a brand from the fire. And, Gate Martha, you will say nothing to the others. Not one word of this, do you understand? It signifies nothing and I will not have silly rumours spread to frighten the children.'

She nodded, and I watched her hurry away. Then I closed the gate behind her, scanning the bushes and trees beyond the path. Were they watching? Then let them. What did they think; that we could be intimidated into casting Ralph out? They did not have the measure of me.

Gate Martha returned and opening the gate a crack, thrust out the brand and sticks. 'I kindled the flames from the eternal light in the chapel.'

'You could have taken it from the cooking fire; it would have burnt just the same,' I snapped, exasperated at her fear, but all the same I clutched the brand more tightly, thankful for what she had done.

'Go inside and shut the gate. Don't let anyone open it until I return. And don't ring the bell to waken them for Prime until I say so.'

I struggled to drag the frame away from the gate. It was heavier than it looked, but I managed to pull it off the path and into a patch of rank weeds. I piled the dry wood over it and set the brand to it. The feathers caught straight away, shrivelling and flashing into a cloud of acrid smoke, then came the smell of burning bird flesh.

Billows of blue smoke rose into the air, blown into spirals by the gusting wind. Beyond the trees other columns of smoke from cooking fires in the distant village rose into the pale pink morning. The world was waking. Far away, the church bell rang for Prime. Our bell would ring late that morning. I would offer no explanation.

The willow frame snapped and crackled as the flames dried it. A twist of ivy uncurled and snaked across the grass in the heat from the fire, smouldering, but not burning. Ivy does not burn.

†

August – St Bartholomew's Day

Patron saint of tanners because he was flayed alive before being beheaded.

Servant Martha

'Mark my words, there's trouble afoot,' Gate Martha muttered, casting a baleful glance in the direction of the guest hall.

'But didn't they give you any indication as to why they have come?' I asked, as I followed her across the courtyard.

'You'll have to ask them yourself. They refused to tell me.' She stomped off back to her gate, evidently much aggrieved by that.

I watched her retreating back for a moment, trying to prepare myself for my unexpected guests. All I had managed to wrest out of Gate Martha was that a man and woman, announcing themselves as the uncle and mother of the anchorite Andrew, had asked if I could spare a few minutes to see them. I knew it must be a serious matter. I could hardly imagine that Andrew had merely sent them to convey her greetings, and as soon as I entered the guest hall I could tell that Gate Martha had been right to predict trouble.

A woman, whom I took to be Andrew's mother, was poised rigidly on the edge of the chair, her eyes darting about anxiously and her fingers plucking at the yellow wimple which framed her lined face. A grey-haired man, who looked enough like her for me to conclude he was her brother, was pacing restlessly up and down the narrow chamber. It was a hot day and his face was beaded with perspiration, but he was too agitated to sit. From the dust on their clothes and their weary expressions it was evident they had travelled some way to see me, and I urged them not to speak until they had taken some refreshments to help them recover. The woman seemed grateful. She shook her head at the platter of cold mutton and cheese, but took a little wine, clasping the goblet tightly in both hands as if she feared it would slip through her fingers.

It was only when I turned to offer meat and wine to Andrew's uncle that I realized there was someone else in the room. A man in a coarse grey friar's habit, with a knotted white girdle at his waist, stood motionless in the shadows in the furthest corner of the room. I recognized him as Franciscan from the simplicity and colour of his robe. His hands were clasped in front of him, hidden in his sleeves, and his head was bowed as if he was praying.

Andrew's uncle wiped his fingers and turned to me with a grave expression as if he could no longer delay the bad news. 'We have come here on a matter of some delicacy . . .' he began. 'We have received a message from Bishop Salmon of Norwich asking us to remove Andrew from the anchorite cell without delay.'

I gaped at him. 'Surely you have misunderstood the messenger or he muddled the words? St Andrew's church would fight from here to Rome to keep her in that cell. She brings so much wealth to that parish. Many pilgrims come to the church just to see her and they all pay good money for candles, food, ale and lodgings, not to mention the emblems and relics. Half the traders in the parish depend on the pilgrims she brings in to make a living. They cannot mean you to take her away.'

Andrew's mother and uncle exchanged uneasy glances.

'Andrew lives in constant prayer now,' her uncle explained cautiously. 'She does not even pause in her meditation to bless the pilgrims. She does not move or speak. She does not . . . she refuses all food and says that she requires no nourishment except the body of our Lord which she receives daily.'

Her mother broke in eagerly, 'But she grows so plump and fat on this holy food, anyone can see it is our blessed Lord Himself who feeds her.'

'Have some questioned it then?' I asked.

Again the two of them exchanged anxious glances before Andrew's mother rose and, turning her face away, stared dejectedly out of the window, leaving her brother to answer.

'There are always some who doubt the veracity of any saint.

But they say ... though I have not witnessed it myself, you understand ... that sometimes when she prays she swells up to twice her normal stature, filling the whole cell. Is this not a mark of one overflowing with the spirit?'

'Some might enquire whose spirit,' I suggested gently.

'Could she take the Host daily and with such joy if that spirit were not from our Lord?' the Franciscan said softly from the shadows.

His voice made me jump. I'd forgotten he was even in the room.

I inclined my head. '*Argumentum ad absurdum*,' I said, humbly acknowledging the foolishness of my remark.

But logical though the Franciscan's argument was, I could see how it might look to others. It would only take one jealous priest in a neighbouring parish, who felt he had lost trade because of her, to whisper the Devil in the Bishop's ear, and her piety would be seen to take on a very different complexion.

I glanced round the room, expecting one of them to add more, but no one spoke.

'So ... why have you come to me?' I asked finally.

Andrew's uncle gave a small sigh of relief as if he had been willing me to raise the subject that courtesy did not permit him to broach.

'My niece needs care, much care, but she refuses to come home. She insists she must stay at the church and that is impossible. No other church will take her, we have tried ... but we thought that she might be persuaded to come here, since you and she are of the same mind. Servant Martha, will you give her shelter here?'

There was such weariness in his eyes that I knew he must have spent many hours arguing with Andrew or pleading her case with others. On the pretext of pouring more wine, I moved away from his beseeching gaze.

Andrew here? It was out of the question. Our very purpose, our whole way of life, was the exact opposite of hers. How could we give shelter to an anchorite, a woman who demanded to be shut away from the world, who made such a public pronouncement of her great piety when we strove to keep ours private? What did he imagine we would do with her here? If she was so absorbed in her own meditations to the point of not even speaking, how could she possibly live the life of a beguine? Did they think we would build a cell for her on the side of the chapel and wall her up in it? It was against everything we stood for to have a woman in our midst attending to nothing except her own soul, contributing nothing, expecting to be waited upon and fed by others.

Yet the Church, which she had served so faithfully, had abandoned her. How could they treat her so, when they had been the ones to encourage her in her life of piety? That priest, her confessor, who had tried to make us all believe he was so concerned about her welfare, where was he to defend her now?

I stared at the lime-washed wall of the room, dazzling in the burning sun, seeing not the whiteness of that wall, but the shadow of a single word carved above the gateway in Bruges – *Sauvegarde* – the place of refuge. Whatever Andrew was, we had a duty to provide such a place for her. We could not close our gates against her.

Three pairs of eyes watched me anxiously.

I forced a smile. 'If Andrew has no other place to go, she will be welcomed here.'

Beatrice

'Lily-livered vermin! Lice of Satan!' Merchant Martha had been muttering furiously ever since we'd left the Bartholomew Fair. I was sure she must have exhausted every insult possible for the Weavers' Guild, but it seemed she hadn't. 'They're all bloodsucking leeches to a man, every single one of them, except leeches do some good in the world.'

The cart rattled along in the sun-baked grooves worn by so many other wheels before, tilting precariously as we swerved around a man trudging with his milch cow up the track. He shook his fist at us as our wheels and horse's hooves enveloped him in a cloud of choking dust. Even when she was in a good mood Merchant Martha hated to be stuck behind anything, and fury did not improve her driving.

Pega sat beside her, gripping the edge of the hard wooden seat with both hands as we bumped over the ruts and potholes. I crouched in the back of the cart behind the bundles of cloth and wool, watching the track retreating behind us. Though my teeth were rattling in their sockets, at least I didn't have to look at the bends and travellers approaching us and only saw the perils when they were safely passed.

Merchant Martha had every reason to be in a foul mood. The cart should have been loaded with the food, wine and grain we badly needed to see us through until the harvest, but instead of returning with provisions, we were returning with every single bale of cloth and wool we'd taken to the Bartholomew Fair.

We'd set off at first light and after three bone-breaking hours on the road had arrived at the fair only to be told that on the Abbot's orders we would not be granted a licence to sell at the fair. A small group of men had gathered a short distance away, listening as Merchant Martha stood arguing with the steward.

They grinned and nudged one another, their smiles becoming broader as Merchant Martha grew more angry, but in the end there was nothing she could do.

'Go easy, woman,' Pega said sharply as the cart gave a great lurch over a stone. 'You'll not make matters better if we've a broken wheel to mend 'n' all.'

Merchant Martha glared at her, but she let the reins slacken a little and the horse's pace steadied. The motion was making me feel sick. I tried to kneel up to ease the pain in my cramped legs and twisted around to face the front.

'Merchant Martha!' I called feebly.

But neither of them turned round.

Pega shifted her broad rump uncomfortably on the too narrow seat. 'I reckon this'll just be the start of it. It's my betting the Owl Masters are behind this. They're trying to drive us out by making sure no one'll trade with us. I've been waiting for something like this, ever since they left their sign at our gate.'

Merchant Martha stared at her. 'How do you know about that?'

Pega didn't answer. I don't know why Merchant Martha bothered to ask. How Pega found out about anything was a mystery, but she always did.

Merchant Martha gave a slight shake of her head. 'Anyway, the blame for this lies solely with the Weavers' Guild. We sell better cloth and cheaper too. They've always hated us. You saw those men standing there smirking, those were Weavers' Guild emblems they were wearing, every one of them. The Abbot can't afford to fall out with the Guild, not with the vast flock of sheep he has on his lands. It's the Guild that puts plump capons on his table and gold in his coffers, so he'll hitch up his skirts and dance whenever they start piping.'

'Aye, we all know whose tune the Abbot dances to,' Pega said. 'But that doesn't answer the question – why now? Guild's been against us from the start, but they've not bothered with us up to now. We don't trade enough wool to be any real threat to them or the Abbot. Way I see it, someone's got to them, and by my reckoning it's got to be the Owl Masters. They don't leave their sign at the door and then do nothing. If one of the Owl Masters is a member of the Guild or they have a hold over one of the Guild members, then it'd be easy enough to get them to stand against us. And if the Owl Masters have got the Guild in their pockets, it won't just be the Bartholomew Fair we'll be turned away from. We'll not be able to sell at any of the fairs or markets round these parts.'

'Is that so?' Merchant Martha said grimly. 'Well, I've a trick or two up my own sleeve. They'll not get the better of me, that I can promise you.'

Now that the horse's pace had slowed, the cart set up a steady swaying. A wave of nausea rose up in me. I felt as if I was suffocating down there among the bales of wool. I clambered precariously on top of one and perched there, clinging on to the sides of the cart with both hands and trying to concentrate on the landscape slipping away behind us.

In the water meadows, scarlet poppies swayed among the purple corncockle and oxeye daisies. The grain in the field strips was ripe now. It had been agonizingly slow to turn from green to gold. It was late, but at least the ears were plump from the rain. The villagers and Manor had not yet begun the harvest, but ours was already cut and stooked in the fields. Another day or two of this hot sun to dry it and it would be ready to thresh.

It was the first good harvest we'd had since we came. We had all prayed earnestly these last few years, five times a day as the Pope had ordered – *frigiscente mundo* – 'as the world grows colder' – but the harvests had continued to fail over and over again. But this year, at long last, God finally seemed to have heard our prayers and the days were turning warm again.

If Merchant Martha kept up this pace we'd soon be back inside the beguinage, and what joys awaited us there. Heavy bales of wool and cloth to be unloaded in this baking heat, soiled bedding to be stripped in the infirmary and pigs waiting to be fed with the mess of scraps. I longed to walk in the fields and feel the grass round my legs and the sun hot on my back, just a few minutes of peace before we were back in the noise and endless chores of the beguinage.

Holding tightly to the edge of the cart, I tried to twist round again. 'Merchant Martha, can you stop the cart? The motion is making me queasy. Let me off here and you go on. I'll walk the rest of the way.'

Merchant Martha reluctantly pulled on the reins and the cart wheels crunched to a halt.

Pega glanced back, all concern. 'I'll walk with you.'

'No, no.' I said hastily. I wanted to walk with my own thoughts, without anyone's chatter ringing in my ears. 'You go on with Merchant Martha; she shouldn't travel by herself with a loaded cart, it's not safe.'

I clambered down and set off at a good steady pace along the track behind the cart. Pega looked back anxiously a couple of times, but I waved cheerfully to reassure her. The cart gradually pulled further and further ahead and, before long, it disappeared from view behind a coppice on the curve of the track. Now that the cart was safely out of sight, I slowed down and let my feet carry me into a patch of fallow land. Slipping off my shoes and hose, I revelled in the soothing coolness of the grass under my feet. Out of sight of track or cottages, I threw myself down in the long grass and lay on my back, gazing up at the rooks lazily flapping towards the distant trees.

A soft hum of insects buzzed around the flowers. Butterflies with purple eyes on their wings tumbled and flipped from one flower to the next. My mother once told me that butterflies are the souls of unbaptized children who cannot enter purgatory or heaven or hell. You must take care never to kill a butterfly, she said, for if you did you'd be killing a child.

I closed my eyes. The sun burned red through my eyelids. It was so hot. The Vineyard in Bruges had been cool in the summer. The canal wound round our walls and slipped in under the boat gate, sparkling and dancing in the sun. The children splashed on the bank and ran barefoot in the cool, damp grass, laughing as it stroked their hot feet. Sometimes I ran with them.

There were always little children and babies there, plentiful as daisies on the green. But they weren't my children. They were never my children.

That last time I convinced myself it would be different, lying in a bed, stifling in the heat of a roaring fire with a swarm of women buzzing round, whispering too softly for my ears. Fingers plucked at my shift and kneaded my belly. Another pain, sharp and short, not like before, then a gush of hot liquid flooding across my thighs and with that came red-raw agony that went on and on, building in waves until I thought it was splitting me in two. I screamed. I couldn't stop screaming even after the pain had gone.

The room grew dark. I was so cold, shivering, despite the heap of covers they piled upon me. When I opened my eyes again the women were gone. I called for them to bring my baby to me, but no one came. I could hear him crying. I could see the crib rocking as he thrashed his little fists in anger. I struggled from my bed and fell to my knees. The floor tipped as if it was a raft afloat on the open sea. I dug in with my fingers and crawled inch by inch across to the crib. It was empty.

I howled. I howled until they finally came running, pressing their fingers against my mouth, trying to make me stop, but they didn't bring my baby. They didn't let me hold my baby.

The midwife swore that this child drew breath and she had baptized him, so the priest would permit him to lie in the family tomb. But we both knew he had not. For more than a week he had not stirred inside me. The midwife gave me a potion to bring on the labour after the fever began, but she spoke of it to no one. The priest took one look at the infant and knew the midwife had lied. My husband wouldn't look at him at all. And my son, *my son* was not buried in the family tomb.

The midwife was a kindly woman. She told my husband that the infant had been born too soon, but I had carried this one the longest and the next was sure to be born alive. But there was to be no next one. That night he took my maid to his bed and I knew he wouldn't come again to mine.

I kept the empty crib beside me for months, hoping, but even as I rocked it, some part of me knew it would always be empty. Even now in the night I still rise, half asleep, at his cry and the creak of his cradle rocking. Pega grumbles at me to go back to sleep, saying it's only the wind whining through the rafters or the mice squeaking in the thatch. But some nights I dream that it's not the wind I can hear, but my child scratching with his tiny fingers at the fastened shutters, trying to come back to me.

I sensed that someone was coming towards me and rolled over on to my belly. A young girl with a wild tangle of long red hair was ambling through the meadow, a little way off. I'd seen her before – Gudrun the witch-girl, the girl without a tongue. I crouched lower in the grass. But she was wandering through the grass lost in her own world, blowing on the puffball of a dandelion, watching the clouds of downy seeds drift around her head. She reached out to grasp a handful and blew them away again, sending them swirling up into the blue sky.

The sun was beginning to sink, hot and red, drifting down to the softly rounded hills. The girl turned her face to it. She pulled her shift over her head and let it fall to the ground. Then, naked as a fawn, she began to dance. Turning in slow circles, her arms outstretched to the source of light and heat, as an infant to its mother. Faster and faster she spun, her flaming hair flying out around her, her arms wide, her back arched. Her ribs slid up and down beneath her white skin. Then, breaking out of her circles, she ran and leapt through the meadow, scattering scarlet poppy petals, which drifted down in dizzy spirals to the golden grass.

A butterfly came to rest on her outstretched hands. She held it out on the tips of her fingers, swaying slightly with the poppies as if a soft breeze rocked her. A second butterfly alighted on her arm, another on her back and on the tip of a strawberry nipple, still more on her shoulders, her buttocks, her thighs and in the mass of her fiery hair. Her naked body was covered by the delicate red and purple wings. Her skin trembled and shuddered in tune with their fluttering. She knelt carefully, facing the sinking sun. The flames of her hair haloed her upturned head as she slowly stretched out her butterfly hands to receive the sacrament of light from the dawn of time.

Suddenly I was drenched in cold fear. I felt guilty, ashamed, as if I had been spying upon a couple committing some forbidden and unnatural act. As if by looking I had committed the sin myself. Without caring if I startled her, I scrambled to my feet and ran from the butterflies and the scarlet poppies. I ran as fast as I could from that hot, bright meadow, and I did not look back.

Pisspuddle

I saw the grey lady run past me. She didn't see me. She was tearing up the track towards the house of women, as if she thought Black Anu was chasing after her. Her eyes had gone strange, dark but glittery, like bright moonlight was shining out of them. I think Gudrun had witched her.

I'd seen Gudrun dancing in the meadow with her hair flying out all around her. She was naked. William and other lads swim naked in the river in summer. But I'd never seen a lass take her shift off outdoors. Maybe that's what witches do to cast a spell. Lettice said when a witch shakes out her hair, it whips up a great storm out at sea. My father knew about storms. He often saw them when he was working at the salterns beyond the marshes. He said the waves turn grey then brown, then they rear up like adders, till they're higher than a man and come crashing down on the shore. He said you have to count the waves. Eight'll fall short and'll not harm you, but if the ninth catches you, it'll drag you so far out to sea they'll never find your body.

The gate of the beguinage opened and three people came hurrying out: Pega the giant, the fat woman who smells of honey and the thin, scary one who never smiles. They rushed past me down the track to where Beatrice was standing, breathing hard and holding her side.

'Beatrice, we were so worried,' the fat one called out. 'We thought you'd returned hours ago, but you weren't at Vespers. Then Merchant Martha told us you'd felt unwell and I was sure you had collapsed on the road somewhere. They should never have left you. Are you all right?' She pressed her hands to Beatrice's forehead, like Mam does to me if she thinks I'm sick.

Beatrice pulled away from her. 'I was tired from walking and sat down to rest. I think I must have fallen asleep.'

The tall, thin one frowned. 'You *think* you fell asleep,' she snapped. 'I always know if I have slept or not.'

Pega put her arm round Beatrice and helped her back up the track towards the house of women; the other two followed. As the gate banged shut behind them, something ghostly pale drifted out over the high fence. I jumped, but it was only a barn owl going hunting.

It was late. The sun had sunk below the top of the hill and the trees had turned black. A big gust of wind made me turn round. Across the marshes the sky was already dark and thick clouds were rolling in towards the hills. Mam would be looking for me.

I picked up my heavy pail of dog dung and tried to run up the track to the village, but it kept banging against my leg. I tried to change hands without stopping, but I tripped and went sprawling on to the sharp stones. My knees burned and stung. They felt wet, but it was too dark to see if they were bleeding.

Then, as I tried to get up, I saw a scarlet light flickering above the track ahead of me. It was the flames of a torch and it was moving fast towards me. I scrambled across to the edge of the track and slithered down into the dry ditch. I didn't want to touch the bottom with my bare feet, in case there were snakes or weasels in there, but I was more scared of what was coming towards me on the track.

I pressed tightly against the side of the ditch and peered up. Four muffled shapes were coming along the track, but I couldn't hear a single footstep. They had great big heads like St Walburga and no legs. Maybe they were ghosts, hungry ghosts who'd been driven out of our cottage and were hunting for something to eat. My heart was banging so loudly I was sure they'd hear it. What if they could smell me? William said Black Anu couldn't see, but she could sniff out little girls.

I held my breath as the creatures came closer and closer, and then they were right above me. The flames of the torch lit up their heads and I saw that instead of faces, they had great hooked beaks and feathers. I clamped my hands across my mouth to stop myself from screaming. But then they were gone, running lightly down the grass on the side of the track, and I realized who they were. They were the Owl Masters.

I dug my bare toes into the side of the ditch and scrambled out. The stones and dirt stung my skinned knees, but I didn't cry. Crouching low, I ran to the corner of the track and hid behind some bushes. I could see the torch wobbling far ahead, the scarlet flames streaming out behind. Then it stopped. The torch was moving from side to side as it lit three others. The torches separated and began to move again. The Owl Masters were walking across a field where the grain lay in stooks, drying. It was the only field where the grain had already been cut and it belonged to the house of women.

One of the Owl Masters raised his torch, his cloak swirling out around him in the wind. He touched his blazing torch to the stook in the far corner and at once smoke and flames leapt up. I wanted to run to the gate and warn the women that the Owl Masters were burning their fields, but I didn't dare move. William said if you ever told anyone what you saw the Owl Masters doing, they'd come for you in the night and cut your tongue out.

I watched the Owl Master brush the flames of his torch over the next stook, but just as he did, a blinding white flash lit up the sky, then came a big clap of thunder. Raindrops, fat and hard as hailstones, pounded down. The flames on the two stooks leapt up and then they were gone quicker than a tallow flame is snuffed out. The witch-girl had shaken out her hair and called up a storm just like Lettice said. But what if the witch dances?

There was a deafening roar of thunder like all the hills in the world had crashed into each other. I leapt up. I didn't care if the Owl Masters saw me or not. I didn't care about my pail. I just ran. Behind me the wind came screaming across the marshes from the sea. I ran faster than I've ever run before, slipping on the mud and splashing through the icy puddles, but I didn't stop. All I wanted was to get home to my mam.

September – St Giles's Day

Patron saint of cripples, lepers and nursing mothers. In Provence he defended a hunted hind from King Wamba, and was permanently crippled by the arrow aimed at the deer.

Beatrice

'Beatrice, wait a moment,' Healing Martha called after me, as I hurried out from the midday prayers in chapel.

If I ignored her, she might seize on someone else to carry out whatever task she had in mind. The afternoon was set to be sunny, the first good day after more than a week of heavy rain, and I'd no wish to spend it indoors stirring some evil-smelling ointment over the fire or cleaning up the old lady who'd fouled herself again. An afternoon spent gathering rushes reaps cuts and blisters, but at least I could feel the sun on my face. But Catherine tugged on my sleeve, so I could hardly pretend I hadn't noticed her. Healing Martha limped up to us, pain gouged deep in the lines of her face and her hand pressed to her back.

'I've run out of water betony and I've no time to go myself, with all the sick in the infirmary. Will you fetch some for me, Beatrice? I believe there was a good patch on the bank further up the river, and you might find some herb Robert thereabouts; bring me as much of that as you can too.'

Catherine was hovering at my elbow, looking eager as usual. 'Stinking Bob? Is that the one, Healing Martha?'

She smiled indulgently, 'That's the one. Why don't you go with Beatrice to learn how to gather it, for I fear that with so many patients to tend I'll have to depend on others in the future to fetch my herbs.'

It was not the sick that kept Healing Martha from gathering the herbs herself, but her back. Some days she could hardly drag herself around, but she was too proud to admit it.

Catherine beamed and rushed off to get the pokes to carry our harvest before Healing Martha could change her mind. But although I wanted an excuse to be outside, I resented being asked. I was not a Martha, so I was at everyone's beck and call to run errands and help with tasks as if I was one of the children.

Servant Martha had let me believe that, as the community expanded, there would be a role for me. I had thought that as Healing Martha became more frail and less able to work, I would take her place, under her at first of course, but later to take over as the Healing Martha. But she showed no sign of drawing me in.

They needed me as a Martha, though none of them seemed to realize it. Servant Martha was in the twilight of her days. Did they think she'd live for ever, and who would take over when she was gone? Healing Martha was even older. Kitchen Martha was only interested in food. Merchant Martha could scarcely contain herself to sit still in chapel until the prayers were over and she could get back to work. Tutor Martha had great learning, but she couldn't even control the children, never mind a whole beguinage. Who was there apart from me who had the skill and energy to manage such a household? But if I was not even a Martha, how could I become the next Servant Martha?

Catherine returned with our cloaks and we left the gate, heading towards the shallow ford. The branches on the trees hung low, their leaves sodden and heavy. As we turned towards the river, I tried not to look at villagers' fields where the grain lay flat, battered into the mud. We had lost some, but at least ours had been cut and stooked, so most of it could be rescued. Two sheaves had been scorched by the lightning, but the rain had doused them before they could set the field on fire.

We stripped off our hose and shoes to wade across the river, giggling like children and holding on to each other as we tried to keep our balance on the slippery stones of the ford. We had to hitch our skirts to our thighs to keep the hems from getting wet. The water was deep after all the rain and so cold. The bones of my feet ached in the chill of it and I rushed the last few steps, almost falling in my hurry to get out, which made Catherine giggle again.

The sun was bright, not hot, but pleasantly warm. I could have danced with the bliss of feeling its light on my face after the misery of the rain. It was such a joy to be outside breathing in the fresh air, heavy with the smell of steaming earth and crushed grass, I could almost forgive Healing Martha for sending me.

A great flock of starlings swished across the blue sky, their feathers gleaming as iridescent as oil on water.

'I can fly across the land and rivers, the forests and the villages and float on the wind.'

Catherine jerked upright, looking horrified, and I realized I must have spoken the words aloud. She stared at me as if she thought I was crazed.

'I mean, wouldn't you love to be a bird, Catherine?'

Catherine shook her head vehemently. 'Some little boy with his slingshot would break my wings and I'd end up in Kitchen Martha's flesh pot. I wouldn't like that.' She stood up, shuffling from foot to foot. 'Oughtn't we to go? It's a long walk.'

I sat up reluctantly and dried my feet on the hem of my kirtle.

'Catherine, do you want to stay here as a beguine?'

She looked puzzled, as if the answer was so obvious she couldn't imagine why I asked the question. Then her confusion turned to anxiety. 'Has Servant Martha said ... I know I'm not clever like Osmanna, but I will try, really I will.'

'Don't take on so, child. Servant Martha hasn't said anything, and I know you'd make a truly good beguine. Cleverness is not the only gift. You have gifts too: faith, gentleness, and you work hard.'

Catherine stared miserably at a daisy-head and absently pulled the petals from it one by one, as if she was making a test of true love. 'But Osmanna reads things. I don't even understand the words, but Osmanna can debate them with Tutor Martha and even with Servant Martha. I've heard her. What does it mean – one God in three persons and three persons in God alone? Osmanna has tried to explain it over and over to me, but I know I'll never understand it, so I just say I do.' She raised her brimming eyes. 'I just want someone to tell me what it is they want me to do.'

I reached over and stroked her hair. 'Osmanna shouldn't even be thinking about such things at her age.'

Servant Martha should have had more sense than to force Osmanna to read such books, never mind discuss them with her. The poor girl was pale and drawn, as if she already lay awake half the night worrying. Servant Martha would never listen to me, but I would have words with Tutor Martha, tell her not to burden Osmanna with books. Someone had to look out for the child.

'Come on. Let's find where the water betony grows. Where do you think we'd best look?'

Catherine brightened at once. 'This way,' she called, confident again, for that was a task she knew she could perform.

We walked alongside the twisting river, following its line upstream, often having to cut away from its banks to avoid the thick pools of mud and rushes. Autumn was approaching much too swiftly, as if it had been fooled by the storm into thinking it was later in the year than it was. But I was still hungry for the sun; it was too soon for the cold and dark to start to close in around us again. Even worse was the thought of the hours we would soon spend dipping those rushes, sweaty, stinking, suffocating hours circling the cauldrons of hot tallow, eyes stinging and arms smarting from a dozen little blisters from the spitting fat.

In the old days, as mistress of my husband's house, I'd simply sent a boy to buy the candles we needed. I gave not a thought to them beyond seeing that none disappeared into the sack of some light-fingered servant. Then in Bruges, our sisters who kept bees made candles themselves from wax smelling of honey and thyme and newly plucked apples. And as if the wax were not sweet enough by itself, they mixed oils of rosemary, lavender and roses in it, so that even in winter the rooms of our houses were filled with the breath of warm, sleepy summer.

I knew it was a sin to look back. Yet I repeated the sin again and again, like a drunkard who would not stay his hand from the wine. I don't know why I did it, for it caused me nothing but pain.

The river cut deep into the fold of the hills and the water cascaded in foaming torrents over stones and boulders. The sides of the valley began to rise steeply around us and we found ourselves scrambling over rocks as we climbed alongside the bank. In the sunshine, tiny rainbows swam above the river in the spray cast up by the crashing water. But there was no sign of the herbs that Healing Martha needed.

At the bend in the river, I scrambled up on to the mound and stared back down the valley behind us. The flat plain stretched out far below us; pea-green patches of grazing land lay between the dark brown strips of ruined crops. The river slithered across the plain, glinting here and there as the sun caught it where it coiled through the trees and rushes. Far in the distance the land tipped into emerald marshes edged with brown and, beyond that, the dark blue line of the sea scumbling into the paler blue of the sky.

It was so quiet up here. The only sounds were the rush of water over stones and the cry of a buzzard circling on the warm air, scarcely bothering to flap its wings. As I turned back to the river I spotted a clump of dark green leaves.

'Water betony,' I called to Catherine, pointing out the patch. 'Not much, but it's a start.'

She frowned. 'But that's brown-wort.'

'Whatever you call it, that's what Healing Martha needs. You gather this and I'll go further up and see if I can find some more. Be careful not to bruise the leaves when you gather it. Cut it, don't try to break it off. Those stems are tough and they'll slice your fingers.'

I scrambled on up the side of the river and was soon out of sight of Catherine. I found another small patch of water betony but the leaves were full of holes and mildewed. Then I saw some more, higher up, which looked more lush. I continued to climb, knowing Catherine would follow eventually or sit and wait for me to return. I was glad of the sensation of being alone. No sound of bells or children yelling. Just the sudden piping of the skylark as it soared upwards, as glad to be out on this day as I was.

I reached a place where the river was squeezed by a rocky outcrop on either side into a raging torrent of water, but on the bend of the river, the bank flattened out into a long shelf of wiry grass. I was so intent on searching for the herbs that I didn't see the cottage at first. One moment there was nothing, then in a single stride I saw it, as if it had mushroomed from the ground in the time it took to blink.

The cottage crouched between the fingers of a rocky out-crop, hidden from both the peak above and the valley below. The wattle and daub walls were threadbare and patched with greenish mud and dung. The thatch had not been attended to for many seasons and had slipped, leaving holes like ringworm in the mildewed straw. It looked as if it had been abandoned for many moons, yet a thin trickle of blue smoke rose from a turf-damped fire outside the door. It was clearly inhabited by someone, but only a hermit, a madman or an outlaw would live so many miles from his neighbours.

A solitary thorn bush grew from the cleft in the rock near the cottage. It was covered with little bunches of dead flowers, ribbons, faded pieces of cloth, teeth, bones, fairings and pieces of tin. They hung from the twigs like thank offerings in a church. But there was no cross and this was no Christian shrine. This was not the dwelling of a hermit and I had no wish to meet the madman or the outlaw. I turned away, trying to retrace my footsteps, treading softly and carefully so as not to arouse any who might be inside.

'What brings you here, mistress?'

I turned sharply. An old woman had appeared by the fire as if she had been conjured from the smoke. Startled, I crossed myself and she grinned mockingly. Bright sloe eyes flashed out from a withered crab apple of a face. She was filthy. It was hard to tell where the rough brown cloth of her kirtle ended and her walnut skin began.

'I didn't mean to disturb you, mother. I was ...' My voice dried up as she shuffled towards me.

'Want a man in your bed?'

I blushed furiously and shook my head, stepping back as she edged forward. But she only laughed, throwing back her head and showing the two remaining blackened stumps in her gums.

'Maybe you've had one already; now you want his seed out of your belly?'

She reached out a long skinny hand and pressed it against my stomach, laughing louder still. Her hand seemed to burn like ice through the cloth. I shrank back.

'Nay, that's not it. There's death in your belly, mistress. Stone babies. That'd be it, that's why you've come: the stone babies.'

I recoiled as if she'd struck me. How could she tell that? No one here knew. I wanted to run, but my feet seemed to have taken root in the earth.

She nodded towards the festooned thorn bush. 'Aye, there's more come to my door now in want of bairns than want rid of them. Cattle won't fall with calves neither, so they say, nor sheep nor hogs. Land's sick. People've forgotten the old ways. Try to wrest too much from the land, then wonder why she turns against them. Still, they know Old Gwenith can get them with spawn. What have you brought me? A gift for a gift.'

'I want nothing,' I said, at last finding my voice. 'I came by accident. I was gathering herbs.' Gwenith, I'd heard that name before, but I couldn't think ...

'None comes by accident. If you weren't seeking me, then she brought you. She can call all manner of wild creatures. She must have seen something in you.' The old woman stared hard at me. 'Aye, I see it too.' She pointed to the hut. 'Go to her.'

I didn't want to, but I found myself walking towards the door. I could feel the old woman's stare on my back. I ducked inside the low door. A ragged grey light filtered in through the holes in the thatch. The beaten earth floor was damp and stank of piss. Bunches of dried herbs hung from the roof wattles, but they were evil-smelling and did nothing to sweeten the air. Near the remains of a fire, a heap of rags covered a pile of last year's bracken. I guessed it to be the old woman's bed, a hard and chilly resting place for sharp old bones. An iron pot and clay jars stood by some charred cooking stones, but there was no table, nor chest, not even a stool to sit on.

Whoever Old Gwenith had sent me in to see was not here. The old woman's wits were wandering – hardly surprising, living all alone in such a place. Perhaps she imagined her long-dead mother waited inside. The aged often think themselves children again and think they see their loved ones near them as if they still lived. It is as if the ghosts of the dead draw close to welcome those who are dying. I turned to go.

A faint slithering sound stopped me in the doorway. I whipped round, my heart thumping. I searched desperately for the source, afraid to move until I found it. As my eyes accustomed themselves to the dim light, I saw that a corner of the hut was screened off by a piece of cloth strung across it. The sound was coming from behind it. I cautiously lifted the edge with the point of my knife and sprang back with a gasp.

A girl sat cross-legged in the corner. She was dressed in a thin torn shift, her wild red hair tangled loose about her shoulders. And, from a face as pale as the old hag's was brown, gleamed a pair of cat's green eyes. It was Gudrun.

Her body was writhing and twisting, yet she sat perfectly still. Then, shuddering with horror, I realized what it was that was moving. Her body was alive with vipers twining themselves all about her. They slithered through her hair and twisted about her neck. A black and yellow bracelet curled about her wrist. She held it up to her face and her little pink tongue flashed in and out of her mouth as the viper flashed his tongue at her. Then, without warning, she looked straight at me and her lips curled back as if she was laughing with delight, but no sound came from her mouth.

I fought my way out of the hut and scrambled down the

hillside, back the way I had come, tumbling and slithering down the slope, only dimly aware of the thorns tearing at my clothes and legs. Catherine came racing towards me and caught me in her arms.

'What's wrong, Beatrice? You look as if the demons from hell are chasing you.'

I glanced behind me. I too feared that. 'An old woman living up there, she startled me.'

Catherine glanced up at the hillside. 'Was it Old Gwenith? Pega said she lived hereabouts, but I never knew where exactly. Pega says she's the gift of second sight. They say it's dangerous to cross her.' She looked at me fearfully. 'Did she curse you?'

I shook my head. 'The old woman's granddaughter was there too.'

Catherine's eyes grew wider. 'You saw Gudrun up close? She usually runs away before anyone can get near her. What was she like?'

I shook my head, trying to remember what I saw. Snakes! Were there really snakes? In that half-light, it was hard to be sure of anything. Who hasn't walked along a track at twilight and seen an old man standing by the path, only to find when you draw close that it's nothing but the stump of a tree? Perhaps she had mazed me after all.

'I ... I didn't see her properly. Come on, you don't want to be late for Vespers, do you?'

I knew that fear of being late for anything would drive all curiosity out of Catherine's head.

As we drew near to the beguinage we saw a solemn procession making its way to the gates. Four men carried a shrouded corpse on a bier. A grey friar paced steadily in front of them. Several women followed silently behind, too well dressed to be from the village, but they were not women from the Manor either. There was no weeping or wailing, just a heavy silence. There seemed to be pitifully few mourners save for this sad handful; the corpse perhaps was someone very old, who had outlived most of their friends and relatives.

I caught Catherine's arm and held her back. 'We'll wait here until they've turned towards the church. It's bad luck to cross the path of a funeral procession. We should pray for the departed soul, whoever he or she might be.'

But to my surprise they didn't turn towards the village; instead they walked to the entrance of the beguinage and laid the bier down before it. The friar spoke to Gate Martha who disappeared inside, closing the gate firmly against them, but they waited and we waited too, not wanting to approach until they had gone. Presently Servant Martha came out with some of the beguines who carried the bier inside. The friar and mourners turned and walked slowly back the way they'd come, eyes downcast, leaning on one another as if in great grief.

Catherine looked up at me, puzzled. 'Why do they bring a corpse to us?'

'Perhaps I was mistaken and it isn't a corpse, but someone very sick. We'd better hurry. Healing Martha may have need of these herbs.'

Servant Martha

Gate Martha called me as soon as her sharp eyes spotted the procession on the road. We watched their slow progress towards us through the gate window. Even from there I could see that Andrew was wrapped head to toe as if she was dead. Perhaps they feared that the people would press about her if they recognized her, or she had asked that her face be covered so that she could not look upon the outside world. The procession hardly seemed to draw any closer to us as it crept down the long track. They carried a holy woman, yet there was no joy in their footsteps, no lightness of step. There was something more there than I'd been told.

At last the bier was laid at my feet, but the figure under the wrappings looked immense, not the wisp of a woman I remembered. Had I mistaken who they brought me? I glanced questioningly at the Franciscan.

'Andrew is much changed of late,' was all the friar said.

Merchant Martha had said the same thing to me, when she returned from the May Fair. I should have listened to her and gone to see Andrew then.

The beguines carried Andrew to a separate room that we had made ready for her and lifted her on to the cot. She moaned as if every movement hurt her. I sent them away and only when Healing Martha and I were alone did I peel back the cloths from Andrew's face. I could hardly believe it was the same woman. She was bloated, her body and limbs so swollen that she couldn't close her fingers. Her thin, delicate face was puffed up as if she had been stung by a swarm of bees, so that she could hardly open her eyes.

Healing Martha unwound the bandages covering her head. The few clumps of broken hair that still clung to her skull were crawling with lice. Maggots swarmed in the festering sores. When Healing Martha and I rocked her over on to her side to cut away the filthy rags, we could see her back too was covered in deep sores from where she had lain for weeks on her pallet without moving. The skin under her armpits was raw and weeping. She was wheezing. It was painful to watch her struggling for breath.

'You are safe among your sisters now, Andrew,' I told her, but I don't think she even heard me or knew what we did.

As we moved her limbs to wash her, she moaned, but she didn't look at us, though her eyes moved. She stared at the sunlight filtering in through the narrow window, her lips constantly murmuring strange words and sounds; it was no human language. A strange, sickly-sweet odour emanated from her and filled the room. It clung fast to me. I could smell it on my clothes and hair.

I saw now, all too clearly, why they wanted rid of her. She no longer drew the pilgrims. What use is a caged bear if it will not perform for the crowds? The mob want a beautiful girl to gaze upon, to watch while she whips herself and rolls on the ground in visions of ecstasy. They're not interested in the purity of the spirit, only in the beauty of the skin, and there was no outward beauty left in her. The priests cared even less about her soul; they had eyes only for the money she brought them. Now she no longer served their turn, they had thrown her out. Perhaps they had already found a new, prettier creature to take her place.

How could any man who daily held in his hands the flesh and blood of our Lord have been so hardened as to have cast this poor woman out? Even the lowliest servant in a manor is granted some straw to lie on and a place near the fireside when he is too frail to work. St Andrew's could have bought the offices of some goodwife to nurse her. Any fool could see that she would not have troubled them long in this world.

Beatrice

Catherine rushed into the kitchen just before Vespers. It was obvious from her breathless excitement that the new arrival wasn't the usual leper or cripple.

'She isn't sick,' Catherine whispered reverently. 'She's a saint and I heard Healing Martha say her mind has already left this world.'

Osmanna interrupted. 'How can she not be sick if she's dying?'

'Oh no, she's not dying. She has *abjured* her sinful body.' Catherine pronounced 'abjured' slowly and carefully as if she tasted a new fruit. 'Servant Martha told me so,' she said triumphantly. 'Andrew eats no food at all, but is sustained by the love of God and the blessed Host which turns to honey in her mouth. And her body gives off a sweet perfume, like roses after a storm.'

'Have you smelt it?' Osmanna asked.

Catherine hesitated, crestfallen, 'Only the Marthas are allowed to see her.'

'She must be so beautiful if she is a saint,' little Margery said. 'Does she have long hair right to the floor like St Catherine?'

'I expect so.' Catherine beamed. 'It'll probably be golden.'

Osmanna opened her mouth to speak, but I managed to catch her eye and shake my head. I could see she didn't believe any of it. I wished she could take more joy from life like Catherine. Osmanna behaved more like an old woman than a carefree girl, as though youth had been ripped out of her. Her face looked more hag-ridden than ever, as if she wasn't sleeping at all. I longed to put my arms around her and comfort her, that was what she needed, but Osmanna wouldn't let anyone come close.

Father Ulfrid

Since first light I'd been sitting at my table in the tithe barn, wait-ing. The villagers shuffled in one by one, twisting their hoods in their hands. Some carried baskets or sacks, but those were half empty. Many came with nothing. The story was always the same.

'The harvest, Father. It's ruined. I can't pay the Church tithe. We've not enough left to feed ourselves this winter.'

It wasn't just the grain; they hadn't been able to tithe the full measure of hay back in June and what little they had had gone mouldy in my barn. Many sheep had died from the fluke and the cold, wet spring had killed half the lambs, so that the tithe on lambs, wools and hides was also far short of what it should have been. Hens and eggs too. It had been the same tale for months. They couldn't pay their full tithe. Some couldn't pay at all.

Alan had been one of the first to arrive with a block of salt wrapped in sacking. He dropped it with a thud on the long wooden table.

'Salt cat, Father, it's what's owed.'

I flicked through the ledger, tracing down until I found his name. 'You're valued at two salt cats a year for the tithe, Alan, and you brought none in spring.'

I flicked back the edge of the sacking. Even I could see that the cone of salt was about a third shorter than it should have been.

I looked up at Alan. He was a burly, thickset man, a hard worker by all accounts. He'd managed to rise up to become a weller, the most skilled job there was in the salterns, for he had to boil the brine and collect the good salt at exactly the right moment before it could be spoiled by the bittern salts that came after.

'It's short measure, Alan. A tithe is not given to me but to

God. It is a grievous sin to withhold what you owe from God.'

Alan folded his muscular arms and scowled. 'You think rain only spoils the crops, Father. Salt mould won't form on sand, not unless sun and wind can get to it. We need dry weather for the salt cats to harden too. We've barely worked half the days we ought this year and the year afore that. Worked like an ox those days we could, all night too without sleeping, but we can't make salt without mould.'

He leaned forward, resting his great hands on the table. Like many workmen's, his hands were bound up in filthy rags to protect them from the rough work.

'It's not just weather, Father, there's the flour. We need flour or sheep's blood to take off the scum from the brine, but if the sheep are dying and grain fails, prices go up and we have to pay whatever merchants charge 'cause we can't make salt without them.'

'I know it's hard, Alan,' I said sympathetically, 'but –'

'No, you don't know, Father,' Alan roared. 'What do you know of sweating over the pans day and night in the steam and smoke of the fires? You think it's easy?'

He picked at the knot in the rags on his left hand and slowly peeled off stained cloth. He thrust the huge hand in front of my face. The skin on his palms was peeling off and between each of his fingers there were deep, raw cracks. He turned the hand over; every joint of his fingers and thumb was covered with great open sores.

'Salt does that, Father, dries out the skin so it cracks wide and won't heal up. You ever felt the sting of salt in an open wound, Father? When you have, you'll know all about *hard*.'

But I had felt it. I knew a salt sting only too well. The scars on my back burned again, as I felt once more the coarse salt rubbed into flayed flesh, the agonizing fire of it, building and building until I thought I would faint, except the pain itself kept from me that mercy.

I stared at Alan's hand, wondering what it must be like to feel that smarting day after day and have to force those fingers to work through that burning. Alan bandaged his hand again with a fumbling haste, as if he was ashamed that he had shown his wounds to me.

I dipped my quill into the black ink. 'I'll record that you have tithed the full amount, Alan. I only have to send a quarter of the tithes to Norwich; the salt you've brought will be enough to satisfy that quarter. Then ... then you can bring what you can for the parish later, when things improve.'

He flinched as if he had been forced to beg and was humiliated by it. He did not look at me as he walked away.

Alan was by no means the last I said those words to that day. I knew what each cottager was supposed to bring. It was all carefully recorded in the ledgers: what each holding was worth; what land they worked; what stock they had. Every croft, toft, field strip, beast and workshop in Ulewic had been valued and assessed. The Church had calculated how much it could wrest from each household, but those calculations were based on good years. There was no allowance made if the harvest was poor or the beasts died. To surrender a tenth of all produce and labour in a good year was difficult enough. In a hard year, a tenth of next to nothing meant starvation.

As evening approached, the trickle of villagers and their excuses dried up and I was left sitting alone. I flicked over the pages of the ledger. Scarcely a figure in the long column of numbers was accurate. If anyone inspected these records ... but they wouldn't. The Bishop would not trouble himself about a piss-poor parish in the back of nowhere. Even in a good year, what St Michael's sent to Norwich must have hardly amounted to a spoonful of all the tithes collected from the rest of his diocese. Bishop Salmon would concern himself only with the wealthy parishes, which had far more opportunity to cheat him. He could never afford the number of clerks it would take to check the records of every little scabby village church.

God, how long would the Bishop keep me exiled in this place? I wasn't suited to be a parish priest. What did I know or even care about the value of a pig or the price of some mangy hen? I had done my penance for Hilary. Hadn't I suffered enough? I couldn't stand another year in Ulewic and if I couldn't get Bishop Salmon to recall me to the Cathedral soon, I would be forgotten and left here to rot for the rest of my miserable life. It had happened to others.

I could still smell the bustling streets of Norwich, the spices and wines of the marketplaces. I could hear the shouts of the merchants and goodwives as they urged passers-by to taste honeyed fruits and sweet pickled herring, pastries sprinkled with cinnamon and sweetmeats flavoured with rosewater. I could feel the soothing musky oils that attendants in the stews massaged into limbs warm and supple from the hot baths. And Hilary. Hilary's soft hand on my buttocks. Hilary's hot tongue licking all the way up the inside of my thigh until –

'Is this the best they can manage, Father? The Bishop is going to be so disappointed.'

I jerked violently. Phillip was leaning on the wall by the door in the fading light, his arms crossed, watching me with amusement.

'Bishop Salmon is a compassionate man,' I said. 'It's been a bad harvest as well you know, Phillip. People can't tithe what they haven't received.'

He shrugged. 'The villagers don't seem to have any trouble paying their Manor dues, but then, the Owl Masters are excellent at encouraging them.'

He sauntered across the barn and perched on the edge of the table, looking down at me. I quickly slammed the ledger shut.

'The Owl Masters could help you collect your tithes too, Father. You only have to say the word. They'd have no trouble filling this barn for you.'

'I don't need to use threats and intimidation in order to gather my tithes. The villagers are mostly good, honest people; they will pay when they can.'

I rose from my stool, clutching the ledger to my chest. It was hard to make my words carry any authority, when Phillip was smirking down at me. 'And since you've raised the matter,

Phillip, you can call the Owl Masters to heel and stop them threatening the house of women. I heard what happened at the Bartholomew Fair, it was all round the village. I told my parishioners and I'm telling you, if those women defy the Holy Church in any way, as a priest ordained by God, I am more than capable of dealing with them, but so long as they do not cause trouble and content themselves with charitable works, I have no quarrel with them.'

'Even when they bring a filthy leper through the village against your orders?' Phillip slid off the table and prowled round the barn, feeling the hides and peering into half-empty sacks. 'And I hear the house of women have taken in another guest right under your nose this very day, the anchorite that Bishop Salmon expelled. Let's hope that doesn't reach His Excellency's ears, Father. It might look as if your authority was slipping – badly.'

He sauntered back and stood in front of me, feet planted well apart in his usual arrogant stance. 'I know you are hoping for a reprieve, Father. You want to go back to your comfortable post in the Cathedral and who can blame you, sumptuous lodgings, good wine and a city teeming with beautiful women. The Owl Masters could help you get all of that back. In a few months, weeks even, you could be lying in a very comfortable bed again. Of course, it would be up to you whether you were lying there alone. I wouldn't dream of encouraging a man of God to fornicate.' He flicked the ledger with his finger. 'All you have to do is ask, Father, and all of this would be over. You think about that.'

He winked and strode out of the barn.

Servant Martha

I blew out the candles in the chapel as the women, yawning, shuffled off to their beds. Finally, when the chapel was in darkness save for the eternal flame hanging above the altar, I closed the door and made my way wearily towards my own room.

The precious hours of dark between Lauds and Prime promised something more important even than sleep, the chance of solitude away from the chatter and noise which filled the courtyard all day long. There were a hundred problems constantly plucking at my sleeve and I found myself longing for just a day, an hour even, away from them. Usually I took great comfort in the kneeling forms of the women wrapped around me in the gentle candlelight, but that night I'd found even their quiet breathing a distraction to my prayers.

Across the courtyard, a glimmer of yellow flame shone dagger-thin through the shutters of Andrew's room. She had been locked away from the world for ten years, for her every waking moment spent in communion with our Lord. She didn't even have to concern herself with who would feed her, still less with who would feed them.

My sister Eleanor was like that. As a child she had no idea what effort it took to put food on the table or clean linen in the cupboard. She simply expected that it would be there whenever she reached out her hand for it, and it was. I kept house for my father, and the household was well run: the accounts in order, always a good table for his guests, the beds sweet and clean and servants troubled him with nothing. Yet I don't think he spoke more than a dozen words a day to me, though his face lit up at the sound of Eleanor's voice if ever her husband brought her to visit, which wasn't often. Her visits become even rarer after our father took to his bed, when he could no longer control his bowels and shook with the palsy. She said the stench made her sick and soured her milk. Dangerous for pregnant women and nursing mothers, she said, and she was always in one condition or the other.

I tried so hard to provide for the beguines and to take in every broken soul that men had rejected. Yet at every turn I found obstacles hurled in my path and sometimes, Christ forgive me, it felt as if the obstacles came not from the Devil, but from God himself. Was God so jealous that he punished us for the time we gave to the wretched and sick that might have been used to worship him? I could not believe that. Yet what if I was wrong? That night I could not find even base words for my prayers, but Andrew's prayers were given angels' tongues.

I was shaken awake. My legs were so stiff and numb that I pitched forward as I tried to rise. It was still dark. I must have fallen asleep where I knelt beside my cot.

Gate Martha caught my elbow and helped me as I struggled to my feet.

'What . . . what is it?' I asked her.

'The grey friar who came with Andrew is outside,' she whispered. 'I told him to go away and come again after Prime, but he says he must speak with you now, Servant Martha. He'll not budge.'

'I thought he had returned home with Andrew's mother. What can he want in the middle of the night?'

As usual she shrugged, but her yawns told me that for once she had no real curiosity to find out. She just wanted him gone from her gate, so that she could return to her warm bed.

Wrapping my cloak around me, I followed the light from Gate Martha's lantern towards the gate. Taking the lantern from her, I slipped outside, instructing her to bar the gate behind me. If there was trouble outside I had no wish to invite it in.

It was a cloudy night. I held the lantern up and cast about me, but saw only trees and the shadows of trees moving. One of the shadows spoke. I spun round, my heart pounding. The lamp only illuminated a thin nose beneath the cowl pulled down low over his face.

'Servant Martha, forgive me for disturbing you at this hour, but it's safer for all of us if I'm not seen here. Can we be overheard?'

I knew he was thinking of Gate Martha. I led the way down the track a few paces to reassure him we were alone. Then I turned to him impatiently.

'What do you want of us?' I was half dead with tiredness and in no mood for courtesies. 'Do you bring another sick soul to us?'

'No, I bring this.'

He held out a small wooden box. In the flickering light from the lantern I could just make out the image of our crucified Lord carved upon its lid.

'For Andrew. It is the body of our Lord. Seven pieces. You must give it to her each day after she makes her confession to you. It is all the nourishment she will take.'

I shrank back. 'You should not even have such a thing in your possession. Where did you get it?'

'Please don't ask me, Servant Martha. It is better you do not know. But you must take it for her sake. You know that your priest will not give her the sacrament daily; indeed it is very likely he will refuse to give it to her at all once he knows that she was sent away from St Andrew's and what is said of her. But she must have it, else she will die in spirit as well as in body.'

'Do you have any idea what you are asking?' I demanded. I found myself glancing round fearfully, even though I knew there was no one near. 'I cannot give our Lord's body to Andrew or to anyone and nor can you. Have you not eyes to see, Brother, I am a woman? You know as well as I do that only a consecrated priest may administer the sacraments. For you, a friar, to dare such a thing is sin enough, but for me ... don't you realize that the penalty for committing such a blasphemy would be flogging and imprisonment at the very least, even mutilation or worse?'

177

He was still holding out the box to me as if I hadn't spoken at all.

'Servant Martha, I know that your sister beguines in the Low Countries have done so before, when the priests have refused them the sacraments. And I ask not that you take it for yourself, but that you offer it as a servant of our Lord to a soul in need. How can that be a sin? The lowliest servant may offer venison to a guest in the King's hall, though he himself owns neither deer nor forest. Did not the first Christians share the bread and the wine among themselves, giving it one to another? You know the love that Andrew has for our Lord. She needs no priest to mediate for her; she is risen beyond that. She reaches out to her soul's love, her bridegroom, and He to her. They have no need of a marriage broker. For her soul's sake and yours, do not separate her from her Lord.'

I shivered and drew my cloak tighter around me. The light from the candle in the lantern danced on the box held out before me and the crucified figure on the lid seemed to move His arms, stretching them out to me. I found my fingers closing around the box and I cried out as they grasped it. It was warm, as if the figure on it was carved of living flesh.

The Franciscan folded his hands back into his sleeves, in a gesture that seemed to say his hands had always been empty and innocent.

'I will come on this day and at this hour every week to refill the box, Servant Martha. Leave it after the midnight prayers in the alms window in the outside wall with the shutter unfastened. I will reach in and find it. We should not be seen meeting again. *Dominus vobiscum.* The Lord be with you, Servant Martha.'

'*Et cum spiritu tuo.* And also with you,' I returned automatically and he was gone, sliding away into the shadows as if he was one with them.

The track was empty. Were it not for the box clutched tightly in my hands, I'd have sworn that I still slept and talked with ghosts in my dreams. Only the trees stirred above my head. The clouds slipped across the moon and the night suddenly grew much darker. I hurried back to the gate, knocking softly until Gate Martha let me in. She was too sleepy even to bother questioning what had transpired, though her curiosity would doubtless return in the morning. I would have to think of some explanation, but not now; I was too tired to think about it now.

Once I was safely back in my room with the door fastened, I looked round for some kind of hiding place for the box and thrust it behind some books on my shelf. My hands were trembling violently. I squatted down by the embers of the fire, clamping my hands under my armpits to keep them from shaking.

Why had the Franciscan asked me to do such a thing? He had no right to lay this terrible burden upon me. Yet Andrew was depending on me. Her soul, everything she had given her life for, was for this one end – to die in God's grace. If the sacraments were denied her now, her whole life would have been a pointless waste. I could not stand by and see a life thrown away. I could not keep her from what her soul needed.

But I was a woman; I could not possibly offer anyone the Host. It was forbidden; it was unthinkable. And yet ... and yet, I was the only one who could give it to her.

September – St Osmanna's Day

Osmanna of Brieuc, an Irish princess who fled to Brittany to escape marriage. She died around AD 650 and is the patroness of Fericy-en-Brie.

Osmanna

It was my saint's day, so for once I was excused all work. Servant Martha had told me I should pray in the chapel. I tried, but in the silence all that filled my head was the same terror that seized me every long night as I lay awake in the dark. I had only one prayer, 'Please let my blood come today. Please let it be over.'

At night as I lay in my cot I ran my hands over my belly. Was it swelling? I tried not to eat. Beatrice had noticed that and coaxed me with tender pieces of meat from her own trencher and honeyed pastries which she pressed on me in the fields. She was kind. But after meals I rushed to the latrines and made myself vomit. I was hungry all the time, but I had to starve that thing inside me so it wouldn't be able to grow. I wouldn't let it feed on me. I had to make it die!

A sudden fusty draught sent the lamp over the altar swinging and the shadows scuttling towards me. Unable to bear it a moment longer, I flung open the chapel door and raced out into the blinding sunlight.

In the outer courtyard, the stout stone pigeon cote squatted contentedly on the patch of green. It had been finished only in these past few weeks after the storms destroyed the old wooden one. It was stout and dry, with good thick walls lined with nesting alcoves right up to the flight platform at the top. It had stone steps built into it, so that you could creep up and slide your hand under the squabs as they sat quietly in their nests, never suspecting that Kitchen Martha's knife awaited them. I'd already discovered that the back of the cote was a good place to shelter out of the wind and out of sight of the other women.

But as I rounded the cote, I almost tripped over Ralph, who was sitting in my favourite spot, his back resting against the stone-wall pigeon cote. A crippled child lay across his lap, her floppy head supported in the crook of his arm. The stick fingers of her tiny hand fluttered beside her face, as if they were trying to grasp at something.

Gate Martha had found the child abandoned on our threshold one morning with scarcely a rag to cover her. Her body was so twisted that she couldn't even sit up or control the movements of her limbs. But the strange thing was that Ralph had taken to her as soon as he saw her.

When Ralph first arrived he'd just sat hunched, staring into the fire for hours, not talking or eating. Healing Martha had tried lavender oil to restore his wits, but nothing did any good until that child arrived. Now he would sit for hours stroking her hair, patiently feeding her and telling her stories. It was as if he poured all the lost love for his family into her.

Ralph was holding out stale breadcrumbs in his free hand as the pigeons fluttered in to snatch the crumbs. When a leper holds out his bound stumps to people, they shy away, twisting their own hands behind them, but the birds didn't flinch from him.

'She likes the birds,' Ralph said without looking up. 'Listen to her laugh. She thinks they fly for her, bless the mite. We come every day to feed the birds, don't we, Ella?'

I crouched down beside them. 'Is that her name – Ella? I didn't know.'

'It's what I call her. Ella means *all*, so I've been told. It's fitting. She's all I have and I'm all she has, I reckon. If ever she was given a name afore, she can't tell me what it was. I don't reckon they'd have given her any sort of a decent name. The Devil's spawn, that's what I heard one old cat in the infirmary call her.'

He turned towards me, his eyes bright with anger. 'What manner of God would curse an innocent bairn with such an affliction? Priests say a bairn is punished this way to pay for the sin of her parents. Me, it's just I'm cursed for I've sinned aplenty in my life, though there's many done worse than me that still sits in health and wealth. But what kind of master would whip a little bairn for his father's thieving?'

'My father would. I saw him flog a potboy with his own hands until he was unconscious just to punish his widowed mother because she confessed she was with child and her husband had been dead for over a year.'

'Can we expect no more mercy from God than from your father when he feels slighted?' Ralph whispered softly, as if he feared to be overheard.

And what would my father do if he ever discovered that demon's spawn was inside me? Potboys were not the only children he flogged. Once, when I was little, my father was raging about some matter to his bailiff and caught me smiling. I was far away inside a story in my head, but my father thought I was laughing at him. He called for a rod, threw me over a bench and thrashed me in front of the entire company. Afterwards he made me kiss his mouth to show everyone I loved him. Even now I can still taste my salt tears running over his fat, wet lips. I hated him for that, not for the whipping, but for that kiss, but I hated myself more because I had lied in that kiss and I hated myself for being afraid of him.

Pater noster, qui es in coelis. Our Father who art in Heaven. Each time I said it, I tasted that kiss again. Each time I said it was a new lie, because a voice inside my head was shouting, 'No, not *pater noster,* not our father, not my father.' I would not pray to a father. I would never call him Father.

Ralph gazed at the face of the child, rocking her and stroking the bare skin of her cheek gently with his forearm. Ella half closed her eyes and her little moans became singsong cries, as if she tried to imitate the notes of a bird or the cradle song of her mother. Her fingers opened and closed, playing upon an imaginary pipe that only she could hear.

'Have you heard any news of your own children?' I asked and immediately cursed myself for saying something so stupid.

His eyes filled with tears. I quickly turned away, pretending not to notice. Ever since that night in the forest I found I couldn't cry any more and other people's tears made me angry.

Ralph cleared his throat. 'Nights I lie awake wondering if they're starving in some ditch. If my poor Joan's been driven to sell herself to put food in their bellies or to sell Marion or my little lads into labour.' His voice was husky.

'Pega says your wife took the children to her own kin in Norwich. You know Pega; if she says it then it's bound to be true.' I refused to look at him for I could hear in his voice that tears still shone in his eyes.

'But her kin won't take them in, not when she tells them of me, for fear she carries the sickness with her.'

I hesitated; I didn't want to upset him again. 'Perhaps she'll have said you had an accident.'

He seemed to brighten a little at the thought. 'Aye, you're right. My Joan's an honest woman, but she'd do anything to protect the bairns. And they'd not refuse a widow and that's what she is, without a word of a lie, for I am dead. Father Ulfrid said as much.' He nodded to himself. 'She'll like as not wed again for she is still pleasing to look at. And her new husband'll surely treat the bairns kindly for her sake. She'd not take to a cruel man.'

'Of course she wouldn't. She'd only marry a good man like you. Besides, the children will soon be grown and have children of their own,' I said eagerly, crowding into his cheerful day-dream.

But he looked down again; the light died in his face. 'And what if their bairns are born like Ella? They say his curse reaches to the seventh generation.'

His grasp on Ella tightened and she opened her eyes wide in surprise. He rocked her, murmuring softly, his mouth against her ear so that she gurgled in the tickle of his breath. Then he held the child away from him and awkwardly, with his clumsy stumps, dragged open his shirt and turned towards me. About his chest he had twisted bands of leather with iron studs sticking through into his flesh. The bands were bound so tightly to his skin that each time he moved, the studs bruised and cut him.

His flesh was purple and swollen on either side of the leather straps. Each time he held the child against him, her wriggles and jerks must have driven the metal deeper into the bruised flesh.

'I wear them sleeping and waking,' he said as he struggled to pull his shirt back and cradle the child against him again.

'But why, Ralph?' I asked, almost unable to believe what I had just seen.

'For the bairns,' he said as if only a simpleton would not know this. 'God must take my penance as enough, and spare the bairns.'

I'd heard that a mother might put herself between a man's fist and the child she loves, but I didn't know that any man could have such tender feelings as to put himself between God's fist and his child. My father wouldn't. God put the mark of his curse on me while I quickened in my mother's womb, but if God cursed me for my father's sins, my father added his own curse to me for bearing it.

'It's quiet here today, Osmanna. Few souls about.'

Ralph's words were so calmly spoken that I wondered if I had imagined the horror beneath his shirt. Ella had closed her eyes again and was lying contented in his arms.

For a moment I couldn't drag my thoughts away to make sense of what he'd said. 'Yes ... yes, it is quiet. Most of the women have gone to the seashore to rake for razor shells and to gather seaweed to dry for winter fodder for the goats. There won't be enough hay to see us through this winter.'

'You didn't want to go with them?' Ralph asked. 'I'd have thought you'd be glad of a day by the sea.' He sighed wistfully.

I felt guilty. I was free to go out, but spent my time inside, while he must have longed to walk by the sea or climb the hills or wander again in all the places he had known as a boy, but he couldn't leave the gates.

'It's my saint's day,' I said. 'I'm supposed to spend it in contemplation.'

'Blessings on you. I wish ...' he began. Then suddenly he thrust the half-sleeping child into my arms. 'Wait, wait here.'

He rose with a struggle and limped off towards the infirmary.

Ella twisted in my arms. She knew I was not Ralph and the anxiety showed in her face. Her body was lighter even than it looked, like a dried fish, transparent and sharp, but her head was heavy as it lolled against me.

Ralph came limping back across the grass, stumbling often. Soon he would need crutches. He would not be able to carry Ella to the cote next summer, if she lived until then. He laid a package wrapped in oiled cloth on the grass beside me, eased himself back down on the grass and scooped Ella out of my arms.

He nodded at the bundle. 'For you, a gift for your saint's day.'

I blushed and stammered in surprise, 'I can't take it.'

'Please,' he said. 'My Joan brought a bundle of things for me the night she fled. I didn't see her. I wish she'd asked for me, but I think she was afraid. I don't blame her. This was hidden inside a blanket. Open it.'

I unwrapped the package more from curiosity than any intention of accepting it. It was a book bound in calves' leather, with fine tooling and traces of gold leaf upon the cover. The lettering was in a fine hand. I looked up. He was watching me eagerly.

'It's a pretty book, is it not? Can you read it?'

I nodded. 'Merchants would pay good money for this. Why didn't your wife take it to sell? She must be badly in need of the money.'

'Poor Joan was always afraid of it. A man gave it me in exchange for some work I did for him. He'd no silver, but he said we could sell the book for more than he owed.'

'Then why –'

'I told you, my wife was afraid. The man told me it came from the Jews in France. There were Jews once in this land too, but that was afore you were born. My father said when they were driven out from Norwich they left many things behind they couldn't carry.' He shrugged. 'Some never reached the ships, but died on the march. But I hear tell they've been driven out of France now too. So maybe those that died were the lucky ones.'

'But the book, was your wife afraid it was stolen?'

He shook his head. 'You can't steal from a Jew. All they had belonged to the King for he owned the Jews, but the only books the King's men were interested in were ledgers of the moneylenders. Besides, they didn't always get there first, and who's to know what a Jew had in his house before it was ransacked?

'No, Joan was afraid because she'd heard that Jews' books are full of witchcraft and evil magic. She thought that if any knew we had the book or we tried to sell it, someone might accuse us of sorcery. She said I was a fool for taking it, though the man said it was a holy book.

'I didn't know what to do with it,' Ralph continued. 'She'd not burn it in case it was holy and that brought down a curse from God, or if it was evil and she burned it, it might conjure a demon.' He studied me anxiously. 'It's not a book of sorcery, is it? My wife blamed my sickness on the book. We can neither of us read and she'd not let me show it to any who could.'

I turned the pages carefully. 'This isn't a Jewish book. It's not written in their tongue. If it was I wouldn't be able to read it, but I can read this. It's in French. It means *The Mirror . . . for Simple Souls*. I don't know why the man said it came from the Jews . . . unless a Jewish merchant bought it to trade or a moneylender was given it as a pledge. I've heard that Jewish moneylenders often took books from Christians as surety. Anyway, this can't have brought a curse on you; it speaks of God.'

His mouth twisted into a crooked kind of leer, but I was no longer frightened by that; I knew it was his way of smiling.

'Then it's a good gift for your saint's day. Take it, it's no use to Ella or me and I've nothing else to give. I'll not forget your kindness that day you brought me here. You've more courage than any man in the village, though you're little more than a bairn yourself. I often think on how you gripped my arm and lifted your hand to cover me when they ...' He faltered, his arm half raised against his face as if he could still feel the sting of the filth and muck they threw. 'If it weren't for you and Servant Martha, God bless her, I ...' He scrambled up as fast as he could, holding Ella fiercely against him. 'Take it for a blessing,' he said, and limped away before I could put it back in his hand.

Servant Martha

I went alone to Andrew's cell. I heard her confession, and absolved her of sins which were so far beyond my under-standing that I was afraid to hear them. Sins of the desolation of a soul sunk to the depths of humility, a soul that saw its own corruption with such burning clarity that it could accuse itself no more and yet accused itself for that very fault. How could I listen to that? There was no penance I could lay upon her that her own spirit had not already taken upon itself.

Trembling, I placed the Host in her mouth and her spirit shot upwards like a lark. She babbled such sounds of joy that I shivered to hear them. Despite her bloated features there was an expression of ecstasy in her eyes, as if she had lost herself entirely. I crept from the room and summoned Healing Martha to sit with her for I could not.

Healing Martha glanced at my face and then at the cloak pulled tight around me to conceal what I carried. I dared tell no one what I did. I wanted to share the weight of it with Healing Martha, to seek her reassurance that I was doing the right thing, but I couldn't. If there was sin in that deed, I had to take it upon myself alone. I'd had a choice. It had been my decision, so I couldn't then force the knowledge of it upon Healing Martha. For this much I knew for certain – even if what I did was not a sin before God, there was danger in the act, grave danger for me and for anyone who knew what I did.

Father Ulfrid

I watched the long, thin finger run down the column of figures in the tithe ledger and the frown deepen. I couldn't bear to watch, but leaving him alone was worse. At least if I stayed in the church, I might be able to divert him.

'Would you care for some wine, Commissarius?'

He didn't look up. 'From what I read in these entries, I am surprised you have any wine to spare, Father Ulfrid.'

He pulled his fur-trimmed robe more closely about him. Although the rain had chilled the evening air, it was hardly cold enough to warrant such a heavy robe, but he had the pinched look of a man who was permanently cold, whatever the weather. Several times he tilted the ledger towards the candle on the table, to illuminate an entry, before dipping his quill and making notes on his own parchment. In the hollow, empty church, the harsh scratching of his quill seemed to reverberate off the stones, until it was all I could hear.

I'd encountered the Bishop's Commissarius only once before, the day Bishop Salmon interrogated me about Hilary, an interview I still relive in my nightmares. The Commissarius had been poised on a stool placed just behind the Bishop. Occasionally he had leaned forward from the shadows to murmur something in Bishop Salmon's ear, but he'd never once addressed me, and those whispers had been far more unnerving than the Bishop's torrent of angry words.

With his face half-obscured in the shadow of the Bishop's high-backed chair I'd assumed the Commissarius was a man of mature years, but now that he was sitting in my vestry, I could see he was only in his late twenties, though his skin had the waxy, unnatural pallor of a prisoner kept for years in a dungeon. He had a long, narrow face as if his mother had squeezed her legs together to try to prevent him coming into the world. His cheekbones were sharp and his eyes sunk deep into dark sleepless hollows, and little wonder, for he had such a tension of ambition in his frame that it would rob any man of his sleep.

'I'm ... surprised that you were sent to look over the tithe ledgers, Commissarius. I thought perhaps the Bishop's Reeve –'

'You thought or you hoped?' he said, running his finger down another column. 'Then my visit must be a great disappointment to you.'

'No, no, it's a great honour, of course ... but I hadn't realized you concerned yourself with such matters.'

Still he did not raise his eyes from the ledger. 'I am concerned with whatever is troubling His Excellency, the Bishop. And he, Father Ulfrid, is troubled about you.' He snapped the ledger shut on this last word and finally lifted his head to look at me.

'Your parishioners would appear to be somewhat reluctant to pay their tithes.'

'But they cannot give what they didn't harvest, Commissarius. You must have seen the fields as you rode here. The grain harvest was ruined and the hay crop was hardly better. Surely it must be the same in all the parishes in these parts?'

'Quite so, Father Ulfrid, as you say, all the parishes in the See are affected.' He smiled, but the smile did not reach his eyes.

'Then you understand the difficulties,' I said, much relieved.

'I understand very well, Father Ulfrid. I understand that all the other priests, priests who are diligent in the service of the Church, have collected their tithes as usual and on time, despite the ... *difficulties*.'

I gaped at him. How could they? It was almost on the tip of my tongue to say I didn't believe him, but I stopped myself in time. 'But, Commissarius, how can they bring a tenth of their crops when they have no crops?'

What did he expect me to do, rip the rags from the backs of beggars? God knows, I didn't want to be here, but if a man is suddenly thrown into chains, he cannot help but feel some compassion towards the other wretches suffering in the same dungeon.

He paused and studied me carefully, pressing the tips of his long fingers together. 'Father Ulfrid, perhaps you have forgotten that the Church accepts wool and crops as the tithe only from its compassion for the poor. What the Church wants, Father, what indeed it demands first and foremost, is money. If the people cannot pay their tithes in grain and beasts, then they must pay in coins. Were you to familiarize yourself with the tithe records of your predecessors, Father, you would find there ample reminders that tithes are collected on time and in full regardless of whether the harvest is good or poor.'

'But with due respect, Com –'

He held up a hand to silence me. 'Ah yes, *respect*, that is at the heart of this matter – the people's respect for the Church. I think you'll find, Father Ulfrid, that excommunicating a few of the more obdurate members of your congregation will serve as a salutary lesson to the rest of the parish. After all, what is a mere tenth of their earnings in this life, compared to an eternity spent in the fires of hell for them and their children?'

'But if the crops have failed, where are they to find –'

'It is because they deny God what is rightfully His that He has punished them with poor harvests. If they had tithed honestly and generously in the past, they would not now be suffering. At such times you should advise them to redouble their efforts to pay in order that His wrath may be turned aside.'

He rose abruptly and tucked the ledger under his arm. 'Come, show me the tithe barn. With so little gathered in, at least there will have been no occasion for error in the counting of it.'

I felt my stomach turn sour. 'Commissarius, surely there's no need to trouble yourself on such a night? The records are accurate, I assure you. You'll get soaked going out in that rain and I'd never forgive myself if you caught a chill.'

He was already at the door of the church. 'I thank you for your solicitude, Father Ulfrid, but I assure you it is no trouble.

I am glad to suffer in the service of the Holy Church, as I am sure are you, Father. Please be so good as to bring the lantern and the key.'

Outside the rain was slashing down. The night was so dark it was impossible even to see across the churchyard. I pulled my cloak tightly about myself and held the lantern up to light the Commissarius' way down the puddle-strewn track. I was praying he'd slip and break his neck, but the way things were going, he'd probably only step in a puddle and soak his boots, which would do nothing to improve his disposition. I fumbled at the door of the barn, trying to turn the great key in the lock. When it finally yielded, the Commissarius seized the lantern and held it up. The trembling flame only seemed to magnify the great gaping spaces between the pitifully few stores.

'Commissarius, you must understand we lost a number of hides. There was an infestation of black beetles. We had to burn the infected hides to prevent the others from becoming holed.'

'Then they were either badly cured, or inefficiently stored. Both are your responsibility, Father Ulfrid.' The long finger was methodically flicking through the skins. 'You must ensure that only the finest-quality produce is given to the Church. The populace will try to pass off their worst goods as tithes if they think the priest is too careless to check. That is why you should insist on payment in coin, Father Ulfrid. Money is never – what was it you said? Ah, yes – infested by little black beetles.'

He strode round the barn, counting sacks here and bales there. He was only doing it to prolong my agony; he already knew the amounts would not tally. The fleeces and hides had never existed. He'd known that before we even entered the barn. The only question was what he would do about it. The rain drummed down on the roof of the barn and wind whistled in through the gap under the door, but it was not the chill draught that made me shiver.

When at long last the Commissarius had completed his circuit of the barn he went to the table and sat down, opening the ledger. His pale finger again traced down the columns. I waited, the old familiar pain in my chest growing stronger with every minute that crawled past.

Finally he looked up. 'As you are doubtless aware, Father Ulfrid, there would appear to be a significant discrepancy between what is in the barn and what is recorded in the ledger.'

I struggled against my rising panic, trying to make my voice sound calm. 'As I explained, the hides –'

'And no doubt you could also explain the missing hay, roots, beans and all of the other items that appear to have vanished. What was it, Father, weevils, mice, floods, fire? I don't doubt you've been smitten with them all. You seem to have been the victim of great misfortune.' He paused and stroked his chin thoughtfully. 'However, since you are a man of God, I shall, of course, accept your tithe ledger as a true and accurate record of what you have received on behalf of the Holy Church.'

I felt myself breathing out hard. I hoped it wasn't loud enough for him to hear, but evidently he saw the look of relief on my face, for he smiled.

'Entirely accurate,' he repeated quietly. 'Therefore, you will deliver to His Excellency, the Bishop a quarter of all the tithes you have recorded in your ledger, regardless of what is actually contained in the barn.'

He paused, and I felt the fear in me ebbing away. It was not as bad as I feared. I had already calculated I had just enough to send what I owed to Norwich and I'd be able to scrape together enough to live on from the tithes set aside for repairing the church and alms for the poor. It would be difficult, but I could do it, and the villagers would surely pay me what they owed when they could.

But the Commissarius had not finished. 'In addition, Father Ulfrid, you will send the quarter set aside for the maintenance of St Michael's church to me and I will personally oversee the settlement of any bills for the church. Likewise you will also send to me the quarter of the tithes recorded in your ledger which are reserved for the poor and needy of your parish. Just for safekeeping, you understand, in case any of it should fall

✝

September – Devil's Nutting Day

Those who gather nuts on this day will be gathered straight to hell or driven mad. Any unwed maiden who gathers nuts this day will reap a crop of bastards.

Osmanna

I felt it move towards dawn. I lay rigid in bed, praying that it had only been a bad dream which had woken me, but I knew it was not. I couldn't pretend any longer. All those weeks I had tried to convince myself there was nothing inside me, but there was. It was alive and it was moving.

I followed the others into the chapel for Prime, but I couldn't pray. All I could think about was that creature growing in my belly. There was another heart beating inside me. I was sure I could hear it. Everyone must surely hear it, that hot, rapid beat that wasn't mine.

'*Aufer a nobis, quaesumus Domine, iniquitates nostras . . .*'

'Take away from us our iniquities, we beseech Thee, O Lord . . .'

As Servant Martha said the words, I felt it flutter for the second time. It could hear the holy words even through my belly and it was fighting against them. I pressed my hands tightly against it, sure that everyone would see the thing moving through my skin, but the tighter I pressed the harder it fought, and I knew that even if I smashed a stone into my stomach, I could not kill it. Its wings were beating inside me. It was biting at my entrails and that's how it would get out; it would eat its way out through my belly. There was a monster growing inside me and I had to destroy it.

I looked up and saw Healing Martha watching me, a frown on her face. I forced my hands away from my stomach and held them together in front of me, pressing them so tightly to stop them shaking that it hurt. Healing Martha mustn't know. She couldn't find out. She would see the bruises on my stomach, would know that I had tried to crush it, and she would lock me up, tie my hands so I couldn't hurt it. I looked around at the faces of the beguines; they were all scowling as if they all knew. They'd force me to carry this thing. They'd make me give birth to this monster. To kill an unborn child was a sin.

She can get rid of warts and more besides. That's what Pega had said that day out in the hay meadow. Old Gwenith, she'd know how to get rid of this creature. Who else could I go to? Who else would help me?

I slipped out of the gates straight after Prime. Everyone was too busy with their chores even to ask where I was going. And where was I going? Pega had said, *Old Gwenith lives far up the river, where the valley narrows.* But I had no idea how far that was. D'Acaster's daughters weren't permitted to wander about the countryside. All I could do was follow the river and pray that somehow I would find the place.

I ran until I reached the ford, desperately afraid that if someone saw me they might call me back to help with some task in the beguinage or, worse still, insist on coming with me. I picked my way across the slippery ford stones, the icy water lapping round my calves. It was only when I reached the other side and my feet began to slip inside my wet shoes, that I realized I had waded across the ford without taking off my shoes and hose.

The river skirted the edge of the forest. Even though I was on the other side, I glanced fearfully across the water towards the dense mass of trees. Though I knew that the creature which hunted in there stalked its prey in the darkness, even in daylight I did not feel safe from it, as if it could slip between the shadows of the rocks or ride in the storm clouds and find me. I ran up the bank as fast as I could, my feet slipping and sliding in my wet shoes, until I had left the curve of the forest behind me.

I do not know how long I walked then. The bank grew steeper and narrower. The crashing of the water grew louder and louder until it filled my head. I slipped several times on the rocks as I scrambled up the hillside, grazing hands and knees, but I could not let myself slow down or even think where I was placing my feet. All the time the river rushed past me, as if it wanted to catch me and drag me back down the hill with it.

I saw the old woman before I saw the hut. I knew it must be her. Who else would live this far from the village? She was squatting with her back to me, pulling at something between her knees. Her back was bent into a hoop and her long, grey, greasy hair swung over her shoulder in a single thin rope.

My legs were trembling from the climb. Now that I was here, I didn't know what to ask. Suppose she couldn't do it after all. Pega had said *warts and more besides*. What if that wasn't what she meant? And if she could, how would she get this thing out of me – with a knife? What on earth was I doing? I began to back away.

'A love potion is it, little maid?' Old Gwenith rocked forward and, picking up a staff from the ground, levered herself to her feet and turned around. A skinned hare dangled from her bloody hands.

I shook my head. My mouth was too dry to speak.

She beckoned with a crooked finger, bright red with scarlet blood. The skin of her face was burnt brown and it looked as if the bones inside had shrunk to the size of a cat's skull, leaving the skin sagging loose and as crinkled as old bark. I'd never seen anyone so old.

'Come closer, my eyes aren't what they were.'

'I made a mistake . . . I have to . . .'

'You've had a hard climb for nothing then.' Her laughter was harsh and rasping, breaking off in a fit of coughing. She spat out a mouthful of brown liquid and wiped her lips on the back of her hand. Her thin chest heaved as she tried to regain her breath.

'All who come here say they want nothing, but they all want something.' She put her head on one side. 'Another grey one. But you've come for me this time, not my Gudrun.'

Another grey one? Did she mean another beguine had been here? But who would go to her, unless it was Pega? What would she have wanted?

The old woman edged closer.

'I see the way of it now. You're no maid after all.' She was staring at my belly and I realized that my fists were clenched across it. I jerked them away, but it was too late.

She laughed again and again. The laughter crumbled into a fit of coughing.

'A lifetime of pain for five minutes of pleasure. Was he worth it, girl?'

'I tried to fight . . .' I found myself blurting out. 'I was forced . . .'

'Aye, it happens.' Her rheumy brown eyes took on a kindly expression instead of mocking. 'You're not the first and you won't be the last. Men think they can take anything they want by force, but what matters can't be got that way. Smash an egg and you'll not get a prize falcon from it, just a mess in your hand. You think on it, lass. He's taken nothing from you that's worth a fart in the end.'

'It wasn't a . . .' I was on the verge of blurting out it wasn't a man who'd done this to me. It wasn't a child growing inside me, but a monster. But if the old woman knew it was a demon who had done this to me, she might be too afraid to kill its spawn, and she had to. There was no one else who could get the thing out of me.

'You can . . . get rid of it?'

'Aye, I can get rid of anything that's not wanted.' She wiped her bloody hand on her skirts and held it out palm up. 'What have you brought me? A gift for a gift.'

'But I haven't got anything. I didn't have time . . . I didn't think . . .'

She shrugged. 'You get nowt for nowt in this world.' She shuffled back towards her hut.

I found myself running towards her. 'Wait, please, I can get something, anything, anything you want. I have money. I'll go back and get whatever you want after you've done it. I promise I'll bring it straight back, but please, you must do this first.'

'Fish promise a good supper, but as long as they're in the river, your belly stays hungry. You fetch a gift, lass, then I'll do what you ask.'

I knew I couldn't go back, not with this thing inside me. I could feel it growing as I stood there. I wanted to take a knife and rip my belly open and tear it out, but I knew I wouldn't have the courage to do it.

'No, no, please, it must be now. I can't bear to have it inside me, not another hour.'

She looked at me curiously. 'You hate him that much?'

I nodded.

'What's that on your chest?'

I groped around and felt a small sharp pin. It must have caught the light and she'd seen it glinting. 'A boar, the emblem of St Osmanna.'

The old woman frowned as if the name was unfamiliar to her.

'Osmanna was a hermit in a forest and gave shelter to a savage boar when it was being hunted. That's how the Bishop found her; he was hunting the boar and it led him to her and seeing how she tamed the wild beast, he converted her to Christianity and baptized her.' I don't know why I explained all that except that I wanted to keep her talking and stop her walking away from me.

'The boar did Osmanna no favours then.' Old Gwenith shook her head as if she could not believe such things. 'So why do you wear this boar? You didn't tame your wild beast, else you'd not be here.'

'My name is Osmanna. She's my namesake.'

The old woman stared at me for a long time, her toothless gums pressed together, until her mouth was a mere slit in the folds of her dark wrinkled skin. She held out her hand again. 'Then I'll take that as the gift.'

I hesitated. I hated the name Osmanna almost as much as Agatha, but the emblem had been blessed. Without it I felt naked and vulnerable. I could not go unprotected, not out here. It was all I had to ward the demon off. I glanced fearfully behind me in the direction of the forest.

The claw-like hand was still extended towards me. For the

third time that day I felt the flutter of those wings in my belly and I reached up and tore the silver brooch from my cloak, not caring that I ripped the fabric too.

She took my wrist and pulled me towards the hut. Her grip was deceptively strong for such frail bones. Before my eyes could adjust to the light, I found myself lying on a heap of mildewed bracken and rags with the old woman pulling up my skirts. I fought the urge to push her away. Cold hands pressed hard into my belly, kneading, pressing and pushing.

'You've left it late, lass. Should have come to me before.'

I clutched at her arm. 'No, please. It's not too late. You must do it. Get it out. Get it out now,' I begged.

'Hush, lass. I'm not saying it can't be done. But it'll go harder with you now that the brat's quickened. Herbs alone'll not do it now. It'll hurt you.'

'I don't care how much it hurts. Just get it out.'

She laughed. 'Easy to say now. Wait there.'

The bracken scratched my bare thighs. The embers of the fire beneath the cooking pot were still warm enough to glow red in the semi-darkness, but the hut felt chill and damp. What did she mean, herbs alone would not do it? What else would she use? An image of the knife swarmed back in my head and I was half on my feet as Gwenith returned.

She pushed me back down on to the bracken. 'Here,' she said, stuffing a wedge of cloth into my mouth. 'Bite on this. I don't want screaming. It frightens Gudrun.'

The cloth stank of old sweat, I almost gagged on it, but a minute later I was biting hard as cold, hard fingers prised open my rigid legs. She knelt, her thighs between mine keeping my legs apart. I smelt her sour breath as she bent over me, the stink of stale piss on her skirts. I couldn't see the expression on her face in the darkness of the hut, just the glitter of two eyes staring down at me.

I felt her bony fingers pushing up inside me, then a long, slender stick sliding over my thigh and being forced up into me. I knew it was only wood, but it felt like burning iron. I squirmed and writhed backwards, fighting to get away from it. Her free hand pushed down hard on my belly. She gave a sudden upward thrust that sent white lights exploding in my skull. Then it was over and she was pulling the stick out.

She threw the stick aside and tugged me until I was sitting. I drew my knees up to my chin, clutching my legs until the pain subsided to a raw, stinging ache. My mouth was so dry it was glued to the filthy rag. I pulled it and tasted the blood welling on my lips as the skin tore away with it.

'Is it . . . is it gone?' I moaned.

'It's dead. Blackthorn's killed it, but it's still in there.'

'No, no,' I screamed. 'You have to get it out.'

Her greasy hand clamped across my mouth. 'Hush, I told you I don't want noise. Here.' She pushed a knotted rag into my hand. 'In this are bay berries. Mind you chew them well, don't just swallow them. Then you'll start to bleed heavy and the dead bairn'll come away with your blood. No one'll know it's not natural. You'll have some cramps, mind, it won't be easy.'

The old woman's head jerked up and she tensed. 'Someone's coming.' She dragged me upright and pushed me behind a ragged cloth that hung across the corner of the hovel. 'Stay hidden.'

I crouched on the stinking earth floor and bit my fist to stop myself moaning from the searing pain between my legs. Then I heard a man's voice outside the hovel.

'So, mother, I hear you've been sending the brat to keep watch on the house of women.'

Gwenith laughed. 'What could my poor little Gudrun tell me of anyone?'

'You can hear the bones of the dead talking. I reckon you've ways of finding out what you want from a dumb girl. The question is, mother, why are you so interested in the women? Do you think you'll be able to persuade them to help you to work against us? Is that it?'

I peered round the edge of the cloth. Gwenith and the man were standing just outside the door of the cottage. The man was much taller than the low doorway and I couldn't see his face, just the long brown cloak of an Owl Master.

'Afeared of the women, are you?' Gwenith's tone was mocking.

The man snorted. 'I think you're the one that's scared, mother. You're the only cunning-woman now, since we got rid of that witch, your daughter. But those women'll not take your part. They're Christians; they'd see you hanged first.'

'Aye, they might. But then again, maybe there's more that binds us than divides us, though they may not know it yet. That leader of theirs has got the spirit of Black Anu in her. You'll not cow them into submission like the villagers. Not every woman falls on her knees at the sight of what dangles between your legs.'

'You witch.' The man raised his fist, but I saw the flash of a blade in Gwenith's hand. He gave a gasp of pain, clutching his arm.

'You've cut me, you vicious old hag.'

'Forgive a poor old woman. My hands get shaky, knife's apt to slip. If I were you, I'd stand back. I'm such a clumsy old besom, I shouldn't wonder if one of these days I don't take someone's eye out.' Her knife was still pointed at him.

He backed a pace or two away. 'There was a time when you and I were on the same side, mother. We could be again. Together we could defeat the Church, turn Ulewic back to the old ways. You know things will continue to go ill with this land until the old ways return.'

'Together?' Gwenith laughed sourly. 'In the hour you spilled the blood of the night-cat, you turned your hand against me.'

'You think you can turn the villagers back to the old ways without blood?'

'There's blood that's meant for the spilling and there's sacred blood that must never be touched.' Gwenith spat on the ground. 'If you follow the path you're bent on, you'll be leading Ulewic into such darkness and destruction that none of you'll be able to find your way out again.' She lowered the knife, but she still held it tight. 'On May Eve you spent the night in the bull oak wrapped in the hide of the white stag. No man's dared do that since my own grandam was a bairn and the last one who did ran mad and was taken by the river afore cockcrow. It takes a rare courage to brave the hide and live to tell the tale, but courage is not enough, not to stand against him.'

'How did you know about the hide, mother?'

'It changes a man, marks him for life. Happen you think if you can survive the horrors of that hide, you can command him. But he'll not be commanded, not by your skills alone. And I'll not lend you ours, so think on it. Remember what's carved above the church door, Black Anu, the maid, the mother and the hag. She was ancient long before the Church was young. She is ours. Without our skills, you have only half the power. You'll not control him. Don't be such a fool as to unleash what you can't master.'

'Your skills! A cunning-woman's skills? What are those – a witch-jar to set the bowels of some poor man afire; a charm to flux some farmer's calf; a toadstone to detect poison? You think a bunch of herbs can master him? Iron, blood and fire, that's what will control him, and I have them. I am the Aodh. I have them all.'

He leaned towards her, 'You said there was blood for the spilling, mother. Take care it is not yours.'

Beatrice

I hated the nights in the infirmary, the patients moaning and whimpering in their sleep, the snores and the constant irritating coughs which you didn't seem to notice in the daytime. Healing Martha couldn't attend night and day, else she'd have ended up in the infirmary herself. But there always had to be someone on duty at night, to fetch a pot for those too weak to get out of bed or a cordial for a fever. So we all had to take turns; not the Marthas, of course, for they had other duties, but us mere beguines who had no domains of our own.

I'd just managed to get an old woman settled when the door burst open and Healing Martha staggered in under the weight of Osmanna who was draped round her shoulders and doubled up with pain. Little Catherine was supporting Osmanna on the other side, white with fear.

'Bring a lamp, Beatrice, quickly now,' Healing Martha said as she and Catherine dragged Osmanna to a cot in the corner of the room.

When I returned with the lamp, Osmanna was lying on her side, legs drawn up, but even in that position I could see her shift was soaked in dark red blood. As another spasm of pain gripped her she bit hard on her fist, closing her eyes tightly against the pain.

'You go back to bed, Catherine, we'll take care of her,' Healing Martha said.

Catherine seemed rooted to the spot, staring down at Osmanna, a stricken expression on her face. 'Is she going to ...'

Healing Martha put her arm round Catherine and led her to the door. 'You did well to fetch me, Catherine, but now try not to worry.'

'She said not to, but I had to ... all that blood.' Catherine was staring back over Healing Martha's shoulder. She looked as if she might vomit.

'You did the right thing. Now get some sleep.'

Healing Martha gently pushed Catherine out into the darkness of the courtyard and firmly closed the door behind her.

Then she returned to the cot and tried to straighten Osmanna's legs, but she twisted away, shaking her head violently.

'It's only cramps ... my menses.'

'You poor child.' I stroked her hair which was damp with sweat. 'I've never seen menses this bad. It could be ague or green sickness. You've scarcely eaten a thing these past weeks. It's those wretched books –'

'Yes, thank you, Beatrice,' Healing Martha said, elbowing me aside. 'Why don't you go and see if you can get Hilda back to bed?' She jerked her chin in the direction of the old woman who was wandering down the infirmary towards us, clearly fascinated by what was going on.

The cot on which Osmanna lay, like all those in the infirmary, was screened on three sides by wooden back, end and side panels, which were too high to see over, and by the time I had settled the woman, Healing Martha had positioned herself so as to block Osmanna from view on the one remaining open side. Every time I approached she kept sending me to fetch things: a bowl, cloth, water or a cordial for pain. But I could hear Osmanna's moans coming at regular intervals, and I could glimpse enough to see Osmanna arch her back, and sink again as the pain subsided.

Suddenly I understood what was happening to her. I'd felt those pains myself, not once, nor twice, but on seven occasions in my life, and I knew only too well what they meant. Osmanna was losing a child before its time.

But how could she be? She was only a child herself, and how could she have got herself pregnant living in the beguinage? She never went out unless she was forced to and then only when she was with a group of us. If she was pregnant it must mean she was already with child before she came to us. Was that why her father had sent her in here, because she had disgraced the family?

I stood in the shadow behind the wooden panel of the cot. Healing Martha was talking softly, so as not to disturb the other patients.

'Osmanna, why didn't you come to me? Did you think we would have cast you out if we'd known? Is that why you tried to get rid of the baby?'

I felt my heart lurch and I swayed, almost knocking against the panel. This was not a miscarriage. That girl had deliberately tried to kill her own baby.

'I didn't ... it just happened.' Osmanna gasped out. 'I couldn't help ...'

Healing Martha bent lower over the cot. 'Listen to me, child. I am not judging you. If there is any sin in this, it is ours. We should have made you understand that we would never have cast you out. This is a beguinage, a place of refuge. Many women came to the Vineyard in Bruges when they were with child that was not of their husbands' getting or when they had no husband. We cared for them and raised their children together. They were as frightened as you and they would have done what you have done, if they'd had no one else to turn to.'

'You don't understand, I didn't ... I didn't,' Osmanna sobbed.

'Child, I've been a physician for nigh on fifty years and I know when a foetus is lost accidentally and when deliberately. I will not ask who did this to you, for I trust it was no one within these walls, but you must tell me all that they did, so that I can help you. If you do not, you may lose your own life too. You must trust me.'

Osmanna moaned again. The bed creaked as she arched away from the pain, but I had no pity for her now. I hoped she was in agony; she deserved to be.

'Healing Martha, you have to understand I couldn't have it ... I couldn't ... It was not like those women ... I couldn't give birth to it. I had to get it out of me. It wasn't a human baby ... it was a monster, a demon ... it was growing inside me. There was no one else who could help me ... I'm sorry, I'm so sorry ...'

'Hush now,' Healing Martha said soothingly. 'What's done is done. I can tell something sharp was used to pierce you, but was anything else put inside you? A herb? A stone? Did they give you some potion to drink? No one blames you, but you must tell me exactly what happened.'

I stumbled away and ran from the room, not caring that the door slammed after me. Not caring that I woke everyone. I had to get away from her.

Not blame her? How could I not blame her? To murder your own child in the womb, what kind of woman could do such a terrible thing? Didn't she know how hard it was to conceive a child? Did she know what a miracle it was, how some women would give everything they had just to have a baby of their own? A child you had carried and given birth to, a tiny fragile life to hold in your arms, someone to love and care for that no one could ever take from you. That's all I wanted. That's all I'd ever wanted, a baby of my own. Hundreds, thousands of women have children, not just one or two but five, six, a dozen even. All I wanted was one. It wasn't much to ask and here was Osmanna throwing my dream away, as if it was a filthy rag. She could have given the baby to me. If she didn't want the child, I would have gladly taken him. I would have loved him more than any child has ever been loved. She murdered the child I could have had. She killed my baby.

Pega turned over with a grunt as I burst noisily into the room we shared.

'What the devil ... Beatrice, is that you?'

'Are you awake?' I demanded.

She groaned by way of answer.

'Do you know what Osmanna has done? What that little slut ...' I paced up and down the tiny confines of the room.

'God's arse, Beatrice, it's the middle of the night. Will you stop thumping about and go to bed.' Pega pulled the covers over her head.

I sat down on the end of my cot and was up again almost immediately, too angry to stay still.

Pega struggled to sit up, the boards of her cot cracking in protest. 'What is it?' she grumbled. 'You may as well tell me now you've woken me. I can see I'm not going to be allowed to sleep until you do.'

I sat down again, this time on the end of her cot, and launched into the tale, hardly stopping to draw breath. There was silence when I finished. For a moment I thought she'd fallen asleep again. The fire had burned too low to see her face properly.

'Aren't you going to say something?' I demanded.

'Is the lass all right?' she asked quietly.

'What? Who cares if she's all right? Haven't you been listening to me? She murdered her own baby.'

'I heard.' Pega sighed. 'Poor little reckling. She must have been scared to death.'

'Aren't you appalled?' I demanded.

'Why would I be?' she said quietly. 'There's many a woman been forced to do what she's done, but none do it lightly. They know fine rightly it could kill them. And if they survive that, there's the fear the law will see them hanged if it's discovered. I pity any woman driven to it. And to think she said nowt all this time. Now we know what was ailing her.'

I could not believe Pega's reaction. I thought she'd be as outraged as I was.

'That's Lord D'Acaster's daughter you're talking about, Pega. Have you forgotten what her family did to yours? That little bitch is no better than her heartless father – worse, much worse.'

Before she could reply, there was a gentle knocking on the door. It opened and Healing Martha peered into the room. 'I thought I might find you here, Beatrice.'

She edged painfully across the room and groped for the end of my cot.

'Do you mind if I sit?'

I said nothing, which she seemed to take for assent, and she sat down heavily on my cot. She was breathing hard. For a few minutes all I could hear was the sound of her laboured breathing and my own heart pounding furiously. If Healing Martha was expecting me to apologize for my noisy departure, she was going to have a long wait.

'Beatrice, I came to ask if you would be so kind as to return to the infirmary,' Healing Martha finally said. 'I need someone to watch them for the rest of the night, if you –'

'I'll go,' Pega broke in. 'I'll not get back to sleep now, anyhow.'

I could feel them both looking at me and exchanging pointed glances with each other. I knew Healing Martha was expecting me to say I'd go back, but I couldn't. I couldn't trust myself to be in that room with that girl. They had no right to expect me to.

Healing Martha eased herself off the cot. 'If you're sure, Pega, thank you.'

Pega, with another glance at me, rose hastily and began to pull her kirtle over her shift. 'Osmanna, is she ... is the lass going to be all right?'

'Beatrice told you –'

'That Osmanna had lost a bairn. Doesn't go easy with a woman, that.'

'No, it does not. She's had a bad time and it's not over yet. Now that everything has been expelled, I've been able to staunch the bleeding a little, but not entirely. But I'm more worried about the danger of the womb festering. Once putrid matter sets up inside a body, it is hard to stop. I will do all I can, but I would value your prayers for my skill and her healing.'

I could not believe what Healing Martha was asking. 'You expect us to pray for her?' I blurted out. 'After what she did, she deserves everything that happens to her and more.'

It was too dark to read Healing Martha's expression, but I could see her shake her head. 'No, we were the ones who failed her. We shouldn't blame any woman for what she does in desperation. The fault is ours that she did not feel safe enough here to confide in us and let us help her.'

I sprang to my feet. 'She murdered a baby in cold blood. She murdered an innocent child. She should hang. You should let her bleed to death after what she did.'

Pega grabbed my shoulder and shoved me roughly back down on the bed. I think she thought I was going to hit Healing Martha. Maybe I would have; I wanted to smash something. I could not believe that they were both defending her.

'She's just a young girl,' Healing Martha said gently, 'and she was terrified, Beatrice. We might have done the same at her age.'

'What she did was wicked . . . . evil! I could never have done that. I'd have given my life to protect my baby, no matter how young I was.'

Healing Martha said more quietly still, 'I know you would, Beatrice. But if it's any consolation, Osmanna's child would not have lived, no matter what she did or didn't do. It was . . .' She hesitated, pressing her hand over her mouth. The knuckles gleamed bone-white in the darkened room. Finally, after a long silence, she collected herself. She swallowed hard. 'I've never seen a foetus so malformed. Trust me when I say there are times when it is better that a baby never draws breath for men would not be kind to such a child.'

Healing Martha shuffled to the door and paused, her hand on the latch. 'I cannot forbid either of you to discuss this with the other beguines, but if you can find any compassion in you, you will not spread abroad what has happened tonight. The fault is mine more than anyone's. Perhaps the Marthas in Bruges were right and I have grown too old to be a physician. I should have realized that first night she came to us, what had happened to her, the bruise on her face, the scratches and her fear. I was blind not to see it. Even now Osmanna will not speak of it, but I do not believe that she consented to the act that got her with child. She has suffered in more ways than we can imagine.'

'Are you going to tell Servant Martha?' I asked bitterly. 'Osmanna is her favourite, shouldn't she know?'

Healing Martha's chin jerked up. 'No, Beatrice, Servant Martha does not need to know. I will tell her only that Osmanna is ill. Servant Martha would only blame herself, and a true friend does not lay another burden upon someone who is already laden.'

October – St Wilfrid's Day

Born Northumbrian and educated in Lindisfarne, in AD 672 he encouraged Queen Etheldreda to leave her husband, King Egfrith, to become a nun, and the King exiled him. He preached against paganism and forty-eight ancient churches in England were dedicated to him.

Servant Martha

The women walked slowly to their tasks that morning, not meeting the eyes of those they passed, as if they were afraid that someone might speak to them. They fastened their gaze firmly upon the frozen ground, taking small, careful steps between the patches of ice. Their breath hung about them like white veils. Each glanced fearfully at the window where I stood, before quickly looking away. It wasn't me they feared, but the room. Andrew lay quiet now, but that unnerved the beguines even more than her screams.

Icicles hung over the casement and glittered on the tips of every twig. Even the moon was unable to stir from the lightening sky, but hung full and bright as if she too was frozen in her place. It was only October; it should not have been so cold. The first frost had come far too early. The patterns of the seasons were unravelling.

I'd been watching from the window since before dawn. Behind me Healing Martha dozed on a stool, slumped forward over the foot of Andrew's cot, her head buried in her arms. The fire was low, the last log burned away to soft grey ash. There was scarcely any heat from it, but I dared not rake the embers for fear of waking Healing Martha. Her face was so white and drawn, I feared that she too would fall sick if she didn't rest. And I knew if I sat down, I'd fall asleep too. My mind was as numb with fatigue as my body.

It had been just over a week since Andrew had fallen seriously ill, her body burning up with fever. We had bled her as much as we dared, but her blood was as pale as if water mingled with it. She wouldn't swallow any medicines and all the ointments that Healing Martha rubbed upon her were to no avail.

For the first three days the anchorite lay as if upon the rack, her limbs twisting and clawing as she cried out in agony. She screamed that demons were assaulting her, pricking her limbs with sharp knives and pouring molten wax into the wounds. They mocked her, offering her dung on golden patens and piss in silver chalices. She wept that incubi had caught her hands and forced her naked into their lewd dances. And though she never moved from her pallet, her limbs jerked and trembled as if she leapt and whirled with them. Such cries of horror came from her lips, such terror was in her wide-open eyes, that if even the most godless of men had glimpsed in her face the purgatory which gaped before him, he would have fallen to his knees to do penance for the rest of his days.

Healing Martha and I tended her constantly, seldom setting foot from the confines of her room except for the offices, for we could not allow any of the women to see her agony or hear her babble such vile tales. Exhausted though I was, when I did manage to snatch some sleep, her shrieks and screams so invaded my dreams that I was almost thankful to be woken again.

Even in the chapel her cries pursued us, cutting through our devotions and punctuating the psalms with cries of torment. I ordered the women to take turns in interceding for her in chapel, so that prayer constantly ascended for her soul without ceasing by day or night. But I scarcely needed to enjoin them to prayer; I could see in the fearful glances that the thoughts of the whole beguinage were focused night and day upon the struggle of the soul in this tiny room.

Then towards dawn on the fourth day she suddenly fell quiet. I opened the shutters and, by the first grey light, I saw that her eyes were closed and felt her skin frog-cold beneath my fingers. I thought her spirit had left her, I was sure of it. I went to the door and called out softly to Healing Martha. She came quickly and bent over Andrew, then laid a feather upon her lips. It stirred faintly. The breath was still in her, though barely discernible.

For the next three days she lay as alike to death as a candle flame is to fire. Her body was limp and still, lids blue-drawn over unmoving eyes. A morbid chill filled the room that was more disturbing to our spirits than all the demonic shrieks that had gone before. Our prayers, so fervent against the howls of hell, seemed to falter before the palpable silence that swelled from her cell, filling every corner of the beguinage. We held our breath, unable to fight against – nothing.

Kitchen Martha tottered across the frozen courtyard, bearing a steaming bowl. Little Catherine trotted behind, a second bowl cradled carefully in her arms.

Kitchen Martha greeted me at the door with a worried smile. 'Now, I've brought you a bowl of good hot broth and some for Healing Martha too. Don't stand there, Catherine, take it in before it freezes. Now, promise me you'll eat this, both of you, while it's hot; you've scarcely eaten a sparrow's crumb for days. Is there any change?'

I had been waiting for this question. I knew this was really why she'd ventured out of her warm kitchen rather than sending one of the girls.

'She rests peacefully and we must give joyful thanks that our blessed Lord has answered our prayers and has driven out the demons that so tormented her. You will tell them that, Kitchen Martha? Tell them to offer prayers of gratitude.'

'I think Andrew is waking,' Healing Martha called out softly.

I closed the door against Kitchen Martha and crossed rapidly to Andrew's cot. The anchorite's arms were flung wide in a cruciform and her eyes were open, but she was not looking at us. I glanced over my shoulder in the direction of her stare. There was nothing to be seen, save for the plain lime-washed wall.

'Look ... even as my Lord hangs on the cross,' Andrew croaked. 'See how like a loving mother ... He offers His blessed breast to me. He suckles me ... from His sacred wound. His sweet blood fills my mouth. He is my tender mother, my virgin ... I am safe in His womb.'

She half rose on her pallet, holding out her arms. Her swollen, cracked lips twisted in a mockery of a smile. Suddenly she turned her head in my direction. For the first time in many days she seemed to know my presence in the room. She grabbed for my hand and pulled me urgently towards her.

'Give me of His flesh to eat. I must . . . I must consume His body for the last time.'

Healing Martha touched my arm lightly. 'You stay here. I'll fetch the Host.'

Before I could answer, she had slipped from the room, closing the door silently behind her. I'd been forced to tell Healing Martha all about the Franciscan's nocturnal visits to smuggle the Host. Cloistered together in Andrew's room for days at a time, I could not have concealed it from Healing Martha. After weeks of bearing the burden alone, it felt almost as if it had been lifted from me when I finally spoke of it. Although I knew in my heart she would understand, I had expected her to be shocked at first, surprised even. But instead she merely nodded as if she already knew.

I struggled to kneel beside the cot. 'Make your confession, Andrew,' I urged her, but I did not want to hear it. I didn't know why I knelt, but I felt compelled to, as if I was the one making confession, not Andrew.

She pulled me close to her; her sour, cold breath made my skin crawl. Angry with myself for my disgust, I forced myself to lean closer until her mouth almost brushed my cheek. She rasped her words at me, but I could not comprehend them. My mind was fogged from weariness.

She recited old sins of neglect and weakness which she had confessed before a hundred times and in the same breath spoke of lewd acts with demons and beasts, as if she could not distinguish those illusions which she conjured in her fever from those sins which she had actually committed in body. Perhaps they were the same. What if her spirit had been transported to some distant place even as her body lay there before my eyes, and in that place she did commit those carnal acts? Witches' spirits can fly out to make mischief even when their bodies are shackled in the chains. But if God was powerless to prevent her blessed soul from being seized by the hosts of darkness, what help was there to safeguard us?

'*Ego te absolvo a peccatis tuis in nomine Patris –*'

I absolved her, but from what I did not know.

Healing Martha hurried in and pulled the small casket from beneath her cloak. I took the Host in both hands as Healing Martha knelt, her gaze fixed upon the body of our Lord in my fingers. The tiredness lifted from her eyes for a brief moment. There was a look of peace on her old face.

I turned towards Andrew and as I whispered the blessed words she levered herself up with her remaining strength, reaching towards me. I placed the sacrament upon her swollen tongue. There was scarcely room in her mouth for her to swallow even so thin a fragment. She leaned back and gave a great sigh.

Healing Martha reached into her scrip and drew out a small flask of oil. She pressed the cold, hard bottle into my hand. 'It's time. She is very near the end.'

I snatched my hand back from her grasp as if she'd burnt me. 'No, I can't. Not that.'

'You've taken it upon yourself to absolve her. You must finish what you've begun.'

The full weight of her words pressed down on me. Suddenly the air in the room was thick and heavy as if it was full of smoke. I couldn't breathe. I had taken upon myself nothing less than the burden of her immortal soul and that of Healing Martha's whom I had drawn into this. And what of my own soul? I had heard the secret confession of this anchorite's spirit. I had stood between her soul and her Lord. I had stood unshielded in the terrible light of God and pronounced His mercy. *What ye loose on earth will be loosed in heaven, what ye bind on earth will be bound in heaven.* Yet no bishop had laid his hand upon me, our Mother the Church had not cloaked me with her mantel. I had no authority, no protection.

Healing Martha was watching me, waiting for me to send this perfected bride spotless to her Lord. But Andrew was no leper, no harlot dying in childbed, grateful for any blessing of mine that would shorten their days in purgatory. I could not, I dared not intervene in such a blessed life, such a mystery.

'Send for Father Ulfrid. Go quickly.'

But Healing Martha didn't move. For a moment I wondered if I had actually spoken the words out loud. There was a long silence. We stared at each other. She stretched out her hand and grasped mine. Her skin felt warm, much warmer than mine.

'Servant Martha, you know that we cannot send for the priest now. If he should ask her when she last took the sacrament ... if he uncovers the truth about what you have done, you would be arrested and after that ...'

After that – we both knew what would come after that – imprisonment, torture, even death. And not just for me, for I had made Healing Martha as guilty as I was by witnessing my crime. There was no going back, no undoing the deed. I had seized the power of the priests like a cutpurse on the road and I could no more return it than a man may restore the King's stolen venison without forfeiting his life. Healing Martha held out the flask of oil again and I took it from her, anointing head, breast, hands and feet. It was finished.

Andrew suddenly cried out and gagged. I rushed to hold a bowl under her chin. Scarlet blood and black bile gushed from her mouth. She fell back, her head twisted round against her body. I didn't need Healing Martha to tell me that it was finally over. We knelt and prayed.

Healing Martha rose before me and began to straighten the body and prepare it for cleaning. I tried to help, but she gently pulled my hand away.

'Leave this. Your place is with the women. You must tell them of her passing, they'll be waiting. And you'll need to organize a place in the chapel to receive her. Send some of the women to help me lay her out. I'll watch till they come.' She wiped Andrew's stained lips with a twist of straw and dropped it into the blood-filled bowl. 'Tell them to bring water for washing and sweetening herbs. Pega has helped before with such a task, she'll know what to bring.'

I knew I had to speak to the women and I would have to choose my words carefully, so that they rejoiced in the anchorite's translation. There must be no sorrow in the beguinage, no grieving. We would give thanks that her soul, freed from the corruption of the flesh, had risen into the light of the blessed bridegroom. I would say that to them, firmly.

I took the bowl from Healing Martha's hand. 'We'd better get rid of this before the women come in. They do not need to see it.'

I tipped the contents on the fire. It hissed and crackled before it flared up again. I wiped the bowl clean with a handful of straw and added the straw to the blaze. I would not permit the sin of grief from anyone. There could be no sorrow for anyone who has gone straight to the arms of our Lord. It was my duty to make them understand that.

Healing Martha waved me towards the door. 'And as soon as you've spoken to the women, you must go to your bed and sleep.'

I shook my head impatiently. 'I have neglected my duties for days. There is too much to do. I'll rest tonight.'

'The world has gone on without you these many days; it can manage a few hours longer. Your eyes are red and you stagger like an old maid with palsy.' Healing Martha wagged her finger in a mocking imitation of a scolding crone. 'To bed with you, my girl.'

I don't know how long I'd slept, but I was jerked awake by a babble of voices outside the window of my room. I heard footsteps running and more shouts and cries. Suddenly afraid, I sprang from my pallet and hurried to the door. All the women in the beguinage seemed to be milling around in the courtyard, chattering excitedly, hugging their cloaks tightly around themselves against the cold. I shielded my eyes against the bright afternoon light. I was still dazed from my abrupt wakening, but it was evident something was wrong.

Catching sight of me, Catherine pushed her way through the crowd and almost fell headlong into me.

'Look, Servant Martha, a miracle, a miracle!'

She pointed to a silver plate that Tutor Martha held reverently in both hands. There was a slightly charred scrap of something lying in the centre of the plate. I couldn't tell what it was. I peered closer. Then I felt an icy hand suddenly grip my stomach. The pattern on the little disc was blackened, but it was unmistakably the same imprint as on the Host the Franciscan had brought.

'Where did you get this?' I demanded.

'When we raked out the fire in Andrew's room, this was lying among the embers,' Catherine blurted out eagerly.

'It was the Host that Andrew consumed this day,' Tutor Martha said in awed tones, still gripping the plate as if she feared it might wriggle from her hands. 'She vomited it as she gave up her spirit and the vomit was thrown on to the fire, but God preserved the blessed fragment for us. Though all the corruption was burned away, the flames could not consume His blessed body.'

'It is a miracle.' The words rippled softly as a breeze through the women.

My bowels had turned to water. I searched the crowd for the face of Healing Martha. She must have told Tutor Martha what had happened. No one else was in that room, no one else could possibly have known about the Host. I could not believe that Healing Martha had betrayed me. She knew the danger. She was the one who had warned me of it in that very room. I'd believed that of all people on this earth I could trust Healing Martha. I had wagered my life on her loyalty.

'Servant Martha.'

I turned my head in the direction of the voice and found Healing Martha standing at my elbow.

'What have you said to them?' I asked. 'How could you –'

Healing Martha gripped my arm and spoke in a low voice, 'Everyone who knew of the anchorite knew that she was sustained only by the Host. And there's not a woman in the beguinage who hasn't heard whispers of the Franciscan's visits. They're not stupid, Servant Martha. Did you honestly think they would not reason the connection? I had no need to tell them why he came. They suspected from the beginning that *the friar* was bringing the Host to Andrew.'

Healing Martha fixed me with deep blue eyes as if she was trying to make me understand something. Then I realized that Tutor Martha had not mentioned me at all when she spoke of the miracle. She had told the story as if she thought I didn't know that Andrew had vomited the Host. She had naturally assumed it was the friar, not me, who had administered the Last Rites to Andrew.

'The beguines have kept the secret of the Franciscan's visits,' Healing Martha continued. 'But if they suspected why he came, then others may also have done so and therein lies the danger.' She jerked her head back in the direction of the infirmary.

I drew a deep breath and tried to recover my wits. My hands were trembling and I clamped them firmly behind my back. I lifted my head, looking out over the crowd of beguines, now standing quite still, waiting for me to speak. I'd have to choose very carefully what I said next.

'It is indeed a miracle that such a morsel falling from the pure lips of Andrew has been preserved. This is a sign that we have indeed had a saint amongst us. God blesses Andrew and we must pray for strength to follow her example. This is her relic and we shall have a fitting reliquary made to house it. But I charge you most earnestly not to discuss this except in private amongst yourselves, until God has made plain to us His will in this matter. You must take every care that this tale does not spread abroad. It would bring grave danger to the Franciscan. Besides, there are many who will be jealous of such a relic and wish to take it from us.'

It was not the theft of the relic I feared, but I dared not alarm them with the real danger. I just hoped the threat of having the relic taken from them would be enough to silence them.

'Now, about your business, all of you. I dare say you all have duties to perform. Tutor Martha, take the fragment to the chapel and see it is locked away safely. And after, bring me the key.'

They hesitated for a moment, then slowly dispersed in whispering huddles of twos and threes, until Healing Martha and I were left alone. I could hardly bring myself to look at her. 'You told them that Andrew received the Host. Are you sure you have not told them anything else?'

Healing Martha sighed. 'After all these years, do you need to ask me that question? Do you really think I would betray you? I have only confirmed what they already knew and they do not know about you, though I suspect Gate Martha may have reasoned it out. She knows the friar did not enter our gates.'

'Gate Martha knows!' I said aghast. 'Do you honestly think she will keep it to herself?'

'She realizes the danger. She may gossip about trifles, but not about this.' Healing Martha blew on her hands to warm them. 'You have many virtues, old friend, but if you have a vice it is that you don't credit others with the intelligence or convictions you have. You demand too much of yourself, but you expect too little from your sisters. You must learn to trust others; it is the only way to win their love and loyalty. Otherwise all you have is their duty and that is a cold companion.'

'You trust too much,' I snapped. I nodded curtly towards the infirmary. 'You said the rumour of the Franciscan may already have reached the infirmary. So how many days will it be before the whole village knows of our miracle?'

She grimaced. 'I've never known a miracle to remain a secret for long.'

'And then?' I asked.

'And then, who can tell? Maybe our miracle will bring fortune, maybe disaster. But this I do know, a miracle never brings peace.'

October – St Frideswide's Day

A princess from Wessex whose suitor, Ælfgar, King of Mercia, was struck blind when he pursued her. She prayed to St Margaret for a healing well whose waters restored the King's sight.

Osmanna

'Osmanna, fetch more water. We'll need some to scald the starlings for supper.' Beatrice tossed two hard leather pails at my feet, forcing me to jump back to avoid being hit.

'Let me go,' Catherine said, jumping up from the stool in the kitchen. 'Healing Martha said Osmanna wasn't to carry anything because it might make her ill again.' Catherine knew I hated going near the well.

'That was over a month ago. She's perfectly capable of fetching a little water now,' Beatrice replied, as if I wasn't even there. 'If she could be trusted to pluck a few starlings without leaving half the feathers on, then I'd fetch the water myself, but she can't.'

Beatrice never talked to me now unless she was forced to and then it was only to order me to do some dirty or tedious task. I sometimes wondered if she lay awake at night trying to think up the worst jobs she could for me.

As I picked up the pails, Catherine darted an anxious look at me and I tried to smile to reassure her. Beatrice pretended to be engrossed in plucking and drawing the sack of small birds. Ever since that night in the infirmary when I had forced that dead creature out of my belly, Beatrice had done nothing to disguise her hatred of me. Healing Martha said none of the other beguines knew what had happened, not even Servant Martha. She'd told them I had the bloody flux. But Beatrice knew what I'd done, I was sure of it.

One night when I'd been sleeping in the infirmary I sensed someone leaning over me and a voice whispered, 'They might have forgiven you, Osmanna, but God won't. You can't ever be forgiven for murdering your own child.'

When I opened my eyes, there was no one near me, but I know it was Beatrice's voice I heard.

And if Beatrice knew, I was certain she would have told Pega. Beatrice told her everything. I had dreaded seeing Pega even more than Beatrice, for though Beatrice is spiteful, she's not clever with words. Pega can use her tongue like a dagger.

But when I left the infirmary and finally ran into Pega outside, all she said was, 'You feeling better now, Osmanna?'

I nodded. It was almost true. The pains in my belly had gone now. During the day, I could forget it ever happened, but not at night. Sometimes I was too afraid to sleep, because every night in my dreams the creature returned. In my dreams it was still inside me. I'd feel it clawing its way out of me. I'd see Mother Gwenith's red-rimmed eyes, feel the raw, blinding pain as she pulled the rod out of me. Then I'd see something in her filthy hands, but it wasn't the rod. She would hold the thing up in front of my face, a tiny black squirming demon with leathery wings and a hooked beak. The beak would snap closer and closer at my face, but I couldn't move. I'd scream and wake myself screaming.

Pega suddenly put out her hand and touched my shoulder. I jerked away, thinking she was going to grab me and make some cruel joke. But when I looked up there was a strange expression on her face, almost ... I don't know ... almost sympathetic.

'Take care of yourself,' Pega said, and walked away. Maybe Beatrice had not told her after all.

I left the warmth of the kitchen and reluctantly trailed out across the courtyard. It was a grey, cloudy afternoon, warmer than it had been when Andrew died, but the wind was sharp and damp.

The well squatted in the corner of the yard. I lifted the wooden cover and peered down. Beads of water sweated from the sides, running down the fingers of green slime into the darkness below, each heavy drop echoing like a heartbeat in a giant chest. The well was never silent.

Sometimes there was a glint of light, a sliver of silver shining on the black water below, a new moon hanging in the midnight sky of some world that lay far beneath me. At other times there was nothing but darkness at the bottom, a darkness that rose nearer and nearer, as I gazed down at it.

Round as an apple, deep as a cup
But all the king's horses cannot draw it up.

I shuddered. Where did the water in the well come from, surging and rushing unheard and unseen beneath my feet? Did those chill black rivers empty into vast lakes or seas with tides and waves crashing in the darkness? Were there plants and fish and birds and animals down there in the bowels of the earth? Who had power to command them? They said the place of the dead was a desert, but what if the realm of the dead and the damned was blessed with water lighter than angels' song?

'Are you well enough to lift those buckets, Osmanna?' I jumped at the sound of the voice and water slopped over my shoes.

Servant Martha was striding across the yard. She looked tired and strained.

'I'm much better, thank you, Servant Martha.'

'Good, good,' Servant Martha said distractedly. 'God be praised that you're restored to health. Then we must resume your studies. I have been trying to catch up with my duties, but we must not neglect your education. Since Andrew left us, there –'

'Was it a miracle, Servant Martha, Andrew's Host being preserved like that? Some of the beguines say it has powers.'

'I gave orders it was not to be discussed,' she said sharply, glancing around, but the courtyard was deserted except for the scratching chickens.

'You said we might talk about it in private,' I reminded her.

'But I expected better of you, Osmanna. That a simple piece of bread becomes the flesh of our Lord is a daily miracle and the greatest miracle of all is that by consuming that fragment we may obtain the life everlasting. That, Osmanna, is the only power that should concern us.'

'But, Servant Martha, I was thinking about that. If a man takes the Host just once in his life, when he is dying, he may still be saved?'

Servant Martha nodded. 'If he has made a true and contrite confession, yes, that is what the Church teaches. Many have been saved in their dying breath.'

'Then why should we need to take the Host repeatedly, if consuming it only once can save you? In a book I was reading it said . . .' I faltered, seeing the frown deepen on her brow.

'Because we repeatedly sin. You surely know this. But I am curious that anyone should question it. What exactly did this book say?'

'I can't . . . remember,' I mumbled, though I knew she wouldn't believe that. I could have kicked myself. I should never have mentioned the book.

Servant Martha took a step closer and stared down at me. I sometimes forgot how very tall she was. 'Where have you been reading about this, Osmanna? I do not recall it from the books I have given you.'

I'd kept Ralph's book hidden at the bottom of my chest, beneath my linens. I could not bring myself to share *The Mirror* with anyone. There were such thoughts inside that I had not known it was possible to think. Such questions, I didn't know you could even ask. To open the pages was like drinking stolen wine, a heady taste of excitement, fear and guilt, which demanded I drank deeper, faster, but I couldn't read it fast enough.

He has freely given me my free will and he will not take my virtue from me. My virtue cannot from me be taken unless my spirit wills it.

The words were so new to me, so hard to understand, I was compelled to read the same lines over again whilst wanting to race on. Yet at the same time I was afraid to read too quickly, in case when the book was finished I was still left wanting.

The soul is transformed into God and so retains her true form which is granted and given to her from before the beginning from the One who has always loved her.

I felt as if my head would burst if I didn't share it with some-one, and I knew Servant Martha was the only one who would understand the excitement of it. But what if she took the book from me? Would she do that? She couldn't do that, not when I'd just found it. I wouldn't give it up.

I felt Servant Martha's gaze boring into me, but I dared not meet her eyes.

'I assume it is a book you have read in the beguinage. Your father did not seem the kind of man who –'

She broke off, wrinkling her nose. At that moment I smelt it too. Smoke, but it wasn't wood smoke from the beguinage fires. It was coming from somewhere beyond the walls, gusted in by the wind, but getting stronger even as we stood there. The stench was acrid, like ... like scorched hair and burning flesh. The ground began to tip sideways.

'Osmanna, are you unwell?'

I staggered, dropping the pails. The water flooded out across our shoes. I felt two strong hands grab me as I pitched forward. I thought I was going to be sick. A wave of cold fear broke over me. I wanted to run to my room and bolt the door behind me, but my legs wouldn't move. It was the same smell as in the forest that night, the smell of the burning saint. I could hear the scream in my head, see the flames leaping upwards. Some-where people were shouting. The sound was coming from the direction of the gate.

'Stay here,' Servant Martha ordered. She began to run towards the gate.

But I was too afraid to be left on my own. I stumbled in the direction of the voices. A group of beguines stood in the gateway staring out at the fields beyond. I squeezed between them. A dozen huge columns of black smoke rolled up from the meadows. Beyond them were other fires, small, but bright with flames as if great stacks of wood were burning. The stench carried on the wind made me shudder violently. Kitchen Martha, feeling me beside her, put her arm about me and hugged me so hard against her that she almost squeezed the breath out of me.

'What is it? What are they doing?' I asked her.

'God have mercy on us, child, they say the murrain has broken out. They're slaughtering the cattle, pigs, sheep – every beast on Manor land.'

'All of them?'

'It's the law, child, they must be destroyed and the carcasses and byres burned alike to stop it spreading.'

'And ours, our cattle, are they also to be slaughtered? Oxen too?'

Kitchen Martha gave me another squeeze. 'Servant Martha has even now gone with Shepherd Martha to look at them. Pray they are not infected, child.'

'St Beuno and all the Saints aid us,' someone murmured.

The *Amen* came from every throat.

Pisspuddle

'Kick me again, you little vixen, and it'll be your throat that gets cut.'

The bailiff lifted me off the ground, holding me around the waist so tight it hurt. I beat my heels against his legs. Then I saw his great fat hairy arm wrapped round me and sank my teeth into it. That made him drop me all right.

'God's fecking arse! I'll have you for that, you little witch.'

He tried to grab me again, but I ran to Mam and hid behind her.

'See what your brat did to me, woman.' The bailiff waved his arm under Mam's nose. 'She wants a good thrashing, she does.'

The two men who'd come with the bailiff stood there grinning as he rubbed the bite. Their faces and hands were smeared with soot and blood.

Mam put her arm round me and held me tight against her rough skirts. 'You lay a finger on my bairn and I'll give you more than a bite, you see if I don't.'

I gaped up at her. If anyone complained about me, she always took their side and I was the one that got the wallop. I wiped my mouth on her skirts, trying to get rid of the taste of the bailiff's sweaty arm.

He glared at me. 'Then keep the brat out of my way, mistress, or I'll not be held responsible. Come on,' he grunted at the two men. 'Let's get these pigs slaughtered as fast as we can. Every hour we waste arguing, the more time it gives the rest of these fecking villagers to hide their beasts.' The bailiff took a step closer to Mam. 'I know what your game is, woman. You think if you can delay us here, it'll give your friends time to spirit their own animals away.' He pushed his face close to Mam's. 'But it'll not work, you hear me? Your neighbours can't keep their beasts hidden for ever. Sooner or later we'll find every single one of them. D'Acaster's out even now in the forest with his pack of hounds, hunting down all the livestock the villagers have driven in there.

'And you can tell your friends this: if we have to waste our time tearing Ulewic apart looking for their scabby animals, they'll earn themselves a hefty fine into the bargain, or worse, much worse. So they may as well hand the stock over now, save themselves time and money.'

'Is that so?' Mam put her hands on her hips. 'I'm not the one standing around blathering. Seems to me, the only person wasting time here is you.'

The bailiff looked as if he'd like to kill Mam instead of the pigs, but he jerked his head at the two men and the three of them strode off round the back of the cottage.

I tried to run after them, but Mam held me back. 'Leave it, lass, there's nowt can be done.'

'If Father was here, he'd stop them.'

Mam sighed and raked back a strand of her hair. 'Aye, he'd try, right enough, and get his head cracked open for his pains. Then where would we be?'

Round the back of the cottage the pigs started to squeal and shriek. Mam winced and closed her eyes tight.

'But why, Mam, why are they killing our pigs?'

'Black bane, lass.' She stroked my hair, but she wasn't looking at me. Her eyes had a faraway look. 'If it comes, it'll kill the pigs anyway.'

'Who's Black Bane? Is he like Black Anu?'

I knew about Black Anu. There was a carving of her over the door of the church. She was an ogre who lived in a deep, dark pool up in the hills where no one ever went. Her face was green and so were her teeth and she had great sharp claws instead of fingers. She came into the village at night looking for bairns for her supper. She couldn't see, but she could hear the softest squeak or whisper. So we had to be very quiet after dark, so she didn't know we were there. If Black Anu heard any bairns crying or being naughty, she'd reach in through the window with her great long arms and snatch them. Then she'd carry them back to her pool and suck out all their blood and bones, and leave their skins hanging on an oak tree to dry in the wind, that's what Mam said.

William said he was too big to be pulled out of the window, but I was just the right size. If Mam went out after dark and she told William to stay and mind me, he'd call out to Black Anu to tell her where I was. I hated my brother. I couldn't wait until I was as big as him and then I'd –

'Black bane's a sickness, lass,' Mam said. 'Beasts get covered in great sores that turn black. If it goes to the lungs and the guts, that's the end of them. Cruel death, it is. You weren't born last time we had it in these parts. Wish to God I'd not been neither.'

'But, Mam, they can't kill Sibley. You can't let them. She hasn't got any black sores. I fed her this morning and –'

'How many times have I told you not to go naming animals?' Mam snapped. 'No good ever comes of it.'

There was a loud wail from the road in front of the cottage. 'May God and His Holy Virgins save us!' Fat Lettice waddled up the path, flapping her skirts over her flushed face. 'They've come for yours too? Of course they have.' Lettice didn't wait for Mam to answer, but peered round the side of the cottage. 'Blood everywhere, don't look, my dear,' she said, as she flapped back to where we stood. 'I swear on my dear husband's grave, God rest him, I'll not survive the winter. This'll be the death of me.'

Something seemed to drain out of Mam and she sank down on the threshold, her head in her hands. 'I don't know what Alan is going to say when he gets back. He's fetching us salt for the pickling when he comes. We shouldn't have waited. If we'd slaughtered last week, we'd have had enough salt pork to see us through the next few months.'

'Who slaughters pigs in fattening month?' Lettice said, spreading her hands wide. 'Summer's been so bad there's not a pick of flesh on them. They needed two full moons feeding on the forest mast, just to put as much fat on as this little mite, and she's as skinny as a piece of thread.' Her hard fingers poked my belly. 'Am I right?' The black bristles on her chin waggled when she talked.

'But even without fattening, we'd have got something off them.' Mam clenched her hands into fists. 'Now we've nothing, no meat, no fat to cook with. I'll not even have the scrimmings to dip the rushes in for candles. Bailiff says the whole carcasses are to be burnt.'

Her shoulders were shaking and she was making strange gulping noises, her face twisting up as if she was trying not to cry. It frightened me. Mam never cried, not ever.

'Mam, don't, please don't.' I tried to put my arms round her, but fat Lettice pushed me out of the way and put her arm round Mam instead.

'There, there, dear. Don't take on so. They're not burning them all, no matter what that bailiff tells you. Most'll find their way into D'Acaster's pickle barrels. His stores will be groaning with the flitches of pork this time next week.'

She looked all round her, then whispered, 'That tall one with the bailiff, one with the squint. Get him on his own when bailiff's not looking. Slip him a coin. He'll make sure there's a dead pig that doesn't reach the cart.' She tapped the side of her nose. 'There's a few carcasses gone missing from that cart round the village. Not that I'm saying anything, of course.'

'Aye, we slipped a few coins to the Owl Masters too. They promised us they'd keep us safe.' Mam's eyes were red and watery, but her face was angry not sad. 'Said they'd stop anything else going wrong this year. Much good that's done us. If they show their faces round here again, you'll not catch me giving them owt but a flea in their ear.'

'Hush! Hush!' Fat Lettice flapped her hands at Mam. The old woman waddled to the corner of the cottage and peered round the side again. Then she sidled back to Mam. 'It doesn't do to be talking about the Owl Masters like that. You never know who's listening. Bailiff could be one of them. Am I right? You heard what happened to old Warren when he refused to pay up? Course you have, who hasn't? Accident, so his wife said, but everyone knows different.'

I remembered the door to the yard where the old man made his pots and jugs had been closed for nearly a week now, but I thought he'd just got the ague.

'What happened to him?' I asked

Lettice jerked her head in my direction. 'Little pitchers have big ears.'

'Make yourself useful, lass, go fetch some water,' Mam said sharply.

'But, Mam, what did happen to Warren?'

'What will happen to you if don't fetch that water. Now, off with you.' She pointed. Mam meant it when she pointed. That was a last warning.

I picked up the bucket and walked away as slowly as I could, trying to listen, but fat Lettice was whispering to Mam and I couldn't hear anything except 'smashed and broken'. There were no more squeals coming from the back of the cottage. I glanced behind me. Lettice and Mam were busy talking. I slipped round the side of the cottage.

Scarlet blood was splashed all over the walls of the cottage and dribbling down the sty walls. There were bright puddles of it on the ground, as if it had been raining red. The pigs were all dead, everyone's in the whole road. They were lying in a big heap on top of one another. The bailiff was bending over a pig on the ground. Its trotters were jerking and twitching. Then they shuddered and stopped. The bailiff's men heaved the last pig on to the heap; it fell with a loud wet slap. Its head dropped back and there was a big red gash in its neck, but its eyes were still open, and it was looking at me.

The bailiff still had his back to me, but he must have felt me looking, because he turned. His hands were red and steaming, blood was dripping from his dark hairy elbows on to the ground. He was holding a long pointed knife.

'You, brat, come here, I want you –'

But I didn't wait to hear more. I ran as if Black Anu herself was after me.

✝

October – All Hallows' Eve

Samhain, when the world of the dead and the world of the living draw close enough to touch each other. The night when the past, the present and the future become one.

Father Ulfrid

For the tenth time that afternoon I cursed as the thread once more slipped from the eye of the needle. The thin strings on my linen amice, which fastened it round my chest, had snapped and I was trying to repair them. I was not accustomed to sewing. In the Cathedral there had been a whole hall full of people kept constantly employed in making and mending the clergy's vestments. Since I'd come to Ulewic, the girl who cooked for me had mended my clothes, and though her work had been clumsy, it was a hundred times better than anything I could manage. But I'd had to let the girl go. It was one of the many things I'd had to sacrifice since the Commissarius' visit. But no matter how much I tightened my belt, I still could not raise the money I needed.

The Commissarius had received his full measure of tithes. I'd had no choice. If I had defaulted by so much as a clipped farthing, I knew the Commissarius would carry out his threat and I would have found myself in chains in the Bishop's dungeon within the day. The villagers couldn't or wouldn't pay the tithes they owed before the month was up, so I had taken the only way out left open to me. I had pawned the church silver to raise the money.

I knew it was foolish. It would cost me more in the end, but I had to buy myself time. The jewelled chalice, the engraved paten, the silver candlesticks and altar cross were only ever used for the High Masses of Christmas and Easter; the rest of the year we used the plain pewter and brass. The valuable pieces were kept locked away in a great heavy chest in the church vestry and I had the only key. So all I had to do was to redeem them in time for the Christmas Mass and no one would be any the wiser.

All I had to do? It sounded so easy. But if I did not retrieve the church silver by Christmas Eve D'Acaster would notice at once that it was missing. I had just two months to recover the pieces. Two months, and I was no nearer raising the money than when I started.

There was only one person in the world I could confide in and trust. I'd sworn I would never see Hilary again, but I'd said that countless times before. We both knew I didn't mean it. If I sent word, Hilary would come to me and would get me the money somehow. I deserved that much at least. I had taken the full weight of punishment for what we had done. I had protected Hilary's identity, even under the most rigorous of questioning. I had never once betrayed my dark angel.

There was a loud hammering at my door and I jerked, dropping the needle again.

'Father! Come quickly. He's gone! He's gone!'

'I'm coming,' I called. 'There's no need to break my door down.'

But the yells and banging only redoubled. I groped for the latch. As the door swung wide, I had to leap back to avoid the wildly beating fists. One of the village women stood on the threshold. It took me a moment to recognize her, for her face was streaked with tears and mud.

'It's Aldith, isn't it?' I said. 'What's happened? Who's gone?'

'Oliver, my little Oliver. He's not there. I went to where ... and he wasn't there.' She broke off in a fit of sobbing, running back and forth in front of my door like a crazed dog.

Several women were beginning to gather on the other side of the path, clutching one another and staring, but not daring to approach, afraid that her madness might be catching.

I seized Aldith by the arm. 'Come now, you must calm yourself, mistress. This won't do you any good. Oliver's dead, don't you remember? I buried him myself three days ago.'

Grief does strange things to a woman. Some refuse to accept that their children or husband are dead. I'd even known women to set a place for the deceased at the table or wash their clothes as if they would return to wear them.

Aldith shook her head violently. 'No, Father, you don't understand, his body . . . it's gone . . . from the grave.'

'What! Are you sure?'

'Grave's empty, Father. I went to lay some meat and drink on it for All Hallows, so he'd not feel neglected, but the grave . . . it was open and his little body was gone.'

She froze, a look of wonderment spreading slowly across her face, then she clutched my arm. 'Father, maybe he wasn't dead, after all or . . . maybe God heard my prayers and brought him back to life. Three days, Father, three days, don't you see . . . I have to go home. He'll be there waiting for me.'

She hitched up her skirts and began to run.

'Wait!' I called after her. 'Aldith, come back. It is not possible. He can't . . .' But she only ran faster.

I snatched up my cloak and hurried down towards the churchyard.

Oliver had been just five years old, and when he had first fallen ill, it seemed nothing unusual at first: a sore throat, a slight fever, some vomiting. It was a touch of ague, his mother had said, brought on by the cold weather. But two days later, little Oliver was writhing in agony, his belly swollen up as if he had the dropsy, and he was vomiting blood. Death had followed within the week.

We had laid the child's body straight into the half-frozen earth, wrapped only in a simple winding sheet. His mother couldn't afford a coffin; it was all she could do to raise the money for the soul-scot. I'd thrown earth on to the small body and watched the villagers add their own clods, while the mother howled and rocked in the arms of her neighbours. Then the grave had been filled in.

I had seen it myself only yesterday, a slender mound of earth, standing out fresh and dark against the surrounding grass and marked with a small wooden cross. What could Aldith have possibly seen to make her doubt her son was in there? The poor woman had been deranged by grief. She must surely have gone to the wrong grave.

As I hurried towards the church I could see a small group of men standing in the doorway under the obscene carving of the naked old hag, which the villagers call Black Anu. Martin the sexton, the blacksmith John and two other villagers were deep in conversation. They stopped talking and nudged one another as I approached, as if they'd been discussing me.

'Martin, Mistress Aldith has just come to me with some tale about her son's grave. She told me . . .' I felt foolish even saying it, '. . . that it has been disturbed. There is no truth in this, I take it.'

'Grave's empty,' Martin said tersely.

'Show me,' I demanded.

The men glanced at each other.

'Your memory going, is it, Father?' The sexton coughed and spat a gob of phlegm on to the church step. 'You know where the grave is, Father, you buried the lad in it.'

'I can still remember who pays your wages. This churchyard is your responsibility. Your job is to ensure that the dead are allowed to rest in peace. So if you've been negligent in carrying out your duties, I want to see.'

Martin at least had the grace to look uncomfortable. With another glance at his companions, he reluctantly led the four of us around the side of the church.

The grave was tucked away beneath an overhanging oak in the far corner of the churchyard. It had not been dug deep; the sexton had complained that tree roots and icy ground had made it hard to go down as far as usual, though I suspected it was because Aldith hadn't given him an extra coin which he seemed to expect as his right.

Even as we approached, I saw that the earth was not heaped over the grave as it should have been, but piled on either side of it. I stared down into the small pit. The outline in the wet earth where the small body had lain was plainly visible, but the body itself had vanished.

My bowels turned to water. Could Oliver have risen as Aldith said, not as our Lord rose, but as one of the revenant dead, the corpses which clamber from their graves and feast on the living? I crossed myself. 'God have mercy on us.'

There'd been such a case when I lived in Norwich. A man, newly buried, had risen from the churchyard and wandered through the streets throttling anyone he encountered. He had been followed by a pack of yellow-eyed cats whose savage yowling terrified all who heard them. In the end Bishop Salmon had commanded the grave be opened and the head of the corpse cut off with the spade that had been used to bury him. When they dug the dead man up, they'd found his body as fat and bloated as a leech, and when they severed his head, a great scarlet spurt had gushed from his neck until the grave was filled with blood.

Was it possible this boy too had become a revenant? He'd had the simplest of burials, it was true enough, but I had been diligent in giving him all due rites of the Holy Church. And the sins of a child that young could surely not have been so grievous as to make him unworthy of a Christian burial.

'Do you think . . .' I stammered. 'Is it . . . is it possible that the corpse has walked?'

The sexton coughed again and spat into the dark hole. 'He'd not be able to leave his grave. I made sure of that myself. I opened it up after his mam had left and hammered iron nails into the soles of the lad's feet, so he couldn't walk.'

I didn't know whether I was relieved or angry. 'You violated a grave after he'd been given a Christian burial?'

Martin shrugged. 'That weren't the ague that killed him. Bairn died from witchcraft, plain as day. Crosses and holy water wouldn't be enough to hold him in the grave, not if he was killed by witchery.'

The other men nodded.

Blacksmith John exchanged a look with the sexton, then cleared his throat. 'Thing is, Father, if the corpse didn't clamber out of the grave by itself, then someone must have taken it.'

I gaped at him. 'But why? Who could possibly want to take a corpse?'

John scratched at a scab on his huge muscular arm. 'The way I see it, Father, is, the one who killed him is the one that's taken his corpse. Why else would she want to put the evil eye on a little lad? She needed his body for her black arts.'

'She? You think a woman in Ulewic, one of my own flock, would –'

John gave a great mirthless bellow of laughter. 'She's not one of your flock, Father. That old witch would never set foot in a church. Her soul's so black, if one drop of holy water was to touch her withered old hide, she'd likely burn to ashes on the spot.'

'Old Gwenith, he means,' Martin explained. 'She never sets foot in the village in daylight, except for the fairs, and then only when she's something to buy or sell. But at night ...' He glanced at the other men. 'At night it's a different story, that's when she comes down from her lair to make mischief.' There were murmurs of agreement from the three other men.

John stared down again at the tiny grave. 'A bairn as small as Oliver would be light enough even for an old woman to carry away with her. Happen that's why she chose him as her victim. And you know what Eve it is tonight, Father.'

I nodded grimly. I knew only too well. It was the night the Church prayed for the souls of the dead, but I knew that others in the village would not have their minds on the rites of the Church, but on the heathen practices of the feast they called Samhain. Aldith had already told me she had come to lay food and drink on the grave. The other villagers would do the same for their dead, however much I preached against it. But that was not all. This was the night when the witches did their worst. God alone knew what this Gwenith intended with the body of that poor child, but whatever devilish rites she was bent on, I swore I would put a stop to her mischief, even if I had to fight the hordes of hell to do it.

'You say this Gwenith lives somewhere beyond the village. Can you take me there?'

The four men as one took a step backwards.

'No, Father, you'll not catch me going up there.' John held up his great broad hands as if to ward off the very suggestion. 'Only a man in Holy Orders, like yourself, would dare set foot near the cottage without fear of her hex. But you know the Latin words and holy prayers to defend yourself.'

'Besides, you'll not need us to guide you,' Martin grunted. 'River'll take you to her. Follow the river upstream. They say her cottage is right by the water's edge, near the top of the hill. You'll not mistake it.'

'You will go, Father, for the sake of the village?' John asked.

I found my mouth was so dry I could not answer him. In my anger, I'd sworn to myself that I'd fight the demons of hell to stop the witch. It was easy enough to swear, but as it hit me that I might actually have to do it, I felt as if I'd been doused in iced water. If these strapping men were too terrified of her even to show me the way to her cottage, what kind of satanic powers could this fiend conjure?

I'd watched men who are trained in such matters perform exorcisms and unmask sorcerers. I'd heard the howls and screams of the possessed, seen objects fly about the room and great black streams of filth burst from their mouths. But the exorcists had done their work surrounded by clergy and holy symbols. I couldn't do it alone and unprotected. No one could expect me to ... I needed books, holy relics ... I couldn't do it ... I wouldn't –

'It'll be a long walk and a steep climb. You must hurry if you want to get there before she's time to do her worst. If she conjures up the evil one ...' John crossed himself.

He was right; there wasn't time to send for help. If I didn't stop her, then God alone knew what the hag would unleash on these defenceless people. I was a priest. I had the power of God on my side. She was merely a woman, an ignorant old woman; she could not stand against the power of the Holy Church.

In a daze, I found myself nodding. The men glanced at one another, relief washing over their faces.

'God go with you, Father.'

It was a longer and steeper climb even than I had anticipated. I was not accustomed to walking great distances and I was forced to stop many times to catch my breath, although I dared not linger until I had fully recovered, for the sun had already disappeared behind the hill. Only a grey ghost-light still hovered in the sky, the last whisper of the sun's dying rays.

The tiny bubble of confidence I'd felt down by the church had long since burst. With each step the pain in my chest grew worse. What would I find if I did reach her cottage? Suppose she had already summoned up the hounds of Satan, how would I fight them alone? I glanced fearfully up at the black rocks rising like devil's horns around me. My body was drenched in cold sweat. Only the knowledge of what evil she might be preparing to do with the body of an innocent child prevented me from fleeing back the way I'd come. I couldn't face the villagers and tell them I'd failed. God knows they had little enough respect for me as it was.

Now the path was nothing more than a sheep's track strewn with stones and rocks. It was so perilously narrow in places that several times I almost lost my footing and came close to plunging into the raging river below. I cursed myself for having neglected to bring a lantern. How could I have been so foolish as to embark on such a climb without any means of lighting my way? Maybe I'd already passed the cottage in the gloom. Surely not even a witch could find anywhere to nest among these rocks. The path vanished beneath my feet and I found myself walking over a flat stretch of grass. The rocks and the hillside rose all around me, like the walls of a fortress, blocking what little light remained in the sky.

Then out of the corner of my eye I glimpsed something moving in the darkness. I turned. A human skull was hanging upside down suspended in mid-air. As I stared aghast, the hollow eye sockets suddenly blazed with flame. I screamed and staggered backwards, slipping on grass and crashing down with such force that I rolled over. The ground disappeared from beneath my head and shoulders.

I had tumbled right to the edge of the bank. I was lying on my back, suspended over the river. I felt the icy spray on my neck and heard the deafening roar of the water crashing over the rocks below. I flailed about, trying to find a handhold on the bank to pull myself back, but the grass I clutched at came away in my hands and I found myself slipping further over the river.

Then I felt someone grasp my hand. I clung to the out-stretched arm and inched myself back on the bank until I was crouching on all fours on the solid earth, my limbs shaking beneath me. I raised my head. I was staring into the stinking, filthy skirts of a woman. I scrambled to my feet. The old witch was standing in front of me, holding the skull with its blazing eyes. Now that I was close to it, I could see that inside the upturned skull was a mound of burning tinder. Red and orange flames licked around the yellowed teeth.

I dared not move for fear I would step backwards into the river. Every word, every prayer that should have protected me, had vanished from my head. I pulled my iron crucifix from about my neck and grasping it tightly in my fist pushed it towards her face.

'Get away from me. I ... I am a priest. God will protect me.'

The old hag cackled with laughter. 'Wasn't God that saved you from a wetting.'

'What evil do you intend this night, old woman? I warn you, whatever mischief you plan, I am here to prevent it.'

'So you've come to stop me kindling my hearth fire, have you? Seems a lot of trouble to go to to stop a poor old soul cooking her supper.'

'Don't lie to me, woman,' I shouted. 'The only fire you are lighting is to brew some deadly potion. What wickedness do you intend to make with that?' I pointed at the skull but, to my shame, I realized my hand was trembling.

The old woman chuckled. 'Don't you know all fires must be doused on Samhain, and lit again from the need-flame to see us safe through the dark winter?' She held up the fire-filled skull. 'You're a priest. You're not afeared of dead things, are you? What harm can a bit of old bone do you?'

The flames danced in the sightless eyes. I couldn't tear my gaze from them. I felt as if I was being pulled closer to the old woman and yet neither of us was moving. Such a small skull, it could almost be small enough to be a child's. I squeezed my eyes shut. St Michael and all angels defend me!

'That's the head of the little boy, isn't it? That's Oliver ... what have you done, you foul hag? Where's the rest of the corpse? The flesh, how did you remove the flesh so quickly? He's only three days dead.' A wave of nausea flooded up from my stomach. 'God in heaven, did you boil and eat ... you did, didn't you? Tell me the truth, you demon, tell me what you did to that child!'

I leapt forward, swinging the iron cross hard at her evil face. It caught her across the cheek and she fell backwards. The skull rolled down her legs, spilling the burning tinder. In an instant, her skirts were on fire.

Horrified, I stood and stared as flames shot upwards into the dark. She was writhing on the grass, screaming and pleading for me to help her. But I couldn't move. I was mesmerized by the yellow flames. With a desperate effort she rocked on to her belly, trying to smother the fire beneath her own body. A lifetime seemed to pass as I stood watching the old woman rolling on the ground and beating at the flames licking around the dark outline of her body; then finally they were gone and we were in darkness.

The old woman lay still. I thought she was dead, but then I heard her moan. I collapsed on to my knees and pushed her over on to her back. The stench of burning cloth hung in the air. In the darkness I could see little of what the fire had done to her, but I saw the glittering of her open eyes as she stared up at me.

'God did this to you, Gwenith, because you lied. God struck you down with fire for your foul deeds. You were screaming when you felt the heat and pain of those flames. Imagine how much more you will scream when you are burning for all eternity in fire that is a thousand times hotter than any fire on earth.'

I was still gripping the iron cross. I ground it against her mouth, forcing her lips to touch it in the semblance of a kiss. 'If you lie now, you damn your soul to hell. If you speak the truth, I will pray that you may be spared a little of the suffering that is about to fall on you. Now, Gwenith, I charge you to tell me what you did with the child you took from the grave. Show me where I may find his body or at least his bones, so that I may return them to his grieving mother. If you do not, I shall see you hanged and I shall send your maleficent soul straight to hell.'

'A bairn's ... been taken ... from a grave?' she gasped.

'You know that, you fiend. You took him. This is his skull.'

'No, no ...' She shook her head. 'That is my daughter's skull ... Gudrun's mother ... it's my daughter who brings the need-fire to us ... I loved my daughter ... I keep her with us ... I'd not leave her in a cold grave all alone ...'

'You are lying!' I shouted at her.

'Pick up ... the skull ... feel it. Those aren't the teeth of a bairn ...' She reached up and gripped the front of my robe with a surprising strength. 'The bairn's corpse, you mustn't let them use it ... three generations ago, five cunning-women joined their powers to send the creature back into the twilight time. My great-grandam was one ... They thought no man would ever have the knowledge to conjure him again ... but Aodh braved the bull oak and the hide ... he has the knowledge ... now he has the boy ... he means to bring the creature back ... I'm the only cunning-woman left. Can't fight him alone ... I hoped the grey women ... but there is not enough time. Only one way to stop the Owl Masters now. You must go back to Ulewic and get the bairn's corpse afore they can use it ...' She groaned. Her grip momentarily tightened, then slackened as she fell back.

I shook her. 'What is this creature? What will it do? Tell me!'

'No time to talk ... go ... hurry. You want to prevent evil this night ... stop the Owl Masters afore it's too late.'

It should have been easier going down the river path, but it wasn't. The moon had risen, but the light that it cast deceived the eye. Shadows masked holes. Rocks which looked solid rolled away beneath the feet. Only the moonlight shining on the tumbling white foam of the river distinguished between ground and water. I knew I should slow down. Several times I slipped and had to clutch at bushes and rocks to stop myself falling right down the hill. My back and arms were bruised and smarting, but all I could think of was what the Owl Masters were even now doing down in that village.

How could I have been so stupid as to let myself be tricked into coming up here? I should have known that there was something odd about the men's story. The sexton must have noticed the grave had been opened long before Oliver's mother found it in the afternoon. Why had he not come to me straight away to tell me about the grave? Had Phillip D'Acaster instructed the sexton to send me on a fool's errand, just to get me out of the way, or did the men really believe that old Gwenith had stolen the corpse?

I heard the hounds howling long before I reached the first of the cottages. All the flea-bitten curs in Ulewic seemed to be joining in. But the streets themselves were deserted. Chinks of light escaping through cracks in shutters showed that not all the villagers had gone to the Samhain fires. Women and children were doubtless cowering behind those closed doors, afraid of the dead or of the Owl Masters. But despite the chill of the night, no smoke rose from any cottages. As old Gwenith had said, all the hearth fires had been extinguished and would not be lit again until the men came home bearing flames from the Samhain fire.

But there was fire somewhere. I could smell the wood smoke on the air and as I rounded the corner I saw it: a crackling bonfire had been lit right in the centre of the graveyard in front of the very church itself. Scarlet and orange flames were twisting into the night sky. Showers of red sparks burst around it, as the wood crackled and spat.

A large group of villagers, men and women, had encircled the blaze and were dancing round it, their hands linked and arms raised. Their feet stomped in a slow, heavy rhythm to the beat of a drum. Some of the dancers were dressed in long white shifts, their faces masked by wooden carvings of human faces or shrouded with white cloth in which holes had been cut for eyes and mouths, crude imitations of the dead, come back to dance among the living.

The drummer sat cross-legged on top of one of the D'Acaster family tombs. He was naked save for a deerskin wrapped round his loins. On his head he wore the skull of a stag. The sharp antlers gleamed white and the drummer's bare skin was bronzed with sweat in the firelight.

I tore through the church gate, hardly able to contain my anger, shouting at the villagers to stop, but no one took any notice. The dancers' heads were thrown back, their eyes closed, as they surrendered themselves to the beat of the drum. I was beside myself with rage. How dare they perform this heathen rite on holy ground, right before the door of the church, trampling over the graves, making a mockery of those Christian remains which lay beneath their filthy feet?

I strode towards the dancers and seized a stout, matronly-looking woman by her arm.

'Cease this godless spectacle at once!' I ordered.

But she flung me off with such force that I bounced on the ground and lay there winded and gasping. Shocked by her strength, I stared up and realized that she wasn't a woman at all. Those dancers I had taken to be village women were all men. There were no women in the graveyard.

I saw that any attempt to break up the dance would be futile.

The men had obviously been drinking and were too carried away by the rhythm of the drum to pay any attention to me. They could wait. I would deal with their sins in the confessional. The important thing now was to find little Oliver's body.

I struggled painfully to my feet, staring around. If Gwenith was right and they intended to use the corpse in some dark rite, it must be somewhere close by. Then I saw them. Four masked Owl Masters were standing in the doorway of the church, beneath the carving of Black Anu, blocking the entrance to St Michael's, as if they were guarding something. They had put the body in the church. Maybe the rest of the Owl Masters were inside, already committing their foul deeds upon the corpse. Perhaps they were performing their rites upon the very altar itself.

I ran round the circle of dancers towards the church door where the Owl Masters stood guard. The flames of the Samhain fire glinted red on the bronze beaks of their masks and on the drawn short-swords in their hands.

'Out of my way!' I made to push past them, but two of the blades flashed upwards and were at my throat before I could take a step.

'How dare you threaten me? I am your priest. I could have you flogged for this.'

But the Owl Masters didn't move. Deep behind the masks I glimpsed the flicker of eyes watching me.

'What is going on in the church? This is the house of God. If you violate a sacred building, God will smite you down and damn you for all eternity.'

I fumbled for my iron cross about my neck and held it up in front of their faces.

I took a deep breath. 'I command you in the name of . . .'

I sensed someone behind me and in the same instant saw one of the Owl Masters gesture with his sword. I half turned, but too late to prevent myself being seized on either side by powerful hands and dragged towards the dancers.

'How dare you lay hands on a priest! I will have you arrested for this.'

But the men only laughed. They had my arms pinioned behind my back. They knew the threat was an empty one. How could I punish them when I couldn't even identify them, for they were both dressed in white shrouds, their faces hidden behind grinning wooden masks and hair of straw.

'You must join the dance, Father,' one of them said. 'Else the dead will think you don't welcome them.'

'Let me go!' I yelled, struggling to get out of their grip, but it was no use. I found myself being pushed and pulled round the circle with the other dancers. A priest's strength is no match for burly villagers, strong as oxen from years of labouring in the fields.

Ducking under the upraised arms of the dancers, one of the Owl Masters entered the ring and strode across to the fire in the centre. He was holding a straw figure in his arms, about the size of a child. The straw figure was more than large enough to contain the corpse of little Oliver. They meant to destroy it, burn it to ashes. And without a body, what hope was there of resurrection for the boy on the Day of Judgment?

'No! No!' I screamed. 'Not an innocent child.'

But even as the Owl Master tossed the straw effigy on to the flames, I saw it was too light to contain a body. The straw smouldered and burst into flames. An unpleasant, pungent stench began to mingle with the wood smoke, heavy and soporific. It was not the smell of burning straw. Some herb or leaves must have been stuffed inside the straw figure, something that was sending up clouds of dense smoke.

I felt light-headed, almost dizzy. I found that I had ceased to struggle. I no longer had the will to do so. The beat of the drum grew louder, until it seemed to be coming from inside my head. I found my feet obeying its rhythm, stamping with all the other feet; it was impossible to do otherwise.

There were shapes moving between the dancers and the fire. They were insubstantial at first, so blurred that I thought what I could see were just our own shadows, but they couldn't be. Across the far side of the circle I could see the shadows of the dancers on the ground, cast by the firelight, but the shadows were behind the dancers and moving with them. We were circling like the sun, towards the right, but whatever was in the centre of our ring was moving in the opposite direction, against the sun. I shook my head, trying desperately to draw in the night air and clear my mind, but my thoughts only became more fuddled. Then the shapes began to solidify.

They were not shadows moving in the circle, they were people. Barefooted girls with thick ropes about their necks were dancing with ancient men, whose beards hung grey to their gnarled feet. Old women with cobweb veils moved stiffly beside pale young men with bloodstained shirts. Old crones, their twisted nails gleaming yellow as old bones in the moonlight, grasped the hands of children with sunken black hollows where their eyes should have been. They lifted their hands as they circled the fire and all their fingers were webbed. More and more of them joined the circle, rising up from the ground, slipping out from between the branches of the yew trees, slithering from between the cracks in the stone tombs. The dead of Ulewic were being called back.

The flames of the fire rose higher, red and yellow snakes striking at the stars. The drumbeat quickened. The stamping grew louder. We were circling faster and faster, until the faces of the dancers opposite were just a blur of mouths and eyes. I clung to the hands that were holding me in the dance. My fingers were locked rigid and I could not let go.

There was a huge bang and a flash of blinding light. The circle broke. Men were falling and stumbling, knocking into one another. For a moment I was blinded, the flash was seared on to my eyeballs. Then the villagers began pointing up at the round tower of the church. Blinking hard, I gazed upwards too.

One of the Owl Masters was standing on the flat roof of the tower, silhouetted black against the moon and stars. His long cloak swirled out about him in the breeze. He stretched out his hands over the churchyard, holding what looked like a rolled piece of white cloth. He raised the bundle in his hands, high above his head.

'Through blood we renew our strength. Through death we renew our life. Through destruction we renew creation. Through fire we make all things fertile.'

'Through fire we make all things fertile,' the villagers echoed in the churchyard below.

On the top of the tower the Owl Master's cloak billowed up behind like wings. 'I call upon the Cernunnos to give him spirit. Triple Goddess, Blodeuwedd the virgin, Anu the mother, Morrigu the hag, I call upon you to give him substance. Taranis, lord of destruction, Yandil, lord of darkness, Rantipole, lord of rage, I call upon you to awaken the Owlman! Awaken the Owlman! Awaken the Owlman! *Ka!*'

The Owl Master let the pale cloth he was holding unfurl in the wind. I could just make out two vertical lines written on it in dark red, on which were many horizontal slashes and marks. Above the lines was drawn a circle divided into four and below the lines, a triple spiral. I could make no sense of what I saw. I heard people crying out in fear. I thought it was the marks on the cloth that they were afraid of. Then, with mounting horror, I realized it was not the blood-red marks, it was what they were inscribed upon. That was not a cloth the Owl Master was holding in his hands, but a flayed skin, a human skin, the size and shape of a small child.

I'd scarcely had time to register what I was seeing when a new cry went up from the crowd of villagers. A trickle of smoke was coming from the church door. For a moment I thought they'd set the church on fire, but then I realized it was not coming from the inside of the church itself. Smoke was writhing out from the gaping cunt of the old hag carved above the door.

At first the smoke was white, but as more and more poured out in a steady stream it began to turn black. Now it was taking shape, the head of a monstrous bird, then huge wings as wide as the church tower. The thing rose in the night air, hovering above the church. Even as we watched it was swelling, becoming denser and darker, blotting out the stars.

The villagers, who had been standing mesmerized, now began to scream and flee. Everywhere men were scrambling to get out of the churchyard, throwing themselves over the walls, not caring where they landed or how, in a frenzy to get as far away from the demon as they could. As if their screams had broken the spell which had transfixed me to the spot, I found myself stumbling and running towards the gate. I did not look back.

November – Souling Day

Third and last day of Samhain. The day on which Christians collected alms to pay for prayers for the souls of the dead in Purgatory.

Pisspuddle

'Put one foot straight in front of the other,' that's what the tumbler's girl said at the May Fair. 'Feel your toes touching your heels, then you don't have to look down. You mustn't ever look down, 'cause that's what makes you fall.'

I got to the end of the trestle without falling off, but then I had to turn. That's the really hard bit. It looked easy when she did it. She put her leg straight out, then sort of swivelled.

'Stare real hard at yon tree,' she said, 'then you'll not slip. Stare at one spot. Don't ever take your eyes off it.'

I swung my leg, wobbled and crashed on to the ground.

'God's blood, whatever are you up to this time, lass?' Mam stood over me, hands on hips, her mouth wrinkled tight like a pig's arsehole. Her mouth always pinched up like that when she was going to clout me.

I quickly began to bawl, rubbing my leg and rolling around. I was good at that. Mam could never tell if I was really crying or not.

'She's practising to be a tumbler, aren't you, Pisspuddle?' William grinned.

'Are you hurt, lass? Where? Show me.' Mam bent down. 'Tumblers indeed, whatever put that nonsense in your head?'

'Isn't nonsense. I'll do it, you'll see. When the tumblers come for the next May Fair, they're going to take me with them. They said they would if I practised and could walk the pole. I'll go all over, fairs and castles and the like. The tumbler's girl said they toss you real gold coins at the castles. And I'll be eating suckling pig every day, twice sometimes.'

Behind me, William snorted with laughter.

'You just wait, fat-arse,' I told him. 'One day I'll be rich and you'll be starving hungry and you'll come to me begging for food and I'll not even give you a bone to suck.'

'It's you who won't have a bone to suck, lass. A bed in a ditch and a kick for your supper is all they'll give you.' Mam pulled me to my feet, feeling my arms and legs. 'And what do you think happens to little girls when they're too big to be tossed on poles? Turned out to thieving and begging, or worse. End on the gallows, every one of them. Just look at the state of you! Muck from head to toe. How's your leg? Can you walk?'

William pushed his face close to mine and whispered, 'Do you know where the tumblers get their suckling pigs, Pisspuddle?'

'Don't call me that. Mam, tell him not to call me that.'

'I'm bigger than you, so I can call you anything I want. And I'll tell you where the tumblers get their suckling pig. They wait for a dark night when the little girls are fast asleep, then they creep up and cut their throats from ear to ear.' He sliced his grubby finger across my throat. 'Then they chop them up and stuff them in pickle-barrels. That's their suckling pigs, silly little pisspuddles like you. But don't worry, they'll fatten you up first; you're so skinny, your arse wouldn't fill a pasty.' He poked me sharply over and over, going for all the soft places.

'Make him stop, Mam. My leg hurts.' I tried to limp away.

'I thought it was the other leg that was hurt,' William smirked.

'Why, you little …' Mam aimed a swipe at my head, but I dodged out of reach. 'You just wait till I get hold of you, I'll give you hurt.'

I darted round the corner of the cottage and smashed straight into Lettice's belly. She staggered back and I tried to dodge round her, but she grabbed me by the back of my neck and marched me back to Mam.

'Have you heard, dear?' Lettice said.

'What?' Mam asked, grabbing hold of my arm.

'Two maids from the Manor, attacked in the churchyard last

night. Ran screaming all the way home. Scarcely escaped with their lives, so they say.'

Mam's eyes were wide. 'Do they know who it was attacked them?'

'Now you're asking, my dear. It's not so much a question of *who* but *what*.'

Lettice looked fearfully round as if who or what might be behind her. She moved closer. 'A great bird, taller than the blacksmith John, swooped right down on them from the church tower just as they were setting out for the Manor.'

'A bird?' Mam whispered.

'You're hurting me, Mam!' I wailed. She still had a tight hold of my arm and her fingers were digging into me. Everyone ignored me. 'Mam!'

'When I say a bird, I mean he had the head and wings of a bird all right, an owl, with a beak big enough to sever a maid's leg and great black talons instead of feet, but he had the body and private parts of a man. And when I say privates of a man,' she raised her eyebrows, 'it was more like a stallion's, so I've heard.'

Mam gasped. 'So it's true then. I heard what happened on All Hallows' Eve, but the men were in their cups. Sow-drunk most of them by the way they went roaring through the village. Most of them couldn't get out of their beds the next day, never mind talk any sense. But if the Owlman himself has been seen . . .'

Lettice crossed herself. 'My old grandam used to tell me tales of him that her mam had taught her. Not just bairns he took, but full-grown men, ripped the flesh off them and ate them alive. Devoured their souls too. He terrorized the whole village for more than a year last time he flew until the cunning-women cast him into a sleep. But that was nigh on a hundred years ago, maybe more. I never thought he'd fly again, not in my lifetime.'

'God save us,' Mam squashed me tightly against her leg.

'Amen to that, for there's not a cunning-woman left in these parts, save Old Gwenith. God grant that her grandam taught her the words to bind the demon, else there'll be no stopping him this time nor them that wakened him.'

She crossed herself again. 'You heard about poor Aldith's little Oliver, of course you have, who hasn't? Still not a sign of the little lad's body. The dear woman's beside herself. In and out of her cottage every day I am, to comfort the dear soul, fair wearing myself out with it. But at the end of the day, what can you say to her? They're dark arts indeed that take the body of an innocent boy for their work.' Lettice inched closer to Mam. 'You want to keep those bairns close by, my dear.'

Mam whirled me round to face her. 'You two, inside now and stay there. From now on neither of you sets foot outside the door till the sun's full up and I want you indoors before the Vespers' bell. You hear me?'

'But Mam,' William groaned.

'Now, inside, both of you, and no more arguments.'

Mam landed a stinging slap on my backside and pushed me towards the door. It wasn't fair. I hadn't said a word. William was the one who was arguing.

William kicked the doorpost as he passed, but he didn't dare say anything to Mam. He threw himself down next to the fire.

'Stupid lasses. I'd not have run away screaming from the Owlman. I want to see him. She needn't think I'm going to stay in.'

'Me neither.' I tried to look as sulky as him and kicked the nearest stool. It tumbled over, scattering a bowl of beans which Mam had left on top. They trickled into the thick layer of rushes on the earth floor. Mam would kill me! Why did she have to put them there? I scrambled to pick up the tiny beans, but every time I grabbed one, it made more of the others disappear.

'You're going to get a really good skelping this time, when Mam sees that,' William grinned, deliberately scattering them even more with his foot.

My stomach somersaulted. I could still feel Mam's hand across my backside from the slap. I crept to the door. I could slip out while she'd still got her back to it, gabbing to fat Lettice.

'Listen, did you hear that?' William said, rushing to the window.

'What?'

'Wings, great big wings swooping down. Look! Quick, did you see it, that black shadow? I wouldn't give much for anyone's chances out there alone.'

Lettice had said it was a bird bigger than John with an owl's head and great big talons. Only the day before, I'd seen a falcon swooping down on a vole. It had perched, with one foot pinning down the little body, ripping out the fur with its hooked beak and tearing at the entrails until its beak was all red with blood. I shivered. What could a bird as big as a blacksmith do?

Father Ulfrid

I started violently as I emerged from the latrine. I hadn't heard the boy creep into my yard. Alan's son, William, was leaning against the doorpost, chewing a twig and idly scuffing his bare toes in the dirt. He grinned when he saw he'd startled me.

'If you've a message you should knock on the door,' I snapped. I was the parish priest, for God's sake. Did they think they could just wander in and out of my house, as if I was a common villein?

'Did,' he said without removing the twig. 'You never answered.'

'That means I wasn't to be disturbed.'

People had been banging on my door all day, especially that old gossip Lettice, but I couldn't face anyone. I still felt sick when I thought about All Hallows' Night and I couldn't stop thinking about it.

I'd made excuses to myself. That straw effigy they burned on the fire had been stuffed with henbane. I'd recognized the foul, lingering stench in the embers of the fire the next morning. Henbane befuddles anyone who breathes the smoke and sends them into a stupor. It's been known to drive men mad. I'd been drugged, robbed of my senses, so how could I have fought that demon?

But deep down I knew that I would not have had the guts to stand against that monster, drugged or sober. Even when I was confronting Old Gwenith, I had not been able to summon up the holy words to protect myself from her, and witch though she undoubtedly was, she was a mere mortal.

William was still watching me with a grin on his face. Had the brat heard that I'd run away and come to gloat?

'What do you want, boy?' I growled.

'Heard something, thought you might want to know, 'bout the house of women. They've got a relic in there that saved 'em from the Black bane.'

'Whose relic?' I demanded.

'A woman. Ann ... no, a man's name ... Andrew, that were it. She was dying and she puked up the Host. They tried to burn it, 'cept it wouldn't burn. It was a miracle, they reckon.'

'Who told you this, William?'

'My sister, that's who. She didn't want to, but I said if she told me a secret, I'd not tell Mam about the beans. Father says girls and women have always got secrets.' He grinned again. 'It's true, 'cause my sister says those women are keeping that relic a secret.'

A relic in this dung heap, was it possible? If it really was a miracle, then no wonder they were keeping quiet about it. They knew they had no right to keep it there. Any pieces of sacred Host, miraculous or not, had to be stored in a consecrated place, in a church or a monastery. Those women were not even nuns; they shouldn't be touching Christ's body, never mind keeping it among their pots and pans. If the Bishop got to hear of it, he would insist that it was removed to Norwich at once.

But how had Andrew come to vomit the Host on her deathbed? I was not summoned to give her the last rites. Had they called in a priest from another parish? If so, he had pocketed the scot that should have come to St Michael's. The insult to me as a priest was bad enough, but I needed every penny of the scots and tithes I could raise. Somehow I had to get money to redeem the silver. And now, as if things weren't desperate enough, I learned that another priest was stealing from me. Was this the only scot he'd deprived me of? How many more of my souls had he shriven or infants baptized?

William looked up at me slyly. 'Reckon that secret's worth something, isn't it, Father?' He thrust out a grubby hand.

'What?' I'd forgotten the boy was still there. 'Come inside, I'll find you something.' I said it without thinking, then with a sinking feeling I realized there probably wasn't a coin in the house to pay him with.

'No, wait. There's something else I want you to find out. Who brought the Host to the house of women? Can you discover that?'

William looked scornful. 'Course I can. But what's it worth?'

'Bring me that information and I'll pay you double.'

William narrowed his eyes like a shrewd old pedlar calculating a profit. 'Pay me for today first.' He pushed his way past me into the cottage, as if to make it quite clear he wasn't going away until he got his money. He was learning fast. How could I blame the boy, when it seemed even my brother priests couldn't be trusted?

Servant Martha

When the judgment of God rides out upon the land, it befits every human soul to fall to his knees and pray that he may be spared. Yet even when the seasons were turned upon their heels and the cattle lay dead in the pasture, men fled not to God for help, but to the evil that had brought them to this pass.

The villagers who crept to our gate seeking food and medicines were bringing that evil with them and poisoning the beguinage with their gossip. A demon they called the Owlman had been seen by a pair of foolish young girls, who ran to the Manor screaming that they had been attacked by a monstrous bird. It was nonsense, of course. The girls had probably returned late having been wanton with some village lads and concocted the tale to escape a well-deserved whipping.

But however often I warned the women not to listen to such talk, it blew through our halls and I could no more hold it back than I could silence the wind. I redoubled my efforts to strengthen our little band, urging them to cloak themselves with the love of our Lord. I assured them even if such a hellish beast did exist, which it most assuredly did not, God would defend us if we were faithful to him.

But whatever madness was raging in the village, I drew comfort from the thought that Andrew's relic lay in our chapel and her prayers were shielding us. Shepherd Martha had lovingly carved a wooden casket to house the miraculous Host and Dairy Martha had made sketches of the scenes she would paint to decorate the box. The painting on one side of the box would depict Andrew's birth, over which an angel hovered protectively. Another would show Andrew kneeling in prayer in her anchorite's cell, with throngs of people stretching beseeching hands towards her. But the last would be of the miraculous

Host itself blazing gold in the midst of the roaring fire, as beguines knelt before it.

The beguines filed past the reliquary every day, touching it reverently, and including Andrew in the saints they called upon to aid them. They were convinced that our beasts had been spared the murrain because Andrew's Host was protecting the beguinage, for had not the Host been given to us just days before the murrain broke out? They said God had forewarned Andrew of the impending disaster and it was for that very reason Andrew had given up her spirit in order that she might leave us the Host to protect us. I had not told them that, but neither had I contradicted the story. I had come to believe as much myself. In those uncertain times we needed to believe that we were protected.

Beatrice came hurrying across the courtyard. 'Servant Martha, wait!' She bent over, her hands on her knees, trying to catch her breath. 'There is a young girl outside the beguinage. She is dumb, but she is plainly distressed and is making signs that she wants me to go with her –'

'Where does she wish you to go?' I asked.

'How should I know?' Beatrice snapped. 'Haven't I just said the girl can only make signs?'

I raised my eyebrows at her tone.

'The child points to the hill,' Beatrice said more quietly. 'She lives ... Pega says she lives up there alone with her grandmother, a woman they call Old Gwenith. I think something may be amiss. Maybe her grandmother has had an accident or is sick.'

'You know this girl well?'

Beatrice flushed a dull red. 'I've ... I've seen her, Servant Martha ... from a distance, that's all. I've never spoken to her.'

'I wonder why she came to you then.'

Beatrice's expression was unmistakably one of guilt, like that of a naughty child who had been discovered in some act of disobedience. I stared at her curiously, but I could think of no possible reason why she should feel guilty that the child had approached her.

'No doubt she saw the compassion of Christian charity in your face, and the instinct God gives to all his dumb creatures told her you would not hurt her. I'm glad of it. We'll go at once. Fetch Healing Martha and get Catherine to help you bring a bier from the infirmary. If this Gwenith is lying hurt somewhere we may have to move her. I will meet you at the beguinage gate.'

'No, you don't need to come. Catherine and I can manage,' Beatrice said hastily.

The idea of my coming appeared to agitate her. But she must surely realize I'd hardly trust her with the decision about whether or not to bring this woman back to the beguinage. And what if this Gwenith was dead? Clearly Beatrice had not even contemplated that possibility. I could hardly imagine that she was equal to dealing with that.

'I rather think I do need to come, Beatrice. In fact I am sure of it.'

Beatrice

What on earth had possessed me to involve Servant Martha? I should have gone straight to Healing Martha to ask for a bier and some herbs, but she would probably only have sent for Servant Martha anyway. She'd keep secrets for that murdering little whore Osmanna, but not for me.

The moment Servant Martha asked me if I knew the girl, I realized I'd made a stupid mistake. I saw again the little pink tongue flashing in and out, like a viper in the shadows. The innocence of her naked body, the trembling butterflies on her flushed skin, her flame-bright hair. I'd felt my face burn and glanced away, unable to meet Servant Martha's piercing stare.

But now that we were toiling up the hill, I kept thinking of Old Gwenith. The girl could say nothing, but the old woman was bound to remember I'd been there before. What would she say in front of Servant Martha? I tried to remind myself I'd committed no sin, but Servant Martha would twist it into some sort of transgression. She could always use her clever tongue to tie you in knots and make you feel ashamed and useless even when you had done nothing wrong.

Gudrun bounded up the path ahead of us, her bare feet so light and sure on the rocks she scarcely seemed to touch them at all. Every so often she'd stop and wait, but as soon as we had nearly caught up with her, she'd skip off again, leaving us breathless in her wake. Servant Martha kept turning back to help Healing Martha over the rocks. It was one of her better days and Healing Martha was determined to struggle up herself, but in the end she was forced to let Servant Martha help her with a strong arm about her back.

Walking at Healing Martha's slow pace, the way seemed twice as long as it did the first time I had climbed it, but finally we stood on the flat, wiry grass beneath the rocks and I saw again the thorn bush hung with faded rags, locks of hair and amulets, and beyond that Gwenith's cottage. Gudrun pointed to the cottage and then ran off and disappeared behind a rock before we could stop her. Servant Martha led the way inside.

The meanest of creatures has a burrow in the earth or a hole in a tree that provides some shelter against rain and cold, but this poor creature's hovel didn't furnish even that scrap of comfort. I had last seen the place when the sun was shining, and thought it miserable enough then, but, dear God, to see it now in the winter, to have nothing but this to shelter you from the snow and rain and biting winds! How ever had she lived so long?

Green pools of stagnant water lay in every hollow in the earth floor. Globs of glistening slime crawled over the stones and crept through the dripping wattle. Old Gwenith lay huddled on a scattering of mouldy straw. The reek of stale piss that hung about her was strong enough to make your eyes water. Her face was as grey as the rags that covered her, and her fingers, clawed over her chest, were so thin, they looked as if they'd snap if you touched them.

I stared aghast at her legs. Her skirts were burnt away, as if she had been in a fire. Patches of charred cloth still hung in rags, but beneath them her bare legs were blistered and weeping. Angry wounds stood out red and sulphurous against the blackened flesh. Healing Martha, holding my arm for support, knelt stiffly in the dirt beside the old woman and gently took one of Gwenith's frail wrists in her hand. She bent closer, impervious to the stench, then straightened up. We helped her to her feet.

'She must have stood too close to her hearth fire and caught her kirtle in the flames. There's still a thread of life in her, though it's so weak her next breath might well be her last. She must be taken to the infirmary. I cannot care for her here.'

'Can you save her?' Servant Martha asked quietly.

Healing Martha shook her head. 'If she were younger, I might be able to heal those wounds, but she is not dying of the burns alone. Old age has caught up with her. There's no herb on earth can undo what time has done, but I can at least lay some soft blankets under those poor old bones and make her warm. She deserves to die in some comfort, for I fear she's had precious little of it in her life.'

Servant Martha nodded and motioned me to take her feet while she slipped her hands under her shoulders. The old woman was as light as a sack of dried chicken bones. I could have easily gathered her up in my arms and carried her out myself. She whimpered in pain as we laid her down on the bier outside. Servant Martha tucked a thick blanket around her and told Catherine to help me bind ropes across the fragile body to keep her from falling as we carried her down the hill. But Catherine was too afraid to touch the old woman and stood helplessly twisting her fingers, until Servant Martha impatiently thrust her aside and helped me with the ropes herself.

We were so engrossed in tending to the old woman that none of us noticed Gudrun creeping up from behind. Without warning she sprang on to Servant Martha's back. Servant Martha was caught off balance and sprawled face down on the ground, while the girl bit her and tore her clothes. She twisted and wriggled, trying to shake her off, but she couldn't get a grip on the girl on top of her.

'Don't just stand there, Beatrice, loosen her grasp.'

I tried to prise the girl's fingers loose, but it wasn't easy; she had the grip of a falcon. At last I managed to drag Gudrun away from Servant Martha. As Servant Martha struggled to her feet, panting, she grabbed Gudrun's arms, holding her from behind. The witch-girl spat and writhed, but she couldn't get out of Servant Martha's grip. Finally she stopped struggling, and began to weep silently, a look of sheer desperation on her pale little face.

'Control yourself, child,' Servant Martha ordered. 'Your grandmother is dying and she should at least die in a warm, dry bed, with the consolation of Christ to aid her passing. If she can be brought to her senses enough to unburden her soul and make a good confession, then God will yet show her mercy.'

The girl's shoulders shook with sobs, but not a single sound escaped her. The silence was unnerving. I knelt down and drew the weeping girl into my arms. But she went rigid and arched away from me as if I was hurting her.

'Hush, child,' I said as gently as I could. 'We mean your grandmother no harm. It's all right, everything is all right now. We'll take her to a safe place and give her hot food and clean clothes. You can stay with her. You can have as much food as you want to eat and you'll be warm and dry. And who knows, she may soon be well again.'

'You shouldn't give her false hope,' Servant Martha cut in, her voice freshly sharpened.

Healing Martha laid a restraining hand on her arm. 'Come now, it doesn't really matter what is said. The child can't understand much beyond the soothing tone of a kind voice. Beatrice is right; a full belly or an empty one is the limit of her reasoning.'

In the end it was Healing Martha and I who cut the rags from Gwenith's body. Healing Martha had asked Osmanna to mind the infirmary while she was gone, but that cold-hearted little bitch kept trying to leave me to deal with Gwenith, making excuses that she had other errands to run. I suppose she thought herself too high-born to be washing the body of some poor old woman.

Gwenith's naked body was a piteous sight. The hair that veils a woman's secret parts was gone and the skin on her belly hung loose and yellow as a plucked fowl. Her arms and hands were burnt too, though the burns were not as deep as on her legs. She was ice-cold, but even naked she didn't shiver. As gently as we could, Healing Martha and I lifted the sticks of her arms and tried to wash her body, but the dirt was tanned into her wrinkled hide and her skin seemed so thin we dared not rub at it. Besides, what was the point? It would add nothing to her comfort and would not lengthen her days.

Healing Martha smoothed unguents on her burns and rubbed a warming ointment on the old woman's chest. The pungent smell of turpentine permeated the room. All this while young Gudrun squatted by the fire, gnawing on a hunk of bread dipped in broth. She ate ravenously, stuffing it into her mouth with both hands as if she feared someone would snatch it from her. Her hair, aflame from the firelight, shielded her face. She was calm, almost as if she had forgotten the existence of the old woman, but she flinched and scuffled away in the furthest corner of the room when she heard Servant Martha approaching.

Servant Martha looked down at the old woman. 'How does she?' she asked, as if she was enquiring about the price of bread. That woman did not have a shred of human compassion in her body.

Healing Martha shook her head. Her meaning was plain; no potion or remedy could detain Gwenith longer in this world.

'Should we bleed her?' Servant Martha asked. 'If she could be roused for just a few minutes, long enough to make her confession.'

'She's so weak, bleeding would only render her insensible and hasten the end.'

'Is there nothing you can give her which would bring her to her senses?' Servant Martha briskly patted Gwenith's hand, but she didn't open her eyes.

'I'll try some warm herbed wine, if she's able to swallow it,' Healing Martha said, limping towards the door of the infirmary. 'But you'd better get to your prayers in earnest, Servant Martha, for I fear it'll take a skill far beyond mine to summon her wits again.'

I woke suddenly with a start. Little Gudrun was bending over her grandmother. The old woman's eyes were open. She was whispering to the girl, but it was impossible to make out what she said. Healing Martha, sitting opposite me near the fire, held up a warning hand.

'Give them a few minutes alone. It can't be long now. Osmanna has gone for Servant Martha.'

Trust Osmanna; I bet that was her idea. And Gwenith's poor little granddaughter would be elbowed out of the way fast enough when those two arrived.

Healing Martha looked reprovingly at me, as if she could read my thoughts. 'Servant Martha has to be told. The old woman must be given a chance to make her peace with God.' She stirred up the fire, sending sparks flying up into the black maw above. 'And it seems Servant Martha's prayers have been answered. I never thought to hear the old woman utter another word.'

'Are you sure it wasn't your wine that roused her?'

Her lined face broke into a twinkling smile. 'Let's give credit to both. Good wine fortified with robust prayer have together worked many a miracle.'

Servant Martha burst into the room with Osmanna hard on her heels. She strode to the bed. Pushing Gudrun aside, she bent close to Gwenith, clutching the thin shoulder urgently.

'Make your confession, mother, so that you may depart this life unburdened. However evil your deeds, if you repent of them even at this late hour our Lord in His mercy will forgive you.'

But the old woman only chuckled weakly. 'No time, mistress, not names enough in the world for all my sins.' Her claw suddenly fastened around Servant Martha's wrist and she pulled her towards her with such fierceness it seemed she intended to drag Servant Martha down to hell with her.

'The Owlman ... I saw him fly ... They've awakened him. The priest was too late ...'

'The Owlman is just a silly rumour, a lot of nonsense spread by empty-headed young girls. Do not waste what little time you have left on such thoughts. You must think of your own immortal soul.'

The old woman tugged at her again. 'Them that waked him had but half the spell ... they can't control him ... priest is too weak ... but you, you've got the spirit of a cunning-woman in you ... you mustn't be afeared, you've got the strength of a woman. You ... remember that.'

Servant Martha indignantly pulled her hand away. 'I have the spirit of Christ in me, as have all here. I can assure you that we are afraid of nothing that Satan may cast at us.'

The old woman was racked with coughing and lay back gasping, her eyes closed.

'My Gudrun ...' she murmured. 'I charge you ... watch over her ... don't let them hurt her.'

The girl stood unmoving beside the cot. If she understood, she made no sign.

'Mustn't cage her ... wild things die in cages ... watch over her and you'll have my blessing. My curse upon you if you fail her ...'

Servant Martha knelt beside the cot and tried again, more gently this time, with a note of pleading in her voice. 'Gwenith, for the sake of your immortal soul, will you not make peace with God?'

'What's there to make peace about? I've not spoken to God, nor He to me, so we've never had cause to quarrel.'

'We are all born in sin, Gwenith. All of us have offended our Lord. But it is not too late to save yourself from the fires of hell.'

The old woman's eyes opened again and she seemed about to answer, but her gaze wandered to Osmanna hovering behind. She curled her claw-like finger and beckoned. Osmanna seemed rooted to the spot.

'What's your name, lass?'

'Os ... Osmanna,' she whispered.

Gwenith waved an impatient hand. 'Not that one, lass. You have another.'

Servant Martha took hold of the frail hand and shook it as if that would shake the old woman's wits back to the purpose. 'Gwenith, your soul is in grave danger. If you die unshriven you will dwell in torment and agony until the Day of Judgment. You must –'

The old woman sighed. 'Tell me your name, lass.'

'I've cast off my other name,' Osmanna muttered, her face crimson now.

'You've cast off nowt, lass ... find your name ... No peace will come to you ... until you find your own name.'

'She's rambling,' Servant Martha murmured. She bent closer to the old woman. 'Listen to me, Gwenith, you are dying, you must turn your thoughts to God.' Servant Martha spoke slowly and loudly as if she was speaking to the deaf.

'Aye, and when did he ever turn his thoughts to me, mistress?'

Old Gwenith's eyes closed. There was a half-breath, a hungry gulp of air that choked before it finished, and her mouth slackened. The only sound in the room was the spitting and crackling of the wood on the fire. Healing Martha lifted the transparent blue eyelids and touched her eyes, then held a feather against her lips. She watched intently for what seemed like for ever, but it did not stir.

Gudrun looked from one to another of us and then at her grandmother. Slowly she reached out a clenched fist, unfurled one finger and gently stroked the old woman's face. She snatched her hand away, as if she had been burnt. She threw her head back, her red mouth wide as a howling dog, but not a sound emerged. Her body was rigid. Before I could reach her she fell to the floor, choking and jerking violently, her mouth foaming. We watched, helpless. There was nothing we could do to help her.

Father Ulfrid

'You could have picked somewhere warmer for a lovers' tryst,' Hilary sang out softly from among the trees.

I whirled around in the direction of the sound, but I couldn't see anyone in the copse. There was still another hour of daylight left, but the clouds had rolled in and light rain was falling, so that it seemed already twilight.

'I thought you said you never wanted to see me again,' Hilary said mockingly. 'But I told you that you'd be begging me to come back, didn't I?'

'Stop playing games, Hilary. Come out.'

I jumped as a hand clapped down on my shoulder.

Hilary laughed and planted a savage kiss on my mouth. 'Anyway, why in God's name did we have to meet in a wood? If you think I'm going to strip off here in the middle of winter, you can think again. That stinking crypt in the Cathedral was cold enough to freeze my balls off, but earwigs and thorns up the arse as well, forget it. Why couldn't we meet at your cottage?'

'We were nearly caught there, remember. And things are worse now. The Owl Masters are watching everyone. They'd spot a stranger instantly and start asking questions. Any one of the villagers could be an Owl Master or be spying for them. It had to be here. I couldn't risk anywhere else.'

The rain pattered softly on the dead leaves underfoot and the bushes trembled. I glanced round uneasily. Rustling and creaking seemed to come from every direction. I'd never realized how much noise there was in the woods. I'd always thought them silent, peaceful places. This hadn't been such a good idea. The old undergrowth could conceal a dozen pairs of watching eyes or listening ears.

'Here, you're shaking, my poor Ulfrido,' Hilary said, grasping my hand. 'You look terrible. Sit down. Has something happened?' His voice had lost its lazy drawl and for once there was genuine concern in his dark eyes, something I'd not seen for many months.

There was a fallen oak close by. I'd sent word that I would wait there. Now, as I half leaned, half sat on the great trunk, Hilary lifted the hem of my robe, sliding his hand up between my thighs. I shuddered as his cold fingers, wetted from the rain, ran lightly across my prick, stroking the length of it, cupping my balls, but gently for once. It was an old familiar gesture. He had not been tender like this for many months and I sensed it was meant only for comfort, not to tease. I ached to surrender my body to his touch, but I dared not. I tore myself away from his hand and stood up, though it cost me every ounce of resolve to do so.

Hilary broke off a twig and began snapping it into small pieces. 'I should be cross with you, Ulfrido. I don't know why I came.' He stuck out his lower lip in a parody of a sulky child. 'Sending me away, then not a word for weeks. Now you expect me to come running whenever you snap your fingers. I had a good mind not to come at all.'

He slouched against the fallen oak, idly scuffing the crumbling brown leaf mould like a bored child. I felt angry and resentful. He had no idea what I'd been through the last few days. For a moment I was tempted to pour out all the events of All Hallows' Eve. But no one who had not witnessed it could understand the horror of it. And what would I say if he asked me what I had done? I could not admit aloud that I, who had been so determined to fight this evil, had simply turned and fled like a coward with all the other villagers.

'Well?' Hilary asked impatiently. 'You dragged me all the way to this arsehole of a village. You must want something. Either talk to me or fuck me, it's all the same to me, but either way get on with it, I'm not sitting here all night getting soaked.'

My anger boiled up again and I jumped to my feet. 'You want to know what I want? I'll tell you. I want money.'

'Money?' Hilary repeated incredulously. 'What could you possibly want money for? You're a bloody priest, for God's sake. Good living. Free cottage, free food, free wine! You've got it all. You don't have to break your back to earn it. Recite a few prayers in Latin and it all comes pouring into your lap without you having to lift a finger. I wish I had it so easy.'

Before I realized what I was doing I had drawn back my fist. Hilary raised his arm to shield his face. I felt instantly ashamed and annoyed with myself. I couldn't afford to drive away the one person I had left. I lowered my hand, and saw a look of contempt on Hilary's face. I knew he despised me because I'd wanted to punch him and also because he knew I lacked the guts to do it.

I took a deep breath. 'The villagers didn't pay all their tithes. I gave Bishop Salmon everything I had in the barn, but it still wasn't enough, so I had to borrow the rest and use the church silver as surety. It's not been missed yet. But I have to redeem the silver in time for the Christmas Mass or D'Acaster will realize it is gone. I have to have the money to get them back.'

'My poor little Ulfrido. I wish I could help you, really I do.'

Hilary moved closer. He stroked the back of my neck. I could smell the sweet, musky perfume of oil that he rubbed on his skin. 'But I'm the one who comes to you for money, Ulfrido. You know I can never keep a coin for more than a day or two without it burning a hole in my purse. It's my nature, I can't help it.'

'But you can get money. Those other men you ... entertain. They'd give you money if you asked.'

'Are you turning whore-master now?' Hilary laughed and pressed still closer to me. He ran a finger across my groin, making me shiver. 'And I thought you didn't want me to *entertain* other men. Or do you secretly get a thrill from it? Do you lie in your cold, empty bed, thinking about me with other lovers?' He suddenly crushed my balls in his fist, making me gasp and wince.

I pushed him away. 'You know I loathe the thought of you

with other men, but I know that you do it. You've always enjoyed throwing that in my face.'

His mocking grin did not deny it.

'Please, Hilary, I beg you, if you ever had any feelings for me, help me. There is no one else I can ask. The villagers won't give me what they owe me, because the Owl Masters are taking every penny from them in exchange for their so-called protection. The church is practically empty.'

Hilary leaned against a tree, staring up at the dripping branches, as if he was already bored by the subject. 'There must be something you can sell, a relic? Every church has those.'

'Not this one.' I said bitterly. 'If I had a relic, the villagers would be flocking into the church, eager to hand over their coins for its miracles and protection. Pilgrims would be queuing up to pay to touch it. All my problems would be over. But you need money to buy relics.'

Now it was I who moved closer, caressing the silky black curls of his hair. 'Please, Hilary. I'll do anything you ask, anything. But you must get me the money. I'm begging you.'

Hilary's lips sought mine, his hot tongue slipped between my teeth, his hand pressed against my buttock, pulling my groin against his, sending a shudder through my body. We pressed hard against each other, feeling those old waves of passion surge through us again. For a heartbeat, I didn't care about tithes or Owl Masters. All that mattered was that perfect, beautiful body I held in my arms.

Hilary bent his head and his soft lips brushed my ear.

'Forget about that arsehole of a village and their poxy silver. Come away with me, Ulfrido, now, tonight. We could go to London. I've always wanted to go there. There'd be just us together. I'll never fuck another man, I swear. I only want you. No one would know you were a priest in London –'

'Hilary, don't you think I would have already done that if I could? I may be walking around freely without chains, but Ulewic is my prison. The Bishop gave me a choice: come to this place or stand trial for what you and I have done. You know the penalties for our crime – mutilation at the very least, most likely death. I had no option but to agree to come here. And the only way out of this village is if the Bishop himself releases me from it. If I try to run away, I'll be arrested, and this time there will be no way of escaping punishment.'

'If you won't come with me then you don't love me.' Hilary pushed me away petulantly. 'You're just like the rest, take what you want, then –'

I seized Hilary's shoulders and shook him violently. 'Look, can't you understand, you spoilt, selfish little whore, that the Bishop's Commissarius was against me being spared from the start? He's only waiting for me to make one more mistake and he'll force the Bishop to have me arrested. Do you think this is some sort of game, something that doesn't concern you? Make no mistake, you bitch, that if what I've done is made public, I'll name you too. So you'd better help me, unless you want to find yourself on the gallows with your own bollocks stuffed in your mouth.'

Fear and hatred flooded Hilary's face and I knew I'd made a fatal mistake.

'Hilary ... I'm sorry ... I didn't mean that, you know I didn't. It's just that I've been so worried ... not sleeping. I lose my temper, but you know I don't mean it.'

His dark eyes stared back at me, cold and contemptuous.

I tried to put my arm around him, but he pulled away from me. 'Hilary, please forgive me. I swear on my life, on my immortal soul, I'd never name you. I will always protect you. Haven't I already done so? I refused to name you even when my Lord the Bishop commanded me to. He had me flogged for that. You've seen the scars. They laid my back open with the whip and still I refused to name you. I'd suffer anything for you. I couldn't bear to see them mar your face or body.'

I knelt down on the sodden leaves, clutching the hem of his cloak. 'You are my angel, my beautiful dark angel. I've given up everything for you. But ... just this once I need your help. I will never ask you again, but I'm begging you now, help me, Hilary.'

'Get up. You look ridiculous and pathetic!'

I struggled to my feet, my face burning with shame and humiliation.

'I'll get your money,' Hilary said coldly. 'But you'll have to give me time. A month, six weeks. I'll have to get small amounts from different people, otherwise they'll ask too many questions about why I want it. Let me go now.'

'But you will come back as soon as you can ... with the money?'

'I said I would, didn't I?'

But the smile was too bright, too brittle, and I knew, deep down, I'd never see him again. I had overplayed my hand and we both knew it. Anyone with any sense would take what I'd said as a warning and get as far away from Norwich as they could before the inevitable happened.

He kissed me before he walked away. One last kiss. It is always the last kiss that betrays.

What had I expected? That Hilary would do what I begged him, because he loved me? Angels cannot love. They have no pity, no compassion. They were created to be adored by mortal men and they scorn those that worship them. They exist only to punish us for our desire of them. They are our temptation and our chastisement. And we kiss the rod they wield, because we are ... ridiculous and pathetic. We deserve no mercy from them and we receive none.

I had learnt one thing that night. I'd had it branded on to my soul. Only the weak show compassion and that is what destroys them. The Commissarius had no mercy for anyone and God had rewarded his ruthlessness by making him one of the most powerful men in the See of Norwich, and doubtless he would climb higher still, even as far as the Vatican or King's Court. But look where compassion had got me – a priest of some piss-poor village in the most godforsaken corner of England.

It was my compassion that had left the tithe barn half filled and the church half empty. It was my charity that made me defend those hags in the house of women from the Owl

Masters and the villagers. It was my pity that made me forgive that filthy little whore, Hilary, and take him to my bed again and again. All that I had once believed were Christian virtues, I now saw were nothing more than my contemptible weakness. I would not make those mistakes again. I would learn ruthlessness from the angels, the favoured ones of God. From now on, I would become as merciless as them.

A relic, Hilary said. But I didn't need money to buy a relic; there was one in the village ready for the taking. A holy relic in a hags' kitchen. Those women had no right to it. The Host had been consecrated by the Church. It belonged to the Church. It belonged to me as Christ's minister in this stinking midden.

If I'd had such a thing in my possession on All Hallows' Night, I would have been able to fight that demon. Even now, if it was in my hands I could send that monster back into the depths of hell from whence it had come. The villagers wouldn't be laughing at me then. They'd be hammering on the church door begging to be allowed back, pleading for my protection. The house of women would have to surrender it to me. I had the authority to demand it. And I would demand it. I would make those whores give it to me.

November – St Winefride's Day

Welsh virgin who refused the suit of Prince Caradoc. In his rage, he cut off her head and where her head struck the ground a miraculous well appeared. Her uncle, St Beuno, replaced her head on her shoulders and she was restored to life.

Servant Martha

The door of the refectory opened, sending the tallow candles guttering wildly and scattering the rushes with fallen leaves. Gate Martha hurried down the long length of the table towards me. At once all the women ceased their chattering and watched her expectantly.

'That pinch-mouthed priest is outside, Servant Martha. He's demanding to see you, but he says he'll not set foot across our threshold.'

'Then that suits both of us,' I said tartly, 'since I would never allow him to enter.'

I sighed and pushed aside a steaming bowl of pork pottage which I had not even had the chance to taste, and rose. Healing Martha also heaved herself up.

'Stay here and finish your supper, Healing Martha. I don't need a chaperone. I doubt that my virtue is in danger.'

'I have no doubt that you would be quite capable of defending your virtue against an entire crew of shipwrecked sailors, but I don't think it is desire for your body that brings the priest to our door,' she murmured, but not quietly enough to prevent Shepherd Martha and Dairy Martha from overhearing, judging by the grins they were struggling unsuccessfully to suppress.

I glared at Healing Martha, but she simply answered me with a serene smile and followed me out of the refectory and across the courtyard to the gate. On my instructions Gate Martha bolted the gate behind us, though I had no doubt she'd have her ear pressed to the wood. It was dusk and the icy wind was whipping the treetops back and forth. Neither of us had stopped to fetch our cloaks and both of us shivered in the wind. The priest was marching up and down the track, his hands clasped behind his back. He came to a halt at a little distance from us as if he was afraid we had some contagion.

'You wished to see me, Father Ulfrid. I assume the matter must be of some import to bring you here on such an inclement evening?'

The priest cleared his throat as if he was about to deliver a sermon. 'It has come to my attention that you have in this house of women a piece of the sacred Host. I am told this Host was vomited by the anchorite Andrew on her deathbed and preserved intact from the flames of a fire.'

So the rumour had finally reached him. Healing Martha warned me on the day Andrew died that a miracle does not bring peace, but I had foolishly begun to believe that, for once, my old friend might be wrong. Andrew's miraculous Host had lain undisturbed in the church for almost a month now and I had begun to hope that God had answered my prayers and the danger was now safely past. But if Father Ulfrid had learned about the miraculous Host, what else did he know?

'Might I enquire who told you this?' I asked.

'It does not matter who told me. The point is, how did Andrew acquire this Host in the first place? I did not give it to her nor, I imagine, did the priest at St Andrew's. So the question remains, who did?'

I swallowed hard, trying to keep my face impassive. I prayed Healing Martha was able to do the same, but I dared not look at her, knowing that the priest would immediately interpret any such glance as a sign of guilt.

'Did not this anonymous informant answer that question for you, Father Ulfrid?'

'Oh, yes. Yes, indeed,' he said triumphantly. 'I know all that has been going on here, mistress, every abomination that has been committed within these walls.' His pale grey eyes blazed in fury. 'How dare you allow a friar to give Andrew the holy bread? Only consecrated priests are permitted to administer the sacraments. You have damned Andrew's soul to hell in this mockery of the rites and you have damned your own soul along with hers. Did you think this friar would not be seen creeping to your gates at night? What other wicked practices did he perform within these walls? Did your women have sex with him? Did you?'

I felt my breath pour out in sheer relief. The priest did not know the truth after all. He believed the Franciscan had given the Host to Andrew with his own hand. I would not attempt to deny it. Father Ulfrid was outraged enough that a friar had usurped his right as a priest, but that a woman might do it was beyond his wildest nightmare. Thanks be to God, he had such a dull imagination that the possibility had not even entered his head.

Father Ulfrid evidently interpreted my silence as an admission of guilt, for when he spoke again, the anger had left his voice to be replaced with cold authority. 'You and all your women will present yourselves at the Mass next Sunday, barefoot and clad only in your shifts. I shall hear your confession before the whole congregation and you shall perform full and public penance for your crimes. You will –'

'For what shall we do penance?' I interrupted him. 'Have you forgotten the news that brought you here? God preserved the blessed Host in the flames. Would our Lord have vouchsafed us such a miracle if His blessed body had been defiled in the manner of its giving? Andrew herself begged for the sacrament, knowing the nature of the one who would give it to her. Could a saint on her deathbed be so misguided and remain a saint?'

Father Ulfrid's face blanched with fury. 'That Andrew was unable to swallow the holy body of our Lord is proof that her sins still lay heavy upon her and God had rejected the mockery of the Franciscan's absolution.' The priest's fists were clenched so tightly that it appeared to be costing him a supreme effort not to strike me. 'That you tried to destroy the evidence of your heinous sin in the fire is proof beyond dispute of your guilt in allowing this travesty. God preserved the holy body from the flames to expose your crime for all to witness.'

He stepped forward and thrust his face in mine, trying to

force me to cower away, but I was taller than him and he couldn't achieve the effect he wanted. I stood my ground.

'Father, am I to understand that you deny that Andrew died a saint? It is strange, is it not, that a miracle should follow on the death of a sinner? I warrant that many have taken the Host with sins still unconfessed lying heavy upon their souls, yet no such miracle has followed their sin.'

For a moment Father Ulfrid hesitated and seemed to be at a loss for an answer. Then his chin tilted up. 'The sacrament was plainly forced upon her without her consent while she lay helpless, in an effort to condemn her. From jealousy and malice, you and that friar sought to drag her soul to hell along with yours. You will present yourselves on Sunday as I have directed and you will deliver the miraculous Host to me on that day and before all the people.

'If you fail to do so, you and all within the beguinage will be excommunicated. You will be forbidden to attend Mass. All the blessed sacraments of the Church will be denied to you and to your women. If you refuse to repent, you will die unshriven and you will be denied a Christian burial. The Devil himself will carry you screaming straight to the eternal fires of hell. I will make certain every man, woman and child in Ulewic knows that no Christian soul shall be permitted to trade with you or set foot within your gates without suffering the same penalty. How many will bring their sick to you then, knowing they are condemning them to everlasting torment?' He crowed the last words out with the triumph of a man who thinks he has won.

'Spare me your threats, Father Ulfrid. You have already excommunicated half the village because they will not pay their tithes. So why wouldn't they come to us, for you cannot ex-communicate them twice over? As for the sick, most are here because the Mother Church in her great charity has already damned them and driven them out. The churches are emptier than a pauper's purse and little wonder, for men get more solace from the alewives than from their priests. More stand now outside your church than within it. What difference does it make if you forbid them burial in the churchyard, since they cannot afford the soul-scot you charge them to be buried there anyway? Those who still look to God make their prayers far away from the church, where the air is sweeter and their voices are not smothered beneath your hypocrisy and greed.'

I was shaking and couldn't trust myself to say more in case my voice faltered. With great deliberation, I turned my back on him and, linking my arm through Healing Martha's, led her back inside.

'I need that relic,' he screamed after us. 'I must have it. I am your priest. You cannot refuse me. In the name of the Holy Church I command you –' He was still shouting threats as Gate Martha bolted the gates behind us. She drew us over to her brazier in the entrance to the little shelter next to the gate. Healing Martha and I gratefully warmed our hands over the glowing wood.

Gate Martha laid a horny palm upon my arm. 'Coming here to demand our relic – I've never heard the like. You pay no heed to him, Servant Martha. He's all wind and fart. The women of Ulewic know fine what you do for them and most are grateful, for it's more than they get from him and his kind.'

Just as I thought, Gate Martha had been listening to every word behind the gate.

'You answered well.' Healing Martha patted my other arm.

I was grateful for their kindness, but exasperated by their easy reassurances. They didn't seem to have grasped what had just happened.

'Did you not hear what the priest said?' I snapped. 'He is going to excommunicate all of us. How many beguines will stay with us when they discover that they will be denied the blessed body of our Lord? What if one of them should have an accident or fall ill and they die without the last rites?'

Gate Martha looked at me as if I was sun-touched. 'But you'll give the sacraments, as you did Andrew.'

I stared at her, unable to believe I'd heard her aright. 'Do you understand what you are saying? It is unthinkable.'

'Why so?' she stubbornly persisted.

'Because . . . because the Church forbids it, you know that.'

Two furrows, like iron bars, deepened between her eyes. 'Church forbade you to give it to Andrew, but you did it all the same. Whatever others may believe, I'm the gatekeeper and I know the Franciscan did not come within these walls, any more than Andrew could walk to the alms' window. So it stands to reason, you must have given it her. Don't fret,' she added, seeing my startled expression, 'I've said nowt to the rest. But the way I see it, if you gave it to Andrew, why not to the rest of us? Aren't we good enough, is that it? We're no saints, that I'll grant, but I reckon sinners stand more in need of His meat than saints.'

Healing Martha had warned me that Gate Martha knew what I'd done, but if she had worked it out, how many of the other beguines had also done so? How long before that rumour reached the priest's ears as well?

I shook my head. 'It's far too dangerous. We have already been betrayed. It could have been a beguine, one of us who –'

'Don't talk daft. It wasn't a beguine.' Gate Martha poked another log into the brazier and rubbed her gnarled hands over the blaze. 'You think the whole of Ulewic hasn't been asking themselves why our cattle were spared the murrain? Owl Masters have spies everywhere. They'll have been watching the track to the beguinage. But there's no reason any of the villagers need find out you're giving us the Host, not if we're careful. Say Mass at midnight; all in the infirmary'll be sleeping then.'

Gate Martha made it sound so simple. Maybe she was right; it was the only thing I could do. I would not lead the beguines in an act of public penance and humiliation. It would devastate the women and destroy any faith the villagers had in us. And neither would I surrender the relic to the priest. The beguines had put their faith in it, and how could I continue as Servant Martha if they saw me intimidated into relinquishing it? But the beguinage would not continue without the sacraments. The beguines were devout, pious women who had dedicated their lives to God; they would never stay if they believed they were condemning themselves to hell.

I sank shakily on to the bench, grasping the reality of the wood, solid in my hands. My fingertips dug into its unyielding form so hard they hurt, but I couldn't seem to let go of it.

The first Christians broke bread and shared among themselves. Why not us? Why should we not do as they did? Women sow the fields, reap the grain, grind it, shape it and bake it, then why do we shrink from placing it in the mouths of God's children?

I thought I glimpsed the faintest of smiles on Healing Martha's face as she watched me. Were my thoughts so transparent to her? I rose without speaking and walked towards the chapel. But even without turning round, I knew Healing Martha and Gate Martha were exchanging silent nods, smugly certain that they had persuaded me.

The chapel was empty and silent. The chill air leached the heat from my bones. My back ached, but I held it rigid, clinging to the shafts of cold and pain to keep me from sinking into sleep. Lights from the candles flickered like moths across the dark walls, setting the painted figures dancing in and out of shadows. The women had gone to their beds. Only Healing Martha knelt with me. I couldn't see her face, so deep was it shrunk inside her hood, but I knew she prayed; I could feel the spirit rising from her. Was she praying for me? I stared up at Andrew's reliquary on the altar, resting like a tiny coffin between two candles.

Andrew had placed herself, body, mind and spirit, under the protection of the Church, that holy shield beneath which all fragile human souls find refuge. The shield of faith and obedience passed from hand to hand in an unbroken chain of male consecration, stretching all the way back through the darkness of persecution to St Peter and through his hand to our blessed Lord Himself. Through that chain a priest may touch Christ's hand and may grasp the very power of God.

Yet here I knelt asking Andrew for her grace, while refusing to submit my will to the Church. Worse than that, seeking, as I asked for her blessing, to take powers upon me that are denied even to ordinary men.

A gust of wind tore at the chapel door and the candle flames guttered. Healing Martha clambered painfully to her feet and limped to the door. I followed, and together we walked back towards our rooms, drawing the sharp night air into our lungs. We paused at the door of Healing Martha's cell.

She leaned wearily against the wall in the darkness, massaging the small of her back. 'You are resolved now?'

'I can see no other way to hold the beguinage together. But will the women accept the Host from my hands?'

'Our sisters in Flanders have given the Host to those whom the Church has cast out. The Marthas know that and they will help you to convince the others. But there is something more you have not yet considered.'

'Can the matter not wait until tomorrow, Healing Martha?' I was so tired. I just wanted to sleep.

She took my hand and squeezed it. 'I wish it could, but you need to understand what you are about to do. The Host which the Franciscan brought – there are only three pieces remaining. Even broken, it will not be enough.'

'Then we must get word to the Franciscan to ask him to resume his visits. He will help us, I'm sure.'

'No, no, old friend, that he must not do. It would be dangerous for him and us. You heard Gate Martha; they are watching the beguinage.'

'Then we must find someone else to bring it, someone the priest will not suspect.'

She shook her head. 'You know what punishments are meted out to anyone caught giving the Host to those who have been excommunicated. We've no right to ask it of others.

'As for us, we must pray the Franciscan is never found. Even the strongest of men can be broken by the Church's interrogators. Father Ulfrid may be as blind as a mole in sunlight, but there are others whose vision is clearer. If the Friar were to confess that he never came within our walls, they would not be slow to reason out your role in this play, and if they did, the matter would not end with excommunication, not for you, not for any of us. Father Ulfrid wouldn't plead clemency for a newborn babe inside these walls.'

I felt like screaming in exasperation. 'Healing Martha, you were the one urging me to give the Host to women. What have we been wasting time talking about this for, if there is no Host to give them and no hope of obtaining any? We have failed. We may as well pack up now, tonight, and return to Bruges. The beguinage cannot survive here.'

As if it heard me, a sudden gust of wind howled around the walls of the beguinage. Doors and shutters rattled and a leather pail skittered across the courtyard.

Healing Martha pulled her cloak tighter around herself. 'There is only one thing you can do, old friend, you must consecrate the Host yourself.'

'No! To give the Host that is already consecrated, that is one thing. I would simply be acting as the servant, passing a dish offered by a host to guest, but I cannot consecrate it. I cannot take bread and turn it into His flesh.'

'It's but another small step and you are already walking upon this path.'

'I cannot do it,' I insisted. 'How could you even think it? I'm not a priest. I am not a friar. I am not even a man.'

'It is not the merit of the priest who turns bread into flesh. It is God who turns bread into flesh, and even when that priest has sinned, still the bread becomes flesh.' Healing Martha grasped my wrists and turned the palms of my hands upwards. 'So why should God not make flesh of bread held in these hands?'

Why was she asking this of me? I was exhausted. Hadn't I carried enough in these past weeks? And now, instead of supporting me, she added this terrible weight. Around me lay the closed shutters of the other rooms, the fastened doors, the impenetrable shadows of the empty courtyard. It was a cloudless night. A thousand stars flickered like distant candles in the violet sky. And behind each candle in the darkness was a face watching, waiting, listening. They were silent. They would give me no sign. They would only judge. They would abandon me to choice and condemn me when I chose wrongly.

Healing Martha pushed the door of her room open. She turned to look back at me. The glow of the fire behind her in the darkened room surrounded her with a halo of light.

'Tell me, Healing Martha,' I said softly, 'how did we come to be walking down this road and not notice where our steps were leading? When did we turn on to this path?'

'It matters not how or when, old friend. We are set on the path now and there is no going back. There is no going back.'

†

November – Andermass

The feast of St Andrew, crucified on an X-shaped cross, patron saint of fishermen. St Rule set sail with the relics of St Andrew to discover where St Andrew wanted his bones to rest and in a storm he was cast ashore in Fife, Scotland. Thus he concluded the bones wanted to be housed in Scotland.

Beatrice

I called her Gudrun as her grandmother Gwenith named her. It fitted her. 'My little Gudrun.' Sometimes when I said it she even turned towards me as if she knew her name. Servant Martha said Gudrun was a heathen name for it means *the gods' secret lore*. So the Marthas gave her a new name, Dympna, because she had the falling sickness. It's cruel to name a child for the affliction that torments her. I bet it was Servant Martha who suggested it. She'd be the first to point out someone else's weaknesses.

Servant Martha tried to baptize the child too, for neither Gate Martha nor Pega could recall her ever being brought to St Michael's, but the Devil would not easily come out of her. She desperately fought the Marthas who held her, as if they were trying to murder her. Finally she managed to break free and ran out of the chapel to hide in the space between the byre and stable, a gap so narrow you'd think a cat could hardly squeeze in. I sat outside with her half the night murmuring nonsense, trying to coax her to come out with offers of food. She did, eventually, but she never answered to the name Dympna.

At first she ranged restlessly around the beguinage, trying to find a way out, while Servant Martha for her part tried in vain to impose some discipline and order in Gudrun's day. It was the first time I'd ever seen Servant Martha defeated by anyone. Gudrun could not be set to the simplest of tasks. She wandered away in the middle of sweeping a room, or else crouched in a chaos of wet linen, staring up at the sky in a trance. During the offices she gazed at the candles and the paintings on the walls of the chapel, frequently wandering over during prayers to trace the outline of a face with her finger. The clanging of the bell terrified her and she pressed her fingers to her ears and ran into one of her hiding places until it stopped. She never seemed to get used to it.

Servant Martha tried to bring her to heel by telling her she would get no food if she didn't work, but Kitchen Martha and I smuggled food to her in spite of Servant Martha's instructions. It was pointless to punish her. She didn't understand. Hunger was so much part of her life before she came to the beguinage that she didn't connect it with her actions; to her it was simply another senseless blow falling without reason. Besides, if I didn't smuggle food to her, she'd only steal it from the kitchen or the beasts, so I was saving her from a worse sin.

She refused to wear the beguine's kirtle, repeatedly throwing it off, scrubbing her skin as if it hurt her. All her life she had worn nothing but a light shift and the kirtle must have felt so heavy to her. But Servant Martha insisted her short, ragged shift was indecent for a girl of her age, so I stitched her a new linen one, long enough to cover her, but light enough for her to bear the weight of it. Servant Martha pursed her lips, but said nothing. Even she recognized that it was better that Gudrun wore the shift than walked around half-naked. Besides, she never left the confines of the beguinage, so who was to see her except us?

Servant Martha had given orders that Gudrun was never to be allowed out of the beguinage. We were not to let her work in the fields for fear that she'd simply wander away and starve by herself or, worse, be drawn to the village to steal food. The villagers already feared her; add theft to her list of crimes and they wouldn't be inclined to mercy.

We didn't even take Gudrun with us when we buried her grandmother. There was no point in asking leave to bury Gwenith in the churchyard. Thanks to Servant Martha, the priest wouldn't grant a Christian burial to any who had lain within our walls, not even on the north side of the church among the unshriven souls. And even if he had, Gate Martha said that the villagers would dig her up again, dismember the corpse and scatter the pieces or drive iron nails into the soles of her feet to stop her ghost walking. If they feared her in life, they feared her twice as much in death.

So we took Gwenith's body back up the hill to her cottage and buried the old woman beneath the stones of her own hearth. In the end, the four of us who had brought her down were all the souls who escorted her back up the river to her grave. We buried her quietly and quickly, indecently quickly. I don't think Servant Martha had forgiven Gwenith for laughing on her deathbed; that's why she was so determined to force her granddaughter through the gates of heaven, just to spite the old woman. But how can a soul be brought to salvation, if she can't understand? And what did Gudrun understand except that the sun was warm and the rain was cold? And her birds, she understood the birds.

Her raven wouldn't enter the beguinage, but he perched on the outer wall each day at noon, croaking until Gudrun came to him. Gate Martha tried to drive him away by waving a broom or throwing stones. She said a raven hanging about the place was unlucky, a death omen, but it was no use, for the bird would simply flap a little way off and perch in a nearby tree, cawing as loudly as ever and watching for a chance to return.

But it wasn't just the raven Gudrun loved. Whenever I couldn't find her I knew just where she was hiding. I'd tiptoe into the pigeon cote and there she'd be, squatting on the flags, with the pigeons on her shoulders, nestling into her warm hair. They'd lie as quietly in her open hands as if they slept in their own nests. She'd a way with them, knowing at once when a bird was sick and how to heal it. Unable to go out to look for herbs, she'd go to the stillroom and take any she needed, pushing aside anyone who tried to stop her. Healing Martha gave her freedom to come and go as she pleased, for she said that Gudrun knew as much about curing birds and animals as she knew of healing man.

Gudrun slept in the cote at night, curled up in a heap of straw on the floor with birds nestling against her as if they brooded her. I didn't try to stop her any more. On cold nights I'd creep in and cover her up with a blanket while she slept. I'd stand and watch her, her face buried beneath her arm, her hair turned to red-gold in the yellow flame of my lantern. I'd listen to the steady breathing, watch her fingers curled like an infant's, her baby lips part as if she was waiting to be kissed. I could watch over my little Gudrun all night.

It was because of Gudrun that I didn't leave the beguinage when Servant Martha told us that Father Ulfrid had excommunicated us all. I should have gone when I had the chance. Servant Martha gave us a choice, if you can call what she offered a choice.

'If any of you wish to return to the beguinage in Bruges, we will arrange immediate passage on board ship for you.'

A sea crossing in the middle of winter – who would be crazy enough to attempt that? It had been bad enough in summer. It was like saying to a prisoner you can rot in jail or you can escape by running through a hall of mad dogs.

She'd assembled us all in the chapel after dark. Andrew's reliquary lay on the altar in front of us, beneath the crucifix and the painting of the Blessed Virgin Mary. The rest of the Marthas sat around Servant Martha, facing us, grave, but composed. Servant Martha rose and stood taller and straighter than ever, the candlelight casting a giant shadow of her on the wall.

The Marthas must have known what she was going to say, but we mere beguines had heard not a whisper of what had been discussed and there was a shocked silence in the chapel as Servant Martha told us what the priest had demanded – the relic and our public penance or excommunication. Little Catherine, sitting beside me, began to sob like a terrified child when the words sank in.

Servant Martha, ignoring Catherine, let us digest these momentous facts for a few moments, then she presented us with her solution. We needed no priest to mediate between us and our Lord; we would consecrate the Host ourselves and give it to one another as the first Christians had done, as indeed, Christ had intended that night He met with his disciples.

'Women feed the world,' she declared, 'from the cradle to the grave, nourishing the unborn in the womb, suckling the infant, feeding husband, children, friend and stranger, the old, the sick and the dying. Is it not the most natural thing in the world that our sex should give the bread of life to the soul just as we give it to the body? Is it not in fact our natural part, our role, our calling?

'We recite each day that God's spirit is in us. Should we not stand upon the truth of what we say or is it just an empty phrase, a hollow piety? If our spirit is with God and as God, if God is in us and we are in Him, then why should we not consecrate His body as He does ours?'

The beguines stared at one another. Servant Martha's gaze swept the room as if daring any one of us to challenge her. I knew what she was saying was all wrong, but I could not put my arguments into words. Surely if anyone could consecrate the bread, the Church would have told us. How, after hundreds of years, could it suddenly be possible for a woman to do what the Pope said only a priest could do? But I knew whatever I said, Servant Martha could defeat with a clever phrase.

Servant Martha said any who believed what she was pro-posing was wrong should obey their conscience and leave the chapel at once. Then she sat down and watched us. All the Marthas watched us, except for Kitchen Martha who stared miserably at her chubby hands, unwilling to look at anyone.

I should have got up and left then. I could have gone back to Bruges, to the comfortable life I had so long regretted leaving. But I didn't move. The sea crossing, yes, that was enough to dissuade the bravest soul, but I was thinking of Gudrun curled up asleep in the cote. I couldn't leave her to the mercy of a woman like Servant Martha who had the warmth and com-passion of a stoat. Someone had to look after the child. Gudrun needed a mother; she needed me.

No one rose and walked through the lines of beguines to the door. I don't know why; perhaps they too knew there was no escape or maybe they really did believe what Servant Martha was doing was right. But that night we all ate the little piece of damnation she offered to us in her hands.

The Marthas rose and one by one extinguished the candles burning round the chapel until only a single candle burned on the altar in front of the miraculous Host. All eyes were turned to it, seeking shelter from the darkness in that one tiny flame. Then Servant Martha stepped forward and lit her candle; when the flame burned steadily she bent to light the one in the hands of little Margery who served at the altar, and sent her into the body of women. We each lit our candles, one after another, the flame passing along the rows, from hand to hand, the light spreading, filling the chapel, driving the shades from us into the deep corners and high up into the rafters.

Wherever these candles shall be set, the Devil shall flee away in fear and trembling with all his ministers.

As the light spread, the dancing began. Some of the women picked out the tune of the *Nunc Dimittis* on their instruments and the rest gathered it up in song as if it was a joyous Easter carol. I stood silently watching them becoming drunk on the light, as I grew more sober. I don't know how long they danced, for we sang the *Nunc Dimittis* again and again, the last amen running into the first note as if they could not stop singing.

Servant Martha seemed content to let it run until the women were exhausted, then she broke the circle and placed her candle before the statue of the Virgin. We each followed her and one by one we added our candles. The light swelled around the Virgin until she floated on a carpet of yellow flame.

Blessed art thou that through thy pure body, redemption came into the world and lifted the curse of Eve from man.

The beguines did not take their eyes off Servant Martha as she said Mass.

We have received your mercy, O God, in the midst of your temple.

She held the Host in both hands. Her hands trembled, but her voice rang out strong and firm as a cardinal's.

Domine, non sum dignus.

The hands of a woman lifted the chalice, His holy blood. I

expected the chalice to shatter in her hand, as it had in the hands of St Benedict when the wine was poisoned. Was I the only one who saw the blasphemy of what she did? But they were all caught up in a rapture I couldn't share. I was a beggar spying on a feast, smelling the food but not tasting it, hearing the music but not dancing. Even Pega, solid, sensible Pega, was as witched by Servant Martha as the rest. She was actually smiling at Osmanna. The two of them were as excited as children unwrapping gifts. None of the women seemed to understand what Servant Martha had done. Not only had she cut us off from the Holy Church and from the sacraments, but now she was putting our very lives and souls in peril.

December – St Diuma's Day

Seventh-century Irish Bishop who was famed for converting the pagan Mercians in England to Christianity, but after the Bishop's death it was widely claimed that the pious Diuma or Diona was in fact a woman.

Father Ulfrid

'But, Commissarius,' I protested, 'Bishop Salmon received his tithes in full. I delivered everything you asked.'

'Indeed you did and in coin too. I am intrigued to know how you managed it.'

The Commissarius sat straight and rigid in a chair drawn up close to my cottage hearth. His face betrayed nothing of his thoughts. His two hands were pressed together at the fingertips, his fingers rhythmically flexing and unflexing. I couldn't tear my gaze from those undulating fingers; it was like watching the throat of some serpent pulsate as it swallowed its prey.

'I ... I did as you advised, Commissarius, I threatened the villagers ... with excommunication.' My throat tightened as I spoke, as if those long thin fingers were squeezing it.

'Good, good,' he said thoughtfully. 'So they found the money after all, did they? I must confess I was surprised, especially when I learned the cattle murrain had reached these parts. I thought you might have a little more trouble persuading them. No?'

He paused, watching me closely. I searched his face, trying to see if he believed me. I could find no clue. Was this another of his games? Was he going to string this out, then without warning demand to see the chest where the church silver should have been? The man to whom I had given the silver in surety had sworn no one would hear of it; his reputation depended on as much, he said. But the Church had spies everywhere.

The Commissarius smiled his grim executioner's smile. 'I am impressed, Father Ulfrid. It appears your parishioners are wealthier than they look.' He leaned forward, grasping the arms of the chair. 'Good, good, that will make it all the easier for you to collect the Christmas tax.'

'But, Commissarius, there is no Christmas tax on the common people. The knights and landowners are obliged to make certain gifts to the Church, but the ordinary people bring whatever offering they can on Epiphany.'

'Quite so, quite so. I see you have been reading your predecessors' records as I advised. Never fear, Bishop Salmon will ensure that the landowners fulfil their Christmas obligations in full. But this year His Excellency the Bishop feels that the ordinary people might be encouraged to bring a little more than they have been accustomed to do in former times. The Church has suffered greatly these past few months. The harvest has been poor on its lands and it too suffered the loss of a great many beasts in the murrain. Bishop Salmon is anxious that the Church may not be able to fulfil its role of bringing salvation and charity to those in need. I wish to assure His Excellency that the good Christian people of this parish will be anxious to help in any way they can to further the great work of the Church.'

My anger boiled over. 'I thought you said, Commissarius, that the failing harvests were a judgment on the sin of the people; if that is so, surely the good Bishop's lands should have been spared, or is God incapable of distinguishing saint from sinner?'

I saw his expression harden and knew I'd made a very stupid mistake. The Commissarius was not a man to stomach his words being thrown back at him.

'His Grace the Bishop is above reproach, but sadly the same cannot be said for those who work in his employ. As you above all people must be painfully aware, Father Ulfrid, many of those who serve the Church are steeped in sin and iniquity. And it is the sins of the priests and other so-called servants of the Church that heaven cries out against.'

He rose and, pulling on his cloak, crossed to the door. 'But rest assured, Father Ulfrid, I will not leave you to carry this heavy burden all alone. It is my role to support parish priests in their great labours. I myself shall attend Mass on Christmas Day in St Michael's, in order that I may preach to the people of Ulewic and remind them of their obligations for Epiphany. I trust I will be addressing a full congregation. I should be most displeased to find I'd had a long, cold ride for nothing.'

He closed my cottage door quietly behind him. He was not a man to slam doors; he did not need to. After a few moments I heard the hoofbeats of his horse clatter away into the distance. But I sat, unable to move from my chair, staring in disbelief at the closed door. A dank chill enveloped my room, as if the Commissarius had brought the stench of the Bishop's prison with him.

I was lost. There was no way out of this. Not only would the Commissarius find the church empty of congregation, but he would see the moment he entered St Michael's on Christmas morning that the silver was gone. I could not possibly raise the money to redeem it in just two weeks. There was nothing ... nothing I could do.

Stealing the church silver was a hanging offence. Other priests could commit cold-blooded murder and still escape death by claiming Benefit of Clergy, but that mercy was up to the Bishop to grant and the Commissarius would take pains to ensure it was not granted to me. And they wouldn't just hang me. The Commissarius would regard slow strangulation on the end of a rope as too merciful a death. He'd make quite sure I suffered for Hilary first.

I found myself staring up at the beam above my head, picturing myself swinging there. A sharp snap of the neck and it would all be over. Not in the cottage, the rafters were too low, but the beams in the church were higher. A man could jump from those if he could get up there, or he might hang himself from the roodscreen. The Commissarius would see the justice in that – a gift for the Church on Christmas morning, the life of a priest. One less sinner in the Church. The Commissarius would think that a fitting tithe.

I yelped as my chair was kicked from behind, tipping it forward. I grabbed at the heavy table and just managed to stop myself crashing on to the floor. I spun round. Phillip was standing behind me, roaring with laughter. I hadn't even heard him come in.

'Caught you napping, did I, Father? Not that I blame you. I saw the Bishop's little ferret riding off. He'd talk anyone into a stupor.' He swung himself down into the chair vacated by the Commissarius. 'I had to listen to that bastard once myself, nearly begged the servants to bludgeon me with a mace and put me out of my misery.' He prodded my leg with the toe of his boot. 'Come on, rouse yourself, man. Is this the way you greet your guests? I want wine, and don't tell me you haven't got any.'

I stumbled across to fetch the flagon and two goblets. My hands were shaking so much as I poured that a puddle of wine spilled on to the table and dripped on to the floor. I didn't care. I couldn't even be bothered to wipe it up. I handed him a goblet and I gulped down my own before he'd even taken a mouthful. I poured myself a second full measure and took a deep draught from it.

Phillip raised his eyebrows. 'Gave your arse a roasting, did he? Now, what have you done to upset the Bishop this time, I wonder?'

I gulped another mouthful of wine. 'If you must know, he came to tell me that he would be addressing my congregation on Christmas morning. It seems the Bishop's coffers are light this year, so the Commissarius intends to encourage them to give generously this Epiphany. And you won't escape either. Apparently Bishop Salmon is going to exact the full Christmas tax from the landowners too, so you might want to warn your uncle.'

Phillip gave a snort of laughter. 'The Bishop can demand his dues from the Manor till he's dancing with the demons in purgatory, but my uncle will find a way of getting out of it, he always does.'

He leaned back in the chair, propping his feet, expensively clad in their new red cordwain boots, up against the wall. Phillip always sprawled in a chair, or stood legs apart, arms akimbo, as if he was determined to fill the world with his great body.

'So the ferret is to give the Christmas sermon, is he, Father? That at least will make two of you in church. You must be getting lonely standing up there with no one to say Mass for except the spiders.'

'After the abomination the Owl Masters performed on All Hallows' Eve, the villagers will come flocking back to the church. You took one of their own children from the grave. Do you think they will forgive you for that? Do you honestly imagine they will continue to pay you for protection after what you have unleashed on them? They will soon realize that only the Church can save them from that demon.'

Phillip laughed. 'The villagers saw you running away, screaming like a virgin maid at the first sight of the demon. They're hardly going to trust you to defend them from the Owlman.'

I felt my face burning and turned away to pour myself more wine.

'And your congregation isn't the only thing that's gone missing from the church, is it, Father?'

I started so violently that the wine spilled over the table for the second time that evening. 'What ... do you mean, missing? Nothing is missing.'

'I think you'll find there is, Father.' He reached into the leather pouch that hung about his waist and pulled out a large iron key, which he dangled idly between his fingers.

I stared at it, and my hand flew to the bunch of keys at my belt. An identical key hung there.

'Where did you get that?' I demanded.

'You didn't think you were the only one with a key to the church chest, did you, Father? As my uncle's steward I have keys for everything in the Manor and the village, including St Michael's. And when I heard you had delivered the tithes in full to the Bishop, I must confess I was curious. We've had a few problems getting the Manor dues from the villagers ourselves after the murrain and I had thought our methods of persuasion were – how shall I put it? – a little more robust than yours. So I thought to myself, where might the good Father find the money to pay off the Bishop, if he couldn't raise it from the villagers?

'My duty is to keep an eye on things for my uncle, see that nothing goes astray. My uncle doesn't like his property wandering from the village. Being a godly man, he naturally tries to follow the example of the Good Shepherd, and seek out that which is lost. So when I found the church chest was somewhat denuded, I made a few discreet enquiries. I think you know what I discovered, don't you, Father?'

I sank into the chair and covered my face with my hands. There was no longer any point in denying it. I raised my head. Phillip was studying me with an amused expression on his face, as he might have watched the misery of a baited bear.

'When are you going to tell the Bishop the church silver is missing?' I asked him bitterly. 'If you'd got here a minute or two sooner you could have told the Commissarius tonight and saved yourself the ride to Norwich.'

'You are even more of a fool than I took you for, Father. Why should I tell the Bishop anything? You spoke the truth when you said nothing was missing.'

My head was swimming from the wine. I couldn't make sense of what he was saying. 'But I thought you said the chest...'

'I said the chest *was* empty, and now miraculously it is full again.'

My shock and bewilderment must have been obvious, for Phillip chuckled.

'Your money-lender friend was persuaded to return the items you gave him to me. The jewelled chalice and all the other items are now safely back in the church chest.' He held up his hand in mock protest. 'Oh, no, Father, don't thank me.'

I stared at him. 'But why would you ...?'

'If you think it was to save your miserable hide, Father, you should know by now I am not that generous. I would have enjoyed seeing you suffer at the little ferret's hands. I regret

I had to deny myself that pleasure. Something tells me our friend the Commissarius could be most creative in the punishments he devised, and he really doesn't like you at all, does he, Father?

'No, I'm afraid I did not recover the church's treasure to spare you. You see, the items in that chest were given to the church by my ancestors. They were brought back from the crusades or made as thank offerings for births and marriages, even, I wager, as penance for the many sins they much enjoyed. So I have a certain ... attachment to them.' He shrugged. 'You might call it a filial duty to the memory of my forebears to guard them. But if the Bishop was to learn how close these valuables came to being lost, he might think they were not safe where they are and be tempted to have them removed to his own palace where he could keep a closer eye on them, especially with his own coffers being somewhat empty at this time. And we don't want to put temptation in the good Bishop's way, do we? Better not to tell him, I think.'

I felt as if I had been pressed under heavy stones and just when all the breath was crushed out of me someone had lifted the weight from my chest. My head was spinning, but whether from abject relief or the effects of the wine, I could not tell. The danger was over, and it had been so easy, so simple.

Phillip waved his empty goblet at me. 'And try to pour the wine in the cup this time.'

The flagon was empty. I went to the cupboard for another. It was the last one I had. I'd been keeping it for the Mass, for I had no money to buy more, but I no longer cared. All I could think about was that I had got the silver back and the Commissarius would never find out what I'd done. I filled Phillip's goblet to the brim.

He took a long draught before setting the goblet down. 'I regret that I will have to ask you for your key to the chest, Father. It would not do to have you led into sin again.' He held out his hand.

'But you can't!' I protested. 'The chest is my responsibility.'

How long would the silver remain in the chest, once Phillip had both keys?

Phillip frowned. 'Now, Father, if you please.'

I knew I was in no position to refuse.

He tucked my key away in his leather pouch, patting the bag with some satisfaction. 'Now, there is just the small matter of the money you borrowed from the money-lender plus his interest, money you now owe to me. To which sum, of course, I will be adding a trifling amount for my trouble and expenses in tracking the man down. But I'm feeling generous, so shall we say payment in full by the Twelfth Night of Christmas?'

I felt as if he'd punched me in the stomach. I couldn't breathe. How could I possibly have thought it was over?

Phillip swung his legs down from the wall and leaned forward in the chair, his eyes suddenly narrow and hard. 'The question is, Father, with an empty church where are you going to get the money to pay me?'

I swallowed hard. 'I ... there ... will soon be a relic in the church. It is presently in the house of women, but ... but I have excommunicated them and warned them they will remain in peril of their souls until they deliver the relic to the church and make public penance for their sins. They cannot hold out for much longer. Once they realize they will be denied the sacraments at Christmas, they will surrender the relic to me. They will have no choice. And when they do, the villagers will return to the church, knowing that it will protect them. And,' I added desperately, 'once word spreads, pilgrims will crowd to the church, which will mean not only money for the church, but for the Manor too. They'll need food, ale, places to sleep, new shoes, candles, all manner of things. A man with your nose for opportunity could make a fortune.'

'You are going to have the pilgrims flocking in by Twelfth Night, are you?' Phillip snorted. 'You haven't even laid your hands on the relic yet. From what I hear, your edict of excommunication is having as little effect on the house of women as it is on the rest of Ulewic. The villagers are still creeping to the women's gate for charity and they are still taking their sick there. The women are laughing at you, Father. You have fired your last arrow and still your enemy is advancing. What have you got left to fight with?'

He leaned back again in the chair. 'Of course, if that bitch who leads the women met with an unfortunate accident, you'd have no trouble getting the others to hand over the relic.' He took a long swig of wine. 'It seems we are on the same side after all, Father. You want the relic and the Owl Masters want those foreign shrews gone. And if you were to help us, Father, I might be persuaded to wait for my money. I'm sure we could work out regular monthly payment from what monies and gifts the relic brings to St Michael's.'

'Me help the Owl Masters? Do you think I have forgotten that you defiled my church and desecrated the grave of a Christian child laid to rest in holy ground? Do you think I would ask you for help after what you did?'

'What the Aodh did, Father. I've told you before, I am but his trusted servant.'

'Oliver's poor mother is beside herself with grief. You might at least have the decency to return what is left of the child to her, so that she can bury him again.'

Phillip picked at a fleck of mud on his sleeve. 'The whore brought it on herself. The Owl Masters warned her to pay up and she defied them. It has been a salutary lesson for the rest of the villagers. And it should be a lesson to you too, Father. I suggest you seriously consider what the Aodh might order the Owl Masters to do to you, when he learns that you are refusing to pay your debts.'

'Do you think I can be threatened as easily as your ignorant villagers?' I slammed my fist against the table. 'Your uncle may be able to order the murder of a serf without anyone outside the village asking questions, but I am a priest. Harm me and the Church will see you hanged and burning in the fires of hell. I may not like the Commissarius spying on me, but as long as he is watching me, you and your Owl Masters can do nothing. As for repaying you by Twelfth Night, you said yourself you daren't tell the Bishop about the silver, so why should I give you any money at all, when there is nothing you can do about it if I don't?'

I felt exhilarated, as if I had broken out of a dungeon. I hadn't released the truth of what I'd said until it burst out of me in fury. Phillip and his uncle were powerless to act against me over the money. They could do nothing to me at all.

Phillip sat quite still for a few moments, his face impassive. Then he rose and walked towards the door. I felt a surge of pleasure. He knew he was beaten. But suddenly he spun round. Too late, I glimpsed the flash of metal. The blow was so savage I was knocked to the floor. White-hot sparks of pain exploded in my skull. Struggling to my feet, I clutched at my ear and cheek as hot blood poured from the gash. An iron spike, shaped like the talon of a great bird, lay in Phillip's hand. He bounced the sharp blade casually as if debating whether to slash again.

'How dare you strike a servant of God?' I yelled in both fear and outrage. 'When the Commissarius learns –'

'When the Commissarius learns that his priest has been meeting a filthy little sodomite here in Ulewic, I think he'll pay me four times what you owe. And as for the exquisite pain the Commissarius will take pleasure in devising for you … I wonder if he'll do to you what Roger Mortimer did to that pervert, King Edward; red-hot poker up the arse, wasn't it? Come now, did you honestly think I wouldn't find out about … what's your whore-boy's name … Hilary?'

My legs gave way and I sank on to my knees, gagging in an effort not to vomit in front of him. I was shaking violently. Blood oozed between my fingers and dripped on to the rushes. The room was spinning and not just from the pain. I was falling down and down into the blackest, deepest pit.

Phillip balled up my white amice and threw it at me. 'Stop snivelling. Get up!'

I clambered shakily to my feet and staggered into a chair, pressing the cloth to the burning gash.

'Now, are you quite sure you don't want to help us, Father?'

I didn't need to look at his face to see the triumph that was written there. I knew this had gone way beyond mere money. 'What . . . what do you want?'

D'Acaster's nephew settled himself comfortably in the chair again and smiled. 'You know, Father, I find your words have touched my conscience, after all. We should return the body of that little boy to his poor grieving mother. First, though, just to show she has learned her lesson, Aldith can perform a little task for us. But we'll need you to put the matter to her, Father. For some strange reason, she doesn't trust us. You are her priest; you can persuade her to do what is required.'

'And what . . . is required?'

'We want her to deliver a message, that's all. Then she will be reunited with her son.' Phillip picked up a poker and stabbed at the dying embers in the hearth, sending a shower of sparks flying upwards.

'Now, Father. This is what you will say to Aldith . . .'

December – St Thomas' Eve

This night at sunset, the Winter Solstice begins. It is a night for divination, when maids stick pins in onions to summon their future lovers.

'Good St Thomas, do me right.
Send me my true love tonight.'

Servant Martha

We had held our Mass in our chapel at midnight. Each festival we celebrated was new and different, for in the past we'd always attended St Michael's church on feast days. I tried to capture the joy of it for the women, but I knew some of them missed the spectacle and colour of the parish church, seeing the village bright with merriment and music, the young people dancing and everyone filling their bellies after the fast, though this year there was precious little feasting or joy in the village.

In the morning we conducted a service in the infirmary for the patients and the poor from the village. We did not say Mass, of course. Many of the village women came to the service, poor thin creatures with dead eyes, and a beaten-down look about them. I was pleased they came to us. It renewed my resolve and purpose. We were not mistaken in our call to come to this land.

But the presence of some villagers did not gladden me. They knelt throughout the service, mouthing their prayers with great exaggeration while their thoughts were fixed only on the meat pies and clothes they knew we'd distribute when the service was over. Their faces lit up, not at the word of God, but at the smell of a goose pudding.

As I stepped out of the infirmary, I had to fight to stop the door being snatched from my hand by the wind. I pulled my cloak tightly about me. Ralph was limping across the courtyard on his crutch, dragging a little trolley behind him, the rope tied round his waist. Shepherd Martha had made it for him, so that he could take the crippled child for her walk. Now they seemed forever chained together as if one sentence had been pronounced upon them both.

'Blessings of St Thomas upon you, Ralph, and upon you,

child.' I bent down and laid my hand on her head. She jerked back. 'How does she fare, Ralph? She looks better today, some colour in her cheeks.'

Ralph looked down at her as tenderly as any doting father. 'Ella's well, Servant Martha. I was afeared I'd lose her these past weeks, for she wheezed so that her lips turned blue and she could scarcely snatch a breath, but Healing Martha cured her.'

'God cured her, Ralph.' I corrected him. 'Healing Martha is but His humble instrument.'

There was a discreet cough behind me. 'God's humble instrument hesitates to interrupt you, Servant Martha, but there is a soul who would speak to you.'

Healing Martha nodded towards a woman standing close to the wall sheltering from the bitter wind. Kitchen Martha was trying to talk to her, but the woman was ignoring her and watching me. She looked as if she wanted to approach me, but was afraid. No doubt she feared the leprosy. Ralph saw the look on her face too and limped away, dragging the trolley behind him.

I beckoned the woman forward, but she remained pressed against the wall. It was hard to tell her age. Her face was haggard with hunger, but her eyes, sunken deep into dark hollows, had an unnatural brightness about them such as you see in those on the edge of madness. I moved closer, but before I could prevent her, the woman fell on her knees in the dirt, clasping my cloak with her webbed fingers, talking and weeping with such agitation that I couldn't make out a word she said. I pulled her up from the ground and gave her a little shake to bring her to her senses.

'Calm yourself, sister. What do you want of us? Is someone sick?'

She shook her head vigorously and fell to sobbing harder than ever.

'What ails you? I cannot help you if you don't tell me what you want.' I was beginning to wonder if the woman was a simpleton; the village abounded in them.

Just when I was about to give up on her, finally she muttered, 'My baby.'

'You have a little son or daughter?'

'Not any more. It's dead. It didn't live but a week or two. And my husband says we must bury it under the midden, before Father Ulfrid finds out. He'll not pay the soul-scot.'

I laid a consoling hand on the woman's shoulder. 'I'm sorry for your loss, sister. God in His mercy grant you strength to bear His will. Do I understand aright? You are seeking soul-scot to bury your baby?'

The woman shook her head and clutched at me again. 'No, you must bury it here, else the Owlman'll eat its soul. You can keep it safe.'

'The baby will be safe in the churchyard. No harm can come to a Christian child there and we'll find the soul-scot for you to give to Father Ulfrid, though you had best not tell him that the money came from us.'

'I don't dare take it to the priest. It wasn't baptized. My husband said he wouldn't name it afore the priest. Said the brat was none of his getting.' The woman was staring around wildly, looking at anything except me. She pulled at her skirts as if she was trying to tear something away.

Healing Martha put an arm around her. 'And is that true? Was the baby not your husband's child?'

The woman shook her head miserably, 'Phillip D'Acaster came calling. We were behind with the Manor tithes ... I couldn't refuse him. When the baby was born it had no ... web ... on its hands. My husband said that proved the bairn was not his.'

I began to understand. The woman had good reason to weep. If her husband would not acknowledge the child before a priest, then she'd be brought to trial for adultery. From the little I knew of him, Phillip would deny his part in it and no one would dare to stand against him. But this poor woman couldn't deny the evidence of her sin. She'd be lucky to escape from the court with a public whipping and a heavy fine that would drive the family into even greater poverty than that which had forced her to those desperate measures. And I'd little doubt that once the court had finished with the woman, her husband would extract his own retribution from her for exposing him to the whole village as a cuckold. A chilling thought seized me.

'Sister, tell me truthfully as you will answer to God on Judgment Day, did the child die either by your hand or that of your husband?'

The woman looked horrified and fell on her knees again, clutching at my skirts. 'No, I swear it by all things holy, the bairn sickened and I could do naught to save it. It'd not suckle, though I nursed it day and night, it just kept wailing. I was up night after night with it, for my man couldn't abide to hear it cry. When everyone had gone to the fields I lay down on the bed for I was that tired with rocking it all night, I couldn't keep my eyes open. When I woke it lay cold aside me. It's witchery, that's what it is.'

Healing Martha patted her briskly on the shoulder. 'Now, sister, let's have no talk of that.' She shook her head at me. 'There's no need to look for evil in this, Servant Martha. This poor woman is so malnourished that I doubt any infant born to her could have thrived, especially if she kept the child hidden in the cold and damp of those village hovels.'

I couldn't let her bury an innocent child beneath a dung heap, but neither could I cast her into the merciless hands of the Church. And besides, even if the Church did grant burial, an unbaptized infant would be laid on the north side of the graveyard among the mad and the unshriven. No fitting place for a babe to wake on Judgment Day.

'We'll give the child a Christian burial close by our chapel. No demon will dare come nigh him there. Now, where is the baby?'

'Hidden in a chest at home,' the woman muttered, still refusing to meet my eyes.

'Then fetch him here.'

She shook her head. 'I daren't bring him in daylight. All the men will be in the forest this night, dancing the sun round the fires for the winter solstice. Women'll keep safe behind their doors. There'll be none to see me.' She pointed to the copse in the opposite direction to the forest. 'In there's a great oak that's tumbled over, but still grows where it lies. I'll bring it there . . . tonight.'

Healing Martha frowned. 'But aren't you afraid to venture out for fear of the Owlman? I heard that no villager sets foot out of doors after dark now, unless they are in a group and well armed.'

The woman's eyes flashed wide and she moaned, pressing her hands tightly across her mouth as if she was afraid to speak, but finally she shook her head.

She grasped my sleeve. 'You will come tonight,' she pleaded urgently. 'You'll come yourself. It must be you . . . if you don't . . . swear you'll come.'

'You have my word that I will come in person,' I told her. 'Return home now and I will meet you tonight at the tree you describe at the Matins hour. But you haven't told me your name, mistress.'

The woman hesitated. 'Aldith,' she whispered, then turned and hurried away.

As we walked away from the gate, Healing Martha fell into step with me. 'That wind cuts right through my old bones. I never thought I'd say it but I'd welcome a good frost or even some snow if only it would calm this nagging wind.'

Healing Martha was very dear to me, but she did have some decidedly infuriating habits, not the least of them making blithe and inconsequential remarks when she knew I was waiting to hear what was clearly occupying her mind. It was always a sign that she disapproved of a decision I had taken.

'Our Lord commands us to bury the dead.' I was annoyed. I shouldn't have to justify myself to her of all people. 'We cannot allow a body of an innocent baby to be thrown on a dung-heap. We can't force open the gates of heaven to receive the soul of an unbaptized child, but we can at least preserve it from the evil one until the Day of Judgment.'

Healing Martha lifted her head and watched a flock of seagulls being tossed and buffeted by the wind. 'Gulls flying inland. It means there's a storm brewing out at sea.'

'I'm not interested in the wretched gulls. Just tell me why we should not bury this child.'

Healing Martha stopped and looked up at me. 'Why was the woman so insistent that you must meet her, when any beguine might collect the child? And suppose her husband asks what she's done with the corpse or she whispers the matter to a friend? It could be all round the village in hours. Have you thought what it would mean if this reaches the ears of Father Ulfrid? We are already excommunicated. If he learns of this he will be furious. There is no knowing what he might do.'

I opened my mouth to answer, but Healing Martha held up her hand. 'Yes, I know what you're going to say, we have no choice. Our duty is to obey God, even if it means disobeying the Church. Forgive me, old friend, but aching bones and this irritating wind sometimes make us ancient ones long for a day or two of peace.' She sighed. 'There are times when I wish the spiritual life was not quite such an adventurous one.'

'But you agree we must bury the baby here.'

Healing Martha smiled wearily. 'I've known you long enough to know that nothing I or anyone else said would stop you doing what you were convinced was right. You are as stubborn as old St Thomas himself.'

'Then . . . will you go with me tonight?'

She chuckled. 'You know full well I wouldn't let you go alone, even if you were going to lay siege to the gates of hell itself.' She patted my arm. 'Someone has to carry the bandages.'

Servant Martha

It was an evil night to be abroad. We pulled our cloaks low over our faces and led our horses quietly out through the gate. I informed Gate Martha that we were going to perform an act of charity.

'In the dark, in this wild weather?' she asked, shaking her head in disbelief.

'Our Lord said, "When you give alms let not your left hand know what your right hand does."'

Gate Martha sniffed, clearly affronted that I would not tell her more.

I helped Healing Martha to mount her palfry side-saddle. I could tell from the way she held herself and the groan that escaped her that her back was paining her even more than usual. There had been a steady procession of village women coming to the infirmary all day to get healing for themselves or their families. They brought children with sores that would not heal or bellies grossly distended with worms from grubbing in the dirt for scraps of food. They came for cordials and potions for elderly parents who were wheezing and coughing. Healing Martha had tended each one and she was exhausted. But I knew she would insist on accompanying me even if I expressly forbade her. Healing Martha had the gall to call me stubborn, but I'd never met such an obstinate woman as her.

The wind tore at our clothes and sent the horses skipping sideways as they tried to turn their faces from the blown dust and grit. Above us the trees creaked and mewled, their branches tossed about like twigs. Clouds, thick as winter fleeces, hid the moon, and our small lantern scarcely penetrated the darkness for more than a hand's space before us.

Fearful that we were being watched, I peered this way and

that into the blackness, but the bushes were swaying and rustling so violently that even if someone was creeping through them, it would have been impossible to distinguish the noise from the sound of the wind. I'd be thankful when we'd collected the baby's body and were safely on our way back. The wooded track offered too many hiding places for cutpurses and outlaws on such a dark night. I held the lantern low and half muffled with my cloak in case its moving light was seen.

We tethered the horses under the cover of the trees, out of sight of the track. Healing Martha called out a soft warning to Aldith of our approach, but there was no sign of the woman. She was probably hiding by the fallen tree, afraid to show herself until she was sure it was us.

'This way, I think.' Healing Martha tugged at my sleeve.

We threaded our way through the trees, trying to avoid being whipped in the face by low branches. I raised the lantern, trying to see if the fallen tree was in sight, and sprawled headlong over a tree root.

Healing Martha rushed to help me up. 'Have you hurt yourself?'

'Nothing broken.'

I'd skinned the palm of my hand. I pressed it tightly under my armpit to stop it stinging. Why on earth had I agreed to meet Aldith here? An open field would have been cover enough in the darkness.

Healing Martha clutched at my arm and pointed to a great fallen oak, half its roots still clinging to the soil, the rest clawing upwards at the sky. But Aldith was nowhere to be seen. Healing Martha called out softly while I swept the lantern around, trying to peer deeper into the copse. Tree trunks loomed towards us, pale in the guttering flame. Swaying branches sent shadows scurrying into darkness, but none was human enough to be the woman.

'Where is she?' I asked.

'Patience, Servant Martha, she'll come soon. She'll be as anxious as us to be abed before the dancing ends.'

The ground was dry enough to sit on and at least we had the solid wood of the tree trunk to lean against and provide some shelter from this wind. I leaned back and closed my eyes, listening to the swish and creak of the branches above us. The pungent breath of wild onion curled about our feet. There was nothing to do but wait. Above the moaning of the wind, a deep rumble of thunder echoed a long way off. The trees shivered.

'She'd better come soon, Healing Martha. There's a storm gathering and it will drive the dancers from the forest as soon as it breaks. I've no wish to be abroad with our burden then.'

'I've no wish to be abroad in a storm at all, old friend. My ancient bones do not take kindly to a wetting and I've a hankering to be warming them at my own fireside before this night is much older.' She shuffled, trying to ease herself into a more comfortable position, wincing in pain, though she tried to muffle the cry.

I was angry with myself for dragging her out on a night like this. At her age Healing Martha could easily take a chill, and with an infirmary full of patients, how would we manage if she had to take to her bed for a week?

'I should have brought Osmanna with me, instead of subjecting you to this,' I said. 'She's young and fit and I trust her to keep her counsel. But for some reason she always seems to find some excuse not to go into the woods, whether it's to gather tinder or fetch herbs. I overheard Beatrice complaining the other day that Osmanna doesn't want to be seen by the villagers performing such menial tasks.'

'Beatrice has resented the child ever since . . .' Healing Martha hesitated. 'Let us just say Beatrice has her own sorrows which make it hard for her to understand Osmanna. But you and I both know that Osmanna is not proud. She will willingly clean up the foulest mess in the infirmary and doesn't care who sees her do it. It's fear, not pride, that keeps her out of the forest.'

'Of what though?' I asked impatiently. 'She made excuses not to go into the forest even before rumours of the Owlman began. Perhaps she heard too many stories in her childhood.'

In the darkness I could hear Healing Martha chuckling. 'Pega might think that boggarts and goblins lurk beneath every sod and bush, but somehow I can't believe that of our sceptical Osmanna.'

'Sceptical! Believe me, Healing Martha, she gives a new definition to the word. She questions everything and accepts nothing without "whys". She's impossible to school, for she'll not be led in any direction unless she's already made up her own mind to go there. Now she is refusing to take the . . .' I lowered my voice to a whisper, 'refusing to come forward at Mass. She says something she has read has caused her to question if the sacraments are really necessary at all. Can you believe that a child would question what lies at the very heart of our faith?'

'But some might say that very fault in a pupil is the virtue in a leader, don't you think, old friend? I seem to remember a young beguine in Flanders who was accused of much the same fault, always questioning, always testing everything for herself. I hear that beguine is now the Servant Martha in England and is still asking questions.'

It was too dark to see Healing Martha's face, but I could hear the teasing in her voice. 'If you are referring to me, I can assure you that Osmanna and I are not remotely alike. I learned meekness and obedience at a very young age, and I learned when to speak and when to be silent in the presence of those who are older and more experienced. Two lessons Osmanna has yet to master.'

A white flash suddenly ripped the sky, penetrating even the dense thatch of branches. Silence was followed by a long low rumble of thunder. The storm was still a way off, but it was drawing closer.

'We can't wait any longer, Healing Martha. I fear Aldith isn't coming. It may be that a neighbour came to sit with her or her husband didn't go to the forest after all. Let's leave before the storm breaks.'

Healing Martha rocked sideways, putting her hand out to lever herself up. She gave a half-stifled scream.

'What's wrong, Healing Martha? Is it your back?'

Healing Martha clambered awkwardly to her feet and, snatching the lantern from my hand, she directed its light towards the base of the tree trunk. In the flickering yellow flame of the lantern, I glimpsed something pale, half-hidden by a clump of dead cow parsley. It was a human hand. It was limp and unmoving. Healing Martha lifted up the lantern and peered around the base of the fallen tree. There, in the hollow beneath the ripped-up roots, lay a woman's body. Her arms were flung above her head, her legs twisted beneath her. Her belly was ripped open. The dark bloody mess of her guts had been dragged out on to the fallen leaves and torn to pieces as if some great animal or bird of prey had been feasting on her.

Healing Martha clapped her hand to her mouth in horror. I fell to my knees and vomited. I heaved and heaved until my stomach was empty, but even then I was still retching. I felt Healing Martha's hand gripping my shoulder hard, though whether it was to comfort me or steady herself I didn't know.

'Is it . . . is it Aldith?' I asked.

The light trembled as Healing Martha turned the lantern on the woman's face. Her eyes were closed and her mouth was agape as if she had died in the very act of screaming. But despite the distortion of the face, it was unmistakably that of the poor woman who had that very morning clung to me, begging me to bury her child.

Another flash of lightning cracked the sky and in the instant of blinding whiteness the woman's eyes opened wide and stared at me. My scream was lost even to my own ears in the crack of thunder. The clouds burst and a torrent of rain beat down upon us. The wind grappled for my cloak as the branches of the trees clashed together above us.

Healing Martha grabbed me by the arm. 'We must get out of here. Take the lantern.'

The shadows around us fought and roared. I heard her, but I couldn't move, gripped by a nameless fear.

She lifted the lantern higher, shining it on to my face. 'Come,

Servant Martha, we must go, and quickly. Whatever did that to her may still be here.'

'But the baby ... we have to find it.' I stumbled around, groping amongst the dead vegetation, but I felt my arm gripped hard.

'Servant Martha, you must listen to me. We will come back and look in the morning, but now we must go.' Healing Martha thrust the lantern into my hand. She forced her arm into mine and tugged me forward. My legs staggered a few steps by themselves, as if they were no longer connected to my body. I slipped on the wet ground and my shoulder banged hard against a tree.

As if the pain had wakened me, I was seized by a frenzy to escape from the trees. Now I was pulling Healing Martha forward, holding her close against me. Someone was yelling, 'Hurry, Hurry,' but I didn't know if it was me or Healing Martha. I sensed something behind me; something was gathering out of the shadows, but I dared not turn round.

We were almost at the track. The horses reared as the lightning streaked down, jerking their reins and rolling their eyes. Rain was streaming down their flanks. It was a miracle they hadn't already broken loose and bolted. I tried to calm them, but they shied at each new crack of lightning. I heaved Healing Martha on to her horse, then I scrambled up on to my own beast and dug my heels into the trembling animal's sides.

The icy rain stung my eyes, blinding me, but I urged my horse forward, trusting that he could see the track where I could not. I knew it was reckless to force him to the canter, but I had to get back to the beguinage. Nothing else mattered except to be inside with the gate safely bolted. The force of the gale beat the trees down on either side of the path. They moaned and shrieked, writhing in a frenzy of wind. I couldn't see Healing Martha ahead of me on the track. I tried to call out, but my words were snatched away by the storm. I turned in the saddle. There was no sign of her on the track behind. She had to be ahead, already beyond the bend of the path. The horse skittered sideways, slithering in the mud.

A flash of lightning lit up the track. In that instant of dazzling light, giant trees seemed to lumber towards me as if loosed from their roots. My horse shied and twisted this way and that. Then the flash was gone and I could see nothing. For a moment I thought I had been struck blind, but it was the lantern that had been extinguished, not my sight. It lay somewhere in the streaming mud. Now, I'd not the merest glimmer of light to guide me. I didn't even know if I was riding in the right direction any more. A branch whipped across my face and I ducked low, kicking the flank of my reluctant horse, urging against all reason that the poor beast could find the track when I could not.

Another lightning flash and suddenly I saw something hovering above me. It was huge, bigger than a bull. It had the head of a bird of prey, with a black hooked beak, as long as a man's hand. Huge round eyes blazed unblinking out of the feathered face, the deep black pupils ringed with red flame. The creature was staring straight at me. But it wasn't a bird. It couldn't be a bird ... between its great wings, the broad chest was covered not with feathers, but bare wet skin that glistened bone-white.

The darkness closed back. I screamed, trying to cover my head with my arms. The wings were beating down, so that I couldn't breathe against the force of them. The great savage beak snapped inches from my face. The twin rings of red fire glowed out of the darkness, coming closer and closer.

With a desperate whinny my horse slipped sideways and I crashed to the ground. There was a searing pain in my right wrist. Clutching it against my chest, I staggered to my feet, sodden skirts slapping heavy as leather around my legs. The wind was shrieking like a mandrake torn from the earth. *Libera nos a malo.* I tried to run. *In Nomine ... In Nomine Patris et ...* But the thunder clapped around me, driving me back.

Lightning sizzled down in a blue vein. The witch-girl was

standing motionless in my path, strands of wet hair writhing around her head. On her shoulder, wings flapping wide, crouched a huge raven, croaking into the wind. Then it all was black again. I staggered against a tree and slid down its trunk, sinking on to my haunches, hugging my wrist and gasping against the pain. The rain dashed against my face. I couldn't gulp air, only water. I was drowning.

A raucous caw echoed inches from my ear. The witch-girl was standing over me. She held out a hand, thin as a devil's claw. I shrank, fearing her talons on my face. She stepped back as if to say she meant me no harm, and beckoned me to follow. Then she walked away, without looking to see if I followed or not. I clambered to my feet, suddenly terrified that she might disappear and leave me alone.

'Wait, please, wait.'

She didn't turn her head, but she stopped and waited until she sensed I was behind her and then walked on at the same rapid pace. The raven swayed on her shoulder. It watched me, as if it was her eyes. I trailed behind her as a small child follows its mother, struggling through the rain and the mud, my skirts and shoes dragging me down at every step. I could just make out the dark figure walking in front of me from the flash of her white wet skin in the rain. Only then did I realize that she was naked.

I held my hands over my head, half crouching as I stumbled forward, terrified that the monster might at any moment swoop on me from behind. I desperately wanted to run, but every grain of strength had been washed out of me. Then, just as I knew I could not take another step, the gate of the beguinage stood open in front of me. I had been staring at it without recognizing what it was. Gate Martha was peering out. She shouted and ran out. Several of the beguines followed close behind, lanterns in their hands as if they were embarking on a journey. Where were they going? What hour was it?

The women crowded round me.

'Heaven be praised you are safe. We feared the worst. We were about to search for you.'

I couldn't speak. My face was numb and my legs gave way. I staggered against them and felt arms wrap round my waist to steady me. I gasped as someone touched my arm.

'Bring her inside, she's exhausted, poor thing. We must get those wet clothes off her before she takes a chill. Is Healing Martha following you, Servant Martha? Where is she? Have you left her to shelter somewhere?'

I tried to drag my thoughts together. 'Is she not here?' The words emerged in a croaking voice that I didn't recognize.

There was a long silence. They all looked at one another, but no one spoke.

Then Kitchen Martha hugged me. 'Her palfry came home riderless, like yours. We thought you must be together. But don't worry, Servant Martha, we'll find her. She'll be right behind you on the road. You walk so fast, no one can match your pace.'

Pega nodded vigorously. 'I know every step of the track, even in the dark. Tell us where you parted company and we'll find her before you've had time to dry your hair at the fire. You get yourself into the warm and don't fret.'

✝

December – St Thomas' Day

'St Thomas grey, St Thomas grey,
The longest night and the shortest day.'

Beatrice

We searched for Healing Martha half the night until long after we were exhausted. We were soaked to the skin and aching all over from a hundred near falls in the treacherous mud. It was a wonder we didn't all die of cold or break our necks, and if we had done, it would have been Servant Martha's fault. I'll tell you this, if she'd been the one lost in the storm, I'd have gone straight to bed and left her out there to find her own way home. If she was fool enough to go out there at night, she'd only had herself to blame, but you couldn't leave a frail old woman out in that rain, could you? And we all loved Healing Martha.

The lightning passed over, but the rain continued to beat down in torrents, turning tracks to running streams and banks into lethal mantraps. I found myself sprawling in the mud so often I thought my boots had been greased, but soon my skin was so numb I didn't even feel the grazes and bumps.

We shouted to Healing Martha, but our voices were drowned out by the howling wind, and if there was a reply we wouldn't have heard it over the drumming of the rain. We clung grimly to one another in the darkness, afraid of vanishing like her, afraid of being snatched away. I cursed Servant Martha roundly under my breath for putting us in this danger, and I can tell you I wasn't the only one damning that woman to hell and back.

It was Pega who called a halt in the end, but no one offered more than a token protest. Healing Martha was not on the track leading to the beguinage, but that meant nothing. She could have been anywhere out there in the enormity of the storm, and in the dark we might easily have passed within feet of her and neither seen nor heard her, nor she us.

It was pointless continuing, we were just groping around in a fool's game of blind man's buff, but all the same we felt so guilty abandoning Healing Martha to the night. What if she was unconscious in a ditch that even now was filling with water? What if she was lying somewhere in agony from a broken leg, praying we'd come, or worse still, believing that we'd never come? Still clutching one another, we battled back through the blinding rain, telling ourselves that Healing Martha had probably taken shelter somewhere or that she might already be safely back in the beguinage. But none of us believed that.

I woke with a start as a log collapsed in the embers of the fire, sending a shower of red sparks spitting on to the hearth. The rush candles had burnt out and a thin sliver of morning light was already sliding in beneath the shutters of the refectory.

Osmanna crouched down to rake the refectory fire, adding fresh logs and banking down hot ash on top to make them burn slowly. Pega, already shod, tossed Catherine's cloak on her lap.

'Up off your arse, lass, and help me fetch a bier from the infirmary.' She nodded at Merchant Martha. 'We'll meet you at the gate.'

Kitchen Martha, struggling to bend down far enough to fasten her sodden shoes, froze half in and half out of one. 'St Andrew and all his angels defend us, Pega, you surely don't think –'

'You mustn't talk like that, Pega,' little Catherine said desperately. 'Healing Martha isn't dead. God will protect her.'

'Have I said she's dead?' Pega rounded on her. 'If Healing Martha was thrown from her horse, which she must have been since the beast came back without her, then like as not she's hurt her back, for it's none too sound at the best of times. If she could walk she'd be here by now, so it stands to reason she must be lying hurt somewhere. How would you have me carry her home, slung over my shoulder like a flitch of pork?'

Merchant Martha nodded. 'You heard her, Catherine. Make yourself useful. Don't stand there biting your nails.' She knelt down and pulled Kitchen Martha's shoe on for her. 'As for you, Kitchen Martha, we need you here tending the pots and pies.

Healing Martha will be in want of a good hot meal when she returns, as will we all.'

Kitchen Martha opened her mouth to protest, but Merchant Martha was having none of it. 'Have some sense, woman. If we all come back hungry and tired, we don't want to have to wait around for hours while you cook.'

For all her brusque manner, Merchant Martha was trying to be kind. Kitchen Martha had barely managed to reach home after the night's search. Such a girth as God had blessed her with was not made for walking. She was as anxious to help find Healing Martha as the rest of us, but none of us wanted to have to carry her home as well.

It was still raining hard. The courtyard was awash with puddles, bubbling like cauldrons under the falling drops. A waterfall cascaded from the roof. We made a dash through it, but icy water splashed up and rain poured down and we were wet beyond caring even before we were halfway down the track. Only Leon, Shepherd Martha's great shaggy hound, seemed indifferent to the rain. He was bounding ahead, stopping every now and then to sniff at a bush or patch of the track.

The deep cart ruts and holes in the middle of the track were filled with water, so we tried to pick our way along the edges, brushing against the dripping bushes, but in places the path was awash from ditch to ditch and we had no choice but to hitch up our skirts and wade through the water. Merchant Martha grabbed my arm to keep herself from slipping and delivered a stream of oaths that would have made a fishmonger blush.

The river was brown and dangerously swollen. A rising torrent of mud and branches hurtled between the banks. Trees and grass on the edge were already standing in water. A dead swan hung by the neck in the fingers of a half-submerged alder. The rain blanked out the hills. The river would continue to rise long after the rain stopped and there was not so much as a crack in the clouds to give promise of that.

Pega stared at the river in dismay. 'The banks'll not hold when the tide in the creek turns and starts pushing this lot back upstream. We'd best pray we find Healing Martha quickly, afore the whole track disappears underwater. Spread out,' she called. 'Search well on each side of the path. We know she set out this way, so if the horse threw her she'll likely be lying just off it.'

The pasture beyond the fringe of scrub and trees glistened green and horribly empty. The massive horned skull of an ox rocked disconsolately on a pole in the middle of the field, a grim warning not to let beasts stray near this place for fear of the murrain. A few tattered shreds of withered flesh and hair still clung to it, but the ravens had picked the rest clean.

We reached the copse and scuttled in among the trees, not that their branches offered much protection against the rain. Rivulets of water ran down the banks and dripped from the trees. Armed with our staves, we poked among the bushes and brambles, calling out to Healing Martha. The old vegetation was so sodden, I could scarcely lift it to search beneath. I was so afraid of what we might find, but more frightened of finding nothing. Please God let her be alive.

The rest of us may have been searching frantically, but there was one person who certainly wasn't. As I glanced up, I saw Osmanna standing a little way off, just gazing into the deep of the trees, not even trying to look for Healing Martha. As usual, she had no intention of getting her hands dirty.

'Aren't you even going to bother to try to find her, Osmanna?'

She ignored me.

'Osmanna!'

But she didn't move. She was standing rigid, her fists clenched, as if she couldn't tear her gaze away from something. My heart began to thump. What was she staring at? Not a body, not that, please don't let it be that!

'Wait there, I'm coming.'

My skirts caught in the brambles. I tore the cloth loose and ran towards Osmanna. I couldn't see anything except the silvery trunks rising out of a mire of dark brown undergrowth. I turned to Osmanna, trying to see where she was looking. Her eyes were fixed wide open, her lips thin and dry. Her breath came in rapid, noisy gasps.

'Did you hear a cry, Osmanna?'

She didn't say anything. She just kept staring into the trees. I knew her little game. She was sulking because for once she wasn't the centre of attention. But if she thought I was going to fuss over her like the Marthas, she was sadly mistaken.

Suddenly she blurted out, 'That smell ... like onion. I've ... I've smelt it before. I ...'

Without warning she threw herself against me, burying her face in my shoulder, gripping me so hard it hurt.

I shoved her away. 'Of course you've smelt it before, you stupid girl. It's ramsons, devil's posies. It's everywhere here. You can't take a step without crushing the old leaves. We'll all stink of onion before the day is out. Why are you twittering about smells? You're not here to pick herbs.'

She was staring at the tangle of leaves around her feet, as if she'd never seen them before. 'Nothing, Beatrice. I don't know what ... nothing.'

'You don't even care about Healing Martha, do you? Why should that surprise me? Anyone who could murder her own ... just look at my kirtle. It's ripped in three places, thanks to you.'

She flushed crimson and began to walk away.

'That's right,' I yelled after her. 'Go off in a sulk and pretend to be lost now, so that we're forced to look for you. Well, I for one won't bother. You can stay out here until you starve for all I care.'

She did not turn round.

God in heaven, would this rain never stop? What on earth had possessed Servant Martha to drag Healing Martha out here in the middle of a storm? Both of them should have had more sense. Servant Martha had given no explanation when she returned. She looked a hundred years old in the lantern light, all drabbled and drawn. When we asked her questions, it was as if she didn't understand us. She walked through us like a ghost.

Pega said she thought Servant Martha had broken her arm. I caught a glimpse of it, and the wrist did seem bent at an unnatural angle, but she wouldn't allow anyone to look at it.

Somewhere deeper in the copse I heard Leon barking excitedly, followed by shouts and whistles. They'd found something. I barged through undergrowth in the direction of Leon's barks. Pega and Merchant Martha were crouched over what looked like a heap of old clothes. Shepherd Martha was pulling Leon aside, patting and praising him as his tail wagged frantically. But all I could see was a pair of worn, muddied shoes. The feet in the shoes were not moving. The other women stood a little way off, holding one another and staring.

'Is she . . .?' I blurted out as I reached them.

Merchant Martha glanced up. 'She's in a bad way. Catherine, Osmanna, fetch the bier. It's close by the track. Hurry, we must get her back, before she perishes from cold. She's lain in this rain all night. Move yourselves.'

Osmanna jerked into action and ran past me. Catherine followed. The others continued to stand and stare. What was wrong? Why didn't they try to help her? I moved closer to peer over Pega's shoulder and clapped my hand to my mouth to stop a scream escaping.

Healing Martha was filthy, her grey hair wet and matted with twigs and dirt. But it was not her appearance that horrified me, it was her face. It was flushed and contorted. Her left eye was open wide staring at us, but her lid was drooping down over her right eye, almost closing it. Her mouth was twisted down at the corner and a stream of vomit and saliva had run unchecked down her neck. It was not a human face but a grotesque, a mocking caricature of the face I knew. She made a gargling sound. Merchant Martha tried to lift up the poor woman's head and shoulders to help her swallow, but it made little difference. Her breath rasped like a dog's strangling on a leash.

'What happened? Has she been attacked?' I asked.

Merchant Martha shook her head. 'No blood or bruises to

speak of, at least not on her head anyway. She's been struck down, that's for certain, but not by any human hand.'

Healing Martha's right arm hung limp, the other grasped at Merchant Martha's cloak. The good side of her mouth worked furiously, dragging the paralysed side into a series of hideous grimaces. A meaningless series of noises crawled out from somewhere in her throat. 'Ga. Gar.'

Merchant Martha and I looked at each other.

'What is she trying to say? *God?*' I bent close to her. 'God has answered your prayers, Healing Martha, we will soon have you home.'

'Gar! Gar!' Healing Martha pounded her fist against the ground.

Merchant Martha shook her head. 'Her wits have gone, poor soul.'

Pega pushed me aside and laid the bier down next to her. 'Merchant Martha, you take the head. Beatrice, can you manage the legs?' She wriggled her arms under Healing Martha's body. 'Catherine, take her right arm and hold it up out of the way. Come on, Catherine, she'll not hurt you. Oh, get out of the way, lass! Let Osmanna do it. Ready? Gently now, lift.'

Healing Martha's legs flopped limply in my hands. She had wet herself. I could smell it, even though her clothes were soaked with rain. I only hoped Merchant Martha was right and Healing Martha was not sensible of her state. But I looked up as we bound her to the bier and saw that she was weeping.

Pisspuddle

'Water's up to the currant bushes now,' William yelled from the doorway.

I scrambled over to the door. The rain was still pouring down outside. Brown, muddy water was swirling round the bushes at the edge of our toft. It had only been up as far as the big stone on the edge of the track last time I looked out. I couldn't even see where the track was any more.

'Mam, Mam, where are you?' I wailed. She'd been gone ages. What if she couldn't get back to the house 'cause of the water? I tried to squirm past William to go outside and look for her, but he caught my plait and pulled it until I squealed.

'Get back inside, Pisspuddle. Mam says I'm not to let you out.'

'But I want to see where Mam is. She might be lost.'

'She's not lost, you daft beggar. She's trying to collect up the hens afore they drown.'

I was still struggling to get past him when Mam splashed round the side of the house with an old wicker pannier in her arms. The broken handle was bound up with a piece of yellow rag.

'What are you two fighting about now? I swear you'll be the death of me. Standing there with the door wide, in this wind, you'll have the hinges ripped off. Get inside, both of you.'

Mam pushed us back in the house with the pannier. I could hear clucking from inside.

'Did you rescue Bryde, Mam?' I tried to lift the wicker lid, but Mam slapped my hand away.

'Don't let them out again, girl. It's been hard enough catching them. I only managed to get three of them. Rest have taken to the trees and the water's round the trunks now. I can't

358

reach them. They'll just have to take their chances out there.'

'But you did get Bryde, didn't you?

'Chickens are chickens, be thankful I got any,' Mam snapped.

I ran to the door and pulled it open. The wind and rain rushed in again, sending everything in the cottage rocking. Mam grabbed me and hauled me back in, slamming the door. I fought her, trying to wriggle out of her hands.

'I have to find Bryde,' I wailed. 'She's only little, she won't know what to do. She'll drown if I don't rescue her.'

'I've got Bryde safe in the basket, now stop fretting,' Mam said. 'And I thought I told you to tie up the blankets. We have to hang everything we can from the beams, keep it out of the water, case it comes into the cottage. Come on, William, don't stand there gawping. You stuff the gap under the door with rushes from the floor, tight as you can. Hurry now.'

It was dark save for the tallow candle flickering on the iron spike in the wall. Mam, William and me sat all bunched up together on the bare bed boards. Mam was clutching the wicker pannier with the hens inside. It was so cold. Mam had wrapped a blanket round me, but I was still shivering. The noise outside was so loud now it was like we were in the middle of the river. The water was already inside the cottage. We hadn't seen it creep in at first. Then William had yelled, 'Look, Mam, the rushes.'

I couldn't see what was the matter with them, but then I saw they were moving; the water had crept up underneath them and they were floating.

'What if it reaches the top of the bed, Mam?' I asked.

'It won't,' Mam said. 'It's come in afore and it's never been more than hand deep. It'll not rise any higher.'

But it had. The rushes were almost floating up to the top of the bed now, but still we sat there. I wondered if the bed would start to float soon. Little trickles of cold water were running over the boards and wetting my skirts. Mam's eyes were closed and she was whispering something over and over. I wanted her to open her eyes and look, but I didn't dare speak, for if she stopped praying the water would get even higher.

I was praying too. 'Mam, make it stop, make it go away.'

There was a huge crash as something was dashed against the door of the cottage. The walls shook. Mam jerked upright. She crossed herself and pushed the blanket off me.

'We have to get out now.'

'We can't, Mam,' William sounded terrified. 'If we open the door more water will come in.'

'Out the window at the back.' Mam pulled me off the bed. I yelled as I sank into icy water up to my knees. I could feel the reeds bobbing round my legs like spiders scuttling over my skin. Mam reached for William and pulled him off the bed into the water. We splashed across the floor.

Mam flung back the shutters on the small window. The wind tore into the house and at once the tallow candle went out. And we were in the dark. I yelped again as something hard bobbed against my leg, I couldn't see what it was.

'You first, William. Get out and then grab hold of your little sister when I push her out.'

William heaved himself over the edge of the window sill and wriggled through. There was a faint splash from the other side.

'William, are you all right?'

His head appeared. 'All right, Mam.' His teeth were chattering and we could hardly hear him over the sound of the rain and rushing water.

'Here, grab hold of your sister's arms.'

Mam tried to heave me over the sill. The sharp edge of the window dug into my ribs.

'No, Mam! No, it hurts! I want to stay with you.'

I tried to pull away, but William's strong hands had tight hold of my wrists. Mam gave a great heave. I slithered over. I yelled and fell headfirst into the freezing muddy water, swallowing a great mouthful. I was spluttering, but the next moment William had hauled me upright again. The water was over my knees and so fast I had to cling tight to William to stand still.

Mam leaned out of the window. 'It's no good, I'll not get out this way, window's too small. I'll have to get out the door. Take your sister up to the church. It's higher ground there.'

'No, Mam, we'll wait here for you.' William sounded really scared.

'I'll not be able to get back round to you.' Mam reached out and touched his cheek. 'I'll meet you at the church. Off with you now. Be a brave lad, make your father proud.'

I heard William's teeth chattering. Mine were too. He grabbed my hand so tight it hurt. 'Come on, you heard Mam.'

'Don't let go of your sister, William, don't let go,' Mam called after us.

I turned round to wave at her, but there was no one there. The dark square of the window was empty.

Ahead we could see the black shapes of the cottages at the back of ours. William was dragging me towards the gap between them. I kept stumbling over things I couldn't see under the cold black water. Something tangled round my legs. I screamed and screamed that it was a snake, but William reached down and pulled it away.

'Shut up,' he ordered. 'It's only an old bit of rope.'

Then we were out from between the cottages. It was so dark. The rain was smashing into my face and I could hardly breathe. Floating things kept crashing into our legs, soft hairy things that made me shudder, hard scratchy things that really hurt. I knew I'd cut my hands and my legs. I could feel the stings, but I couldn't see if there was blood.

The water was swirling round me and kept tugging me backwards. It was much deeper now, up to my waist. I couldn't stand up against it. I was sobbing and hanging on to William's hand. He bent down.

'Climb on to my back. I'll piggy you.'

My legs and arms were so cold it took ages to get up. I clamped my fingers round his neck.

He bent forward, pushing through the water. We were wading up the track, except it wasn't a track any more, it was a river. William kept slipping. Several times he fell to his knees and the freezing water would splash over my head. I knew he was getting tired. He was going more and more slowly. What if he couldn't get us there?

Ahead of us I saw some other shapes splashing along. I couldn't see who they were, it was too dark. Maybe one of them was Mam. She'd come back to get us. 'Mam, Mam!' I yelled, trying to make her hear over the wind and the roar of water. But no one stopped. No one came. The shapes disappeared.

I didn't know where we were any more. It wasn't that far to the church, why weren't we there already? Maybe we were going the wrong way. The rain was falling so hard that I couldn't open my eyes properly to look. I squinted around. There was a faint glow in the darkness ahead. It seemed to be floating high up, appearing and vanishing again through the rain.

William almost fell again. 'Have ... to get down ... can't carry you any more.'

My hands were so cold they wouldn't come apart, but he prised them off his neck and I slid down, whimpering, into the icy water. He grabbed my hand.

The black oily water was creeping up to my armpits. It was too heavy to walk through. My legs were so cold they wouldn't move properly.

'I can't ... William ... I can't walk.'

'You can ... see, there's the churchyard wall. All you have to do is get to the wall ... then you don't have to walk any more ... Come on.'

He was pulling me forward. Then something hit me hard in the side, knocking me backwards. My head went under the water. I was choking and thrashing. I couldn't stand up. William still had hold of my hand, but the water was dragging me away from him. I thought my arm was going to break.

'Hold on to me!' William screamed, but I couldn't. I could feel William's fingers slipping out my hand. My slippery webbed fingers couldn't curl round his.

'Help me,' William was yelling. 'I can't hold her.'

I was so cold, I didn't want to hold on any more. Maybe I was turning into a frog or a mermaid. My feet were growing webs just like my hand. I'd swim away right down the river to the sea where father was. I couldn't hear William any more, just a funny booming noise. I was sinking down and down.

Something heavy was splashing in the water beside me. The next moment I was swept up in thick hairy arms and the water was pouring away from me in a big torrent. I was coughing and spluttering.

'I've got her, lad.' John the blacksmith was carrying me into the church.

He set me down, but my legs wouldn't work. I crumpled on to the rushes and was sick. I heaved again and again. Finally I stopped. My belly ached and my throat was burning. I sat up shivering and blinking in the candlelight.

The church was full of people. Everyone looked wet and muddy. Babies were crying and grown-ups were shouting. Some were clutching sacks round their shoulders, a few had blankets, but most were just dripping wet like me. My brother staggered over to me and crouched on the floor. He was shivering and his lips were blue.

'Y . . . you cold?' His teeth were chattering.

I nodded miserably, trying to wrap my wet arms round my body.

'Don't move.'

He disappeared into the crowd of people. He was gone so long I thought he wasn't coming back, but when he did he was holding a rolled-up piece of sacking. He pushed it at me. It was heavy and hot.

'Hold it against you. It's a stone warmed in the fire. Can't get you near the brazier, too many people round it, but I pinched one of the stones they were warming.' He looked sort of white under his brown skin and there was a big graze on his forehead that was oozing watery red blood.

'Come on . . . you know what Mam always says, dry your feet first, so you don't get a chill.' He bent down and tried to undo the laces of my soggy shoes, but they were too wet and his fingers were too cold and clumsy. 'Stupid, stupid fecking things!'

'William!' I gasped. Mam would skin his backside if she heard him say that word, but as I looked up I saw there were tears in his eyes. 'William, where's Mam?' I was suddenly frightened again.

He dashed his hand furiously across his eyes. 'I can't find her ... she's not here yet.'

I began to sob. 'But she said ... she said she'd be here ... I want her ... I feel sick ... I want Mam.'

William sat down beside me on the rushes, and awkwardly pushed his wet arm round my shoulder.

'Don't you dare cry, Pisspuddle, else next time we go gathering wood, I'll nail your plaits to a tree and leave you there for the Owlman to get you. Mam'll come. She said she would, didn't she? Mam'll be walking through that door any time now and she'd better not catch you gurning, else you'll be for it.'

I didn't care if she did catch me crying. I didn't care if she was as angry as a whole nest of wasps. I just clung shivering to William, praying for that door to open and my mam to walk through it.

December – St Chaeremon,
St Ischyrion and the Martyrs

Chaeremon, the elderly Bishop of Nilopolis, fled with a young companion into the mountains of Arabia to escape the persecution of the Roman Emperor Decius. The pair vanished and their bodies were never found.

Osmanna

The cold water in the vat began to bubble violently as Pega tumbled lime into it.

'Keep well back, else it'll be all over you. Cover your eyes, Osmanna, you too, Catherine. You get even a speck of lime in them and it'll feel like someone's jabbed a red-hot pin in your eyeball. Bastard stuff this is, blinds you.'

We backed away to the furthest corners of the barn as Pega, with a cloth clamped across her mouth against the fumes, carefully stirred the lime water. She had made us rub butter round our eyes and on our arms and hands for she said you don't notice a splash on your skin until it begins to burn and then it is too late.

Earlier that morning Shepherd Martha had lugged two dead sheep into the barn. She said there were other sheep, floating and tangled in the refuse of the flood, but they were not worth risking a life to retrieve in those powerful currents. Besides, they were most likely too bloated to use for meat.

How many others we'd lost she didn't know until she could reach the hill pasture on the other side of the river. But the little wooden bridge had been swept away and there was no crossing the ford in its present mood. At least the beguinage itself was on high ground and was safe, but the great expanse of brackish water spread out across field and pasture as far as the eye could see.

Having left the carcasses in the barn, Shepherd Martha had immediately gone out again to search for other stranded beasts, with Leon lolloping at her heels, leaving Beatrice, Pega, Catherine and me to gut and butcher the dead sheep.

We ferried the spoils to the kitchen and soon there was no trace of the poor beasts save their bloody skins. The heads, which would not keep, Kitchen Martha set to boil at once and the tails and scraps went into the flesh pot. The rest of the meat would have to be smoked or potted for there was precious little salt left to spare. But Kitchen Martha had to preserve the meat by some means for we desperately needed it.

If my mother could have seen me smeared with blood and dung, dismembering a carcass, she'd have fainted. But for once, I wanted to do it. I needed to chop and saw until the sweat poured down my face. I wanted to smash bone and flesh again and again until my arms were too tired to move. I wanted to hack the forest out of my mind, to smell blood and shit instead of wild onions and rotting leaves.

Ever since we'd returned from the forest yesterday, I'd not been able to rid myself of its stench. I worked most of the night in the infirmary, for I knew if I tried to sleep, the demon would come for me in my dreams. But even the stinks of the infirmary had not obliterated the smell of the forest. That creature was still out there. And it was waiting for me.

You murdered your own, Beatrice said. She did not say baby, but she didn't need to; I saw the savage hatred in her face. Did that creature also know I had murdered its spawn? If it could strike Healing Martha so savagely that she was disfigured almost beyond recognition, destroy her speech and paralyse her limbs, what would it do to me if it discovered what I'd done? I shuddered and tried to blot the sight of Healing Martha's face from my head, but I couldn't stop seeing it.

'You finished cleaning those skins?' Pega called out to me.

Beatrice elbowed me out of the way, tutting over the tiny shreds of scarlet threads still clinging to the greasy hides. 'There and there,' she pointed. 'Can't you be trusted even to do that?'

Pega came across to examine the skins. I expected her to join in Beatrice's sneers, but she didn't.

'Stop mithering, Beatrice. That'll do fine. Lass here's been up better part of the night tending to the infirmary and she's still worked like an ox this morning, which is more than young

Catherine's done. You intending to do anything to help, lass?'

Catherine didn't seem to hear. She was huddled miserably on an upturned pail, her face and hands smeared with sheep's blood.

'Poor child,' Beatrice said. 'She's so upset about Healing Martha, bless her. She's scarcely eaten a thing since yesterday. She's shivering. We should send her inside.'

'Aye, well, she'd not be cold if she got off her bloody arse and did some work. Sitting there moping isn't going to help Healing Martha. Over here, Catherine, and help get these skins in the lime. Sooner we get done here, the sooner we can all get into the dry.'

Catherine stumbled across, not looking at any of us. The rain drove in through the open barn doors, swirling the blood in the puddles.

Pega glanced over at me. 'So how is Healing Martha? Any better?'

I shook my head. 'She doesn't seem to be able to speak. Just keeps saying the same word she did in the forest, except it isn't a proper word. I gave her some lavender to help restore her wits, but –'

'Who gave you the right to physic Healing Martha?' Beatrice snapped. 'You know no more than the rest of us, a great deal less I should think. Healing Martha was the only one with the skill to mend others and now she has neither the wit nor speech to tell anyone how to heal her.'

Catherine made a little high-pitched sound like a puppy whimpering. She stared towards the infirmary, her eyes brimming, her hands shaking helplessly by her sides.

Beatrice put a protective arm around her. 'She is in no state to work, her hands are like ice. I'm taking her inside to get warm, otherwise she'll be ill herself. And we don't want to tax Osmanna with another patient, do we?' she added, glowering at me.

Beatrice gently guided her out of the barn and across the yard. And as the rain wetted her again the dried blood on

Catherine's hands began to run and dripped from her fingers into the puddles as she walked.

'Looks like it's just you and me, lass,' Pega said. 'Come on, grab the skin.'

We carried the heavy skin across to the vat and edged it in, trying not to splash ourselves with the lime.

'You seen aught of Servant Martha since the night of the storm?' Pega asked, her gaze fixed on the delicate task of sliding the skin in without touching the burning liquid.

'I don't think she's left her room. She let me bind up her arm, but she didn't speak. She just sat, staring at the wall, and there was such a strange expression on her face as if she'd seen ...'

'A demon?' Pega finished.

I glanced up at her to see if she was taunting me, but for once I could see she was serious.

I nodded.

'The Owlman,' Pega said gravely. 'Servant Martha didn't believe in him afore, I reckon she does now. She's the strongest woman I've ever known, but I tell you, when she staggered towards us out of the storm she looked near to broken, as if she'd been put to the rack.'

'Have you ... have you ever seen the Owlman, Pega?'

Pega shook her head vehemently. 'No, and I don't want to. My grandam told me the last time he flew, though it was years before she was born, the Owlman caught a villager in his talons one night and carried the man right up to the church tower. Still alive he was. They heard him crying for help as he was carried over the cottages. He was still screaming from the tower for hours after, but no man dared to go up to rescue him. Then at the darkest hour the screams stopped and in the morning, there was a pile of bones lying beneath the church tower, picked clean, but still bloody. They say –'

'Shepherd Martha told me of the sheep.' We both started violently as a voice rang out from the door. Servant Martha, looking almost as wet as she had that night, strode across to us, limping slightly, but trying hard to disguise it.

She threw back her sodden hood and peered into the vat. She still looked deathly pale. There were dark hollows around her eyes and she cradled her arm protectively.

'Servant Martha! I didn't expect ... are you feeling better?' I asked.

She looked down at me. 'You attended to my arm most efficiently, Osmanna. I've no doubt it will fully recover.' Her tone was brittle as if she was trying to force a cheerfulness she did not feel. 'Where are the others? I understood Beatrice and Catherine were assisting you with this task.'

'Beatrice took Catherine inside,' Pega said. 'State little lass was in, she was no use to man nor beast. This business with Healing Martha has scared her half to death. Others too.'

'I do understand Healing Martha's condition has distressed them, Pega. I am not entirely blind or deaf. And I acknowledge that I am at fault in not speaking to all the beguines immediately. But I needed time to ... pray.' The crisp voice suddenly faltered and Servant Martha swallowed hard, as if she was trying to choke back an emotion she would not permit herself to betray. 'It was hard ... difficult.'

Pega gripped Servant Martha's shoulder. 'Whatever you saw in the woods that night, you can speak of it. You needn't be afeared folks'll not believe you.'

'I don't know what I saw ... the lightning ... the raven ... I can't ...' Servant Martha closed her eyes tightly as if trying desperately to shut something out. Then she took a deep breath and drew herself upright.

'There is a great deal of work to be done. These floods will cause severe hardship in the village, but then I do not need to tell you that, Pega. We must offer every assistance.' She nodded curtly to Pega, then to me, and walked towards the barn door, a little more slowly and stiffly than she had done when she entered. As she pulled her hood back over her head, she turned.

'At this testing time, Osmanna, all the beguines must be of one mind and one purpose to support one another. Strength in the community is forged by us partaking of the one Holy Bread.

We must lay aside our own spiritual quests and strive for unity. The Mass on Sunday will be said both in gratitude for God's mercy in sparing Healing Martha and to pray for her recovery. I know how much you want to see Healing Martha restored to full health and strength, Osmanna, and therefore I trust you will demonstrate as much on Sunday – to everyone.'

Servant Martha ducked under the waterfall cascading from the barn roof and disappeared out into the driving rain.

Despite the cold, I felt my cheeks burning. I turned away, trying to hide my face by pulling stray shreds of flesh from the remaining hide.

'That woman never uses one word if she can torment ten,' Pega said. 'Why doesn't she just tell you she wants you to take the Host?'

She picked up the other end of the skin. I could feel her looking down at me, just as Servant Martha had done.

'There's a few not coming forward to take the Host now that you've refused. But I'd not have thought you'd be the one to disapprove of a woman leading the Mass, Osmanna. Beatrice, now she's different. There's always been a rub between her and Servant Martha. But I'd have wagered you for one who'd have had your heart set on doing it yourself someday.'

'Is that what you think,' I blazed, 'that I'm refusing the Host, because the Church says it's forbidden?'

'Isn't it?'

I stared at her. 'You know it's not. You know none of the women think that.'

She shrugged. 'How am I to know why you're refusing it? You talk about it to others, but you've never explained it to me.'

'I didn't think you'd be interested in anything I've got to say. I'm D'Acaster's daughter, don't forget. I thought you hated all our family.'

'You're D'Acaster's brat all right.' She held up her webbed hand. 'You think because I've got this, I'm as thick as pig shit, an ignorant whore who can't read or reason.'

'You're not stupid, Pega, far from it. You're so clever you can take anyone's words and twist them up into a rope to hang them. You want to know why I don't talk to you? It's because this is too important to me to have you ridicule it, like you do everything else.'

Pega flinched. For the first time ever I saw pain in her eyes. She dropped the edge of the hide and wiped her hand across her eyes, leaving a glistening smear of blood and grease on her forehead.

'Aye well, maybe it's true,' she said softly. 'But you learn to do that. Sometimes words are all you've got to defend yourself. I'm strong, yes, but still no match for a strapping work-hardened man. You think I wouldn't have got beaten to shit a hundred times over, if I'd not learned how to turn a drunk and make him laugh? Becomes a habit after a while, but it doesn't mean, I . . .' She looked away.

I fingered the sticky wetness of the hide, hating what I'd just said and the hurt on her face. I wished that she'd come back with one of her barbed taunts, but I knew she wouldn't.

'Ralph gave me a book called *The Mirror of Simple Souls*. It was written by a beguine in France. I don't understand some of it, but she writes things I've never heard Servant Martha say. Wonderful things. That a soul who truly loves God does not need to seek Him through sacraments. Pega, I know Servant Martha is right when she says we don't need a priest or the Church, we can take the sacraments for ourselves. But the book says why do we need the sacraments at all? Servant Martha is just making another Church. It is ten times better than Father Ulfrid's Church, but we are still doing the same thing as we did at St Michael's. Why can't each one of us just speak to God for ourselves?'

I had not looked at Pega as I spoke, but now I risked glancing up. There was no mocking grin on her face, instead there was a look of deep concentration. She nodded slowly.

'What you say makes sense, lass. But question is, you going to do what Servant Martha wants on the Sabbath to keep the peace? Like she says, the Mass is for Healing Martha. Some might take it amiss if you refuse.'

I bit my lip. What was I going to do? I didn't want to hurt Servant Martha or have anyone think I didn't care about Healing Martha. But I didn't believe in the bread any more. I'd told everyone that. I couldn't take it now, not when I'd convinced others not to take it. She couldn't make me do that.

'I can't, Pega. I won't!'

Pega smiled for the first time that day. 'You've got the guts of a fighting cock in you, I'll give you that. But you want to think long and hard on it, lass. Servant Martha's not a person to take on lightly when it comes to a fight. You're both as stubborn as each other. You pit yourself against her and I reckon you'll both come out bruised and bloody.'

She walked round to where I stood. She placed her broad warm hands on either side of my face and tilted it upwards.

'There's no shortage of punches life'll throw at you. It's my guessing you've had a few more than your share already, but you don't need to go looking for fists to throw yourself against. Just you be careful, lass.'

She bent forward and kissed my forehead.

I went rigid, my body frozen between the warm tenderness of her mouth and the flood of revulsion that welled up in me. I felt my father's lips again on my child's face. For a moment I could not move, then I tore myself out of her grasp and fled the barn.

Pisspuddle

Someone was shaking me awake. William was squatting in front of me, holding a small stone mortar which had steam rising from it.

'Here, we'll have to share. There aren't enough bowls to go round. You take first swallow, then I'll take next.'

'That's not for drinking from,' I protested. 'That's for grinding, like the one Mam uses for grinding beans.' Then, with a sudden sick feeling, I remembered. 'William, has Mam come? Is she here?'

He bit his lip. 'Not yet. But she'll come now it's light. Hurry up and drink some of this, else I'll have it all. I'm starving.' He thrust the mortar at me.

I was hungry too and thirsty. We'd not had any supper last night, but the broth smelt like mouldy leaves.

'What's in it?'

'Dunno,' William shrugged. 'But it's all there is.'

William held it while I took a gulp. It was hard to get my mouth round the thick curve of the stone. It didn't taste of anything much, sour ale and herbs, water mostly, bitter and muddy, but my belly was rumbling and I drank it.

Light was trickling in through the faces of the yellow saints in the window. People weren't shouting any more. Most just sat huddled on the rushes staring at the floor, drinking their broth like William and me. Up at the altar Father Ulfrid was saying Prime. A few people were kneeling, and praying in front of the roodscreen. Some of the grown-ups were crying as they prayed. I could hear them sobbing.

But lots of people were ignoring Father Ulfrid. They just carried on talking or sat on the rushes suckling their babies as if they didn't even know they were in church. There was one old man who kept coming round asking everyone if they'd seen his wife, but no one had and after a while they got fed up being asked the same question over and over and shouted at him to sit down, right in the middle of Father Ulfrid's prayers.

Afterwards Father Ulfrid came round blessing people where they sat or stood. Some made the sign of the cross, but others scowled and turned away as if they didn't want to be blessed. Father Ulfrid didn't seem miserable like everyone else. He seemed almost pleased, as if he thought everyone had come to church because they wanted to pray.

He stopped in front of William and me and made the sign of the cross, then pressed his hot, sticky hand down on our heads. William jerked his head away.

'Bless you, my children. Now, remember this is the house of God and you must behave yourselves in here. No playing games or spitting, and you make sure you go outside if you want to pass water. Is your father still away at the salterns, William?'

William nodded.

'Then you must pray for him. If the storm was bad here it will have been worse on the coast. Pray diligently like good children, just like your mother taught you, and God in his mercy will hear your prayers. Where is your mother?' He gazed about as if he thought she was with us.

William grabbed my hand and pulled me to my feet. 'Come on.'

We ran to the heavy church door and dashed outside. It was still raining a bit, but not so hard as before. The air felt cold and sharp after the smelly church. We ran to the churchyard wall and scrambled up on the rough stones to peer over.

It looked as if we were on an island. Brown water lay all round the graveyard. Where the path should have been, ducks were swimming and diving among the rubbish. The water was thick like pottage, with leaves and branches and all kinds of things from people's cottages and gardens floating in it. There were reeds from the floors, bits of furniture, lumps of tar and rags. It looked as if a giant had picked up every cottage and shaken everything out of them into the water and then put the cottages back empty.

Men were wading through the water, picking up stools and pots, rakes and hoes. Most of them were smashed, but they were picking them up anyway and splashing off with them down the street. Two men saw the same wooden chest bobbing in the water at the same time. They both started towards it, their legs jerking like spiders as they tried to run in the water. They both grabbed the chest, tugging it and punching each other until one slipped and fell into the water. The standing man tried to make off with the chest as fast as he could, but the other one caught up with him and leapt on his back and they both fell with a great splash into the water, rolling over and over on each until they were out of sight beyond the bend.

'William, look, that's our pannier. The one Mam put the hens in.' I pointed to a shape caught up against the trunk of a tree.

'It's just a basket.'

'No, it's ours, I know it is. Handle's wrapped with a yellow rag, just like ours, see.'

William scrambled over the wall and jumped into the water. It was as high as the top of his legs. He splashed towards the basket and dragged it back towards the wall.

'Here, take hold,' he said, pushing it over.

But I couldn't catch it properly and it tipped over as I pulled it. It rolled on the ground and the top fell off. Three limp, draggled little bodies slithered on to the grass. Their feathers were sodden, their beaks wide open and their eyes too, but they weren't moving.

'Mam said Bryde was safe in the basket, but she's not in here. Mam didn't rescue Bryde, she didn't even try.' I burst into tears. 'Where is Mam? She said she'd come. She promised. She's a liar. Just a big fat liar. I hate her! I hate her!'

'Stay here,' William said fiercely. 'You wait for me, right?

You're not to move.' He clambered back over the wall and waded away.

'William, come back,' I called frantically. 'Where are you going?'

'I'm going to find Mam.'

Beatrice

The voices in the refectory were subdued. Kitchen Martha had cooked a special dish to try to raise our spirits – a mutton spicy pie with the head meats and brains of the sheep and the last of the dried fruits of winter. The sweet and savoury aroma filled the room, a rare treat at this season of the year, but few seemed to have much of an appetite. We politely offered each other dishes and urged one another to pass them along, knowing they were not wanted, but simply to fill the silence with a rattle of words.

I hadn't expected Servant Martha to be here. I thought she'd take her meals at Healing Martha's bedside as she had with Andrew. But instead she was talking to Merchant Martha as though nothing had happened, except that her right arm was bound up. She ate clumsily, unaccustomed to using her left hand, but she supped steadily, her appetite undiminished. She was probably discussing the price of cloth or the shortage of salt.

I'd always known she had the compassion of a pike, but I thought if there was a mote of affection in her it was for Healing Martha. It seemed, however, she had plucked even that out. She sat straighter than ever, her back upright and stiff. Even sitting she was a full head taller than Merchant Martha. Did she have to hold her head quite so cloud-capped?

There was a sharp rap of a knife on wood. Servant Martha rose to her feet and cast around the room to see that she had everyone's attention.

'My sisters, as we give thanks to God this day for our food, our tongues should not merely recite the duty they owe, but our spirits should soar on wings of praise that once again God has vouchsafed such mercies to us.'

We all sat up and leaned forward eagerly. Had He worked a miracle for Healing Martha?

'Our Blessed Lord shelters us in His arms, for while our neighbours are driven from their homes by the flood, we are safe and warm in ours. While our neighbours struggle to find a scrap of bread which has not been ruined by the water, we eat hot food and drink good ale.'

Yes, yes, but what of Healing Martha? Why didn't she come to the point?

'We must pray for the souls in the village whose cries are unheard by God because of their sin and faithlessness. But if we pray for help for them, we ourselves must be willing to be the instruments of answering those prayers. If we say, "Lord, send them food and comfort," then He will turn to us and say, "Daughters, give them food and comfort." This very day God delivered two fine sheep into our hands, just as He gave the ram to Abraham, as a sign of what we must do.'

Pega muttered, 'Not much of a gift, if you ask me; they were our sheep anyway.'

'God has given us the sacrifice and we will offer it. Tomorrow we will go to the village with meat, bread and ale. After the evening prayers, instead of sleeping, I ask any who are willing to come to the kitchens, for there is much cooking and baking to be done if we are to have enough food for all who need it.'

She paused to take a gulp of ale. Round the room the women glanced at one another, nodding approvingly, before all eyes turned back to Servant Martha. There must be more to come. She must speak of Healing Martha. Surely she must.

'There is another for whom we must pray tonight even as we work.' She paused.

You could feel the tension in the room. No one moved.

'As you all doubtless know, two nights ago our beloved sister, Healing Martha, was struck down not by any human hand nor by the hand of God, but by the legions of the Devil. Healing Martha fought with a terrible demon, but her faith prevailed and she vanquished it.'

'The Owlman!'

The name reverberated around the room from a dozen mouths. Servant Martha must have heard it, but she ignored it and strode on through her speech with not so much as a flea's breath of hesitation.

'Like our blessed Lord Himself in the wilderness and all the saints who have followed Him, Healing Martha was attacked by the forces of darkness, because her love for God was so strong it struck even to the depths of hell and wounded the Devil himself and he wanted to destroy her. But Healing Martha has so girded herself with the armour of the Lord and her shield of faith is so strong that all the arrows of hell could not pierce it, nor any demons conquer her. God preserved her, both body and soul, to His glory.' She bowed her head. 'May we all strive to be worthy of such a test.'

She looked slowly around the silent room, fixing each of us in turn with her gaze as though measuring our worth and finding us wanting.

'Tomorrow we will say a special Mass to give thanks for His protection and preservation of our sister.'

'Praise God!' The cry was loud, but without feeling. Many looked perplexed.

'Does that mean Healing Martha is well again?' Catherine whispered urgently in my ear.

Muttering broke out around the room. Catherine was not the only one who was confused. Merchant Martha tugged at Servant Martha's arm and whispered rapidly. Servant Martha, frowning, took another draught from her cup.

'I have to tell you now that Healing Martha is sorely wounded from her great battle, as you would expect. For who could face such a trial and come through unscathed? But they are honourable wounds she bears, as those of the saints and martyrs before us who have defended their faith and virtue against great evil. The burning touch of the demon paralysed her side, as our own Lord was wounded in His side by evil men. She does not speak to us, for to tell us of the horror and evil of the demon who assailed her would be too great for us to bear. But she needs no discourse with us, for our Lord Himself speaks to her and she to Him in tongues beyond our understanding.'

'Praise God! Praise God!'

Some of the women looked pleased, grateful even, but they'd not seen her. Catherine's expression relaxed too, as if Servant Martha had somehow explained everything and all was right with the world again. She smiled eagerly at me. Did she remember how Healing Martha looked when we found her or was that picture now diffused with martyr-light, a twisted face made pretty with gold leaf and an animal grunt sweetened to angel song?

Servant Martha rapped the table again. The speech was not over.

'It's evident that Healing Martha will not be able to perform her duties in the infirmary for some time. She was an elderly woman when she came here and after a lifetime of service many of her age might expect that they had earned the right to doze in the sun and have others care for them, but we all know that Healing Martha was never one to do that.'

There was a ripple of affectionate laughter round the room, but it had a sad edge to it.

'When she is restored to health, and we pray that is soon —'

'Amen.'

'— then, we must persuade her to rest and let younger, stronger women take up her load. We must treasure her as a fine book, seeking her wisdom, but not allowing her to squander her precious energy on tasks that others could perform. Therefore we must appoint another Martha to take up her duties. Once we have done all we can for the village and the flood waters have receded, the Council of Marthas will meet to discuss the matter. You are each enjoined to pray that God's Holy Spirit will guide our decision. Now we shall kneel for the Grace.'

There was much shuffling and Catherine nudged me in the ribs.

'That'll be you, the next Martha. Everyone says so.'

'No,' I hissed, blushing scarlet and wishing she would not whisper so loud. 'There are many others who could be chosen.'

'None with as much learning as you, nor been a beguine so long,' she persisted blithely. 'They have to choose you.'

Pisspuddle

It was nearly dark when William came back. I'd waited all day, sitting on a big high tomb so I could watch the bend where he had disappeared. I knew he'd come back round there again with Mam. William would be waving, shouting he'd found her. Mam would say I was a good girl, to wait, like she said.

All day people were wading to and from the church. Some came back with big bundles of dripping things tied to their backs. They said it was too wet to sleep in their cottages. Others said they were going to stay in the cottages even though there was still water in them, in case their things got stolen. But some came back angry or crying, saying all their things were gone, taken by the river or their neighbours. Some of the cottages were gone too, smashed to pieces by the flood.

By the afternoon the water was going down a bit. I didn't see it go down, but if I looked away for a long time, when I looked back I could see that the top of a stone which had been covered right over was now poking out of the water. I tried to make William and Mam come back. *When the water is half-way down that stone, they'll come. When the water is three withies down that gate, then they'll come.* But they didn't.

It was freezing cold sitting on the grave. Lettice had given me one of her old kirtles to wear while my clothes dried. She looped it up with a bit of rope but it still came right down over my feet. I wrapped the long sleeves tightly round me. I wanted to go back inside the church in the warm, but if I didn't keep watch William wouldn't be able to find Mam. I had to stay and wait, like William said, or my prayer wouldn't work.

The priest said to pray for Father, but I couldn't do that. God might not know which prayer I wanted Him to answer. Father Ulfrid said there'd been a storm at the coast, but my father said there were always storms there. He'd watch the great grey horses galloping to shore, tossing their white manes and tails, but he wasn't afeared of them. So I didn't need to pray for Father, because I knew where Father was.

Lettice came out in the afternoon. She saw me on the tomb and waddled towards me. She looked even fatter than usual 'cause she'd got lots of her clothes tied round her waist, in case someone stole them.

'There you are. I've been looking all over, dear. Whatever are you doing sitting out here? You'll catch your death. Inside with you.' She caught hold of my arm and tried to pull me, but I squirmed my arm away and clung fast to the stone.

'I'm waiting for Mam and William.'

'And what do you think your mam is going to say, when she finds you hanging around out here in the cold? As if she hasn't enough troubles, poor soul, without you taking a chill. She doesn't need a sick bairn on her hands.'

'Don't care. I'm not coming in.'

'There's a little of that hot broth left, dear, don't you want some?' Lettice wheedled.

'No. It was horrible.'

'There are some naughty little girls who should be grateful they've anything to eat at all. Very well, you sit here, but don't come crying to me when you're hungry, because there'll be none left.' She stalked away.

I was starving, but Lettice didn't understand. I had to keep watching or William would not be able to find Mam.

When the sun went down it was colder than ever. Then it started to grow dark. *Please make them come. Make them come now.* The candles had been lit in the church and light tumbled out through the windows, making shadows creep through the graveyard. The trees began to creak and moan. I hadn't heard them when it was light, but now there were all kinds of noises I hadn't noticed before. I cringed against the stone as something black flew across the graveyard. It was only small, a bird or a bat. It swooped over me without a sound.

My heart started thumping. I looked fearfully up at the church tower. Lettice had told Mam the Owlman had flown down from there and pounced on two lasses in the graveyard. He could be up there right now, sharpening his beak and flapping his wings ready to swoop down.

I jumped up and tried to run towards the safety of the church, but I tripped over Lettice's long kirtle and went sprawling on the ground. I yelped as my knee banged hard against a stone.

'Pisspuddle, is that you?' a voice called behind me.

William was climbing over the wall. I hitched up the long skirt and ran down the graveyard. I threw myself at him, hugging him so tightly he staggered backwards. He was sopping wet and stank of mud and shit, but I wouldn't let go.

'Watch it, you daft beggar. You'll squash her.'

He pushed something warm and soft into my arms. I heard the chirruping gurgle. I turned the bundle towards the light from the church windows. There, nestled in a bit of sacking, was a little brown chicken with a white flash on her wing. It was Bryde, my Bryde. She was safe. I pushed my nose into her warm feathers and breathed in the new-bread smell of her.

William rubbed his arms and shivered. 'Stupid bird was roosting up in the rafters in the cottage. Reckon she went in there looking for you. You'd best put her in the pannier and keep her hidden, else someone will have her for supper.'

'Thank you for saving her.' I stretched up on tiptoe and kissed him.

'Get off!' He pushed me away, scrubbing at his cheek with his sleeve. 'Here, you're perishing cold. What are you doing out here anyway? It's almost dark.' He glanced fearfully up at the church tower, grabbed my shoulder and pushed me towards the church door.

'But where's Mam, William? I thought you were going to find her?'

He stopped and rubbed his fist against his eyes. 'She's not here then? I . . . thought she might have come a different way . . . kept telling myself she'd be here.'

'She hasn't come. I've been waiting all day, William. I didn't move, like you said, but she still didn't come. Wasn't she in the cottage?'

'Door was open. Bed was smashed against the wall, but there weren't no sign of Mam. I've looked everywhere, Pisspuddle, all over village. I can't find her.' He turned his face away and his voice sounded strange, as if his nose was running.

I clutched his hand. It was as cold as a frog. 'I expect Mam's gone to find Father, to tell him to come home. That's where she's gone, William, isn't it?'

But he didn't answer.

Beatrice

After the steaming heat of the kitchen, the sudden shock of sharp night air took your breath away. The wind still had a wetted edge to it, but at least the rain had stopped. Pale clouds were scudding across the moon, but the skies were clearing. The bell would ring for the midnight prayers soon, but the food for the village was prepared at long last. The pots would simmer slowly until morning. The wind hungrily devoured the rich aroma of herbs and mutton, wafting it out into the night air. I wondered if the wind would carry it as far as the village. If they could smell it, sitting there cold and wet with rumbling bellies, they'd curse us to hell and back.

Holding the lantern aloft, I tiptoed into the cote, silently closing the door behind me in the face of the wind. Gudrun was curled up in the corner, her head resting on a wad of straw. Two pigeons were bedded in her hair. She'd thrown off her covers again. Her shift was so thin, I knew she must be cold. I crouched down to pull the covers up around her. I noticed her arms were covered in scratches and bruises and there was a big purple bruise across her thigh. What had she been doing? Gudrun didn't seem to notice pain. A knock that would send another wincing and wailing did little more than make her blink. Yet if someone stroked her arm in sympathy, she'd snatch it away as if they had laid a branding iron on her skin.

Except for the gentle rising of her ribs, the child didn't stir, but four bright eyes stared at me and wondered. I sat down on a heap of straw and watched her. I loved to watch her sleeping, but that night I was so weary. We'd scarcely slept for two nights and had been working every hour between. I longed to curl up in the straw by my Gudrun, bury my face in her long, soft hair, like the pigeons, and sleep holding her in my arms, my little one, safe and warm. But it was no good even thinking of sleep; that bell would ring any time now, summoning us to the chapel.

Would Healing Martha hear the bell? Would she struggle to rise to it, without knowing why, as a dog comes to a shepherd's whistle? Prayers would continue without her. All of life would go on without her. It seemed impossible, indecent even, that it should, but you can't hold life back.

Healing Martha lay in the infirmary, not a leader and physician, just a body to be washed and anointed, to be talked about, but no longer talked to. And who would replace her? It would have to be someone skilled in the healing arts and I didn't possess a tenth of Healing Martha's knowledge, but who among us did? My little Gudrun probably knew more than any of us of herbs and potions, but they'd not permit her to treat a hanged man let alone themselves, even if they were all dying and she had the certain cure in her hand. Pega had helped Healing Martha with the rough work and she must have picked up some knowledge, but what use was that when she couldn't read labels on jars or recipes in books?

I knew as much as any of the others about the curing of common ailments. I had run a household in Flanders, treated the maids and manservants and my husband too, when they fell sick with agues or fevers. I would have learned more in the beguinage, but I'd never been encouraged to work in the infirmary. I was always being asked to do the hard, messy jobs in the field or kitchens and kept from learning anything skilled. Want kirtles washed or grain threshed? Send for good old Beatrice, she'll do it.

I learned quickly though. I always had, though I'd been given precious little time for study. But all that would change when I became a Martha. Then I'd have the time to study the herbals. I wouldn't be called upon to waste my days in washing and grinding. The infirmary would be my responsibility and I'd work night and day to make it run efficiently. I'd never be as skilled a physician as Healing Martha, of course, I didn't have her training, but I would be a good healer. I could be equal to any of the other Marthas here or in Flanders. I wanted that. I'd earned it and Catherine was right for once; who else could the Council possibly appoint?

December – St Stephen's Day and Hunting the Wren

A day when the Church gives alms to the poor. The wren, king of the birds and the underworld, is hunted and killed to despatch winter and allow spring to return.

Pisspuddle

The Owl Master slipped out of our cottage. I held my breath and crouched as small as I could behind the bushes. His big feathered head turned this way and that, like he was watching what everyone did even through the walls, then he slipped between the cottages. I crept to the corner of the cottage to see where he'd gone, but he'd just vanished.

As soon as he'd gone, Lettice beckoned to me from the cottage door. She was always in our cottage now. I wished she'd go away and leave me and William alone. I dragged my feet over to her as slowly as I dared.

'You're as filthy as a beggar's ear. Whatever would your mam say? This infernal mud.' She spat on the corner of her apron and scrubbed at my face with it. 'Now, you listen. Owl Master said those outlanders have come back to the village to hand out food. But you're not to take anything from them. You hear?'

'But I want something to eat,' I wailed. 'I'm so hungry.'

'Hungry or not, that food is witched. How else would they have so much food when there's not a bite left in the village?'

'It's not witched. I've had . . .'

'Had what?' Lettice demanded. 'I hope you've not been near those women, my lass, or your father is going to give you such a thrashing when he gets back from the salterns.'

'I haven't, honest, I haven't.' But I felt my cheeks burning. 'I just meant that I saw some women taking food from them yesterday and they didn't die or turn into toads or anything.'

Lettice snorted. 'You can be witched and not know it. I knew a poor woman who was overlooked by old Gwenith's daughter. She started to have terrible nightmares of monstrous birds that pecked away at her. In agony she was, poor soul. She wasted away and died afore the year was out. Now those outlanders are harbouring that Old Gwenith's granddaughter. She's the cause of this flood and those outlanders are helping her. There was no trouble in Ulewic until they arrived, and we've had nothing but ill-fortune since. Am I right?' She crossed herself. 'So you mind what I say and stay away from those women.'

'You're not my mam. I want my mam!' I shouted.

Lettice shook her head sadly, 'Wanting won't bring her back, my dear.'

I followed the grey women out of the village and back along the track. They didn't see me, 'cause I darted behind the bushes and they were too busy talking.

The village looked like a mire. Green waterweed clung high up on the walls. Great pools filled the hollows in the fields. The water had mostly gone from the roads except for big puddles, but everything inside the cottages and outside was covered in thick, squelchy mud, so deep it came right up to my calves.

Beatrice was pressing the corner of her cloak over her nose. 'That stink. I can even taste it. I suppose we should be thankful the wind's blowing it away from the beguinage.'

'Be thankful you're not living in it,' Pega said.

'Why don't they at least burn the corpses of the drowned animals?' Beatrice grumbled. 'That dead cat lying in the road was so bloated its guts had burst open. I retched from one end of the street to the other from the stench of it.'

Pega laughed. 'A newborn babe pukes less than you do, Beatrice. You've the stomach of a princess. Eaten too good all your life, that's your trouble. Villagers have enough to do digging the middens out of their homes and scratching around for a bit of dry straw and bracken to lie down on of a night without bothering about what's lying in the street. Besides, I reckon there's fever taking hold in the village. That bairn curled up in a doorway, he was ailing and no mistake.'

Several of the women nodded. 'I saw a few like that. One had a nosebleed.'

'And I saw two little girls, vomiting and scouring.'

"I'm sure it's nothing serious, just the runs,' Beatrice said. 'Those children will scavenge anything. Most likely they've been eating some putrid scraps they've found. I've seen no sign of D'Acaster's men in the village. Hasn't his steward sent anyone to help?'

'From what I hear, Phillip's got every man out hunting meat for Manor.' Pega spat into the ditch. 'He'd watch a bairn drown in a puddle at his feet sooner than bend down and pull it out, even one of his own bastards.'

She stopped and turned, peering in my direction even though I was sure she couldn't see me. Then she grinned. 'Come out, little mouse. There's no one from village to see you now. You hungry?'

I looked carefully up and down the road before I crept out. Pega held out a big piece of cold mutton in her giant hand.

I reached out and then drew back. What if it was witched and I died from the birds pecking at me? But I was so hungry and the mutton smelt so good. I snatched the meat from her hand and tore at with my teeth. I didn't care if I died, I had to eat it.

The women all smiled, all except the tall, fierce one. She'd hurt her arm. Two flat pieces of wood were tied tightly to it. She looked down, frowning. 'Tell me, child, why are many of the villagers refusing to take food from us? They must be hungry like you.'

''Cause Owl Masters say it's ... witched,' I whispered. 'Lettice has made a witch jar. She pissed into it and stuffed it full of pins and thorns. Then she put it under the hearth. She says when the fire gets hot, it'll scald your bowels and stab you till you confess.' I glanced up, suddenly afeared. 'You're not burning now, are you?'

The women laughed and shook their heads.

But the fierce one looked crosser than ever. 'Did no one teach you such practices are wicked, child? If you are afraid of anything you should pray and God will ... He must surely hear the prayers of a child.'

She looked sad and worried. Maybe someone she loved got lost in the storm, like my mam. I wanted to give her a hug to make her feel better, but I was too scared of her.

Servant Martha

The infirmary was peaceful and quiet after the mess and chaos of the village. I paced slowly from cot to cot, blessing the occupants. Ralph waved at me respectfully. The twisted child lay cradled asleep in his lap. I longed to climb into one of the cots myself and sleep for a month.

The pain in my arm kept me awake most nights and I used the prick of it to drive me to my knees in prayer. That at least I should have been able to do, keep vigil through the dark hours. Even if my limbs were hacked off, my tongue torn out, my eyes blinded and my ears sealed, I should still have been able to perform the work of prayer. But I could not pray. Healing Martha's distorted face floated constantly beneath the surface of my thoughts like one drowned.

If I had gone back to look for Healing Martha, instead of following Gwenith's granddaughter, could I have protected her? If I'd had the faith and courage to fight that demon, could I have saved her? But the question that tormented me the most, the one I could not push away, was why had she been chosen to face that battle alone and not me? Was her faith so much greater than mine?

I stood before His altar and held in my hands the deepest mysteries of life, both of this world and the next. It was my words that transformed base bread and wine into His very flesh and blood for others to consume. But I was only the ditch through which water flowed, leaving me behind, empty and cold. Yet what right had I to ask for anything more? A priest is but an instrument, a knife, a spoon, a bowl. When all is said and done, it is women's work, this feeding.

I finally made my way to the bedside of my old friend. I'd wanted to move Healing Martha back to her own room, but I knew it wasn't practical to do so. Andrew could be left for hours at a time, except in her last few days, but Osmanna, who had been working in the infirmary ever since the night of the storm, assured me that Healing Martha must be watched constantly. She struggled sometimes to clamber out of her cot and if she slipped she couldn't right herself. Osmanna had found her choking on her own saliva when she was lain too flat. We couldn't spare someone to watch her in her own room day and night, at least not yet.

Healing Martha smelled of lavender and stale urine. She'd slipped down the cot and her head was lolling to the side like a hanged man's. She peered at me with her open eye and her good fist clutched at the cover.

'Gar.'

'What is it, Healing Martha, what are you trying to say?'

She took a deep breath. 'Gar. Gar. Gar!' she shouted, her good hand pounding her leg in frustration.

I couldn't believe that such a fury could emanate from any so weak, let alone Healing Martha. Osmanna came hurrying up and slipped her arms under Healing Martha's arms and hauled her back up the bed. Then she carefully arranged her head on the pillow, as if she was tidying John the Baptist's head upon the platter. Healing Martha sank back, both eyes closed, her breath rasping.

'Is that what she was asking for, to be lifted up?'

Osmanna looked pained. 'I don't know. She makes that sound over and over to whoever is near. Sometimes she shouts it, other times she whispers. No one understands what it means.'

'I dare say it has no more meaning than a baby's cry. How is she?'

'She's quiet most of the time, staring for hours into space, and I don't know if she is awake or sleeping. Sometimes, Servant Martha . . .' she hesitated and glanced uneasily back at the spectre in the bed, 'when I look at her she's weeping. I can't tell if it's because she's in pain. I don't know if I should give her something.'

'Healing Martha would not weep for pain. Look how she suffered with her back without complaint these many years. She weeps for the evil she has seen. Her tears are prayers, Osmanna, prayers for those who have not repented. Didn't our Lord Himself weep over the stiff-necked people of Jerusalem?'

Osmanna looked unconvinced. Perhaps I sounded unconvincing. I hoped that's why Healing Martha wept. I prayed it was.

'You look weary, Osmanna. Have you been in here all day?'

'I don't mind. I want to.'

'I'm glad of it, but get yourself some ale and take it out in the courtyard. The cold air will revive you. I'll watch here.'

She smiled gratefully and walked away, her feet dragging in the rushes.

I took Healing Martha's right hand. It lay like a dead fish in mine. I squeezed it, but there was no response.

'I've neglected you, Healing Martha. Forgive me. You know that I'd spend every day at your bedside if I was free to do so, but I'm not. The women are frightened. They depended too much upon you. I'm guilty for not having recognized it long ago. They shouldn't depend on any save God alone. I must show them that the beguinage will continue without you. I can't be seen to keep vigil over you as if I also missed you.'

Her expression didn't change.

'In a few days we are to elect a new Martha. Someone must take responsibility for the infirmary. Not that they will ever replace you,' I added hastily. 'I've prayed these past days for guidance, Healing Martha, but I'm no closer to the answer, for there's no one who clearly stands out as your successor, no one who has your skill and maturity. I wish you could be with us in the meeting. You could always examine a seedling and tell which way it would grow.'

Healing Martha made no response. Her head lay at ease where Osmanna had placed it on the pillow. Osmanna handled her well and the rest of the patients too. Ralph, old Joan, they all seemed to respond to her. The infirmary looked ordered and calm, almost as if it was under Healing Martha's rule. Not as tidy, but the patients appeared content enough.

But Osmanna was much too young to be appointed as the Healing Martha. She was scarcely more than a child. Then again, perhaps it was young blood we needed. A new beguinage needed young beguines who would carry on the vision long after we ancient ones were dead. If she was trained up as a Martha, allowed to sit in Council and listen to the debate, she would learn, and maturity would come in time.

I leaned closer to Healing Martha. 'Is that what you meant the night of the storm, when you said, *The fault in the pupil is the virtue in the leader*, that we should make Osmanna a Martha?'

Healing Martha's eyes did not flicker.

I squeezed her hand. 'I know the Marthas think I should never have taken you out that night. They do not say it to my face, but I see the reproach in their eyes whenever they speak of you. And their condemnation is nothing compared to my own guilt over what I've done to you. But God ordered us to bury the dead. I was doing what God commanded, and I trusted Him to keep faith with us.

'I have searched alone in that place since and there's no trace of either the baby or that poor woman's corpse. Aldith's body simply vanished. But it *was* there. The woman had been ripped apart. We both saw it. I touched it. Did the Owlman devour them both? If that's so, I not only failed you, I failed to protect the soul of the child she entrusted to me. I've always believed that faith could defend me against anything. Where was God that night? Why did He abandon me?'

Healing Martha's good eye opened and I realized I was shaking her arm. Tears trickled down, settling in the wrinkles of her face. 'Ga,' she whispered. Her face twisted into a devil's mask as she struggled to make the animal sound. That demon had destroyed her mind and body as if he had eaten her from the inside.

I closed my eyes and saw that creature again, those eyes, ringed with fire, the great black bottomless pupils that seemed to draw me closer and closer until I was swallowed up in the darkness of them. What evil lay at the bottom of them? What horrors had Healing Martha seen in them to freeze her face for ever in this glimpse of hell? I had not believed that such a monster could exist and now, now he was more real to me than God. Each time I tried to pray I saw his face. I heard the crack of his savage beak and smelt the foul stench of his breath. That demon reared up before my face as if the prayers I was offering were made to him. And God was silent; he was nowhere and nothing.

✝

December – St Egwin's Day

To prove his innocence of a crime of which he was accused, St Egwin locked his feet in irons and threw the key into the River Avon before walking to Rome. There he bought a fish which he cut open in front of the Pope and inside was the key.

Servant Martha

The Marthas entered singly into the chapel, each from their appointed realms. Gate Martha was already seated. She was used to waiting without impatience. Her eyes seemed permanently fixed on a far horizon, from perpetually squinting down the road to see who approached. Her hands were, as ever, busy with her spindle while her mind slipped off by itself to who knows where.

Kitchen Martha, scarlet and sweating profusely, waddled in and flopped down on the bench, fanning herself. 'Thank the Lord, it's cooler in here. The heat in my kitchen's fit to roast a pig in ice, for we've to keep all the doors and shutters fastened against the wind. That wind is so strong it could pluck a fowl. One day we're near drowned, the next we're flayed to death. God alone knows what it'll be next – snow, I shouldn't wonder. It was a wise decision, Servant Martha, to hold the Council in the chapel where we've stout walls. A body can't hear themselves think with the wind howling round that refectory.'

'Thank you, Kitchen Martha, though I did not convene the meeting here for our comfort. This decision must be guided by the Holy Spirit through prayer, for it is God's choice we must wait upon, not ours. I hoped the chapel might remind us of that.'

Kitchen Martha lowered her gaze, looking discomfited, as though I'd reprimanded her. Why did all the women take everything I said as a criticism when it was simply meant as an explanation?

The door banged open and Merchant Martha strode in so quickly, I feared she wouldn't stop in time and burst straight out again through the wall on the other side.

'Am I the last?'

'As always, Merchant Martha,' I said.

She nodded as if she expected no less and was certainly not abashed by it.

The others chuckled quietly. Merchant Martha was for ever trying to cram a full day's work into each and every hour. She'd no doubt been busy with some task that she didn't trust anyone else to perform. But it was as well she was last for she'd only fret and fume if she was obliged to wait for someone else to arrive.

'Sisters, as we consider who will be elected Healing Martha, let us remember that we sit in the presence of the Blessed Host of Andrew and of our Mass stone, given into our hands by the priest at Bruges when many of us were commissioned to come here. Weighty decisions were made then and must be made again this day. So, in the knowledge that others pray for our guidance, let us begin.'

Each looked at the other, but no one spoke. Finally, Merchant Martha shifted forward in her seat. I knew she wouldn't be content to dither long.

'Beatrice is the obvious candidate. She's been longest among us as a beguine and is a hard worker. Who else is there?' she asked in a tone which suggested, that matter now being settled, we could all leave.

Several heads nodded in agreement around the room.

Shepherd Martha frowned. 'Beatrice is a dedicated beguine, there's no doubting that, but the Healing Martha is different from other Marthas. Whoever is chosen must have the skills to tend the sick and prepare cordials and ointments. Just to discover what ails a person is no simple task, never mind to reason what will cure them. Has Beatrice these specific skills?'

'Do you think any here have those skills?' Merchant Martha asked tartly. 'Healing Martha studied a great many years and attended the finest school of medicine in Flanders before she settled in the Vineyard. We'll not find another like her, so we'll have to make shift with what God's seen fit to grant us. No use fretting for roasted swan when you only have herring.'

Kitchen Martha waved her hand in a timid gesture. 'Is she to be called Healing Martha?'

'We've not yet decided that Beatrice *is* to be appointed Martha,' I explained, trying not to let my impatience show. The events of the past weeks had left us all exhausted, but Kitchen Martha could at least attempt to pay attention to the discussion.

'No, no ... I mean, whoever is appointed a Martha, if she is to be called *Healing* Martha, what will our own Healing Martha be called? We can't take her name from her, can we, not while she lives. It's been her name for so long and ...' she hesitated and bit her thumb, 'and as ill as she is, she might not understand another name.'

Kitchen Martha was absolutely correct and I was annoyed with myself for not foreseeing this problem. To be a Martha is a responsibility, not an honour, but the beguines had come to look upon the title as a badge of respect and would think we were insulting Healing Martha if we stripped her of it. Besides, what had been her beguine name before she became a Martha, or her baptismal name before that? If I who had known her longest couldn't remember, who could? It would be in the records in Bruges but, as Kitchen Martha said, would she recognize it?

'Obviously, we'll have to give the new Martha a different title,' Merchant Martha said impatiently.

Everyone nodded and smiled, relieved.

'So it's to be Beatrice, then?' Gate Martha said.

All eyes turned to me. It must not be Beatrice, of that at least I was determined. There was a bitterness in her, a festering splinter that I couldn't pluck out. She was sullen as a child, with as little control over her own emotions. She refused to bare her soul to me in confession. I knew that she said what she thought I wanted to hear, guarding her real thoughts from me.

And it was not just her thoughts and sins she hugged to herself. Of late, I had observed that she had become uncommonly possessive. Kitchen Martha would never mention it in open Council, but I had seen her forced to stand outside the door of the pigeon cote, waiting like a scullion for Beatrice to hand her out a basket of squabs. It was to be commended that any beguine took charge of some aspect of husbandry, but Beatrice had gone much further than simply caring for the cote; she refused to let anyone, except the dumb girl, set foot inside. How could you trust a woman like that to make decisions that would affect all our lives?

I knew the Council of Marthas was waiting for me to speak, and I made them wait, fixing each pair of eyes in turn. I wanted them to be quite clear that I would not be swayed on this.

'I don't believe that Beatrice seeks this office and it would be wrong to force this responsibility upon her. She is too close to Pega and some of the other women to want to lead them. And she openly shows favouritism among the young beguines, indulging some and being overly critical of others. She fusses over the dumb girl as if she was the child's mother. I do not dispute that a little maternal care might be good for the girl, if Beatrice would discipline her as a mother should, but instead she encourages the child to run wild. If Beatrice cannot exercise control over one young girl, how is she to be entrusted with the running of a beguinage? No, if Beatrice had wanted responsibility, she would have taken it already. She's content to be guided and directed. Women like her find responsibility frightening.'

Merchant Martha frowned and shuffled forward to the very edge of her seat, as if she was about to leap out of it. 'I don't agree, Servant Martha. Beatrice has a deal of common sense, which is what we need on this Council. And she wants to be given the opportunity, any fool can see that. I've often heard her grumble that she is sent too often to the fields and not entrusted with more weighty duties.'

'Thereby demonstrating all too plainly that she's not ready to be a Martha,' I retorted. 'Marthas are elected as servants of the beguinage. They should never grumble about performing humble tasks and most particularly they should not complain of such to the other women and encourage discontent. We need

Marthas who will uplift the spirit of the beguinage, whatever their personal feelings. And we need Marthas who can keep their own counsel.'

The women exchanged sidelong glances with one another.

'Does no one else have another candidate to propose?' I asked, willing someone to propose the name that was in my thoughts. It must be seen to come from one of them. Then they would accept it. 'Tutor Martha, what about you? You've told us nothing of your thoughts on this matter. Whom do you propose?'

Tutor Martha looked up eagerly. 'I know you'll say she's too young, but have you considered Osmanna? Look how she's already taken charge of the infirmary and the care of Healing Martha and she learns quickly. I'm sure such responsibility would hasten her maturity.'

A small sigh of relief escaped my lips. 'She is very young, Tutor Martha, but, I agree, shows every sign of making an excellent leader.'

Dairy Martha pursed her lips. 'I've no objection to Osmanna personally, nor do I have any quarrel with appointing one so young, But ... I hate to say this, many of the local women are uncomfortable being around her. She never seems to make any effort to befriend any of the other beguines. I know I should not say this ... but I've heard them describe her as cold and well ... proud. They might not respect her as a Martha, they might even resent her. And besides, as Merchant Martha says, Beatrice expects to be appointed. She'll be very hurt if she isn't.'

I raised my eyebrows. 'Dairy Martha, have I heard you aright? Are you seriously suggesting that we should appoint someone as a Martha simply on the grounds that they will cry if we do not?'

She flushed. 'No, Servant Martha, that's not what I meant. I simply –'

'I am most relieved to hear it. As to Osmanna's popularity among the women, unfortunately we cannot be liked by every-one. I dare say some of the women dislike me.'

Kitchen Martha chuckled nervously, but no one contradicted me.

Merchant Martha coughed pointedly. I tried to ignore her, but everyone turned expectantly. This time, unable to sit still a moment longer, Merchant Martha rose and began pacing the chapel, her hands clasped behind her back.

'There's another objection to Osmanna that no one seems to have mentioned.' Merchant Martha glanced back at me, frowning. 'We all know that the state of the soul is known only to the penitent herself, her confessor and God. Nevertheless, when we are considering that person for a position of authority . . .' She paused and surveyed me with dark, inquisitive eyes.

'Continue, Merchant Martha,' I said. 'Say what is on your conscience. I know it will not be divulged outside this room.'

'Some of us have observed of late that Osmanna has not received the Host during Mass, nor even attended upon the altar. Naturally as her confessor you cannot divulge the sin, but . . .'

I knew she'd raise that. I'd seen the looks pass between her and Kitchen Martha each time Osmanna did not come forward to receive the Host.

'I can assure you, all of you, that Osmanna has not been refused the Blessed Sacrament because of any sin. On the contrary, it is Osmanna's own desire to abstain. Something she has read in these past weeks has caused her to question whether our blessed Lord intended us to take His words literally regarding the bread and wine. She asks whether it is right to seek the presence of God through physical elements at all, when God is spirit.'

There was a gasp of horror and outrage from some of the Marthas.

'She is mistaken, of course,' I said quickly. 'Nevertheless, I rejoice that Osmanna desires to seek the truth for herself and I have no doubt, no doubt at all, that when she has meditated upon such questions and searched the will of God, she will again receive the Blessed Sacrament with renewed joy and understanding.'

'Then, Servant Martha, until she has resolved these matters of faith, we can't consider her for the position of a Martha, where she must give leadership to others.' There was a note of triumph in Merchant Martha's voice. She thought she had won.

January – Feast of Fools

A week of general licence in abbeys and monasteries. An Abbot of Misrule was appointed, monks burned old sandals instead of incense, drank, swore and farted in church, sang parodies of hymns and ate black puddings in a mock Mass.

Osmanna

Servant Martha laid her quill down with a sigh. 'As I told you last week, Osmanna, you will continue to work in the infirmary until a new Martha is appointed. My instructions have not changed.'

But I wasn't a physician. I could keep the place in order and continue to give the existing patients the same treatments as Healing Martha had done, for she had written down exactly what each person must be given. But if anyone came with a new sickness or injury I wouldn't know what to do. And what of Healing Martha herself, how was I to treat her?

'But, Servant Martha, when will a new Martha be appointed?'

'Were you not listening when I explained to the whole beguinage that the Holy Spirit did not confirm who was to be the next Martha?'

'Yes, but –'

'Then you already know the answer to your question.'

But that was the point, I didn't know, no one did, though there were endless whispered speculations. 'Being of one mind is the sign that the Holy Spirit has put His seal upon a decision, for he plants His will in each of our minds,' Servant Martha said. But the Marthas had not been of one mind. Everyone said that they had argued, and since everyone expected Beatrice to be named Martha, it could only have been over her. But which of them had opposed her?

Beatrice was angry and hurt. She spent as much time as she could with Gudrun, ignoring all the stares and whispers. She'd always doted on the girl, but now she seemed be occupied with nothing else, fussing over Gudrun as if she was a newborn baby. They spent hours together in the cote and if Gudrun ever managed to slip out, Beatrice would abandon anything she was doing and clamber up to old Gwenith's cottage to look for her, no matter what the weather. I didn't blame her. Gudrun was the only person who didn't realize the humiliation Beatrice had suffered and Gudrun couldn't gossip behind her back.

Servant Martha had taken me aside after she'd spoken to everyone in the refectory. It was obvious from her clipped voice and hardened jaw that she was annoyed about what had happened in the Marthas' Council. Her instructions to me had been curt and to the point. I should continue in the infirmary until a Martha was appointed. That would be my only duty from now on and Pega would help me.

I was relieved that someone was to help me, but half of me wished it had been someone other than Pega, and the other half of me was glad it was her. I wanted a chance to explain to her why I had run out of the barn on that day she kissed me. I wanted to say to her, hold me again and this time I won't run. But she seemed to go out of her way to be busy whenever I tried to approach her.

I often caught her looking at me when she thought I was occupied. Whenever I felt her watching, the place on my brow where she'd laid her warm mouth seemed to burn as if her lips were still there. I cursed myself a thousand times over for running out of the barn. It was only a kiss and she was only trying to be kind. A hundred times a day, I tried to think of something to say that would mend what I had done and get her to talk to me again, but everything I thought of sounded foolish, even in my head.

'Servant Martha, I don't have the skill for the infirmary. I'm sure there is someone else who could do it much better. Perhaps, Beatr –'

'Nonsense!' The mole on her chin quivered.

If Servant Martha had lived in the time of Noah and God had told her that He was going to send a flood to destroy the world, she would have simply said, 'Nonsense.' And He wouldn't have dared to do it.

'I'm very disappointed in you, Osmanna. I didn't think that

you of all people would refuse to take on a little work, when you know how grave is the need.'

I opened my mouth to protest indignantly that I wasn't refusing to work, but she didn't wait for an answer.

'God requires this task of you; therefore He will equip you to perform it. Do you think that some good fairy simply bestowed the skill and knowledge on Healing Martha at her christening? She earned her knowledge through long, tiring hours of study and practice. And you will acquire the skills you need if you apply yourself diligently to the mastery of them.'

I knew that she was in no mood to be questioned, but I blurted it out before I could stop myself.

'Servant Martha, doesn't the parable of the talents teach us that each of us is born with different gifts which we must use in different ways for God's service?'

Her back stiffened and she rose slowly from her stool, like a father before he strikes a rebellious child. She moved past me to stand in the open doorway, staring out at hard grey skies beyond the walls.

'The parable speaks not of gifts, Osmanna, but of coins, which are entrusted to us for safekeeping. A gift may be used as the recipient pleases, but the master requires a reckoning of the money entrusted to a servant. A coin must be spent to fulfil its worth, else it remains a useless disc of metal. The coin that God saw fit to place in your keeping is your intelligence, Osmanna, your quickness to learn. Do not squander such a purse on clever arguments and vain questions, but on acquiring such knowledge as may save your soul and that of your fellow man. Read the herbals, Osmanna, read the Psalter and put other books aside until you are able to bring a goodly measure of knowledge and mature judgment to the studying of them.'

I felt my cheeks burning. I knew exactly which book she meant. When I finally confessed what I'd been reading, I expected her to order me to destroy the book or, at very least, surrender it to her, but I should have realized that she wouldn't. Servant Martha had spoken so many times in the chapel of the folly of seeking to silence knowledge. She always said that if the words on a page were true, then burning the book would not destroy the truth of them, and if they were false, then their falsehood would be exposed in God's good time, so that all men might mock it. However much the book angered her, she would never break faith with her principles and destroy it.

Servant Martha turned from the doorway and glared down at me, her lips pressed tightly together. I had irritated her from the first moment she saw me in my father's hall. Every answer I made to her was the wrong one, but I couldn't seem to keep my mouth shut. I had to answer back; even when she declared the discussion closed, I couldn't help myself. But for once I wished she'd talk to me, really talk. There was so much I wanted to know. I wanted to ask her what she felt when she elevated the body of Christ, that moment when she is become Christ. What did it feel like to touch the mind of God? If only she had told me that, perhaps I could have understood why taking that little piece of bread was so important.

Servant Martha gripped the edge of the doorframe, as if she was suddenly weary. 'Osmanna, I know that you are young and the infirmary is a heavy responsibility for one of your tender years. But you can always seek advice from others. It is not a burden you have to share alone. That is the whole essence of a beguinage, no woman is alone with her burdens. But know this, I would not have entrusted you with the task if I did not believe you were equal to it. I have had to persuade others that you are capable of this, and believe me, there are many who think you are not, so do not make me a fool in their eyes, Osmanna. I will not forgive that.'

Father Ulfrid

'Is your father at home, William?'

The boy glanced apprehensively back over his shoulder into the cottage, then finally he drew back a little from the doorway so that I could squeeze past him. Like all the cottages in Ulewic, this reeked of the dung heap and decay. The sodden rushes had been gathered up from the floor and thrown into rotting piles in the street. But the earth floor and walls had been soaked in flood water awash with all the excrement and refuse from the cottagers' middens, and there was no way of throwing out that stink.

Alan sat hunched over a smoking fire that only served to draw up a foul, clinging mist from the earth floor, chilling the bones. His eyes were unfocused and his hands trembled slightly. I'd seen those signs in many of the villagers since the flood. They were drinking some concoction made from the dried heads of the white poppies that infested the marshlands. It fuddled the mind like strong wine, and blunted the edge of their hunger, numbing the misery. But it was an evil substance, for it robbed a man of all will to labour and eventually sent him mad. I was shocked to see a strong, hardworking man like Alan under its influence.

I coughed, but he did not stir or rise to offer me his seat. 'God keep you and the children, Alan.'

'God will keep us, will He?' he growled. 'He'd best do it then ... I can't. Salterns have gone.' He flung his arm wide in a wild, uncontrolled gesture. 'Sea took them, took it all back. My father worked them and his father afore him. Been working them so many generations, no one knows for sure who made them. But they're gone, just like that, in one night. There's nowt left.'

'But at least your life was spared, Alan. Many of the other men and boys weren't so fortunate.'

'Fortunate – that what you call it? Some fortune. How am I supposed to feed the bairns now? You got an answer for that, Father?' Alan spat a glob of yellow phlegm into the flames, which hissed and spat back at him. 'D'Acaster'll be demanding his rent for this pigsty. Church'll be screaming for their tithes, isn't that right, Father ... all you ever want is money, whole fecking lot of you ... Owl Masters too, you're all a pack of scavenging dogs fighting over our guts. What good are any of you to us? You with your Latin prayers, Owl Masters with their bonfires. There's not one of you could stop the river taking what she wanted.'

What was I supposed to say to him – pray and repent? God will forgive and all shall be restored? I knew better than anyone that whole seas of prayers would not induce God to forgive and restore.

I'd prayed that St Michael's would be filled for Christmas and it was. God had sent a flood to herd the villagers into the church, a captive congregation for the Commissarius to see, but God's vicious joke was that very flood had also kept the Commissarius away. As the waters receded, the villagers ebbed away again. And as soon as the roads became passable, the Commissarius would return. Like a tethered bird, a wing-beat of escape was all I'd been granted, and now it was only a matter of time before I was brought crashing down.

Alan peered up at me from beneath heavy lids. 'Why did you come here, Father? See for yourself, we've nothing left. Between the Church, the Manor and the Owl Masters, you've taken it all, and what you didn't get your greedy fists on, the river took.'

I gritted my teeth. 'I came to discuss a Mass for the soul of your poor wife.'

'They've found Mam?' a voice whispered. I turned to see William standing behind me, his small, thin body tense and alert.

'No, no, I'm sorry. They've found nothing yet.'

'But they'll keep looking, won't they?' William said desperately.

'I told you, boy, your mam's gone,' Alan bellowed. 'There's no use you hoping she's going to come back. Your mam's dead, boy, dead and gone. If Black Anu takes you as her prey, that's it, boy.'

'Only God takes life, Alan,' I snapped. God's balls, I couldn't take much more of these numbskull villagers and their stupid superstitions! Why did I even bother to waste my breath preaching to them? The church pigeons took more notice of me than they did.

I took a deep breath and tried to swallow my anger. 'If your poor wife has drowned, we will make every effort to recover her body and give her a decent Christian burial in holy ground, so that she may rest in peace.'

'Let it alone, Father. You'll not find any in these parts that'll take a corpse from water. If they do, they or one of their own family will drown afore the year is out. Same'll happen to you, if you try. Cross'll not protect you, no more than it did in the churchyard at Samhain,' he added, sneering.

I wanted to punch him. I'd been drugged, for God's sake. What could I have done? 'I'm no coward! I know that's what you and rest of this devil's arse of a village thinks, but I'm not afraid of –' I faltered as a terrible stench filled the room, overpowering even the stink of mildew and decay. Someone was whimpering in the corner.

'William,' Alan roared. 'I told you to take that brat outside to shit.'

'I did,' William protested, scuttling over to the corner. 'But I no sooner take her out than she does it again.'

He pulled his little sister up from the pile of rags on which she lay. Green excrement was running down her legs and dripping on to her bare feet, and the child was moaning and clutching her belly. Her head flopped against William's shoulder as he dragged her out of the cottage.

I turned to Alan, who had slumped back in his chair. 'That child is very sick, Alan. Have you any physic for her?'

He wiped a weary hand over his eyes. 'How am I supposed to know what to do for her? Her mam did all that. I can't take care of a sick bairn.'

Alan heaved himself from the stool, bracing himself against the wall, his legs too unsteady to support him. He groped along a shelf until he found a small jar and scraped a little of its black, sticky contents into a beaker with his fingernail. I grasped his arm.

'No, Alan, you must keep a clear head. What would your poor wife say if she was here? Your son's a good lad, but he needs your help.'

He shook off my arm violently, almost hitting me in the face as he flailed out.

'William's not my brat, haven't you eyes to see that? Let Phillip D'Acaster take care of his own bastards. If you want to meddle, Father, try starting with those whores and witches in the house of women. How is it they've got food, when there's none in the village? How come none of their beasts got the murrain and the flood didn't even touch them? 'Cause they put the evil eye on us, that's why. All this is their doing.'

He stumbled back to the stool and crashed down heavily on to it again. 'You want to know something else, Father?' He wagged a trembling finger at me. 'I heard tell that even when the Owlman was sent out against them, they escaped, and I'll tell you for why, 'cause they've got that relic. Protects them against anything and turns the curses back on us. As long as they've got that relic, there's no one can touch them. Ulewic won't be safe till we get it away from them.'

I knew he was thinking I was useless. The whole village was laughing at me because I, a priest, could not make a gaggle of women obey me. Those women would pay for making a mockery of me, they'd pay dearly.

I clenched my fist around my iron cross. 'I swear I will get it, Alan. One way or the other I will force them to give it to me.'

January – St Distaff's Day

The day when women returned to their labour, especially spinning and weaving, after the days of Christmas.

Osmanna

Hunching forward on the stool, I tried again to spoon the warm pap into Healing Martha's mouth. A little of it dribbled out from the corner. I scraped it up with the spoon and shovelled it back in again. It was an improvement. A few days ago nearly all I spooned in would leak back out again, but either she swallowed better now or I'd mastered the trick of tipping the spoon towards the good side of her mouth. She sank back, worn out by the effort of eating. The edges of her veil were wet where she had puked, as was the front of her shift. I'd have to change them or they'd stink as they dried.

Her good eye missed nothing, for all that she couldn't name it. She pointed at anything she saw amiss in the infirmary and, if we couldn't see it, she grunted her one sound over and over, till she shrieked with frustration. She wouldn't rest until it was put right: a fouled cot cleaned, a loose bandage fastened or a smoking fire stirred to flame. She never used to be so impatient and angry. But then she was always busy; now she could do nothing but watch.

She wept often. Sometimes silent tears rolled down her face and ran into rivulets on her wrinkled neck, wetting her pillow. Other times she made great noisy sobs with her mouth open and snot hanging from her nose, beating her good arm against the wood of her cot until it was purple with bruises. I rubbed oil of lavender on her then to restore her wits and she quietened, but I don't think it was the oil which dried her eyes but her own pride, for even in her state she remembered what the perfume signified.

Some of the beguines, like Catherine, refused to come near her. She said she was afraid she'd cry and upset Healing Martha. I think she was afraid that she'd somehow be struck down too, as if Healing Martha had some contagion. But others did come; they couldn't keep away. I seldom passed her bed in the evening without seeing someone sitting there, one of the beguines or another patient. They came after dark mostly, when the tapers in the room burned gentle and mellow and her face was veiled in the shadows of her narrow cave.

When daylight came she was left alone save for little gifts tied to her bed: ribbons, sweet-smelling dried herbs, or pressed flowers, their colours faded like ghosts of summer. Votive offerings laid at the feet of the statue of a saint. But what could she grant them? They leaned into the shadows and whispered for hours, vomiting all their thoughts. She uttered nothing but her one impenetrable grunt. Yet they went away, looking content, as if there was absolution in that sound. She, not Servant Martha, was the sovereign bee in our hive, helpless and flightless, while we workers gladly danced attendance on her as if she was our liege lord.

I held a cup to her lips. 'Try to drink a little of this, Healing Martha. It's good for you.'

She glared at me. 'Gar!'

'Please, Healing Martha. You've written it in your own herbals; lily of the valley distilled in wine will restore speech. I prepared it exactly as you have written.'

Would it heal her? If only I could be certain. Her hand had also written that the physician must have patience. 'Healing waits upon time,' she'd written in firm, steady strokes. If I could be sure that it would restore her in time I'd have gladly waited. But what if I waited for weeks, for months, and all the while I'd not been giving her what she needed?

A hand touched my shoulder. I glanced round to find Merchant Martha standing behind me.

'How is she?' she asked, inclining her head vaguely in the direction of Healing Martha.

'Why don't you ask her?' I said, sliding off the stool.

She took Healing Martha's useless hand in her own and patted it heartily. 'Getting stronger, Healing Martha? That's

426

good,' she bellowed, as if Healing Martha was deaf. Then, still clutching Healing Martha's limp hand like a lucky rabbit's foot, Merchant Martha turned to me with her real errand.

'There are women at the gate. They bring their sick, three children and an old man. They've the fever.'

'Sick?' I repeated stupidly.

'The same fever we saw in the village. Must be spreading. Where shall we put them?'

Merchant Martha shuffled her feet impatiently as if she already held them in her arms and was waiting for me to tell her where to lay them down. Her beady gaze darted round the overcrowded infirmary. 'It's to be hoped the whole village don't bring their sick here. Still, I doubt they will, seeing as we are under sentence of excommunication. That priest probably did us a service, else we'd have had them all at our door, with Servant Martha insisting on feeding the whole pack of them with no thought as to where we are going to buy more food.' She shook her head as if such recklessness was beyond her comprehension. 'Still, we'll have to deal with those that have come. Best put them in the pilgrims' room next door. You'll not want them in here in case the contagion spreads.'

I nodded gratefully, thankful that she had made the decision. What was I supposed to do for them? *Deal with them*, Merchant Martha said. She made it sound as easy as milking a cow. But what did I know about fevers? And what if it did spread and the beguines caught the fever as well? I could already feel Healing Martha's good eye staring at me from her cot, telling me in her one sound that I'd killed them.

I tucked the coverlets unnecessarily firmly around Healing Martha, but she didn't stir. Placing her limp hand, which Merchant Martha had now discarded, tidily on the covers, I smoothed down the fingers to make them lie at ease on the bed. The arm lay at an unnatural angle. I turned it, but still it looked no better. I stared at it, trying to visualize how an arm at rest should look.

'Come along now,' Merchant Martha urged. 'They're waiting.'

Merchant Martha scurried ahead and I had to trot to keep up with her, but she always walked as if she had eight legs instead of two, so I could tell nothing about the urgency from her speed. She clutched my arm and steered me to the open gate of the beguinage.

The entrance to the beguinage was blocked by a handcart as if the owner was determined that nothing would precede him through the gates. An old man lay crumpled up inside, his grey head sagging against a lumpy sack. His beard was matted with vomit, his scarlet face beaded with sweat. He panted, mouth open, like a dog. A younger man squatted on the ground in the shelter of the cart, sunk into a stupor. His eyes were closed and he seemed content to doze, knowing that nothing could get past the cart without disturbing him.

Gate Martha was clucking like an old hen, clearly vexed that she couldn't get her gate closed. I followed her through the open gate, squeezing past the handcart. Outside two women crouched on the ground, their backs to the wall, hunched up against the bitter wind. They looked worn out. A small girl lay across the knees of one of them, sweating and fretful. Her mother kept up a regular rhythm of patting the child heavily on the back. It didn't appear to soothe her, but it was as if the mother had been doing it for so long she had forgotten how to stop.

An older boy rested his head in the second woman's lap. She couldn't have carried such a lanky child so far, he was almost as tall as she, but perhaps he had come on the handcart with the old man. Beyond them a little girl lay curled up alone, whimpering. She'd messed herself and lay in a stinking puddle of liquid shit the colour of pea broth.

Gate Martha peered around, then looked down at the solitary child. 'There was a lad with this one. William, he called himself, said he was her brother, but by the looks of it, he's run off. I reckon that's the last we'll see of him.'

Crouching down opposite the woman with the little girl, I touched the child's leg. She was burning up.

'How long have the children had this fever?' I asked.

But neither of the women answered or even looked at me and I began to wonder if I had actually spoken aloud. They gazed down unseeing at their own stained clothes, their thoughts so turned in that if St Michael himself had appeared with his sword of flame, I doubt they'd have noticed him. Gate Martha nudged the grime-streaked toes of the nearest woman with her shoe. The woman squinted up at her.

'Lass asked what ails the bairn,' Gate Martha said.

The woman protectively pulled her child closer to her, half smothering her. The child wailed and struggled feebly.

'We've come for the cure, for the bairns.'

I tried to smile encouragingly. 'We'll take the children to a room near the infirmary. They'll be comfortable there.'

The women frowned at me as if they didn't understand.

'There are good clean beds, dry and warm,' I added eagerly. Anyone would think I was an innkeeper trying to sell the virtues of his lodging to a passing merchant. 'We'll give them what tinctures and herbs we have to help them.'

They continued to stare blankly at me and I sensed that I was not telling them what they wanted to hear.

'We can't promise to cure them, but we'll try what remedies we know and if God wills it . . . we'll all pray for them.'

The woman struggled to her feet, weighed down by the burden of the child in her arms. She glowered at me as if she thought I was refusing to help.

'We want the cure,' she said with the grim determination of a cheated housewife demanding her full measure of flour.

'We can bathe them, give them cordials, bleed them, do whatever we can but –'

She took a step forward, angry. 'We can wash our own bairns and we've not brought them here for potions. We've come for the cure. Let the bairns touch it, that's all we want.'

I turned in bewilderment to Merchant Martha. 'What does she mean – the cure?'

Gate Martha beckoned Merchant Martha and me aside.

'Host that was saved from the fire,' she whispered. 'That's the cure they've come for.'

'Andrew's Host?'

Gate Martha nodded and Merchant Martha looked as grim as I'd ever seen her.

'But why do they think it'll cure the children? There's been no healing.'

The Host had lain in its painted wooden reliquary in the recess near the altar. Everyone said it had protected us from the murrain and even the flood, but no one had claimed it had healed them of any infirmity or sickness. It had not cured Healing Martha.

Gate Martha shrugged, but offered no explanation. The woman came across to where we stood, swinging her child in her arms like a battering ram.

'You'll not deny the cure to the bairns. We've money for candles,' she said defiantly. She jerked her head towards the young man still snoring on the ground under the cart. 'He's got money an' all, so don't let him tell you he hasn't. I saw his wife give it him, though he'd sooner spend it on ale and let the old 'un die. He's wanted him out of the way for years, says the old pisspot's a useless mouth to feed.'

The little girl lying by herself gave a convulsive shudder and turned over. Even through her coarse shift, I could see her belly was swollen up like a drowned sheep. Her flushed face crumpled in pain. She cried out and another stream of green shit oozed out of her. But she didn't open her eyes.

Merchant Martha gripped me fiercely by the arm. 'If they're demanding the relic, I'd best fetch Servant Martha. She'll want to know about this. Meanwhile, you take that little girl inside. If her brother has left her here for us to care for, I warrant that child at least will be grateful for a warm room and a dry bed.'

Pisspuddle

Black, black water is creeping towards me. My legs are heavy. They won't move. I can't get my arms free. I'm trapped in the stocks and the water's rising up. It's running round my feet in a little trickle, like spiders' feet. It's crawling up over my belly.

'Mam, Mam, get me out!'

Why doesn't she come? It's cold. It's so cold. My teeth are chattering and I can't get warm. There are monsters swimming in the water, things with big eyes and beaks, sharp beaks stabbing at me, tearing me. I can't fight them off. I can't get my hands free.

'Don't leave me here, Mam. Where are you?'

Water's getting deeper. I'm so thirsty I want to drink the water, but the beaks are jumping out of the water at my face. Sharp beaks, hot beaks, hotter than pincers from the furnace. Black Anu's in the water, she's biting my belly with her big teeth. She's eating me.

'It hurts. It hurts so much. Mam, make her stop!'

'Hush, lass, hush. She's getting worse, Osmanna. I've seen bairns taken like it afore and there's nothing can save them when they get this bad.'

'Keep wiping her with the cold water, Pega. We have to cool her, she's burning up.'

'Mam?'

'Your mother's not here, child. It was your brother who brought you here. Try to drink some more of this, please. It'll make you better.'

'No, Osmanna, leave the bairn be, she only pukes it back up again and it just makes the poor mite more miserable every time. There's nowt you can do for her now. She'll not make it through the night. Let her rest.'

'No, Pega, she won't die. I can't let her die.'

'Bairns die, that's the way of it. When they get this bad, there's nothing can save them.'

'There's another way ... I remember ... I saw Healing Martha do it once on a babe that wouldn't suckle. Turn her on to her belly, Pega. If the medicine won't go down, perhaps we can get it up.'

✝

January – St Pega's Day

Anchoress and virgin sister of St Guthlac, she lived not far from Crowland. When Guthlac realized he was dying, he invited his sister to the funeral and she sailed down the River Welland. Following Guthlac's death she went on a pilgrimage to Rome where she died.

Servant Martha

All eyes were fixed upon the white wafer raised high above their heads; such a tiny, fragile thing yet it was the very presence, the very substance of the omnipotent God who created all heaven and earth. I held in my hand a drop of water that is an ocean, a flame that is the essence and being of the whole fire.

'*Salus, victoria et resurrectio nostra.*'

The blessed mystery, bread made by my hands and trans-figured by my words into His very flesh. Upon that fragment stood our immortal souls, the eternity of our existence. My hands had become Christ's hands. I had climbed the sacred mountain for *them*.

But the mountain top was deserted. I stood barefoot and alone in the holy place and saw that it was empty. Nothing came back from all my prayers and questions except a hollow, mocking silence. I could make bread into flesh for them, but in my own mouth it had turned to dust. My hand trembled and drops of red wine spilled on to the white cloth.

I busied myself in the chapel cleaning the vessels until I saw Osmanna rise and make her way towards the door. I called her and she paused with her back to me. Hesitated, just for a moment, a scintilla of defiance was all, but it was enough. Then she turned and walked back meekly, eyes wide and questioning, the semblance of obedience.

I'd had days to think about this moment, yet I'd still not decided how to begin it. I folded the linen cloth. The wine had seeped through it and beneath there was a small blood-red stain on the white stone of the altar on which the Mass stone rested. I scrubbed at it with a little water, but it would not come out.

'Was there something you wanted me to do, Servant Martha?'

God in heaven, could she not at least wait for me to speak? Her arms were thrust behind her back and she stood watching me, her head on one side and her eyebrows raised quizzically. Did she really not know why I'd asked her to stay?

'Did you observe, Osmanna, that eight women did not come forward to receive the blessed Host tonight?'

Her gaze flinched away from mine and she swallowed hard. At least she appeared to retain some slight awe of me. That was something.

'I was lost in my prayers, Servant Martha ... I didn't notice who went forward. Surely we're not supposed to watch –'

'*Lost* is indeed an apposite term for you, Osmanna, and for that very state in which you now find yourself. I foolishly trusted that you sought only to come to a greater understanding of the sweet mystery that is the sacrament, but not only have you not returned in all humility to the table of our blessed Lord, you have incited others to follow your example and turn away.'

I found myself pacing up and down the chapel and was suddenly aware that my voice had risen to a strident pitch. I forced myself to lower it.

'Some of the women are not blessed with your reason. They were content in their faith and you have deliberately set out to undermine it. To wrestle with our own doubts is part of every religious life, but it must be done in private. To infect others with that venomous worm –'

'I have no doubts, Servant Martha.'

She stood by the altar, glowering at me. Her face was flushed, her hands clenched at her sides as if she was struggling to hold them in check. She looked as she did that first day I laid eyes on her in her father's house. I was beginning to think he was right about her after all.

'You have *no* doubts, Osmanna? Then forgive me, for I see you are indeed blessed above all God's saints – I know of no other who makes such a claim.'

'I didn't mean ... what I ... Servant Martha, you yourself say our souls may reach out directly to God and He to us. We don't need anything else.'

Blessed Lord, forgive her youth. 'I do not need reminding of what I've said, Osmanna. I may seem ancient to you, but I can assure you my wits are not wandering yet. I'm flattered that you attend to me so well and, that being so, it makes your refusal to take His blessed body the more inexplicable. God laid hands upon me in spirit to consecrate the bread and wine as He lays his hands upon every one of his servants. Even you, Osmanna, could do this one day if –'

'No, you don't understand!'

How dared she raise her voice to me, and in here? Still, at least it was evidence that my words had penetrated that armour of self-possession. I met her gaze unblinking and she finally had the grace to lower her eyes.

She took a deep breath. 'Servant Martha, don't you see, that's the whole point.' She spoke unnaturally slowly as if she was struggling to keep control of her temper. 'You said … I mean … doesn't it say that God is spirit and we should worship Him in spirit? So why do we need to eat bread? Why should this little piece of wheat and water have any more power to save us than the loaves that we share daily in the refectory? It is only our faith that makes it so and our faith does not need physical signs. You taught me that.'

'It was our Lord's command that we should do it. That should be enough for you. Did Abraham question why God commanded him to slay his son?'

'When the women were afraid to take Ralph in, you sa … you *said* God is in each of us, Servant Martha. So if God is already in me, why must I take His flesh into my body? All I have to do is reach out for salvation and take it. I don't need you or anyone else to give it to me.' Osmanna thrust out her chin as if she could take the world with a snap of her fingers.

It took every grain of self-control I possessed not to slap her. 'Osmanna, I give you nothing. I am merely the channel of His love and mercy.'

437

'No, Servant Martha, you are not a channel, you are a guard barring the way. The priests won't let the people speak to God except through them. They tell us that no one can be saved unless they eat the bread that they alone have the power to consecrate. They control who will eat and be saved and who will be refused and damned. Like some pedlar in the market-place, they offer an elixir of life and they decide the price. You haven't changed anything, Servant Martha. All you have done is to take their place in the gateway. Now you stand between us and God instead of them.'

Holy and blessed Mother of God, hadn't she understood how far we had come? Didn't she realize the power we had taken into our own hands? And now she thought to cast it aside as if it was a mere nothing, an empty eggshell, to be discarded on the midden.

'Do you dare to presume, girl, that the disciples who were with Jesus daily had less faith than you? Yet did Jesus not command them to eat the bread after His death? And the blessed St Peter who had walked with our Lord, did he not instruct the first Christians to eat of the bread though they did so in fear of their very lives? How dare you presume that you do not need to obey God in this? It is not for us to know what divine plans are accomplished through this act of obedience.'

'Servant Martha –'

'Be silent! I will not debate this with you. To claim that salvation may be obtained without the sacraments is heresy. Don't you realize that the words you've spoken today, if they were heard outside these walls, would be enough to have you convicted of the most heinous crime that any man or woman may commit. Do I really need to remind you of the punishment which awaits those so condemned?'

Her eyes opened wide in alarm. She stared at me in horror.

'But I didn't . . . I didn't mean . . .' she stammered.

At last I had succeeded in driving home the enormity of what she had done. For once there were no clever words forming in her mouth, no blaze of truculence in her eyes. She was a frightened child, waiting for me to tell her what to do.

But what should I tell her to do? I could insist upon a public retraction before all the beguines, but if I demanded that of her I would have to demand the same of all those who had dissented or I would make a martyr of her, and I didn't need a martyr on my hands. Let her, let all of them slip back into the fold without any fuss as if they had never been away. If we ignored it as though it had never happened, it would more quickly be forgotten.

'Next Sunday at Mass in chapel, Osmanna, you will receive the Host again. The others will soon follow your example, and if they don't, I will speak to them privately and encourage them.'

She opened her mouth to speak. Her expression had suddenly changed and I could see her words were not going to be those of meek acceptance. I stepped rapidly towards her and grasped her shoulder. I felt her stiffen under my hand.

'Osmanna,' I said as soothingly as I could. 'Think of it in this way; if, as you claim, the sacrament is but an outward symbol of a spiritual action, then what harm can there be in consuming the bread as an example to those whose understanding is not as great as yours? We must not put stumbling blocks in the way of our weaker sisters.'

Her mouth was trembling, but her fists were clenched.

'Osmanna, we cannot afford divisions now. The villagers blame us for the sickness. You saw the mood of those women when they demanded their children be allowed to touch Andrew's relic. If the fever continues, as I fear it will, their hostility towards us can only increase, and as we have already incurred the wrath of the priest, I feel sure he will do nothing to calm their fear of us. I need the support of all the beguines to stand firm against them, especially you. That the other women have followed you in refusing the sacrament proves you have the gift of being able to influence others. Use it for us, Osmanna, for the beguinage.'

I released my grip on her shoulder and turned back to polishing the vessels, making it quite clear that the discussion was at an end. From the corner of my eye, I could see her staring up at the face of the Blessed Virgin. Her expression told me nothing. I had no idea if I had succeeded in convincing her. Would she defy me at the next Mass, and what would I do if she did?

She turned away without looking at me and strode towards the door.

'Osmanna,' I called out after her, 'where would you go if you had to leave the beguinage?'

Her backbone jerked upright as if she had been struck from behind. She paused for a moment, but did not turn. Then she tugged the door open and ran from the chapel without answering, leaving only a puddle of moonlight on the floor.

January – Plough Monday

Gangs of youths, or Plough Jacks, dragged a plough from house to house demanding money. If they were refused they ploughed up and wrecked the garden. Bawdy and violent Plough Plays were performed by mummers.

Beatrice

Patches of the night frost still lingered in the hollows on the hill, glittering oddly against the dark, sodden grass. The morning sky had turned pale, almost white against the bare black branches of the trees. Across the river, a flock of sheep ambled across the slope of the hill and I could just make out the familiar shapes of Pega and Shepherd Martha on either side of the flock.

But there was no sign of Gudrun. I hoped she might have gone with them. I'd not seen her since I had gone to check on her in the cote after the midnight service. She was sound asleep then, her lips parted slightly like a baby's, her breath soft and sweet. But when I went to the cote in the morning to take her some bread and pottage, the cote was empty.

She had become adept at slipping out of the beguinage, though I never saw her do it. Sometimes she was away all day, not returning until near dark. Kitchen Martha always kept some supper back for her, however much the other Marthas disapproved. Merchant Martha said if she didn't work she shouldn't eat. I suspected she'd complained of it to Servant Martha more than once, but Servant Martha seemed to have given up any attempt to control Gudrun. I sometimes caught Servant Martha staring at the child, frowning as if she was puzzling over something. Maybe she'd given up the struggle or perhaps she'd mellowed since Healing Martha was struck down.

Mellowed? What was I thinking? Servant Martha wouldn't mellow if she lived as long as old Methuselah. You might as well have tried to soften a stone in a vat of oil. If anything, Servant Martha was more cold and distant than ever, especially to me. I didn't need to be told who objected to me being elected a Martha. And no matter what the other Marthas thought, they wouldn't have stood up to her, even if they all opposed her. That was the real reason she opposed my election, because she knew I would. At least I had my child, my Gudrun, and she couldn't take that away from me, Martha or not.

On any other day, I wouldn't have worried about Gudrun so much, but being Plough Monday there'd be all kinds of mischief abroad. The day might begin with processions and mummers' plays to roust the witches and bless the plough, but it always ended in drinking and fighting. No girl's virtue was safe. My little Gudrun knew how to take care of herself in the hills and forest, but she was such an innocent in other ways, and besides, against two or three strong lads bent on sport what could she do? I couldn't rest until she was safe inside the beguinage again.

But my feet were too swollen and painful with chilblains to go chasing up the hill on a fool's errand, especially in this cold. Pega and Shepherd Martha would have to return across the ford, so I sat down on a rock by the river and waited for them to cross. No sense in making my feet worse by plunging them into that icy water. Pega would have spotted Gudrun if she was making for the ruin of her grandmother's cottage. She wouldn't come to any harm there. The villagers didn't dare go near the old cottage for fear of old Gwenith's ghost.

I pulled my feet up under my cloak. My chilblains itched unbearably, they kept cracking open, and some mornings when I woke they were covered in blood where I'd rubbed them in my sleep. Last year, Healing Martha had given me some thick, foul-smelling ointment to rub into them which had soothed them, but I wasn't going to ask that bitch Osmanna if she had any. I'd rather suffer.

Shepherd Martha whistled Leon to heel as she and Pega strode towards the ford. They pulled off their boots and hose. Pega hitched her skirts and lumbered down into the ford, cursing and swearing as the cold water rose up her calves. She splashed across, taking the last few paces at a run. Shepherd Martha followed more cautiously.

'Sheep,' announced Pega, 'are the most cussed beasts ever to come out of the Ark. I'll never know how you can abide to be around them all year, Shepherd Martha. If you wanted a sheep to stay out of the valley it would go in as soon as look at you. Ask it to go, and you'd think you were trying to murder it.'

'Not so different from men, then,' Shepherd Martha chuckled. 'You don't need to work with sheep very long before you see why our Lord likened His disciples to them. But when it comes to finding a dry, warm place to sleep, they've far more sense than cattle or even old Leon.'

She whistled, and Leon bounded enthusiastically out of the river, waiting until he was up close before shaking his thick black shaggy coat vigorously all over us.

'Get away, you great brute,' Pega yelled, pushing his chest, but Leon seemed to take that as a mark of affection and happily rolled at her feet, drooling as Pega obligingly rubbed his belly.

'Pega, you've not seen Gudrun today, have you, up by the old cottage?' I asked.

'She's not gone up the hill. Leastways, not unless she's doubled back, 'cause I saw her going that way earlier.' She pointed behind us, to the track that led to both the forest and the village. 'We called after her, but she took no notice, not that she ever does, and I'd not the time to go chasing after her.'

Shepherd Martha patted me on the shoulder. 'Don't fret. I dare say she's wandering round in the forest with that raven of hers.'

'I need to make sure,' I said anxiously.

Pega rubbed her great broad hands and blew on them against the cold. 'Leave the poor bairn be, Beatrice. She'll be back when she's hungry. Besides, you'll never find her in the forest; she could be anywhere. I dare say she knows places in there even the verderers have never found.'

I clambered to my feet. 'But what if she's gone into the village? She's had nothing to eat this morning; she might go there looking for food if she gets hungry.'

Shepherd Martha glanced at Pega and shook her head. 'It's no use, you may as well tell the ewe not to bleat for the lamb. She won't rest until Gudrun's back.'

I knew they thought I was fussing, and even I told myself I was. Gudrun had disappeared for a whole day before. There was no reason for me to be anxious. No reason, except for a feeling I couldn't name even to myself.

We'd been to the village to take food several times since the flood, so I knew at once that there was something wrong as soon as I reached the outlying cottages. There was no one peering from the windows or hunting for dog dung outside. There were no children playing in the road, or women fetching water or firewood. It had been quieter of late because of the fever, but even so, there was usually some half-naked infant sitting on the track stuffing fistfuls of dirt into his mouth or a woman sitting in her doorway picking over beans. But I couldn't see anyone. What if the fever had spread? You hear of whole villages being deserted when a sickness takes hold, the sick fleeing and leaving the dead to rot where they lie.

The path between the houses was empty but for the winter midges. They hung in a thick cloud over the ditches where stagnant river water still ran among the refuse and stinking mud. A dark stain was wrapped around the wall of each cottage and strands of dry, yellowish-green slimeweed clung to wattle and fence, marking the height of the water.

The hairy back of a solitary pig poked up from a ditch as it snuffled and rooted among the refuse. It grunted contentedly as if nothing could go amiss in its world. How it had survived the cull, I didn't know. Most likely one of the villagers had hidden it, or it had wandered out from the forest.

'Think yourself fortunate to have survived, do you, little sow? Well, take my advice, mistress, you'd best follow the example of the noblemen's wives and get yourself in litter soon with any boar that passes or you'll not live to see Candlemas.'

The sow gave another grunt, its snout buried deep in the

carcass of some creature that was too far rotted to own a name.

A couple of moth-eaten hens with long scaly legs and wilted combs scratched beside a doorstep. The door of the house was closed tight and the shutters too, as if that was going to keep the fever out, but it was too late, you could smell it was in there. The stench was unmistakable; it clawed at your throat even through a closed door.

The door to the tanner's yard lay open, but there was no sound of beating leather. A scraper lay abandoned on the stretched skin. The skin needed wetting again; it was drying out in the cold wind. It would be the devil's own job to clean that if the fat dried. But what master would be so lax as to let his apprentice run off leaving a hide to spoil, unless he'd been suddenly struck down? What would take master and apprentice together in the midst of their work and in so much haste they didn't even stop to put the skins in soak? Not even the fever could do that.

The Owlman! A shiver ran down my back. I spun wildly round and round, staring up at the milky sky, terrified that he might be crouching up there in the bare branches of the trees, watching me. I started running back the way I'd come, desperate to get to the safety of the beguinage. I stumbled and went sprawling on the sharp stones. Shaken, I crouched on the ground, trying to get my breath.

There was a harsh croak above me. Covering my head, I threw myself against the wall of a cottage. I cowered there, my heart thumping, but nothing happened. Cautiously, I glanced up. It was only a raven. It had settled on the roof of the cottage and was peering down at me.

A raven! Gudrun's bird; that meant she was here, somewhere in the village. No, it was silly to think that. There were hundreds of ravens; how could you possibly tell one from another? There was no reason why this one should be hers.

Then I heard it, a sound like a great wave breaking on a shingle beach. I couldn't tell if it was a roar of fury or excitement. It was coming from the centre of the village. I wanted to run in the opposite direction, but I couldn't leave Gudrun. If she was here, I had to find her. Sick with fear for her, I set off in the direction of the sound.

As I emerged from the lane, the noise of the crowd exploded in my ears. Every man, woman and child from the village who could walk was there, crowded together around the pond at the far end of the Green, children perched on their fathers' shoulders for a better view, women at the back standing on tiptoe on upturned buckets or barrels. Another cheer rose, but was abruptly severed, as if the heads of the crowd had been chopped from their bodies in mid-roar.

One man, sensing I was there, turned to look at me. He touched his neighbour on the arm and they both moved away from me. Others turned, sensing the movement behind them. They stared at me sullenly, mutinous, like sulky children. There was a movement at the front of the crowd. Father Ulfrid pushed his way through and stood in front of me, his hands tucked into his sleeves as if he was in his own church doing God's work. His narrowed eyes glittered with triumph, but his body was trembling as if gripped by the kind of giddy relief you see in young boys after battle.

'Crawl back to your nest of vipers, woman. You've no business here. There will be no more souls from this village coming to your door. The sickness is over.'

He bellowed these words for the benefit of the crowd, who made a half-hearted cheer in response, but there was strangely little rejoicing in the sound.

I tried to muster what dignity I could. 'Praise God for it, if it is so. But can you be sure?'

'Oh, I'm sure. We know the cause. We know who brought the evil upon us and you can rest assured, mistress, the malefactor will not trouble us again. Take this as a warning back to the house of women. We have dealt with one of your number, and should any further misfortune strike this village, we will see to it that the rest of you suffer the same fate. You tell that to your so-called leader.'

'Dealt with?' A dreadful coldness gripped my bowels. 'How dealt with?'

He turned and gestured. The sea of people divided and parted. A brown-cloaked man stood at the pond's edge, legs planted firmly astride, arms folded across his chest. He had a man's body, but his head was the head of an owl. His bronze beak was hooked and sharp as a wetted scythe. The tawny feathers were smoothed and glossy. His eyes were hooded deep within the feathers, so that I couldn't see if they were the eyes of a man or a bird. He pointed down at his feet with a slow, extravagant gesture, but I couldn't tear my gaze from his head.

Someone pushed me from behind and I stumbled forward, my legs shaking. It took all my will and concentration to force them to bear me up. I followed the pointing finger. A body lay face down in the mud at his too-human feet. She was naked. Her red hair snaked in thick wet strands across her shoulders. Her wrists and ankles were bound, tied so tightly that the skin was cut and bruised purple where she'd struggled. They had whipped her, lashed her slender back again and again. The water had washed the blood away, but the cuts were bright as poppy petals against the bluish-white of her skin. The whip had curled around her side, its tip cutting into the small mound of her stomach, biting deep into the soft flesh of her little breast.

I dropped to my knees, heedless of the stinking mud, and turned her over, tilting her face towards me as if I needed to see, as if my mind could still cling to any shred of hope that it was not her. Tenderly, I plucked the wet weeds of hair out of her wide-open eyes. Livid bruises covered her face and arms, purple as a summer storm. Her lip was swollen. She had not died gently.

All my fear was consumed in fury. I wanted to tear the face off the man who stood there.

'Why did you do this? She was only a child. You put her through the ordeal by water and she sank in front of your eyes, proving she was innocent. You could have pulled her out before she drowned, but you all stood there and watched her die. How could you do that? She'd never done you any harm.'

The man in the owl mask neither moved nor spoke. In the silence we stared each other down. Father Ulfrid nudged Gudrun's body with the toe of his shoe as if to ensure she was really dead.

'She stood accused of malfactorum. Many worthy witnesses testified on oath that she danced up a storm and raised a flood against this village and that she poisoned the water with her evil eye so that our children sickened and died. She was whipped to encourage her to confess her sins and save her soul, but she was so steeped in sin that she stubbornly refused to make confession –'

'She was dumb,' I screamed at him. 'You knew that. Each and every one of you knew that. If you had tortured her upon the rack, she could not have uttered a single word to save her life.'

'If she couldn't speak it is yet further proof of her malice, for her soul was so far given over to Satan that he stopped her mouth so that she could not confess and receive divine grace and forgiveness for her sins.'

'She didn't feel no pain neither,' yelled someone from the back of the crowd. There were murmurs of confirmation from those at the front. 'Even when the Owl Master was laying the whip on her good and hard, she never screamed.'

'Not natural, that. Even a grown man cries out under the lash.'

'It was the Devil protecting her.'

'Don't you understand?' I pleaded. 'She couldn't cry out however much agony she was in.'

But no one was listening to me. All eyes were riveted on Gudrun's body. A great cry of horror went up from the crowd and they shrank back, crossing themselves. I looked down. Her mouth had fallen open and a green frog was crawling out from between her lips.

January – St Paul the Hermit's Day

Paul was buried in the desert by two lions who dug his grave with their paws, at the request of St Antony.

Servant Martha

The women crossed the courtyard in twos and threes, chatting companionably to one another in the glacial winter sunshine. As I stood in the doorway of my room, watching them, a wave of loneliness washed through me. Their solidarity only sharpened my isolation. They could complain to each other, cry on each other's shoulders and receive a friendly arm of comfort, but I couldn't undress my weaknesses before anyone.

Healing Martha lay in her cot, as withdrawn from me as if she lay across the sea. Perhaps she heard me when I talked to her, but even if she did, she couldn't answer. Looking back through all those years when we were friends, I don't think I ever really told her anything. I never needed to. She had a way of seeing through the most closely veiled silence and would say the word that could lance a boil, however carefully concealed. Now, even if she could understand what troubled me, she couldn't offer me any words of advice or comfort. A seer without a tongue is as useless as a blind watchman. Until I lost her, I never realized how much I needed her.

The gate burst open and Beatrice stumbled in. Her hands and the front of her kirtle were covered in mud. She staggered as if she was drunk, and didn't even seem to see me standing in the doorway of my room. I hurried out.

'Beatrice?'

She stopped and stared up at me, as if I was a stranger. Her eyes were swollen and her face was blotched with red marks.

'Have you taken a tumble?'

She shook her head, but I knew something was wrong.

'Is there some problem with the livestock? The murrain has not struck again?' Merciful God, not that. We needed every shred of meat we could store this winter if we were to survive.

'Why didn't you at least beg them for her body?' She spat out the words with a look of such venom on her face that I almost took a step back.

'Why did you let them kill her? You could've stopped them. The fever was none of her doing. She didn't cast the evil eye on them. She wasn't a witch, she was just a child ... an innocent child.'

She gabbled her words so fast that it took me a moment or two to make sense of what she'd said.

'Do you mean Gwenith's granddaughter? Beatrice, you know perfectly well that I knew nothing of this matter until you yourself told me of it last night. I'm as appalled as you by what was done to the girl. It was a wicked and evil act, but if anyone could have prevented it, it was you. You insisted on the care of the girl. You encouraged her to wander abroad instead of schooling her to tasks within these walls. It was only a matter of time before she came to grief. I've no doubt that Pega warned you of the fear the villagers had of her.'

'What did you expect me to do, lock her up? How could I stop her? She wanted to go out.' Beatrice twisted a handful of her cloak tightly between her hands, as if she was trying to wring water out of it. But the cloak, though filthy, was dry.

'If you'd ever had children, Beatrice, you'd know that infants can't be allowed to wander freely, however much they might want to, for fear of them falling into a stream or being trampled beneath a horse. Sometimes you must tether them to keep them from harm and you said yourself she was just a child with no more sense than a babe-in-arms.'

Beatrice's head jerked up, her eyes glittering with rage. 'What does an old hag like you know about children? You've never wanted a baby, have you? Everything about them disgusts you. Remember what you said about Andrew?'

Beatrice screwed up her mouth in what I assume was intended to be a vicious parody of me. '"Andrew has so mastered her body that God healed the wound of her menses and returned her to the pure state that Eve knew before this curse

454

of filth came upon us." You said that we should all pray daily that this curse would be lifted from us too. What kind of a bitter, twisted prayer is that?

'Don't you understand that when your menses are gone, so is your hope? But that didn't matter to you, did it, because even before you were a withered-up old crone, you were never a normal woman. You could never have loved a child because there isn't a grain of love in you for anyone.'

For a moment I was so stunned, I couldn't reply. Then I gripped her shoulders and shook her hard. 'Control yourself, Beatrice! This is a disgraceful display in a woman of your age. I think it as well that you were not blessed with children since you seem incapable of behaving any better than a spoilt infant yourself.'

I could feel her trembling violently beneath my grip. I tried to speak soothingly. 'I understand that stumbling across the body of the girl in such circumstances was a great shock to you, as it would have been to anyone. But why are you saying all this now?'

She stared wildly around her, clenching and unclenching her hands. When she finally spoke, it was barely above a whisper.

'I went to fetch her little body home, but I was too late. They'd already buried her at the crossroads ... like a common murderer. Beggar Tom told me. I found the place. Tried to dig her up with my hands to bring her here. But they've laid her too deep ... have to get a spade to dig ... I can't reach her ...'

She tried to tear herself away from me, but I held her firmly.

'Beatrice, it is pointless to go running back there. I give you my word that we will fetch the body and bring it here. But it must be done after dark when the villagers are safely behind their doors. I'll see to it that the child is given a proper resting place here. Though she died unshriven, nevertheless she died innocent of the crime of which she was accused and for that alone she deserves a hallowed resting place.

'Now, go to the wash-house and clean yourself up at once, before anyone else sees you. And for heaven's sake, Beatrice, conduct yourself with some decorum. Pray for her soul from your charity if you will, but such unseemly displays of grief, especially for one such as her, are quite unnecessary. After all, it's not as if she was your own child.'

She flung off my hand from her shoulder, her face twisted with hatred. I leapt back as she struck out, her fingers clawing inches from my face. A single cry escaped her, the shriek of a wild animal in pain. She stood rocking backwards and forwards. Then she seemed to collect herself and walked stiffly away towards the wash-house, her arms wrapped tightly about her chest.

I retraced the few steps to my room, closed the door and stood over the small blaze in the hearth, warming my hands and trying to stop myself trembling. Beatrice had seemed almost possessed. Was it fear of what the Owl Masters had threatened? I should not have accused her of neglect. For I knew I bore the greater guilt for the child's death; she had been entrusted to my care. And if she had not been out on the night of the storm . . .

Every time I closed my eyes at night, I could see the girl standing over me, her naked body glistening white in the flash of lightning, the rain streaming down her bare legs and that great black bird flapping its wings on her shoulder. How had she got there? Why had she come to me of all people? She had always tried to run away from me before.

Had the girl saved me that night or had she been the cause of the horses rearing? I knew in my heart that I had made no effort since then to keep her safe inside our walls; perhaps I was afraid of her and had wanted her to run off. I owed it to the girl to bring her body home, however much I shrank from the task. It would be my penance.

But there would need to be at least two of us to dig her up and lift her out of the grave. They'd doubtless buried her as deep as they could dig. We'd also need two people to keep watch on the approaches to the crossroads, to give us warning in case any should see us and try to prevent us taking the body, or worse still, try to seize us and swim us.

We'd have to go at dusk with just enough light left to see the place without needing torches or lanterns. On the open road, the flames of a torch or even a lantern would attract attention from miles away. We'd have to take a cart to carry the body back and something to cover her nakedness, for it seemed unlikely they would have covered her in a shroud or winding sheet before they dumped her in the grave.

The question was who to take. Certainly not Beatrice, I couldn't trust her, especially if we discovered the body had been mutilated or dismembered, as was often the custom with any corpse people feared might walk. Pega, of course – she had no fear of the villagers. Shepherd Martha – she was another with brawn. Between the two of them they'd dig the body up in no time and we didn't want to linger longer than we had to.

Who else? Osmanna? She'd make a useful lookout, and if I showed her that I put my trust in her perhaps it would make her more willing to do what I had asked of her at Mass. Besides, the sight of Gudrun's body might be no bad thing. It would bring home the dangers of the path she was treading far more effectively than mere words. I would tell –

There was a frantic hammering on the door of my room and before I could answer, Gate Martha burst in.

'There's villagers at the gate, a crowd of them.'

Her hand darted back and forth as if she would like to grab me and pull me out to the gate with her, but I'd no intention of flying out at every alarm.

'If they've brought more of their sick, have them taken into the pilgrims' room with the others. If there isn't enough room –'

'They've not brought their sick.'

'What is it then? Food, is that what they've come for?'

Gate Martha bit her lip. 'The blessed Host of Andrew.'

'We have already explained to them when they brought their children that we do not know that the relic has healing powers. But tell them I will bring it out and they may touch it and light a candle for healing.'

457

'They'll not be content with touching it this time. They say the fever passes over us because we've Andrew's Host in our chapel. They want to take it back to their church and keep it there to protect the village. They say . . .'

She hesitated, then gabbled as if reciting something learned by rote, 'God continues to punish them with the fever, because the miraculous Host has been left in the sinful hands of those who've been excommunicated. Servant Martha, we must give it them. They're saying they'll take it by force if we do not.'

'They'll do no such thing, not while I live and breathe. I see Father Ulfrid's hand in this and I intend to put a stop to this nonsense once and for all. Come along.'

I strode out into the courtyard. Gate Martha hurried along in my wake. The gate was wide open and a crowd of people jostled on the threshold, mostly men, but there were a few women among them. Two of the men had pushed their way inside.

'Why didn't you lock the gate and make them wait outside?'

Gate Martha made some vague gesture towards the crowd. 'Too many of them. They pushed against it and wouldn't let me shut it.'

'Then why open it in the first place?'

'Said they'd sick, Servant Martha, and I thought . . .'

I would have words with her later about what she *thought*.

A little knot of beguines huddled to one side of the gate. They seemed unwilling or unable to do anything, but Osmanna stood with her back to me directly in front of the men. She appeared to be remonstrating with them, though I couldn't make out what she was saying above the murmur and mutterings of the crowd. Whatever her faults, at least she'd the mettle to challenge them. Courage often walks with stubbornness. But what she was saying was having little effect; the crowd was jeering. Suddenly Beatrice broke from the group of beguines and pushed her way in front of Osmanna, her fists clenched in fury.

'What are you asking Osmanna for?' she shrieked. 'Don't you know she doesn't believe in the sacraments? She thinks the

Host is no more holy than the crusts you throw to your pigs. She says faith is all you need to save you. So where are your Owl Masters? You've got faith aplenty in them, haven't you? You don't need a mouldy piece of bread.'

'Beatrice!' I grabbed her and tried to drag her back, but she pulled away from me, screaming at the men.

'Don't you know the fever has gone? You sacrificed an innocent girl to stop it, so it must be so. If your children are still sick, go and ask your Owl Masters why. Go ask your priest. They murdered her. They promised you her death would rid you of the fever. Why come to us? Don't you know we sent you the fever? Do you want us to send you something worse? Get out! Get out!'

Beatrice raised her right hand, the fingers spread like claws pointed towards them. For a moment they held their ground, then as one they turned and ran. She slammed the gate behind them and leaned on it, visibly shaking. Gate Martha hurried up and swung the beam across the gate.

The beguines clustered around Beatrice, stroking and soothing her, patting her on the back, praising her for sending the villagers packing. They were all smiling and joking in their relief. It was hard to know if Beatrice was laughing hysterically or crying.

The only one who didn't move was Osmanna. She stood where Beatrice had pushed her. She was deathly white, her eyes wide with fear and shock. We stared at each other in silence. I knew she wanted me to reassure her, to tell her that no one would take any notice of what Beatrice had said. Her eyes were pleading with me to say that the villagers wouldn't understand.

I knew what she wanted me to say, but I couldn't say it. I couldn't lie, not even to comfort her. I felt the blood draining from my own face. I turned away. Beatrice was still being congratulated and comforted. Had she any idea what mischief she had done? There was no undoing her words. All we could do now was wait and pray.

✝

January – St Ulfrid's Day

Ulfrid was an Englishman who tried to convert the people of Sweden by preaching against paganism. In 1028, after chopping up a statue of Thor with an axe, he was lynched and his body thrown into a marsh.

Father Ulfrid

The Bishop's Commissarius stood on a mounting block peering in through the single slit window of the village jail. Ulewic's jail was not a large one, but then it didn't need to be, for it contained no furniture. It consisted of nothing more than a round, reed-thatched room, built of stone, much the same size and shape as the Manor cote. At present it had only one occupant, although it could accommodate three or four men, six or eight if they were forced to stand pressed together.

The jail boasted a stout wooden door and a narrow barred window set too high in the wall for a prisoner to see out or anyone to look in unless, like the Commissarius, they were standing on something. The bars on the window were unnecessary, for only a starving cat could have squeezed through the small gap between the thick stones, but its builders had taken no chances. No one would escape their stronghold.

The Commissarius' expression betrayed nothing as he stared down into the cell. Though it was only mid-afternoon, the sky was grey and heavy, as if it was already twilight, and it must have been even darker inside the cell.

'We didn't know when to expect you, Commissarius,' I said, still breathless from having run from my cottage. 'If I'd known you were arriving today, I would have had the bailiff waiting here with the key. But I can send for him now if —'

'That will not be necessary. I have seen all I wish to see.' He turned and sprang nimbly to the ground. 'We are on our way to speak with Lord D'Acaster.' He beckoned to a thin, round-shouldered youth who hunched miserably against the wall of the jail, blowing on his blue-knuckled hands. 'Take the mounting block back to the inn, boy; I will speak to Father Ulfrid in private before we ride on to the Manor. You may bring our mounts to the church and wait for me there – outside!'

The lad nodded vigorously as if he wanted to leave no doubt that he would carry out the instructions to the letter. He started off in such haste that he stumbled over the wooden mounting block as he tried to pick it up.

The Commissarius booted him up the backside as he tried to get up, which sent the lad sprawling over the block again, but his master ignored the boy's yelp of pain and, turning, marched off in the direction of the church.

I had waited for this moment for days. I'd hardly been able to sleep or eat, thinking about it. It was as if the heavens had opened and the Holy Grail itself had fallen straight into my lap. First, the witch-girl had come wandering straight into our hands, and now this. It was as if everything I did was suddenly blessed by God. Finally, finally, He had turned the tide my way. God had kept faith with me. I had been cast into a pit and thought myself abandoned, but God had remembered me in Egypt and was about to bring me forth.

I had prayed for the relic and instead I received something far better, a heretic. That prize was surely enough to cancel out any transgression I had committed in the Bishop's eyes. I would soon be back in the comfort of the Cathedral at Norwich and the Owl Masters could do what they liked with this shit-hole of a village; it would be far behind me.

The church was dark, for little light penetrated the coloured fragments of the stained-glass windows. Only the ruby glow of the eternal lamp above the altar stood out from the shadows, but it illuminated nothing. The Commissarius prowled around, peering into the vestry and bell tower to assure himself that the church was empty. Finally, he slid on to one of the stone seats which lined the walls where the old or weak rested during the services.

The wall behind him was painted with the Harrowing of Hell. I could hardly make out the figures in the gloom, save for the gold of the halo above the head of Christ, but I knew it well enough. Christ standing before the prison of Hades in his winding sheet, breaking the prison door down and offering release to the dead who crowded behind it. It seemed to me in that moment the most blessed of omens, that the Commissarius should have chosen to sit before that painting of redemption and liberation. His first words were also gratifyingly comforting.

'I must congratulate you, Father Ulfrid,' he said. 'You appear to have wasted no time in bringing this grave matter to our attention.'

'When I learned what had transpired at the house of women, I was naturally appalled. I sent a letter at once to Bishop Salmon.'

'Quite so.' The Commissarius nodded encouragingly.

'When the Bishop sent the warrant for her arrest, I saw to it that it was acted upon immediately. I was ... a little surprised, though, that His Excellency ordered the girl to be held here. I thought he might wish her to be held at his own jail in Norwich. But now that you are here to take the girl back to Norwich for trial, that will be a great relief to the village. Although ...'

I hesitated, not wishing to be seen to offer advice. 'Forgive me, Commissarius, I couldn't help noticing that you have only one lad with you. Naturally I will accompany you to Norwich to testify and, of course, a young girl will hardly be able to offer much resistance. We will be able to manage her between us, I'm quite sure. But perhaps ... we should take a few other men with us, just as a precaution, in case the foreign women attempt to rescue –'

'Lord D'Acaster's daughter on trial in Norwich?' The Commissarius pressed his delicate fingers together. 'I think not. You must understand that any accusations brought against a noble family have to be handled with great delicacy. His Excellency, Bishop Salmon, has no wish to publicly humiliate one of our leading families.'

For a moment I couldn't seem to catch my breath. I felt winded, as if he had just kicked me in the stomach. Surely he wasn't going to dismiss this crime, because she was D'Acaster's daughter? I felt as if I had grasped a rope to pull myself out of the mire only to have it come away in my hands.

'But, Commissarius, she's a heretic. Countless witnesses will testify to the fact. Surely the Bishop wouldn't turn a blind eye to such a crime because the girl is highborn?'

'Father Ulfrid, are you suggesting that the Bishop weights his scales of justice in favour of the wealthy or powerful?' The Commissarius' voice crackled with ice. 'Just because he was unduly lenient with you, Father, do not imagine that he allows crime to go unpunished.'

'Of course, I didn't mean ...' We both knew that was exactly what I did mean. 'Forgive me, Commissarius, but I don't understand. You just said the girl would not be brought to trial, then how will justice ...'

'The girl will not face trial in *Norwich,* Father. But there will be a trial, make no mistake about that. The Bishop has graciously entrusted me to conduct it myself, here in Ulewic, and if the malefactor is found guilty, the sentence imposed for the crime will also be carried out here.

'His Excellency desires discretion, Father Ulfrid. There is no need to make a public spectacle of such a tragic affair. One does not punish the father for the sins of the child. Lord D'Acaster is a generous benefactor to the Church. One would hardly wish to see such a devout and godly man publicly shamed for the heinous crimes of his wanton and rebellious daughter. She has surely heaped misery enough upon her father's head. But you need have no fear, Father Ulfrid, the girl will not escape justice.'

The Commissarius shuffled slightly on the stone seat, revealing a little tongue of red flame among the dark figures on the wall at his back.

'If the trial is held in Ulewic,' he continued, 'it will make it easier for witnesses to come forward, particularly those who might be a little reluctant to testify. It has been my experience that simple men, who have lived all their lives in a village, are apt to become tongue-tied if paraded before their betters in the splendour of a great Cathedral building. They are inclined to become confused about what they heard. And we don't want our little fish wriggling from the net because some village idiot muddles his testimony, now do we?'

The Commissarius gave a slight smile, lifting his chin to study me more closely. 'I am sorry if that disappoints you, Father Ulfrid. No doubt you were looking forward to leaving the village, perhaps renewing old acquaintances in Norwich, or one friend in particular?'

My heart lurched. The band of pain tightened. Had Phillip told him about Hilary coming here? No, if he had I would be sitting in that jail now instead of D'Acaster's daughter.

'I only wished to serve His Excellency in this matter,' I said hastily, glad that the church was too dark for the Commissarius to see my face.

The Commissarius studied his fingers. 'However, Father Ulfrid, I did not bring you here to discuss the conduct of the trial. There is another issue which ... concerns me.' He paused before pronouncing the word *concern* as if he had devoted much thought to the selection of the word.

'As I said, you are to be commended for your diligence in reporting the matter of the heresy, Father Ulfrid, which makes it all the more puzzling as to why you did not immediately report the fact that you had excommunicated the house of women in its entirety. If I am to understand your letter correctly, it would appear that you took this step two months ago and yet you only thought fit to tell us of it now.'

'But, Commissarius,' I protested, 'it was you yourself who instructed me to use the penalty of excommunication if the people would not pay their tithes.'

'Quite so. But your letter suggested that you did not impose such sanctions for a failure to tithe. If I have understood you correctly, you excommunicated them for their defiance in refusing to make public penance for a far graver crime, a crime that should have been brought to our attention immediately. Had you done so, the matter might have been resolved long before this girl committed her heinous act, thereby saving

467

Bishop Salmon the embarrassment you have subjected him to and saving me a great deal of trouble.'

The Commissarius shifted on the cold stone again, revealing more of the flames painted on the wall behind his back. It was too dark to see the details, but I didn't need to; I knew every detail of that painting by heart. The fire burned beneath a great cauldron in hell in which the tormented, their limbs hacked off, were being boiled alive.

The Commissarius tapped his mouth with a long thin finger as if he was deep in thought, but I was certain that he had already planned every word he was going to say to me.

'It would appear, Father Ulfrid, that you have knowingly permitted a nest of vermin to breed in your midst, a nest which has been brooding a most evil and wicked heresy, while you have stood by and done nothing. I think, Father Ulfrid, you had better tell me all that has transpired from the beginning concerning these women. And I caution you not to leave anything out, otherwise I may indeed be returning to Norwich with a prisoner for trial, but it will not be the girl.'

Beatrice

Every time I went into the cote I looked for my little Gudrun, expecting to see her crouching there with a bird nestling in her hair, as if the past days had been nothing but an evil dream. She'd simply wandered away as she often did. She wasn't dead. My Gudrun wasn't dead.

Every mother wails to all who will listen that all kinds of disasters have befallen her missing child, only to feel so foolish when the child walks in with a grubby grin, all blithe and innocent, to be startled by her mother's fierce hug, her slaps and tears, her laughter and her scolding. So, each time I opened that door I expected to be made foolish. I'd shout and cry and she wouldn't understand. She'd have lost track of time. She wouldn't even know I'd been searching for her. She never did.

I had peeled the wet strands from her face with my own fingers. I could still feel them tangled in my hand, but that was not death. The body I touched wasn't real. It was a trick, a deception contrived by mummers, a doll made to look like the living, stuck with pins or bound with thorns that could not hurt it for it was made of wax. The lips painted blue, the green eyes carved out to resemble real eyes, that doll, that pretty semblance of a virgin saint, was not my Gudrun. It was not my Gudrun dead.

Gudrun's straw pallet still lay against the wall and I saw her there, curled up like a cat beneath the covers, but as my eyes grew accustomed to the dimness I looked again and saw her bed was empty. Her breathing form was turned to straw, which no spinning of my prayers would turn again to gold. It was as if I saw with two pairs of eyes, a pair that lied and a pair that revealed the brutal truth. I wished to God that I only had the lying eyes.

The pigeons missed her too. Every now and then one flew down and alighted on her bed as if it too saw her there. They wouldn't come to my hands, nor let me snuggle their warm bodies, fluttering away if I reached out to them, but at night there were always three of them, her candles, nestling together where her head used to lie. We were the only ones who missed her, the pigeons and me, for we were the only ones who'd ever loved her. Everyone else continued with their lives as if she had never been.

I was the keeper of the cote. No one came in except Gudrun and me. I had to sleep in the cote now, in case the others sneaked in during the night. I had to keep them out. They mustn't know that Gudrun's bedding was still there. They'd tell Servant Martha and she would order it removed. 'A waste of good blankets and straw,' she'd say. 'A morbid obsession, unfitting for a beguine. The sooner all traces of that dumb girl are removed, the sooner Beatrice will pull herself together again. It is for her own good. She has no right to grieve. She was not her mother.'

But that pallet was all I had of Gudrun, my only keepsake. She had nothing to leave, except her smell that still lingered on the linen. If they took it away, she couldn't come back. She knew her own bed, you see, like the pigeons. If you destroy their nests, they circle round and round. They won't land. They won't come home.

Pega took me to the place where she said they buried her, close by the chapel wall, hidden from a casual glance. Just a little strip of newly dug earth, swollen and livid in the grass like a fresh weal laid upon a naked back. That was Servant Martha's doing, hiding her away in a forgotten corner like you'd bury a dead cat. Her precious saint, the pure, virginal Andrew, was given an honoured place under the chapel floor, but not my innocent murdered child; she was nothing more than a gnawed bone to be tossed out of sight.

Only a week had gone by since Servant Martha and Pega had buried her, yet already the earth was settling back. Old brown

470

leaves were drifting over it, blown against it by the wind, and the rich brown of the newly dug soil was turning grey and dull. There were no flowers to lay on it. No stone marked it. Rain would rinse it away. Frost would trample it flat. By spring it would be gone. That's what Servant Martha wanted, to obliterate all signs that my child ever lived. That's what they had always done, tried to pretend that my little ones had never existed.

None of my graves survived until spring. I'd watched them all fade away. Tiny, insubstantial things, they none of them outlasted my grief. Stone babies without a name, without a voice, without a breath. They fled from me, slipping out in a scalding torrent of pain and blood as if they could not bear to be inside me a moment longer. Little fish escaping back to the river. I tried to hold on to them, even when I could feel them escaping. When the blood began to flow, I knew I had lost them, but still I tried to hold them inside me. But they knew I was not fit to be their mother and they wouldn't stay. They didn't want me.

I remembered a face. I'd slept – some opiate the midwife had given me – and I woke to see a face floating above me in a white haze, so distant, so blurred I could only make out the eyes and mouth, but it was my baby's face, so like my husband's, his eyes, his mouth. He would be overjoyed to have a son who favoured him. The mouth moved and I thought he cried for me. I stretched out my arms to hold him and felt a stinging slap striking my hands away.

'Don't touch me, mistress. There shall be no more embraces between us. Yet another born before its time. I might almost think you had taken some pernicious potion to rob me of my sons for spite, but the physician says it is your wanton lust that kills them. It's the overheated blood which poisons them. Do you pleasure yourself, mistress, or satiate your appetites in another's bed? For as God is my witness I have taken every care not to arouse you. You are a whore, and it's well you have not borne a child for you are not fit to be a mother.'

Once the blood is washed from the linen people say you

never had a child. See that woman over there whose infant lived a few months, then died, she has the right to cry and mourn and be comforted. She is to be pitied, but what do you know of losing a child? But I did, I did. They were my children no less than those who drew breath and I cried for them, for I had cuddled them inside me. They had drawn nourishment and life from me. I had felt them swell and move, my secret children. I shared them with no one. I felt them quicken and kick. I had nursed their life. But no one would let me grieve for them, my nameless ones. They were dismissed from life as easily as phantasms born of the moon-crazed. They were buried as menstrual rags.

I used to sit in the casement of my house in Flanders looking down on the waterfront. For hours I'd watch the men loading and unloading the barrels of wine, baskets of herring and bales of cloth. Shouted greetings and bellowed orders, cries of sellers and seagulls were carried upwards to my window on a rich current of sea salt, leather, spices and sweat. I'd see the women waddling past, one hand pressed to aching backs, the other cradling bellies stuffed full as pomegranates with new life. I'd hear the squeals of children daring one another to run between the legs of horses or climb up on stacks of teetering bales. I'd watch them swing from ships' ropes and play tag along the very edge of the quay, while their mothers gossiped or haggled with merchants, indifferent to the danger.

Why them and not me? How could that whore, Osmanna, that blood-smeared bitch, swell with child from some filthy groping with a drooling stable boy, when I, who had never once betrayed my marriage bed, remained barren? I would have made a dozen pilgrimages on my knees for just one of the infants sluts like her spat out as so many grape seeds into the mud. I would have doted on my child, never letting it out of my sight, alert to every kind of danger, attentive to every need. Why should other women burst open every year, pushing out a healthy, lusty infant with no more effort than a sow, when I couldn't manage to produce even one?

But I know now. I know why I could not have a child. My

husband and Servant Martha were right; I was not fit to be a mother. I had pleaded and begged and worn God down until he had finally granted me a child of my own. And just like all of those careless mothers I had condemned, I'd let her run straight into danger.

But there wouldn't have been any danger if Servant Martha hadn't turned the priest and villagers against us. If she'd given them the relic, they wouldn't have taken my Gudrun. But she wouldn't, because she wanted them to kill my child. Servant Martha didn't want me to love little Gudrun, because she can't love anyone. She didn't want me to have a child. She and Osmanna, they both murdered my babies. They don't want me to have anything that I can call mine.

The iron ring on the door turned and I braced myself against it, holding it shut.

'Beatrice, are you there?' Catherine called out.

The handle jiggled again. Catherine never had the strength to push open the door easily, even without a body as weighty as mine leaning against it.

'Beatrice, Servant Martha wants you.'

Servant Martha mustn't come in here. I jerked open the door. Catherine fell into my arms. I pushed her back out of the doorway and closed it behind me.

'What does she want?'

'There are men with Servant Martha. The same ones who took Osmanna.' Catherine shivered and looked up at me, her forehead wrinkled in concern. 'I heard them say they were taking you to testify against Osmanna, but you won't, will you?'

A wave of nausea and irritation rolled over me. 'I have to look after the pigeons. Tell Servant Martha, tell her I have to look after the pigeons.'

'They're taking Servant Martha to the trial as well.'

'Trial?'

'Beatrice,' Catherine wailed, 'you know Osmanna was arrested, because of what you ... They are putting her on trial.

473

But Beatrice, you won't say anything, will you?' She clutched at my arm and peered anxiously up at me.

'It's a sin to tell lies, Catherine. Ask Servant Martha. Thou shalt not bear false witness. Thou shalt not . . . speak.'

January – St Wulfstan's Day

Accused of being unworthy to hold office, Bishop Wulfstan pushed his crosier into the shrine of Edward the Confessor. He challenged his accusers to pull it out, but no one could for it was stuck fast. Then Wulfstan effortlessly drew the crosier from the shrine himself, proving his fitness for office.

Servant Martha

We waited in St Michael's, pressed side by side on the assortment of small narrow benches and stools brought down from the Manor and carried in from any cottage that still had a stick of furniture worthy of the name. Braziers had been lit inside the church and the air was stifling, fetid with dung-caked shoes, wet wool, wood smoke and stale sweat. The thick yellow flames of the tallow candles curdled the faces of the people, souring clothes of red, green and brown to a single hue of rancid butter. The tallows added their own oily fumes to the stench. Father Ulfrid was evidently not going to waste good wax candles on this affair, for who knew how many might be burned before this trial was over.

Two ornate empty chairs, flanked by several lesser ones, stood upon a dais before the altar. They were empty. The Bishop's Commissarius was dining with D'Acaster and Father Ulfrid. So the villagers were obliged to kick their heels and wait until their masters had finished filling their bellies. I had no doubt they would be well filled, for D'Acaster would want a good report made to the Bishop. There was no sign of Osmanna, but a small gap had been left in front of the dais that no one had filled, a hexed circle in which none dared tread.

All around the men, for they were mostly men, fidgeted, farted, laughed and gossiped, waiting for the play to begin.

Beatrice was seated beside me. She had not said a word to me since we left the beguinage. Her eyes were clouded as if her spirit inhabited some distant place. I had tried to convince Father Ulfrid that she was not well enough to testify, but the more I argued, the more determined he seemed to bring her.

I had managed just a few whispered words alone with Beatrice, cautioning her to say as little as possible. I warned her that if anything should come to light about the Masses we had conducted, her life would be in danger no less than mine. I hoped that would be enough to bring her to her senses and make her guard her tongue, but I could not be sure. She would not even look at me.

I knew it wasn't Osmanna's blood that Father Ulfrid wanted; it was mine. The Church would try to use her to trap me. It was not just Osmanna who was on trial here, it was the whole beguinage. I could only pray Beatrice understood that.

The crowd stirred as the church door was flung open and their masters entered. A few made half-hearted attempts to stand and make small, ungainly bows as D'Acaster passed through the crowd, but most kept their seats.

Robert D'Acaster's face was shiny and dripping with per-spiration as if he was carved of melting tallow. His foot missed the step and for a moment he teetered between falling back-wards and tipping head first on to the dais. Phillip D'Acaster hastily grabbed him and hoisted him up. He flopped down into one of the carved chairs, which visibly bowed under his weight. Dinner had evidently been well washed down with large quantities of wine.

Father Ulfrid took one of the lesser chairs on the dais, while the other great carved chair was occupied by a man who looked as if he had dined on nothing but dried bread and bitter herbs. At first glance he seemed to be an aged man, with dark hollow eyes and sharp cheekbones. Even his gestures were ponderous and ancient, as if he had sat for many years in some great debating chamber or in a library poring over books, but on closer inspection, I could see that he was no more than thirty, probably a deal younger.

The man crushed on the other side of me on the narrow bench elbowed me in the ribs. 'That's Bishop's man, that is. You want to watch him. They say he caught his own brother lying with a man and he witnessed against him. Then he watched while they sliced off his brother's nose and ears. What kind of bastard would do that to one of his own?'

The Bishop's Commissarius gathered his fur-trimmed gown closely about him, as if he feared a draught, though no one could possibly have been cold in that church unless he had iced water in his veins instead of blood.

The crowd began murmuring again as the door opened for a second time and Osmanna was led in by a rope bound around her wrists. Some of the villagers hissed. Others crossed themselves and drew back as she was led between the benches, as if they thought she might have some contagion.

Osmanna stared straight ahead of her. She was pale, but there were two unnaturally bright spots of colour on her cheeks. She was not wearing her beguine's cloak. She looked fragile and vulnerable without it. Wisps of straw clung to her skirts. Her long hair was loose and tangled as it had been that first day I saw her in her father's house.

A venomous murmur swelled up around the room as if a swarm of bees was gathering. Phillip D'Acaster leaned forward, regarding Osmanna with an undisguised leer as he might look at a tavern wench. Clearly, the sight of a young girl bound and dishevelled aroused the basest of desires in him. I felt sick with disgust.

The Bishop's Commissarius swept his gaze around the room and all fell silent. He nodded to his clerk sitting at a small writing desk below the dais. If the Commissarius was young, his clerk was still younger, scarcely out of clouts with the pimples of youth sprouting fresh upon his face. He was hastily slicing quill after quill as if he thought he would be called upon to copy out the whole Bible before the afternoon was out.

The Commissarius coughed impatiently, which only made his poor clerk start violently like a birched schoolboy, sending his quills rolling to the floor. A rough gale of laughter ripped through the room as he scrambled to retrieve them.

The Commissarius slowly looked from Beatrice to me and back again. Then he unfurled a ringed finger and beckoned to me. I stood.

'Mistress, I judge you to be the leader of the women, the one they call the Servant Martha, is that correct?'

I nodded, trying to steady my breathing.

The Commissarius turned to D'Acaster. 'She will not be required to swear an oath, for she is excommunicated and the lips of the damned shall not be permitted to blaspheme the name of God. Such persons may not bear witness against a godly man, but against other malefactors they may be heard, for the devil will denounce his own.'

He turned back to me, jerking his chin up as if he was about to order a scullion to empty a pot.

'Mistress, we solemnly charge you to speak the truth before us this day, lest you find yourself under the sentence of this court, if indeed any woman so lost to the mercy and grace of our blessed Lord is capable of distinguishing truth from falsehood.'

'Commissarius, we are ever mindful that our blessed Lord is witness to all our discourse in both light matters and grave, in private and in public, therefore we speak the truth by custom. Unlike some, we need no oath to chasten us so to do.'

I could hear a collective intake of breath from the villagers behind me. Father Ulfrid leaned forward as if to speak, but the Commissarius silenced him with a raised hand without taking his eyes from mine.

'I sincerely pray for your sake that it is so, mistress. Very well, let us begin.' He turned to the clerk. 'You may record that no oath was taken, therefore her words are to be accorded little weight.'

'If our words are to be paid so little heed, may I ask why you have troubled to bring us here?'

The mouth of the Commissarius curled in a slight smile without engaging his eyes.

'It takes but a feather to tip the scales of justice, mistress. But that aside, His Excellency the Bishop wishes to know how far this poison has spread. Are we here to lance a boil, mistress, or must we sever the whole limb?' He stared pointedly at Father Ulfrid, who gnawed his lip as if he feared the warning might be directed at him.

'The girl Agatha resides with you under your care and authority, does she not?'

'Osmanna is a beguine. She lives and works with us.'

'But *Agatha*,' he enunciated the name as if I was deaf, 'obeys you and your rule.'

'*Osmanna*,' I countered firmly, 'obeys God and God's rule. Beguines keep no rule, but that which God Himself dictates to them.'

There was a whimper from the clerk beneath the dais and all eyes turned in his direction.

'Well?' The Commissarius spat out the word.

'I beg pardon, sir, but what am I to write?'

'Write, boy? You scribe what is said, no more no less, surely that is simple enough even for a dolt like you.' He raised his eyes to Robert D'Acaster. 'My own clerk fell sick with a fever, God damn him. So they saddled me with this numbskull.'

The hapless clerk half rose, sat again and rose hastily once more. 'But, sir, I meant what name? Agatha or –'

'*Agatha*, you blockhead, that is the name by which she was baptized. Now sit down and write, boy, before I kick your backside so hard you'll be hopping like the frog-wit you are from now until St Stephen's Fair.'

The crowd rocked with laughter. Phillip grinned and winked at Father Ulfrid, who shifted uncomfortably in his chair.

The Commissarius held his hand up for silence. He waited until he had full command of the room.

'Mistress, a man of good report has sworn on oath that the girl, Agatha, cast the blessed Host of our Lord into the mud to be trampled by filthy swine. What say you to this?'

There was an exaggerated gasp of horror from the room, though it could not have been a new revelation to anyone, if it had already been testified.

'Commissarius, you yourself have told the court that we are excommunicated,' I said. 'Where would she have obtained the Host to desecrate? Has Father Ulfrid given it to her?'

Father Ulfrid leaned forward and whispered rapidly to the Commissarius, who nodded before continuing.

'I am informed that a certain Franciscan friar was in the habit of bringing you the Host. An act which is against all the precepts of the Holy Mother Church, as I'm sure you are aware, mistress, and for which you were rightly excommunicated. Doubtless it is from the same source that the girl obtained the blessed Host for her abominations.'

'Commissarius, Father Ulfrid himself has set watch for the Franciscan since he discovered the matter. Surely you cannot think that the friar slipped by so diligent a watch?'

The Commissarius glared at Father Ulfrid, who looked decidedly uncomfortable. Phillip D'Acaster smirked with satisfaction, clearly enjoying seeing the priest lost for words.

The Commissarius turned impatiently back to me.

'Obviously, Father Ulfrid has not allowed the Franciscan to come nigh you since you were excommunicated.' He fired another angry look at Father Ulfrid as if this was far from obvious. 'Nevertheless, mistress –'

Robert D'Acaster staggered from his chair to the back of the dais and stood with his back to us. There was a loud hissing and splashing as he pissed copiously into a pot.

'Nevertheless, mistress, I warrant –' the Commissarius began again.

But it was impossible to ignore the noise as the piss thundered into and over the pot, a stream of yellow liquid trickling down the side of it. D'Acaster shook himself dry and groped his way back to his chair, waving a damp hand at the Commissarius to bid him continue.

'I warrant, mistress, you kept a store of the Host that the Franciscan brought you, thinking to use it in God alone knows what wicked abominations.'

No one had mentioned that I had been consecrating the

Host. Osmanna had clearly said nothing of it; I blessed her with all my heart for that. But I knew I must choose my next words carefully.

'The Host of our blessed Lord is as transient as the manna which fell from heaven, Commissarius, and as subject to corruption.' I tried to keep my tone steady and calm. 'How long do you think we could have kept it? Father Ulfrid himself will testify that Andrew's Host is a miracle precisely because it has been preserved from corruption.'

Father Ulfrid studied the floor, desperately trying not to meet the furious gaze of the Commissarius.

D'Acaster's elbow slid off the arm of the chair and jerked him from his doze. He looked around him dazed, as if he couldn't remember what he was doing there, and clicked his fingers vaguely in the direction of a beaker that lay on a small table just out of reach of his slumped form. D'Acaster had not looked once at his daughter, nor she at him.

'I am growing tired of these games, mistress.' The Commissarius raised his voice sharply. 'Answer me plainly, did Agatha take the Host of our blessed Lord and cast it before the swine?'

'I will tell you plainly; she did not.'

He turned to Father Ulfrid. 'There is nothing to be learnt by questioning this woman. She is dismissed.'

I breathed a sigh of relief. If Beatrice kept to the same answers, they could prove nothing. We might all yet get out of this unscathed, but would Beatrice be able to control herself? I glanced over at her; she was staring at rushes on the floor. I wasn't sure if she'd even been listening.

I whispered, 'Stay calm, Beatrice, think.'

The Commissarius frowned. 'I gave you leave to depart, mistress.'

'By your leave, I will stay.'

'As you please, mistress.' His frown deepened, then a slight smile flickered across his mouth. 'Yes, yes, perhaps you should stay, but you will keep silent.'

The Commissarius' eyes flicked across to Beatrice.

'Stand, mistress.'

She didn't move or even glance up.

'Mistress!'

I pushed her to her feet, but still she didn't look at him.

'You are known as Beatrice, I believe.'

She gave the briefest of nods.

'Though doubtless that is not your God-given name, that is the name which shall be recorded, for my idiot clerk will most likely shit his breeches if we confuse his feeble brain with another.'

Laughter broke out again and the Commissarius raised his hand for silence. Beatrice stared fixedly at the dried head of a tansy flower drowning among the rushes on the floor.

'Now, my dear,' he said kindly. She glanced up at the sudden change of tone and he smiled. 'There is no need to be afraid. All you have to do is speak the truth and all will be well. Do you understand?'

The leg of the man sitting beside me was trembling against mine, though whether from excitement, apprehension or the palsy I couldn't tell.

Beatrice nodded warily.

'Good, then let us begin. Agatha did not take the sacrament, did she?'

'No, she's excommunicated . . . we all are.'

He nodded encouragingly. 'And naturally she was distressed by this, by being denied the comforts of the Holy Church?'

'We . . . we all were.'

'Quite so, as any Christian soul would be.' He pressed the fingers of his hands together as if he was deep in thought. 'But, tell me this, did Agatha seem more distressed than the others?'

Beatrice hesitated, glancing wildly at me. 'Not more.'

'Not more distressed, Beatrice. Well, then, perhaps it was less?'

'No . . . not less.' Her voice was tremulous.

He bowed his head. 'I stand corrected. Of course, you are

right it was not less. In fact it was not at all. She was not distressed at all, that is what you are saying, is it not, Beatrice?'

'I didn't —'

'You see, we have it on good report that Agatha declared that the sacraments are not necessary for salvation and that the Host is not transformed into the body of our blessed Lord in the hands of the priests, but remains common bread. Isn't that right, Beatrice? Isn't that what you told the villagers when they came to the gate? Don't even think of denying it, Beatrice, a dozen men will swear by God's hand that they heard you say it.'

Servant Martha

The first drop of rain slips softly into the pond. Only the hermits and the madmen observe it, but they say nothing. Then another falls and another, little ripples spreading silently outwards, disturbing the smoothed reflections. We who live in this world do not have time to stand and stare at reflections. We do not notice them tremble. What is one more drop in so much water? Only when the drops begin to tumble fast and furiously do we see the rain falling through the air, feel it pricking our skin and wetting our clothes, but by then it is too late to seek shelter. Is that how the Great Flood of Ages began, with a single tear falling unnoticed and unmarked? If I had seen that first drop fall, would I have understood the danger? Could I have prevented all that we had worked for crashing down like this?

The Marthas crouched on their stools in the dark chapel, their heads bowed, their faces hidden in the shadows. No one moved. No one spoke. No one would even look at me. I sat as torpid as the rest. I had exhausted my own words. What more could I say? How often could I recite the same story, the same defence?

A vicious wind had sprung up and now howled round the chapel. The shutters shook in the casements and the charcoal in the brazier spat. Only the inanimate had voice that night. We huddled deeper into our cloaks, like beggars in straw. It must have been nearly two hours past midnight. We were all tired and should have been in bed, yet I had no more strength to rouse them to it than they had to stir themselves to go.

'But there must be something we can do to help her. There has to be.' Kitchen Martha's voice was thick with tears.

'I've told you,' I said wearily, 'her fate lies in her hands now, Kitchen Martha. There's nothing more we can do.'

'You said the Commissarius ordered us to surrender the miraculous Host to the church within seven days; if we offered it to them now they might …' She looked up at me with the eyes of a beseeching child.

Under the flickering candle flames the gilt on the reliquary ebbed and flowed as if the box was dissolving away. I shook my head, not even bothering to reply. This matter had gone way beyond Andrew's Host. Didn't she understand anything I'd said? No bribe would rescue her, no miracle was needed, just two little words, but Osmanna would not utter them.

Merchant Martha spread her hands over the dying embers in the brazier. 'The girl will see sense and recant, once she's had time to reflect on the matter. If you speak to her firmly, I'm sure –'

'I *have* spoken to her,' I shouted.

Kitchen Martha's face crumpled. I knew I shouldn't lose my temper, but I was so tired I couldn't bite back the anger. They all blamed me for this, but it was Osmanna's stubbornness and Beatrice's loose tongue that had brought this about.

'I've talked with Osmanna at great length,' I said more softly. 'But she has hardened her heart and she only has two days left.'

'But she can't mean to persist to the end,' Tutor Martha said. 'Perhaps if I speak with her … that is, I don't mean to imply, Servant Martha …'

I knew exactly what she meant to imply. 'Pray continue, Tutor Martha, you may as well speak your mind. Everyone else has.'

'I only meant that perhaps it has become a matter of pride. You know how obstinate she can be when faced with anyone she regards as an authority. Perhaps if I or someone else …'

'You're welcome to try, Tutor Martha, you or anyone else. I wouldn't want it said that we did not attempt every means to bring her to reason.'

Tutor Martha nodded, looking much relieved.

'But you should take someone with you,' I cautioned mechanically. 'There's much hostility against us in the village.

Remember what happened to the dumb child.' Why bother to warn them? They wouldn't take any notice.

'I'll accompany you,' Merchant Martha announced firmly.

Tutor Martha swallowed hard and inclined her head. 'I'm most grateful for your offer, Merchant Martha, but do you think . . . that is, I wonder if . . .'

'I believe what Tutor Martha is struggling to say,' I explained, 'is that she thinks that, like me, you lack the skill of sweet coaxing.'

'I know exactly what Tutor Martha thinks of my tongue, Servant Martha, but if she'd had to deal with as many rogues and clodpolls as I have in my life, she'd soon learn to keep hers well sharpened. And just you think on this, Tutor Martha, hunger's a sharper edge than my tongue, as you'd soon know if I stopped using it to bargain for our food. Maybe if you'd been harder on the girl yourself and not flattered her into thinking she was clever, it wouldn't have come to this.'

'Enough, enough, this is no time to turn on each other.' God grant me patience. I couldn't endure another argument tonight.

'I ask your pardon,' Merchant Martha grimaced. 'You're right, a crabby old woman like me is not the best person to reason with her. I'd likely lose my patience and box her ears. I give you my word, Tutor Martha, not one word shall she hear from me, but I'll go with you all the same, to drive the cart and keep an eye on you. I can smell the fart of trouble coming even before the maker lets rip.'

Tutor Martha smiled and extended her hand, gripping Merchant Martha's for a moment or two.

'I'll go too,' Shepherd Martha said. 'At least the sheep have never complained about my tongue.'

'If that's settled, you should all get some sleep,' I said hastily, seeing Kitchen Martha about to open her mouth again. 'Leave the candles. I'll pray here awhile. Alone.'

They lumbered stiffly to the door and dragged it open. The wind rushed into the chapel, extinguishing half the candles and scattering the charcoal in a shower of sparks. The door banged shut behind them.

Whatever they said to her, I knew Osmanna would not recant. Something happened in the church that afternoon, something that put her beyond fear. One minute she was a frightened little girl, willing to say anything, do anything to save herself, then that look on her face which came from nowhere. What was it that made her change in an instant? It was as if a demon had entered her. I watched it happen repeatedly in my head, but I couldn't make sense of it.

When the Commissarius pronounced the sentence of 'death by burning', even the villagers seemed stunned. Osmanna's knees buckled and her face turned the colour of parchment. I thought she was about to collapse. She stood trembling, her eyes pleading for someone, anyone, to rescue her. The Commissarius paused, waiting for the full measure of his words to take root in her and the gasps of the crowd to die away. Robert D'Acaster looked at Phillip and nodded. It was as if they already knew and approved the sentence. Then the Commissarius spoke again and the crowd held their breath.

'There is a way you may be spared the flames, Agatha. Make full and public confession of your heresy, leave the beguinage and marry. Your excommunication shall be lifted and you shall receive the Host publicly before all; then you will live out your full span as an obedient wife and faithful daughter of the Church.'

Osmanna lifted her head with an expression of such abject relief and gratitude upon her face it seemed she would have hugged him if her hands had not been tied. He was watching her closely and a flicker of triumph crossed his face.

'Like the father of the prodigal son, your father has been most generous and forgiving, Agatha. He has offered a fine gift to the Church as a penance for your sins and he has already found you a suitable husband, a widower who has nobly agreed to take you of his charity.'

The look of fear was subsiding on her face. Like a drowning

man feeling a rope pulling him to the shore, she saw that her rescue was assured. If she had only replied then, all would have been well. She would have agreed to anything they demanded of her. I could see from her face that she would have gladly wed the foulest ass in Christendom if it pulled her from the flames.

But D'Acaster chose that moment to lumber from the dais. He lurched drunkenly towards her and clapped a heavy hand on Osmanna's shoulder to steady himself. She almost buckled under his weight.

'Never fear, girl. Your betrothed's well past his prime. Old age has dimmed his sight, so be grateful he won't see your blemishes. And if he still has the filthy appetites of lust, he can always ride his whore-bride in the dark.'

The crowd shrieked with laughter and Osmanna, her cheeks scarlet, hung her head in shame. The shock of the sentence had left her thoroughly cowed, and if he had led her out there and then, she'd have followed him, meek as a nun. But D'Acaster, encouraged by the laughter of the villagers, spun Osmanna round to face them. He stood behind her, his arm around her waist and his mouth against her neck. He grabbed a fistful of her loose hair in his hand, jerking it up and down like a small boy playing ride-a-cock-horse.

For an instant she seemed to go rigid. Her eyes widened in horror, then her face became a mask of pure hatred. I have never seen such a look on any maid's face, not even on a man's before he plunges in a dagger. Her expression was so grim that those men closest to her abruptly stopped laughing as if they too realized that something had changed. Despite her wrists being tied she jerked her elbow back, striking her father in his belly with such viciousness that D'Acaster loosed his grip on her and staggered backwards, gasping and clutching his side. She whirled around to the Commissarius.

'I will not marry and I will not receive the Host. If you want my life, you take it, for I'd rather die and burn in hell for all eternity than owe my life to that man you call my father.'

She spat out the words with such force that every man in the room seemed to have the breath knocked out of him.

D'Acaster lurched towards her again and gave her a resounding crack across her face with the back of his hand, sending her sprawling against the dais. The crowd let out their breath in a roar of approval.

'I'll send you to hell myself, m'lady. I knew from the first day I clapped eyes on you that you'd come to this. You were born under Lilith's star and that demon-temptress marked you as her own. I tried to rid myself of your curse by fire with my own hand. I tried to make you pure like your sisters, but God saw the whore you were in the cradle and branded you with your fate.'

He hauled her to her feet and, spinning her round once more to face the crowd, tore down the front of her kirtle and thrust her at the gawping men. Her right breast tumbled out, small, white and perfect, but it was not that that the men were staring at. It was her left breast, or rather the place where it should have been. Instead of a breast there was a fist-sized hollow in her chest, covered by puckered skin, scarlet as an open wound – the mark of St Agatha. The church was abruptly silenced.

'There, do you see, do you see it?' D'Acaster urged them, thrusting Osmanna towards them. He was clearly not getting the reaction he expected. Men stared horrified at the breasts, then averted their eyes, embarrassed and unnerved.

No one moved. As if to break a spell, the Commissarius stood up and gestured to the man who had brought Osmanna into court to take her away.

'Leave her alone to think awhile. I've know many a heretic more obstinate than her come to their senses when they've had time to reflect upon the agonies that await them at the stake. Did not the blessed St Paul himself say it is better to marry than to burn?'

Father Ulfrid laughed dutifully, but no one else joined in. All were trying to leave the church as fast as they could struggle through the door. The Commissarius, bellowing for his young clerk to follow, swept from the dais. As he drew level with me, he stopped and leaned towards me, his lips almost brushing my ear.

'Do not think this matter will end with her, mistress. Father Ulfrid may be a fool and easily deceived, but I am not. I know there is more to be uncovered here.'

He drew himself away from me and addressed Father Ulfrid loudly enough for any left in the church to hear.

'Beguines are pernicious tares sown by the Devil to destroy the order of man and God. It was women that destroyed the order in the Garden of Eden, Lilith refusing to lie beneath Adam, and Eve seducing him into forbidden knowledge. Now they are hell-bent on destroying the very priesthood itself, and with it the Holy Church and all Christendom. They will drag you to hell with them if they can. I caution you not to suffer them to take root here, lest all you hold dear is destroyed and thrown in chaos.'

He stared back at me one last time, then strode from the church, pushing men aside as he elbowed his way through the crowded doorway.

The shutters rattled in the casement of the chapel. I thought of that cold prison where Osmanna was lying at this very moment. I tried to imagine her thoughts, the terrors that must be filling her head. Yet when I left her she hadn't cried or pleaded. She had stood there, arms at her sides, watching the door close.

It wasn't a calm resignation, more as if she was frozen, beyond speaking, hearing or feeling. Her gaze was empty, turned inwards on some revelation that seemed to consume her. I told the Marthas that I had spoken to her, but what in all truth had I really said? What could I have said? I should have told her to give up the life of a beguine and marry, but I only had to look at her to know that the argument was futile.

As for the sacrament, I'd urged her to take the Host before in vain. Would my arguments have carried any more weight this time? And what if she had agreed to take the sacrament to save her life? If it had turned out to be a principle not worth dying for, a conviction not strong enough to sustain her through the flames, could I have persuaded her to that, knowing I would despise her for being so persuaded? Worse still, if it were to prove a belief so easily surrendered, then I had allowed the beguinage to be brought to this grave danger through nothing more than a young girl's game. I would not, I could not, live with that.

Yet, if I couldn't persuade her to recant, I should have strengthened her resolve and comforted her. I should have told her that the fleeting pains of this fire would save her from the agonies of the eternal fires, that as a martyr she would rise straight to heaven, but I couldn't. I couldn't even convince myself that somewhere heaven still existed. What if, after all, there was nothing and no one beyond the grave? If my prayers were not answered, because there was no one to answer them? What if none of it mattered; if Host and wine, prayer and Mass, and everything we had worked for, had been nothing but mist blown away by the wind?

Agatha

The laughter of the crowd in the church roared in my head. Over and over I felt his hand yanking my hair, my head jerking back and forth, the heat of his groin against my buttocks, the trunk of his arm against my ribs pulling me tighter and tighter to his stinking, scalding breath. He crushed me into him until I couldn't breathe as the hardness of his prick swelled up and uncoiled against me.

And still I didn't understand the reason for my cold sweat of fear. I couldn't put a name to the choking panic rising inside me until suddenly the reek of wild onion burst in my head and mingled with his sweat. And then I knew. I knew and I couldn't wipe the knowledge from my mind. It was not the demon who raped me that night. It was him.

I'd been dragged back down into the tangle of his forest and nothing could lift me out. I stank of him and I couldn't wash it off. I'd doused myself with the little water they gave me to drink. I scrubbed my skin with the coarsest straw I could find in the cell until my skin was raw, but still I smelt him, felt his damp paws gripping harder than a wolf's bite. The stench of onion filled the cell, choking me. Even though the wind howled through the open bars, I couldn't gasp in enough air to breathe.

Fornication is the wickedest of sins, my father declared, but all along he had been the fornicator. He knew that night as he forced me down among the ramsons and the brambles exactly who it was he violated. He knew the next morning in his hall when he saw the marks on me. He knew when he hit me and called me a whore. He called *me* a whore. He made me feel filthy. He made me filthy. He put his seed inside and made me pregnant with his monstrous child. But he didn't feel anything,

494

no guilt, not then and not since. The shame has all been mine and he will never feel it.

I scrubbed my lips until they bled, but the blood would not wash away the hundred child-kisses I was forced to give his mouth. Hating, hating him even then and feeling the guilt of hell because of it. Evil child. Wicked child. Child of Satan. Honour thy father. Honour thy father the priest. Honour thy Father God. Obey them. Love them. And what is the duty of a father to a child? Beat it, chastise it, bend and break it to his will and call it love. Then call the broken thing obedient, redeemed in blood. Is this what our Father God wants, the cringing, fawning, faithfulness of a whipped dog, the frightened tears of a child crying in the night? Does he pleasure himself on our fear?

January — St Agnes' Eve

This night is the night for divination to discover your true love. This night, too, the Hounds of the Underworld howl, foretelling impending death or disaster.

Beatrice

'What on earth are you doing, woman?' Pega grabbed my wrist and pulled me away from the jars.

I had almost finished. Nearly every jar and flask in the infirmary was bare and waiting for me to write on it in my hand. Just two left. I tried to struggle out of Pega's grasp, but her grip was too strong. She was hurting me.

Kitchen Martha was standing staring down at the fragments of parchment on the floor. 'All Healing Martha's labels torn off. The notes in her books all ripped out. Why, Beatrice, why?'

I hadn't heard them come in. I'd been too busy. She sounded surprised, though I couldn't imagine why.

'I have to write new ones,' I told her patiently. Kitchen Martha was so slow-witted. You had to explain the most obvious things to her.

She bit her lip, glancing at Pega. Then stroked my arm soothingly, as if she thought I needed comforting. 'But, dear, now we don't know what any of the herbs or cordials are.'

I prodded the torn pieces with my foot. 'This was written by Healing Martha, and this and this. I couldn't leave them like that. I have to organize the infirmary. Osmanna isn't coming back, you know. So I'm the Martha now. I must write everything myself or no one will know that it's mine.'

'If this is you in charge, God help us,' Pega snapped. 'Why didn't you do it one jar at a time? How're you going to fathom what's what now?'

I stared at her. Pega wasn't making any sense. You had to get rid of all the old ones and start afresh. How could you write your own labels when you could still see the old ones? They wouldn't be yours, they'd just be copies of hers.

A cart rattled across the courtyard, answered by the cries of half a dozen voices raised in alarm. Pega was at the door before me. Tutor Martha was being lifted down from the cart. Her head lolled against Shepherd Martha's shoulder and her eyes were half closed. They were both splattered with mud and filth. Pega swept her up and carried her into the infirmary. Shepherd Martha and several of the women followed.

Merchant Martha remained sitting, hunched like a crow, on top of the cart, with the reins in her hand. She didn't seem to have noticed the cart had stopped. She too was covered in muck, as if she had been pelted in the stocks. A rotting cabbage stalk was caught in the folds of her cloak. They should never have gone into town risking their lives for that little slut, Osmanna. She was the one the crowd should have been pelting and with rocks too, not cabbages. There was a small, shallow cut on Merchant Martha's forehead, oozing a watery blood. I put my hand on hers; it felt deathly cold.

'You're hurt, Merchant Martha. Let me help you into the infirmary.'

Merchant Martha looked up, almost startled to see me, and rapped my hand away.

'I must speak to Servant Martha at once. Where is she?'

'But your head's bleeding. You must let me see to it first. It will fester if it isn't dressed. It's my responsibility.'

She put her hand up and touched the place, staring at the smear of blood on her fingers in surprise. 'It's nothing, don't fuss, Beatrice.' Merchant Martha pushed me aside and clambered down impatiently. 'Where's Servant Martha?'

'In the chapel, I think.' She never seemed to be anywhere else these days. 'But you have to let me make you better.'

She didn't reply, but shook out her cloak and strode off in the direction of the chapel.

In the infirmary, the beguines were clustered around Tutor Martha. 'One of the village men grabbed me here.' She passed a hand vaguely in the direction of her breasts.

Pega, hunkered down by the fire, stuck a red-hot poker into a beaker of ale, which gave off a great hiss of steam. 'Here, drink this whilst it's hot. So did he hurt you?'

Tutor Martha shook her head. 'But he … he said …' Her words jerked out in heaving sobs. 'Said …'

'Said what? Spit it out.'

It was Shepherd Martha who answered quietly from the corner. Leon was sitting with his great black head resting on her knees and gazing sorrowfully up as if he knew something was wrong.

'He accused us of unnatural practices,' Shepherd Martha said quietly. 'You know, immoral acts between women, though he didn't use those words.'

Pega let out a great snort of laughter. 'I bet he didn't. Well now, that's the first time I've been accused of that. *Strumpet* and *slut* I've had aplenty, but that's a new one. And I dare say he thinks Servant Martha's the bawd of this lively whorehouse. It's a wonder they're not queuing up at the gates. What strange little fancies men do have.'

She slapped Tutor Martha firmly on the back, making her cough and splutter on the wine. 'Come now – a few names, a roving hand and a rotten egg or two. I've taken worse and called it a good night out. But to the point, did you see the lass?'

Tutor Martha shook her head. 'You don't understand. They blocked the road and wouldn't let us pass. We tried … They were screaming and jeering, a whole mob of them with cudgels and stones. Father Ulfrid was standing watching them. He did nothing. If Merchant Martha hadn't hit the man with her whip and pulled me back on to the cart …'

She broke off in renewed sobbing. I put my arms around her and held her.

Pega nodded grimly. 'The Owl Masters are rousing the villagers and we all know who's controlling the Owl Masters. Osmanna's more spirit than I gave her credit for, standing up to that old bastard.'

'Too much spirit,' I said. 'Look what trouble she's caused for the rest of us. This is all the fault of that stupid girl, all of it!'

Pega stared at me for a moment before she answered. 'Maybe so, but all the same, I think I've misjudged that lass. I'd stand up against D'Acasters out of sheer devilment, have done many a time, but I'd not have the mettle to face the fire for it. That's more than stubbornness – that takes the courage of a sow badger and more faith than St Peter.'

'What are you defending her for?' I screamed. 'She's a murderer. She killed her baby ... her own baby. I know you all blame me for what happened to her. I've heard you whispering behind my back. You think I don't know what you're saying, but I do. But you're all wrong. You can't blame me. She brought this on herself. I hope they do burn her, she deserves it. She deserves to burn in hell for what she's done!'

No one looked at me. They all knew it was true.

The door crashed open. Catherine burst into the room. The wind sent up a swirl of rushes around her feet. She stared round, her face stricken as if she'd seen the dead walk.

Pega frowned. 'What is it, lass?'

But Catherine just stood there, her breath jerking out of her in little mewling sounds.

Pega clamped a broad hand on her shoulder. 'Out with it, lass.'

'The oxen ... the ones we use for ploughing. Dairy Martha and I went to fetch them from the pasture for the night and ... they're dead!'

Shepherd Martha leapt to her feet. 'The murrain! God defend us.'

Catherine burst into terrified sobs. 'Not black bane. Something attacked them ... great slashes .... blood everywhere ... It tore out their eyes ... The Owlman ... It was Owlman!'

Servant Martha

As I knelt in front of the altar, I heard the chapel door open and close, and the scuffling of the rushes behind me, but I did not turn round. I hoped that whoever it was would say her prayers and leave me in peace. I couldn't bear one more woman looking at me sorrowfully and asking the same question over and over.

'Isn't there anything we can do for Osmanna, Servant Martha? Isn't there anything we can do?'

There was silence in the chapel save for the wind whistling around the rafters. I don't know how long I remained on my knees, but eventually pain and stiffness forced me to rise, and when I turned I was surprised to see Merchant Martha sitting on a stool at the back of the chapel, her head resting against the wall and her eyes closed. I'd never known Merchant Martha to be content to sit and wait before. While she would never actually interrupt anyone's prayers by speaking to them, she would usually stand behind them, coughing and fidgeting, until she'd attracted their attention. I noticed the blood on her forehead. Alarmed, I hurried over to her.

'Merchant Martha, are you ill?'

She opened her eyes, 'I didn't want to disturb you, Servant Martha.'

'You are hurt. Do you feel faint?''

She waved her hand impatiently. 'It's nothing.'

'The villagers?' It was as I feared, but I had warned the Marthas of the dangers. Still, it gave me no satisfaction to be proved right.

'They're in an ugly mood, as you said. This business with Osmanna has got their blood lust up and that damned priest is goading them on.' Merchant Martha pressed her hand over the cut on her head. 'Something's brewing. I've seen it before.

Instead of acting as a warning, a public execution sometimes stirs the mob up and they go on the rampage looking for more victims. If they do burn Osmanna, it's my belief it'll only be the start. They'll likely take blazing brands from that bone-fire and try to start another here.' She paused and glanced up at the reliquary on the altar before continuing, 'Servant Martha, I never thought I'd say this, but we have to close the beguinage and return to Bruges immediately. We should start out at first light tomorrow if we can.'

I stared at her, unable to believe what she was saying. 'Run away? Is that what you are proposing, Merchant Martha? I might have expected such advice from Kitchen Martha, but I never thought I'd hear it from you. I thought you were made of stronger metal.'

Merchant Martha leapt up from the stool. 'I'd stand fast in the path of a hundred men even if they were armed to the teeth with pikes and spears,' she declared indignantly. 'And if they cut the legs from under me, I'd still go down fighting. I'm no coward, as well you know. I've faced more than my fair share of danger in my time, and I've never run away in my life.'

'I know that, Merchant Martha. That is why I cannot believe you of all people should be suggesting that we should crawl back to Bruges and tell them we failed, that we gave up at the first sign of trouble.'

Merchant Martha sank wearily back on to her stool. 'There's been conflict twixt us and the village since that day you took Ralph in.' She held up her hand to stop me before I could interrupt. 'Not that I'm saying we shouldn't have done that, but all I'm saying is, this is not the first time there's been trouble.'

'Exactly,' I said, 'and we have overcome it before. There is no reason why we should not gird ourselves to do it again.'

'But this time it's serious. I can read a crowd, better than you can read a book. They mean to destroy us and the Owl Masters are behind them. You and I may be prepared to go down fighting, but what about the rest of the women and children? If a mob's blood is up, they lose all sense of reason and decency and they don't spare anyone. As Marthas we've a responsibility to care for the other beguines and we can't protect them here.'

'Seek refuge in Bruges, you mean.' I could not contain my anger. I found myself pacing up and down the chapel. 'You want us to hide ourselves away like a bunch of frightened nuns. Merchant Martha, you and I became beguines to work in the world, to stand up and fight against its injustices whether they are perpetrated by Church, King or baying mob. What kind of example will we set for the beguines now and in the future if we scuttle back to Flanders?'

Merchant Martha's eyes blazed with fury. 'So you are determined we should stay here to demonstrate a principle, is that it, Servant Martha? You'd rather the beguinage went up in flames and us with it to prove our faith. Are you sure it's faith in God that keeps us here and not your stubborn pride?'

She walked rapidly to the door. 'Think about it, Servant Martha, but do it quickly. The execution is set for the day after tomorrow, unless D'Acaster intervenes to save his daughter, and from what I've heard, a bull is more likely to give milk than he is to save her.'

She turned at the door and gazed around the chapel as if she was looking at it for the very last time. 'You're good at speeches, Servant Martha. Doubtless you think you can turn even an angry mob around with your tongue and maybe you can. But there's something else, Servant Martha – the Owlman. If they've that demon on their side, all the logic and reason in the world won't prevail against a creature from hell. You want proof, go and look at Healing Martha. Take a long, hard look, and ask yourself if you are really willing to risk that.'

✝

January – St Agnes' Day

Thirteen-year-old Roman martyr, who refused marriage, was put in a lunatic asylum, then sentenced to be burned. When the fire would not light she was killed by the sword. It is thought unlucky to name a child Agnes, for she will go mad.

Osmanna

They brought me gifts – a thin white shift and a tall, conical hat, pointed like the horn of a unicorn – offerings for a virgin. Three of them crowded into my tiny cell, locking the door behind them: Father Ulfrid, my cousin Phillip and a slack-mouthed youth, Phillip's page. They filled the cell, blocking out the afternoon light. I pressed against the rough wall, sick with fear at what they would do under the cover of the twilight they'd brought with them.

Phillip made a mocking bow. 'Oblige me, m'lady, by removing your clothes, all of them, then clad yourself in this.' He held up the loose white shift, but when I reached for it, he snatched it back.

'Don't be so hasty. You must strip yourself first.'

He leered and moved a step closer as if he hoped I'd refuse so that he could do it for me. They waited. I wanted to turn my back, but that would only make me more vulnerable, so I faced them, trying to slip my clothes off without taking them away from my body. Father Ulfrid at least lowered his eyes. Phillip smirked, cracking his knuckles, and the boy blushed to the roots of his straw-coloured hair as he stared frog-eyed up and down the length of me. I was naked. I clutched my kirtle against me, trying to keep covered, my back pressed to the cold, sharp stones of the wall. Phillip snatched my clothes away. I wrapped my arms across my body, trying to cover my hideous scar with my hand.

Father Ulfrid stared contemptuously. 'Modesty? There're no dresses where you're going. Have you not paid heed to the paintings on the church walls? They're put there for the instruction of foolish girls like you. Heretics bound together in the eternal fires of hell, bare and naked for all the devils in hell to mock.'

He dragged the shift out of Phillip's hands and thrust it at me. I hurried to drag it over my head, feeling their gaze groping my body as I struggled to cover myself.

'She'll be bare-arsed long before the devil comes for her.' Phillip laughed. He leaned over me, crushing me against the wall, his hand resting on the wall beside my head. I could smell the wine on his breath. He twisted a curl of my hair round his fingers. 'As soon as the flames touch you, this pretty little shift will shrivel away and every hair on your body along with it. You'll be trussed up there on that bonfire as flesh-naked as a scalded pig. The whole village will see what you're marked for before your flesh melts away to tallow.'

The young boy giggled nervously. 'Maybe we'll put a grease pan under her to catch the drips. Lay the rushes in it and we can burn her all winter.'

'All winter?' Phillip pulled away from me. 'It's precious little light you need then, boy. There's not enough fat on her to dip a pennyweight of rushes.'

The floor was writhing under me. My face was burning, but I was freezing cold. My legs buckled under me. A wave of bile rose in my throat. I crouched against the wall, vomiting on to the stinking straw, shivering uncontrollably.

'Are you cold, my sweet cousin? Never mind, you'll be warm enough tomorrow.'

He cuffed the pageboy around the head, 'Get on with it, boy, there's a flagon of wine waiting for me at the Bull Oak Inn.'

It was only then I saw that the boy was holding a pair of sheep shears.

I tried to scramble to my feet, but Phillip seized both my wrists, crushing them together. The boy leaned over me and grabbed a handful of my hair. There was a grating rasp and he tossed the hank of cropped hair down on the straw in front of me. He grabbed another handful and that too fell, then another and another, until all my hair lay among the vomit in the straw. I hadn't realized I had so much hair until I saw it scattered in front of me. My scalp felt raw and cold, as if someone had tipped ice over my head. Phillip let me go and I crumpled down on to the straw. I couldn't move. It was as if this was happening to someone else and I was hovering somewhere overhead, watching it. Perhaps I wasn't there at all. I was a ghost. I was invisible.

Father Ulfrid thrust the tall hat in front of my face. 'See there.' He shook me. 'Look at it, girl.'

I tried to focus my eyes to read the name written on the hat in red letters –*Lilith*.

'That's your rightful name. You cannot be allowed to die with a saint's name upon you. You need a demon's name to send you straight to hell.'

He stood the hat opposite me, the name turned towards me, like a judge. The door crashed open and shut again, the key grated in the lock. I was alone again.

I sat where I was dropped, as cold as a drowned man. My legs were dead. My scalp prickled, but I didn't want to touch it. I couldn't have lifted my arms even if I did. My body didn't obey me any more. I stared at the long brown curls lying among the straw. Heretics, harlots and nuns – all shorn. Why do men fear our hair so much? The stones dug into my back, but the feeling was far removed from me. I floated somewhere beyond it. I knew what they said they would do tomorrow, but it couldn't happen. It wouldn't. It was only a bad dream and I would wake up soon.

Servant Martha

The infirmary was silent. The shutters were closed against the cold and only a few tapers burned, barely penetrating the twilight. Most of the patients had gone, those who still had families to collect them. Maybe Merchant Martha was right and the villagers knew the Owl Masters were planning to attack the beguinage, so they'd rescued their own relatives while there was still time to get them out.

Beatrice was gone too. We knew something was wrong when we saw the door of the pigeon cote flung wide open and the birds wheeling round the top. At first I feared she might have harmed herself in there, but she'd not done that. The cote was empty, save for the candles. She must have collected up every wax candle in the beguinage and set them all burning. It was a wonder they hadn't set light to the straw.

Pega and some of the others had looked for her, but she was not in the fields or barns. I knew we wouldn't find her. Guilt over Osmanna had doubtless weighed heavy on her mind and perhaps she thought the other beguines blamed her, so she had simply slipped away. I should pray for her. I had let her down as I had the others, but I couldn't even pray for myself.

A soft hand gently stroked mine. Healing Martha was watching me. I could see the embers of the fire reflected in that one open eye. 'I am tired, Healing Martha, so very tired. Tomorrow they will burn Osmanna and all my thoughts should be with her, and there is nothing I can do.'

Healing Martha's hand squeezed mine gently as if encouraging me to continue.

'Merchant Martha thinks we should return to Bruges. They are all packed and ready, waiting for me to give them the word, but I can't give it. I have failed so many people – you,

Osmanna, Gudrun. I cannot fail again. The decision I make, I must make for the whole beguinage, not just for the beguines here now, but for all the women who will join us in the years, even centuries, to come. And for the first time in my life, I don't know what to do. If the pagan hordes were massed against us, then our duty would be clear, but when it is the Holy Church itself that seeks to destroy us, on what do we stand? *Pater misericordiam*, why will God not answer me?'

'Gar.'

Not that noise again. Why was that sound the only one left to her, a mockery of a word, so utterly meaningless?

'What do you want, Healing Martha, a drink perhaps, is that it?'

'Sa ... gar.'

'Yes, I heard you. Are you cold? Shall I stoke up the fire?'

What was I doing in the infirmary? My duty was to be in the chapel praying, but my prayers disappeared into a void. I didn't even know if Healing Martha could hear me, but at least her one sound, senseless though it was, was better than cold silence.

'Sau ... garde.'

I stared at her. 'What? What did you say?'

'Sauve ... garde.'

This time there was no mistaking it. Sauvegarde – the inscription written above the gateway to the Vineyard in Bruges.

'Is that what you've been trying to say all these weeks? No, Healing Martha, no! You cannot ask me to go back to Bruges. We might as well be nuns sheltering from the world, hiding behind thick walls. But we are not called to be safe. I thought you of all people understood that.'

She winced and I cursed my own tongue. Hadn't I hurt her enough?

'Forgive me, Healing Martha. I've been selfish. You're old and sick and it's right that you should return to spend your last days in the Vineyard with people to care for you properly. I should have listened to you with more patience and realized you were asking to be sent home.'

There was a surprisingly sharp slap on my hand. I rubbed my skin more to acknowledge the rebuke than because it stung.

'Sauvegarde!' She tapped the side of my head and then her own.

'I believe she's asking you what Sauvegarde means, Servant Martha.' I jumped at the sound of Merchant Martha's voice behind.

'We all know what it means, Merchant Martha,' I snapped. 'Refuge – the place of refuge.'

'Refuge for what though?' Merchant Martha asked. 'I think she's saying you have not understood it.' Merchant Martha sat down on the edge of the cot. 'Tell me why you became a beguine.'

'To serve God,' I said impatiently.

'Then why not serve God as a nun or anchorite or wife? What did you find in a beguinage?'

'Freedom, somewhere I could be –'

'That's it, Servant Martha, you'd the freedom to be yourself, do what you thought was right, not what others told you to do. Thoughts, that's what Healing Martha is trying to tell you. What we safeguard is not our bodies, but our freedom to think.

'I don't hold with what Osmanna did, you know that. There was a time when if I'd had the care of her, I'd have taken a strap to her backside, as well you know. But that day in the Marthas' Council you said, "Osmanna desires to seek the truth for herself." You gave her the freedom to do that. You and me, we may not have liked the truth she found, but she'd the right to try to find it. And if there is to be true refuge for the thought, then we must be free to explore any path without let or hindrance. That's what you taught me that day in Council, Servant Martha. It's taken me a while to accept it. You know me, I'm a stubborn old goat, but even old goats can change.'

Merchant Martha slipped off the cot; she touched my shoulder, just for a moment, before she walked away.

Healing Martha squeezed my hand again. For a moment I thought I saw her smile, then a sudden spasm of pain twisted her face. Her hand clutched at her chest. She coughed, choking and wheezing, struggling to reach for a cup of herbed wine beside her. I held it to her lips. She drank and slumped back, shaking with the effort. A few drops of the red wine had spilled into her open hand. She gazed at them wonderingly and slowly closed her fist, letting the drops run through her fingers and fall on to my open palm. By the glow of the fire's embers, I watched her eyes close. Her good hand fell limp in mine. The flame on the rush candle guttered and died, leaving only a wisp of smoke.

Pisspuddle

'If the two of you don't give over squabbling, I'll tell your father and then neither of you'll be going to the burning tomorrow. There's me trying to help your poor dear father out of the goodness of my heart and all you two can do is mither me until my head's fit to burst. And *you* can get out of here and all.' Lettice flung a ladle of water at the dog trying to slip in through the door behind her. It growled, but slunk off.

'Now see what you've done,' William hissed in my ear. 'It's all your fault, you little pig's turd.'

'I can't be doing with you two under my feet all day,' Lettice grumbled. 'Make yourselves useful, fetch some water, and not from the well – that's still cursed and will be until that wicked girl is ashes. You go down to the river, draw the water from there, and mind you find a nice clear patch, don't be bringing me back a pail of mud. Now off with you, before I tell your father to take a switch to the pair of you.'

She hung a pair of leather pails strung together with a rope over William's shoulder and shooed us out of our cottage.

William shoved me aside and hurried ahead of me down the path, trying to leave me behind. I had to run to catch up with him. It really annoyed him if I walked with him, that's why I did it, even though I'd sooner walk by myself. It was hard keeping up with him. Although I was better, my legs still felt wobbly.

I didn't remember much about being sick. It was all a jumble, the flood, being ill, the Owlman. Sometimes I didn't know what had really happened and what was just a bad dream.

I don't know how long I'd been in the house of women, but I woke up in a room that was bigger than two cottages together and had lots of beds in it with people moaning. I was scared. I'd eaten the food the grey women had given me and it was witched, and now I was going to waste away and die. I'd felt the birds pecking me, like Lettice said. I was so afeared I yelled and wouldn't stop yelling, but Lettice came to rescue me, not a moment too soon, she said.

I thought Mam would be waiting for me at the cottage. But she wasn't there. Father said she wasn't ever coming back. I didn't believe him and I kept crying for her till Father smacked me. I still cry, but only at night, and I stuff my blanket in my mouth so he can't hear me.

'Stop trying to walk next to me,' William said, deliberately nudging me into the bushes. 'You think I want everyone to see me walking with a girl? And you needn't think you're coming with me tomorrow, 'cause you're not. I don't know what you want to come for anyway. You'll be pissing yourself and crying for Mam ... Anyway, you'll be bawling before the flames even touch her.'

'I won't so.'

'You will too. You don't even know what happens, do you?'

'Neither do you,' I said. My legs were shaking, but I wasn't going to drop behind.

'I do, 'cause Henry told me,' William said, looking all smug. 'He's seen loads of burnings in Norwich. Shall I tell you?'

I knew it was going to be horrible and I didn't want him to tell me, but if I said no, he'd make me listen. I shrugged, trying to look as if I really didn't care.

'First all her clothes burn off and you can see her bubbies and everything. And her skin starts to blister and pop, then it melts and starts running down her legs. The stench is powerful. Just one whiff of it and you'll be sick as a dog, and she'll scream and scream and you'll never be able to get the scream out of your head.'

I pressed my fist against my mouth and shuddered. I already felt sick.

William grinned down at me. 'See, I told you, Pisspuddle, you're scared.'

I ran a few steps ahead of him, so he couldn't see my face.

'Doesn't bother me. I'm going to go to the Green afore it gets light, so I can get right in the front.'

'Oh yeah.' He grabbed me by my plaits. I wriggled and tried to kick him, but his arms were too long and I couldn't reach him. I bit him hard on the arm, hard as I could. He squawked like a strangled goose and let go.

'Just wait till I catch you, you little turd.'

I ran down the path as fast as I could, round the tanner's yard and up towards the Green. My legs felt heavy and shaky. William was pounding after me, but the pails slowed him down. My legs had cramp and I'd got a stitch in my side.

I tore round the corner so fast I didn't even see the Owl Master standing in the shadows until he grabbed me. He clamped his leather-gloved hand across my mouth, and before I knew what was happening, he'd pulled a stinking sack over my head and arms. He tipped me over his shoulder. He was walking fast. My chest was banging hard against him and it hurt. I struggled and kicked, but I couldn't get free. I heard a heavy door creak open, then he stopped. And he dumped me down on the rushes. I curled up tightly in a ball, too scared to move.

'Here's the brat, Father.'

'Did you have to bring her like that? You've frightened her half to death.'

I heard a man laugh, but it wasn't a happy laugh. 'Doesn't the Church teach that fear is the beginning of wisdom? Just make sure she does the wise thing, Father. Otherwise I'll be having that little chat with the Commissarius about a certain pretty lad of your acquaintance.'

I heard scuffling in the rushes and Father Ulfrid yelped as if someone was hurting him.

'Make no mistake, Father, one way or the other the Aodh is determined to finish that foreign woman tonight, her and her whole house of witches. You will bring her to him, or you will be pleading for death yourself before dawn breaks.'

A door banged with a great hollow echo.

I shrank as I felt fingers tugging the sack off my head.

Father Ulfrid was bending over me. He pulled me to my feet. We were standing inside the church.

'Are you hurt, child?'

I shook my head, glancing round to see if the Owl Master was still here, but he wasn't. I tried to edge towards the door, but Father Ulfrid caught my arm.

'There is nothing to be afraid of, child.' Father Ulfrid knelt down and so his face was close to mine. He was sweating, even though it was very cold in the church. 'Listen carefully, child. There is something you must do for me. It is very important. Do you know the foreign women that live outside the village?'

I shook my head.

Father Ulfrid frowned impatiently. 'Yes you do. You were taken there when you were ill, remember?'

'I never talked to them, ever.'

'I need you to talk to them now. I want you to go there and ask the woman on the gate if you may speak to the leader, the one they call the Servant Martha. Can you remember that?'

'Mam says I mustn't go near them, 'cause they take little girls and sell them as slaves across the sea.'

'But you were in their house and they didn't sell you, did they?'

'Only 'cause Lettice came and rescued me afore they could.'

'Enough of this nonsense.' Father Ulfrid struggled up from his knees and stood over me. I backed away, but he held my shoulders.

'You were seen talking to the women before you were ill. You took food from them. You know what happens to little girls who tell lies, don't you?'

He pulled me round and pointed at the wall where demons with bird heads on their chests were poking the screaming sinners into the flames of hell.

'Now, child, you are to go to the house of women and ask for Servant Martha. When she comes you are to give her these.'

He pulled something out of his pocket. 'Hold out your hands, child.'

I shoved my hands behind my back, scared he was going to hit me with a switch, but he grabbed my wrist and pushed something into it. It was soft, and when I looked down, I saw it was only a lock of curly brown hair, tied up with a piece of torn grey cloth.

Then he took my other hand and pushed a single long feather into it.

'You are to give these to Servant Martha, but you must put one in each of her hands, like I have done to you. Then you must say just one word – *choose*.'

'Choose what?'

Father Ulfrid shook his head. 'Pray you never need to know that, child. Now, you go and do exactly what I've told you. And if she asks you who sent you, you must say the Owl Masters. You must not mention me, do you understand?'

I didn't understand. Why did I have to take a stupid feather to that woman? What if she asked me who gave it to me? Father Ulfrid had just said I'd go to hell if I told lies. She'd get angry if I wouldn't tell her. I wouldn't do it. I wouldn't.

I dropped the feather and the hair and ran towards the door, but it was too heavy. I couldn't wrench it open before Father Ulfrid caught me. He dragged me back and spun me round to face him.

'If you don't do exactly what I tell you, the Owl Masters will take you to the top of the church tower and leave you up there alone in the dark for the Owlman. Are you going to do it, or shall I call them? They're waiting.'

Servant Martha

'If I have not returned by midnight, Merchant Martha gather the other Marthas, and act as God directs your spirits this night. I know you will do what is right for the women.'

Merchant Martha held the candle higher and peered up into my face, frowning as she tried to read what was written there. 'You are going to see Osmanna, to try to persuade her to recant?'

I couldn't answer her. 'If I do not return, don't search for me. Promise me you will not do that or allow anyone else to do it. Your duty is to the women.'

'I know my duty, Servant Martha,' she said gruffly. 'I hope you remember yours.'

As I walked away from her room, I heard her call softly behind me, 'God go with you, Servant Martha, and keep you safe.' I was grateful for those words.

I swung myself up on to my horse and urged him forward at the trot. The night was still and quiet. I had grown accustomed to the roar of the wind in the trees and the rattling of doors and shutters, but now that the wind had died away the silence was deep and unnerving. Sounds which had been masked before were now magnified: the boom of a bittern crouching somewhere in the reeds, the rustle of the grass as some unseen creature wriggled through it, and the clatter of my horse's hooves on the loose stones of the track, a sound which I was sure must be heard for miles. A sea mist had rolled in across the marshes. A great white curtain hung over the dark fields. Wisps of fog were edging towards me, curling around the horse's flanks.

At the fork I stopped; the right track led to the village and Osmanna, the left to the forest. I reached into my scrip for two small scraps – a strand of hair and a single feather. I held one in each hand just as the child had given them to me. 'Choose,' she said, as if it was a game.

Right hand or left, how could I choose between what I held? They were both as soft and unsubstantial as air. Surely such ethereal fragments could not carry the vastness of eternity upon them, but they did. They say the Archangel Michael, when he holds our souls in his scales balanced between salvation and damnation, weighs our deeds against a single feather. Now those scales were in my hands, swinging between life and death, heaven and hell, but for which of us? The choice had been given into my hands. Three of us watched through this night, Osmanna and the Owlman and me. By this time tomorrow, one of us would be dead and one of us would be in hell in this world or the next. But would any of us be left alive in this cursed valley?

I had failed all the women. I had failed myself. *Confiteor Deo omnipotenti, beatae Mariae semper Virgini.* But what could I confess? To say *mea culpa* was not enough. I had failed, yes, but how, how had I failed? What had Old Gwenith said? 'Not names enough for all my sins.' And a sin must have a name or it can be neither confessed nor absolved. Merchant Martha was wrong; it was not pride that kept me from returning to Bruges, it was fear that I had committed the greatest sin of all, the one that God will not name and will not forgive.

I would have changed places with Osmanna if I could. I would have faced death for Christ. I would have embraced it. I was not afraid of losing my life. I was not afraid of pain or disfigurement. My sin was that I was not willing to sacrifice my mind and my reason for my Lord. 'Go and look at Healing Martha,' Merchant Martha had said. 'Ask yourself if you are really willing to risk that.' God had called Healing Martha to fight for him that night, for she was willing to surrender everything and I was not, because I could not be certain that sacrifice would not be in vain. To give all and discover you had given it for nothing. To climb the holy mountain and find no God there, that is both the unforgivable sin and the eternal punishment.

I pulled on the reins and turned my horse on to the left-hand track. Not until that moment did I know for certain which I would choose – the hair or the feather, Osmanna or the demon.

The mist was rolling in behind me and by the time I came to the edge of the forest, it was already slinking in among the trees. I dismounted and tethered my horse to the branch of a tree, right on the edge of a track where I could be sure to find it again. I patted the leather scrip tied about my waist, where I had placed a crucifix and Andrew's Host in a small wooden box. Then I lifted the lantern and cast about me into the trees.

I knew the Owlman was here. I could feel it. On that first night in May I had seen the Beltane fire glowing above the trees in the forest. Whatever evil had been hatched in the fire that night was the beginning of all this and this is where I was determined it would end. There were no fires burning tonight and the forest was vast, but the demon had sent me his sign. He would find me as surely as he had found us that night in the storm, and if he did not, I would call him forth.

I strode into the trees. The mist rubbed around the trunks and curled over the boulders. The feeble yellow flame of the candle couldn't penetrate the dense fog, and white trunks loomed out of it inches from my face. All the time I was listening, conscious of the snapping of twigs and crunching of dried leaves under my feet, wondering what hidden creatures in the forest were even now tracking my footfalls. The damp mist clung to my clothes and skin in tiny beads, soaking them faster than rain. Nothing was stirring. It seemed that I was the only thing moving out there in the darkness. All the beasts were still, listening and waiting.

Then I heard it, a deep echoing *oohu-oohu-oohu*, the call of the eagle owl hunting. I felt the hairs on the back of my neck prickle. I glanced fearfully upwards but the mist was pawing around the branches, blocking out even the dark sky above.

Perhaps it was only a harmless owl. I stood listening, trying to remember which direction the sound had come from. For a few minutes, I could hear nothing except the sound of my own breathing.

Oohu-oohu-oohu. The call came again. This time I knew it was no ordinary bird. It was too strong, too deep, like a pack of bloodhounds baying across the sky. The cry was coming from ahead and to the left. I touched the leather scrip again to reassure myself and stumbled towards the cry.

Several times I crashed into trees or tripped over rocks and brambles, but I pushed on. Whenever I stopped to look around, the cry would echo again, as if it knew exactly where I was, and it was leading me deeper and deeper into the forest. I was aware that I was climbing; the ground was sloping upwards and boulders became more numerous. To the left of me was the sound of crashing water. I must be somewhere near the river. I turned away from the roar of water, afraid that in the dark and mist I might walk straight into it.

Then a huge dark shape lumbered out of the mist towards me. I just had time to throw my arm up before my face was smothered in something wet which wrapped itself around me, clinging to my face. I screamed and fought out of its slimy grasp, falling backwards with a crash on to the ground. The lantern rolled out of my hand. I covered my face, expecting the thing to pounce again, but nothing happened. Slowly I edged my hand towards the lantern. It had fallen on to a great heap of old leaves and thanks be to God had not smashed or extinguished. I pulled it towards me and tilted it upwards.

I was lying beneath a great bull oak, its hollow large enough for half a dozen men to stand inside. A tattered length of cloth dangled from one of the low, bare branches. That must have been what I had walked into. Feeling foolish, I clambered to my feet and reached to touch it. But it wasn't cloth, it was a kind of leather, pale and soft, but as thin as parchment. The mist had wetted it, making it slimy. There were markings on it, crude symbols drawn in red. I held the lantern closer. Two long vertical lines with smaller horizontal lines bisecting them. Other symbols too, a spiral and –

'The flayed hide of a child, mistress,' a voice rang out behind me, 'an ancient spell to summon the gods.' Before I could turn, I felt the prick of a sword in my back.

'Hang the lantern from that branch and walk into the oak.'

My heart thumping, I did as I was told, careful not to make any sudden movements which might cause my captor to drive that blade home.

'Turn around.'

A burly man filled the gap in the entrance to the hollow oak, holding the sword ready to strike if I should attempt to push past him. In the pearly mist, the light of the lantern hanging from the branch behind him made a shimmering halo of his outline. At first I thought he was hooded for I couldn't make out his face; then, as he turned his head to the side a little, I saw it was covered by a mask of the great horned eagle owl. The candlelight glinted from a hooked bronze beak.

'I knew you'd come to me.' The speaker's voice was deep and distorted inside the mask. 'Phillip was sure you'd choose to save the girl, but he always underestimates women, a foolish thing to do.'

'Phillip D'Acaster? Is he your leader?'

The man laughed. 'You think a strutting cock like him would have the knowledge to bring the Owlman forth? No, mistress, I am the Aodh. I am the fire.'

'Then it was you who unleashed that demon upon the village. And you who were responsible for the vicious attack on Healing Martha. She was an old woman and a skilled physician who had done nothing but good all her life. Your demon left her a cripple without speech or reason and now she is dead. God will punish you for that. But you failed miserably if you thought your demon would take her soul. All the demons of hell cannot prevail against such faith as hers.'

Outside the hollow of the oak the mist prowled round the trees, stirring softly as if it breathed in the candlelight. But inside the hollow of the trunk there was no mist at all, almost as if there was an invisible door keeping it out. It was very dark and still inside the tree.

'Poor foolish Aldith was sent to draw you out, but we did not expect the old one to come with you.' The man lowered his sword, but kept a firm grip on it. I knew it could flash upwards again faster than I could reach the entrance.

'Then you intended that demon should kill me,' I said coldly.

'Your death would have been useful to us, but dead or frightened away from Ulewic, either would have served our purpose. In the end, though, you served us better than we could have hoped for.'

'I served you?' I said, taken aback by his words. 'I would never –'

'But you did. The Owlman is as much your creation as mine, mistress. I called it back from the shadows of the gods, but the day you swore that your friend had fought it and vanquished it you gave it power. You proclaimed to all that you believed the Owlman existed. When a priest says he has exorcized a demon, he has in that instant created the demon by his word. You, mistress, gave the Owlman life because you made of him a demon to be feared and fought.'

I stared at the dark figure. With sickening dread, I knew that I had unwittingly played right into their hands. I had been so intent on turning this evil deed into good, making them see Healing Martha as a victor, that I had acknowledged this creature before all the women. I was the one who'd told them of his great power and horror.

'If I made him, then it will be all the easier to destroy him,' I said. 'And that I promise you I will do this night, even if I die in the attempt.'

'They told me you were clever, but you still haven't understood, mistress. In attempting to destroy him, you would only strengthen him.'

He laughed. The sound was more chilling coming from the hollow of the blank, expressionless mask. 'Isn't that what your

Church teaches? Your martyrs and your Christ, who would ever have heard of them if people with your zeal had not set out to kill them?

'Mark this, mistress, and mark it well; the Owlman cannot be killed. We have unleashed a legend in this valley, you and I, and legend cannot be destroyed. You can slay a human. You can slaughter a beast, but you cannot kill a demon or a god. They are immortal because we make them so. To fight them is to give them ever greater power.'

He lifted his sword and pointed it at my heart. The steel blade glinted in the candlelight. 'In the morning they will find you bound to this oak tree, dead. I cannot tell you how the Owlman will kill you; maybe he will rip out your bowels, like poor, foolish Aldith, or tear strips from your flesh and devour them while you live. Perhaps he will blind you first or tear out your tongue. But he will come before dawn and he *will* take his prey.

'I'm going to make a martyr of you, mistress. It's what you want, isn't it? That's why you've come here. You will be remembered. Whenever they talk about the Owlman, they will speak your name too. Then the villagers will remember the old ways, and turn back to them, back from the Church which cannot protect them, and back from the Christ who cannot protect you. Order will be restored. Your death will breathe life into the Owlman. That is the true resurrection, the one we have known since this land was formed from Anu's blood and bones.'

I felt sick. He was going to stake me out for this demon. I thought of Healing Martha's tortured face, the mutilated body of that village woman lying behind the fallen oak. Is that how they would find me? And what if he was right, what if my death only served to terrify the village into serving that creature? I would have damned the souls of innocent men and women and children, maybe for generations to come.

Beyond the oak the fog swirled, forming into miasmas and dreams, then just for an instant the mist curled up behind the

Owl Master, so that it looked as if there was an old woman standing behind him.

Somewhere, as if the mist of a memory was gathering in my head, I heard the whisper of a dying voice. 'They only have half the spell. You mustn't be afeared, you have the strength of a woman ...' For a moment the white phantasm raised its blank hollow face as if to look at me, then the shape melted back into the whiteness, like ice in water.

Anger swelled inside me. The Owl Master was right; he needed me to give this demon life and I would not give him that. I had to get away. If the Owl Master was going to bind me, he would have to lay down the sword. If I rushed at him and struck him, I might be able to throw him off guard long enough to get past him. In this mist he would never find me.

I swallowed hard. 'If you propose to kill me, at least have the courage to show yourself. Do I not have the right to see the face of my murderer?'

He laughed again. 'Curious, are you, mistress, curious to see who has bested you? Yes, I think you should know me.'

He pulled off his owl mask and stepped back a little from the tree, so that the light from the lantern fell on his face.

'Now do you remember me, mistress? We're not strangers, you and me. We met one day on the Green when you ordered me to release the child from the stocks. You thought you could command the whole of Ulewic back then.'

I gaped. 'The blacksmith ... John? You are the Aodh? But I thought D'Acaster or one of his men would –'

'Would be the Aodh. Robert, you mean? He's a fool. Like all of the noble lords, they are descended from outlanders. They're not part of this land. They don't know how to use its power.' His grip on the sword had relaxed and now it swung loosely at his side. 'You disappointment me, mistress, did the name not tell you?'

'Aodh – fire. I should have known.'

'Yes, mistress, you should, but like Father Ulfrid and the D'Acasters you think those of lowly birth are simpletons. It's a dangerous mistake. Blacksmiths have worked the alchemy of fire and iron and water since the earth was young. We are the horse whisperers and the bloodcharmers. Who else could keep the knowledge of the old ways? I have faced the ordeal of the hide and I –'

He had stepped far enough back from the tree for me to take my chance. I ran for the gap. Caught off guard, he only saw what I was doing when it was too late. He raised his sword as I rushed past him, but I grabbed the hanging skin and swung it into his face. I heard his muffled cry as the clinging hide enveloped his face, but I did not look back. I fled into the mist.

I'd been so intent on getting away that it took a few moments to comprehend the deafening roar; then I realized it must be the crashing water of the river. It sounded as if I was almost on top of it, but in the mist I couldn't make out where exactly the noise was coming from. I stopped, afraid to move in case I plunged into it in the dark. I could hear him crashing through the bushes behind me.

I felt for a tree and crouched against it, praying he would run straight past. The water was so loud that I could no longer hear where he was or even if he was still moving. He could be a yard away, creeping up on me from out of the mist, and I'd not know until I felt the sword in my back. I peered this way and that, trying desperately to see through the swirling white, but the ghostly outlines of shapes that loomed in and out of the mist might be trees or men; it was impossible to see.

'The mist will not shield you, mistress,' John's voice rang out over the roar of the water. 'He will find you. He can smell you wherever you hide.'

The voice seemed to be coming from somewhere close by, but fog distorted the direction, so that I couldn't hear if he was behind or in front of me. I crouched lower, clasping the leather scrip which held Andrew's Host.

Then the blacksmith's voice boomed out again, louder and deeper, reverberating through the silent trees. 'In the names of Taranis, lord of destruction, Yandil of ice and darkness,

Rantipole spirit of rage, Owlman, come forth and take your prey.' He gave the same deep sonorous *Ooohu-ooohu-oohu* that I had heard earlier that night.

As the echoes of the cry died away, there was a moment's silence, then came an answering call: *Ooohu-ooohu-oohu*. But this call made the breath freeze in my throat. The cry seemed to cleave the night in two. Whatever made it was of monstrous size and power.

I felt the rush of silent wings overhead, beating down on the mist, sending it boiling round my head. I caught a glimpse of talons, sharp as daggers, the flash of a huge beak in the mist. Then I saw, blazing out of the mist, the twin fires ringing those terrible dark pupils. I was pulled deeper and deeper into their blackness, until the strength was dragged from my limbs. I was consumed in the despair of that icy flame. My legs collapsed beneath me and lay in the dirt, shaking and sobbing, waiting to feel those giant claws rip into my back. There was nothing I could do to save myself.

God has ordained you. A young girl, a child, was crouching in prison, waiting like me for the end, but she could have walked free. Osmanna did not have to die, but she would, because she was not looking for God in that cloud on the mountain. She did not demand an answer to her prayers for she knew he *was* the silence. And in that very silence lay the answer. *God is in you.*

I forced myself to my feet. I made my arms fall from my face to my side. I stood upright, taller than I had ever stood in my life, and I shouted into the forest, 'I am the body. I am the blood. I am creation. Do you hear me, demon? In the name of the God who set His spirit within me I deny you life.'

There was a rush of wind over me, and looking up, I saw the eyes of fire circling, coming closer. I threw back my head, waiting for the talons to tear at my throat, but it did not strike.

There came a terrified cry, 'No, no, get back! Not me! I am your master!'

Someone was crashing wildly through the bushes.

'I command you –' John roared, but the words broke off in

a long-drawn-out scream. There was a heavy splash. Then nothing.

I stood there for a long time, terrified that the demon was still there hovering above me, but all was still.

'John,' I called softly. 'Where are you?'

But there was no reply. I fell to my hands and knees, crawling forward through the mist towards the sound of crashing water. I felt the ground disappear under my outstretched hand and knew I was kneeling on the river bank. I crouched on all fours. The mist hovered about a foot above the water. Below it, the white foam boiled down over the rocks.

'John, are you hurt?' I called again, but my voice seemed to be smothered by the white blanket and I wasn't even sure I would hear his answer over the sound of the water. Then the mist parted for an instant and I could see something moving in the centre of the river. A man's head, the face turned towards me, his eyeballs glittering white in the darkness. He was clinging on to the rock in the centre of the river. The icy water was cascading over his fingers as if they had become stones in the river bed.

'Hold on!' I yelled. I struggled to get my cloak off, twisted it and knotted it top and bottom. I threw one end, but it was not long enough. The knot splashed into the water.

I needed a long stick or branch, but it would have been impossible to find one in the mist. I pulled the belt from my waist and buckled it through the knot of the cloak; it only lengthened it a little, but I prayed it would be enough. I lay flat on the bank.

'I'll throw it again. This time you must reach out. Now!' I yelled, as the mist closed again.

I heard the end of the cloak fall into the water, but no hand grasped it, and I felt the cloth being dragged downstream. Again I hauled it out.

The mist parted briefly again. I could see his fingers, white with cold, were slipping from the rock.

'John, let go with one hand and catch this when I throw. You must trust me or you will be swept away. It's your only chance.'

I threw again and the end of the cloak fell into the water within inches of his hand, but he made no attempt to reach out for it.

'No ... no ... mistress, you can't take back from Anu what she has claimed for her own ... Remember, mistress, you cannot destroy a legend ... a legend can only die ... if no one speaks its name.'

From above our heads, a piercing shriek rang out like high, mirthless laughter – *Kraaaaaah.* A great bird came swooping down through the swirling mist towards the river. It hovered, its huge body stretched out over the water. The skin of its torso and long human legs gleamed bone-white; black talons clawed the air. But the head was the face of hell itself.

The stroke of its wings was so powerful that the water was beaten back beneath them into a great hollow with towering white waves rearing up around it. For a moment I saw John's body lying exposed on the rock. Then something green reared up out of the water, an ancient woman, her hair rippling out behind her like wet weed, her massive wrinkled breasts swaying against the rocks. Her mouth opened wider and wider like a huge fish, showing rows of sharp, pointed teeth.

John threw up his arms to cover his face, screaming until the whole forest echoed with the horror and despair. But with one sweep of her powerful arms Black Anu had embraced him and dragged him down with her into the raging torrent.

Osmanna

I'd watched the pale light in the tiny slit of the window turn pink and grey, then shiver into hyacinth. But now there was nothing, not night nor day. Just a shimmering whiteness in the tiny oblong high above my head. I thought I had slept without knowing, and already it was dawn and they were coming for me, but it couldn't be daylight; that whiteness was not the sun.

I was so cold. I had not known how cold my head could feel without my hair. The white hat waited for me by the door, waited for me to put on my new name. It was too dark to read it any more, but I did not need to read it. Know your own name, old Gwenith had said, but deep down I had always known it. It was there at my birth, the demon star, Lilith's star, the evil eye that winks at man from the heavens. It was my star now, for under that was I born and under that would I die. Birth and death: they are the same; the one curses the other.

My nursemaid told me that I was born with her sign. It was only a little thing, a tiny red mark on my chest, shaped like a crescent moon, Lilith's symbol and Lilith's curse. Three days after I was born my father had taken a hot iron from the fire and made her strip me of my swaddling bands and stretch my little body out. Then he laid the red-hot metal to my mark to rid me of the curse. It would keep me chaste, he said, drive out the demon-whore, for as everyone knows, fornication is the greatest sin and my father demanded chastity. My nursemaid said she pleaded with him to stop, but he held it there, determined to obliterate every trace of the curse. It burned deep into the flesh beneath. I had taken many moons to heal and she feared I wouldn't live, but I had.

Lilith, the night-hag, the winged demon with hairy legs and goat's feet. The bloodsucker who rides the night, who invades men's dreams and steals their seed. She fled Adam before the Fall, before he brought death into the world. She is immortal. She cannot die. She cannot die in the flames. They will go on burning her for ever and she will not die. There cannot be an end to her pain. She will be bound there for ever, naked and screaming.

If willpower alone could have made my heart stop ... but it wouldn't stop. It just kept on beating as if I wanted to live. I'd taken off my shift and twisted it into a noose. I tried to climb the wall to the bars on the window to hang the noose from, but I couldn't reach them. For hours I had searched every inch of that cell, trying to find a nail to scratch open my veins or a sharp shard buried beneath the straw; even in the dark I went on searching with my fingertips. Feeling through the straw, sweeping my hands over the cold flags trying to find one scrap of something I might have missed. Let them not burn me. Blessed Virgin, let me not burn. Please let me die now. I cannot bear it. I know I cannot bear it.

There were voices outside the window, a woman's voice and murmuring words too low to be distinct, excited laughter, then a thump against the wooden door.

'I told you, she's not coming. I saw her ride off towards the forest,' the woman said.

'So the bitch really believes she can stand against the Aodh, does she? It will be her last ride.'

'Don't you fancy a ride, master? Come on, it's a pity to waste the evening.'

The man laughed. I knew that deep, mirthless laugh. It was my cousin, Phillip.

'I usually prefer them young and tender, but why not? Most of the women in this village think they have to put up a show of resistance. It gets a little tiresome. They are all strumpets under their skirts; it makes a change to find an honest slut.'

There was a resounding slap on well-rounded flesh and the woman laughed.

'God's blood ... what're you wearing?' Phillip was panting.

'It would be easier to bed a virgin abbess, and don't think I haven't tried.'

'If you're too weak, I'd best find a man who can keep his end up.'

Another slap, a squeal and low chuckle.

'I could fuck you till dawn and still have strength enough to whip you bloody for the whore you are.'

'Could you now? Why don't you put your prick where your mouth is and prove it then?' The voice belonged to Pega!

Phillip was grunting hard like a farrowing sow. I stuffed my fingers in my ears, but I could still hear the moans and pants as they copulated against the wall. How could they? How could she? She must have known I could hear them, why else would she have come here? I wanted to scream at them to go away, but they'd only laugh and do it all the more. A final groan and it was over.

For a long time I could hear nothing except their deep, panting breath. Then finally Pega spoke. 'I've wine here, that'll get you going again. Come on, drink up. I warrant it's better than that arsehole of a priest is supping tonight.'

'I can swear to that,' Phillip said. 'I've suffered the pig's piss he calls wine more than once. Where did you steal this from?'

'The house of women, of course. The leader doesn't stint herself there. Straight from France, this. Sit yourself down and rest awhile. Get your strength up; you'll be needing it. I've a few tricks to show you that I warrant none of your high-born ladies can teach you.'

'I bet you learned ... a thing or two from those women ... heard those foreign whores can ...'

Phillip's voice trailed off into heavy snores. There was what sounded like a heavy kick into a mass of flesh, but the snores continued unabated.

'Osmanna?'

Pega's outline suddenly filled the window, blocking out the white. Only someone as tall as her could reach it. In the darkness I couldn't make out her expression, but I could smell his sweat on her. I crouched against the wall. I couldn't bear her taunting, not now.

'Osmanna!' The whisper was more urgent this time. 'Osmanna, I know you're awake. Stand up where I can see you.'

'Won't there be time enough to mock me tomorrow?' I said bitterly. 'Why must you come tonight? I've no doubt you're going to watch me burn. That's what you've always wanted, isn't it, revenge on my family?'

'Osmanna, listen to me, I –'

'I've already heard you, Pega. Do you creep out to whore every night? Or did you find it amusing to do it outside my window and force me to listen? So you've had your fun, now for pity's sake, go and leave me alone.'

'Listen to me, you sour-faced little cat,' Pega snapped. 'No one from the beguinage can get near this place. Tutor Martha, the others, they tried. The only way I could do it was to fuck that bastard Phillip to get him off guard. You can't just walk up to a man and give him drugged wine. He'd have known something was up. There are ways of dealing with a man, which you'd know if you'd ever had to survive in the world for yourself, m'lady.'

'Am I supposed to be grateful that you sacrificed your virtue just to speak to me? It didn't sound much of an effort from here. Don't tell me they've sent you as my confessor?'

'Nobody sends me anywhere,' Pega retorted. 'I came 'cause I'd a mind to, though God alone knows why I bothered. You are the most stubborn, stuck-up vixen that ever drew breath. Anyone who offers you their hand in friendship gets their whole arm bitten off.'

'So why don't you go and leave me alone?'

''Cause I'm as stubborn as you are. I heard about the way you faced down old D'Acaster. Though how he ever came to spawn a salty brat like you is a mystery only your mam can answer. For all my talk, I'd not have the stomach to see this through, not to that end. You've the faith to equal any saint. I wish I'd a gill of it.'

'You couldn't be more wrong, Pega,' I said softly. 'It's not faith, it's hatred.'

'Is it now? Aye well, that I can understand. I've seen hatred drive many a man to face the kind of death that would make faith shrivel in its tracks. You hate your father so much then? It seems we've something in common after all.'

I rushed towards the window and tried to reach up to her. I wanted to touch her. I wanted to feel a warm human hand in mine. 'I'm scared, Pega, I am so frightened. You cannot begin to know how much. I can't face it ... haven't the strength ... help me, Pega, please help me!'

I tried not to cry, but the tears were forcing their way out. A rough hand pressed down on mine, solid and warm, as if Pega had the strength to pull me through the tiny space and out into freedom. I clung to her hand like a lost child, wanting her never to let me go, as if she could keep me from all the terrors of this life and the next.

'Pega,' I pleaded, 'give me something sharp, your knife or a piece of broken flagon, anything, so that I can kill myself before morning. I can't face the flames, Pega. I can't do it.'

'You think I came here to help you kill yourself? I've thieved, lied and fornicated for you this night, lass. You think I'm about to add murder to the list?'

'It wouldn't be murder if I did it. Pega. Please help me. Please, I beg you. Don't let them burn me, Pega, please.'

'Course I'm not going to let them burn you, lass. What do you think I'm here for? But we have to hurry. Your cousin's snoring away like an old boar now, but I don't want to be around when he wakes up. The pig'll have a head like a swarm of wasps when he does and serve the bastard right.'

'What are you going to do?'

'Get you out of here of course; what did you think I came for? The Commissarius kept the key himself, he'd not entrust it even to Phillip. So we'll have to take you out through the roof, lass. It's only thatch.'

'But I can't reach it.'

'No, but I can. They don't call me the Ulewic giant for nothing. I've a rope I can use to haul you up once I've made a hole. Someone must have been praying some pretty powerful prayers for you, lass, this sea fret is sent from heaven. It'll cover us while I work and our tracks while we make off.'

Her face disappeared from the window and I heard the sound of the reeds being torn away above my head. Gradually a bright white patch began to glimmer through the dark roof.

'But we can't go back to the beguinage, Pega. They'll come looking for me there and you too. Phillip's bound to tell them what you did.'

'Phillip'll never admit he let himself be tricked by a whore. But he'll come looking for me, make no mistake, and I've no intention of being around when he does. No, lass, you and I are going to have to disappear. Boat to France, then who knows where? I've a hankering to see more than this poxy village before I die. We might not make it, and if they catch us, we'll likely burn together. But they'll have to catch us first and we'll give them a run for their money. What say you, Osmanna, you willing to take a chance? You and me together, lass, I reckon with your learning and my brawn, together we could take on the world.'

January – St Vincent of Saragossa's Day

A Spanish martyr and the patron saint of drunkards, he refused to sacrifice to heathen gods and was roasted on a gridiron and left in the stocks to die. Six ancient English churches bear his name.

Pisspuddle

It was the highest tree I'd ever climbed. I could see for ever, right over Ulewic and the hills beyond it. I was balancing on the branch and I wasn't even holding on. I just had my hand pressed against rough bark above, but I wasn't gripping it, just resting my hand. I could walk that branch without holding on if I wanted, but I wasn't going to, not yet.

There'd be a fair next May Day, I knew there would be. The tumblers would come again and this time they'd take me. I'd be ready by then; if I practised all winter, when the spring came, I'd show them. I'd show everyone. I'd steal Father's big sharp knife and cut the webs between my fingers and then Ulewic would have to let me go, for I wouldn't belong here any more. With the tumblers I'd travel way beyond the hills to castles and towns bigger even than the forest. And one day we'd come back here to the fair. I'd be wearing a red and gold costume and William wouldn't even recognize me and I'd not speak to him.

I'd walk the whole length of the springy pole and when the two men holding it on their shoulders bounced it upwards, I'd somersault and land on it again, my fingers spread wide like flowers. Everyone would cheer, especially William; then I'd speak to him, but only so he'd know it was me.

I'd be rich then. Father would beg me to stay the night in the cottage and say that I could have all the best bits from the pot and tell William he'd have to sleep on the floor, but I'd not go. I'd be feasted at the Manor. Father and William would have to wait in the rain in the courtyard outside. If they were nice to me, I'd have a few scraps sent out to them from the table, but only if they were really nice, otherwise I wouldn't.

'Get down here, Pisspuddle!'

The sudden shout startled me. I slipped, grabbed for the

branch and hauled myself back up again. My knees stung like fire, skinned on the rough bark. It hurt. It was all William's stupid fault, bellowing like that. He made me slip. I hated him.

'I'll leave you here in the dark by yourself and the Owlman'll get you!' William bellowed.

'No, wait, I'm coming, William, don't go.'

I looked round, trying to find the quickest way down. I couldn't remember how I got up here.

'I'm going right now!'

Below me I could see him walking away from the tree.

'No, wait, wait. Look, the sea fret is coming in again. I can see it from here. Look, William, look!'

A thick grey mist was rolling across the fields, tumbling over itself, sliding along the ground, then rearing up again.

'This'd better not be one of your games.' William swung himself up into the tree and quickly reached the branch below me. He was good at climbing.

'Isn't, look there.'

The huge grey wall of fog drifted beyond the village. William sniffed the air and fetched me a clout across my head. I had to grab on tight with both hands to stop myself falling off.

'What did you do that for?'

'You wouldn't know it if your own arse was on fire. That's no fret, that's smoke, that is, you daft beggar.'

'What's afire?'

William shrugged, 'House of women, I reckon.'

'Are they burning the women too?'

'Lettice says they're gone,' William said, craning to get a better view. 'She said Father Ulfrid went out there and there wasn't a soul left. It was like they'd all vanished in the night.'

The girl they were going to burn was gone too. The door of the jail was still locked, but there was a big hole in the roof. Father Ulfrid said the Owlman had come in the night and torn the roof open with his talons. He ripped her heart out of her chest with his beak and ate it right in front of her while it was still beating. Then he carried her soul straight to hell in case she repented in the flames and Satan was cheated of her. Father Ulfrid said she was his greatest prize because she was so wicked, but I didn't believe she was wicked at all.

I was sorry they'd gone. Servant Martha hadn't got angry when I gave her the hair and the feather. She held them in her hands for a long time, staring at them, and then she said softly as if she was remembering something, *'He has freely given me my free will.* How easily we forget that we have chosen what we are and can choose what we will become.'

She looked at me then and gave a tiny sad smile. I'd never seen her smile before. 'Remember to choose, child.'

William whacked my leg. 'C'mon, we've to get going. It'll be dark soon. What did you have to climb up here for anyway, you daft beggar, you'll fall.'

He held my ankle and pushed my foot down safely on to the next branch, then the next, till I was down.

Mostly I hated William, but sometimes since Mam got taken and Father went strange, he looked out for me. Sometimes it felt like William was all I'd got left. It was just the two of us now. When the tumblers came in spring, maybe I'd take him with me. William didn't have a web. So we could run away together, far, far away, and nothing could ever pull us back to Ulewic. Maybe that's what we'd choose to do one day, very soon.

Epilogue

Smoke billowed up from the ruins of the beguinage. Only the buildings burned. They had been stripped of anything movable as soon as the women and their curse were gone from the village. Looted for valuables first by the Manor, as was their liege-right – even thieves know their place – then by the villagers gleaning for broken furniture, food, pots and out of sheer curiosity. The Manor found little worth the bother of their efforts save the livestock, wine and the stores of grain, but the villagers were always glad of any prize they could snatch from their neighbours, be it a straw pallet or a patched blanket. Tables and benches rejected as too rough and plain for the Manor were carried off on cart or foot. They were far too big to fit inside the cottages, but good wood was hard to come by and they could always be made into doors to keep out the cold, or hurdles to keep in the sheep. Even the dead got their dues, for a tabletop makes a serviceable bier.

The villagers stripped the beguinage to the bare bones, but in this world even bones have their scavengers, and finally the beggars were allowed their turn at the carcass. They all took something; even the slowest and feeblest cripple scuttled away with crocks and scraps, for the meanest rag is a fur robe to a naked man.

Too occupied with fighting for the spoils, no one so much as glanced at the two slender mounds in the dirt outside the chapel walls. One was almost grassed over now, invisible. The other, smaller strip was still bare. A small wooden trolley stood at the foot of the grave. A boy snatched it up; it would make a fine toy. The villagers trampled the tiny grave flat, not knowing or caring that the wasted body of a child lay just below their feet. It was only little Ella, that was all. But she had been loved. Ella and Gudrun, they had both once been loved, and love needs no cross to mark it.

Father Ulfrid hurried straight to the chapel. The green altar stone with its blood-red flecks, the chalice and the paten were all gone. Carefully wrapped in wool, they were safely stowed in the beguines' chests on the ship bound for Flanders. There was nothing left to show that women had ever served at this altar.

Father Ulfrid was not expecting to find anything of value, but even so he had convinced himself that the reliquary containing Andrew's Host would be there, waiting for him. The Commissarius had ordered the beguines to surrender it to the Church, and the Commissarius could not be disobeyed for he held the keys of hell in the next world and in this.

But the reliquary was not standing on the altar where Father Ulfrid expected it to be. Unable to bring himself to accept that his last hope of salvation had vanished, he spent a long and fruitless time turning the chapel upside down inch by inch, even brushing the rushes aside to see if there were any signs of it having been buried in the ground. White with frustration, he scoured the walls of the chapel, trying to see if there was any loose stone or niche that he had overlooked. But at last he had to admit that the miraculous Host was gone.

He glared up at the walls, choking with rage. He had been so desperate to find the reliquary that he had barely glanced at the wall paintings, but now he saw them. The paintings were finished at last. The serene eyes of the dying beguine looked down on him, her triumphant smile undisturbed by his rage. Her long hair flowed from under her invalid's cap, bright and shining as if she was a girl again, and the Son of God Himself held out a hand from heaven towards her, a bridegroom welcoming His bride. Every muscle and bone in the priest's body were so racked with hatred that he felt as if his sinews were tearing themselves apart. He snatched the knife from his belt and gouged into the plaster, chipping and scratching away at that painted face like a cornered rat.

'Whore! Heretic! Blasphemer! Cunt!'

He tore at the body like a torturer with a flesh rake, obliterating breasts, loins and hands until only a space remained, a hollow outline of an empty woman.

As he spun away, he stumbled hard against the stone altar. A small, dark red stain, the size and shape of a holy wafer, marred the whiteness of the stone; for a moment Father Ulfrid thought that it was his own blood. Without thinking, he reached out to wipe it away, but as his palm touched the red stain, he yelped in surprise, clamping his stinging hand under his armpit. He examined his palm. A burning, livid red sore was etched deep into it, as if an iron nail had been driven right through it. Aghast, he stared at the wound, then he fled from the chapel, leaving only the Virgin staring sadly down.

Outside, the Owl Masters were waiting, blazing torches at the ready. Dry straw and rags had been dipped in tallow and stuffed under eaves and in the crevices. Piles of dry rushes had been heaped inside the open doorways.

'Do we burn the chapel too?' they asked Father Ulfrid. Even they would not presume as much without the voice of God to give authority.

'Burn the viper's nest out, burn every stinking stick of it. There will not be a stone left standing to remind anyone that this foul abomination ever existed.'

It burned and was burning still. But there was something that escaped the burning. It lay outside the gate, half hidden in a patch of weeds, its wrappings crumpled up nearby. A villager had snatched up the bundle, not troubling to find out what it was, and then discarded it as soon as he'd unwrapped it. It was a battered thing, bound in calves' leather, a book, just an old book. Tomorrow it would be picked up by a pedlar, a camelot with a badly scarred face, on his way to a fair in a distant town. It might not fetch much, but the camelot was learning that anything was a profit on nothing and someone, somewhere would even buy an old book, if he spun them a good enough tale.

High up on the hill above the burning beguinage, a woman squatted on the bank of the river by old Gwenith's tumbledown cottage. She could smell the smoke and if she had looked, she would have seen the distant lick of flames climbing into the darkening sky. But she did not raise her head.

The woman's clothes were sodden and so caked with mud, you could scarcely see the grey of her kirtle beneath the dirt. Mud streaked her face and hands, but she wasn't aware of that, nor of the way her hair tumbled loose down her back. She had discarded her grey cloak even though the air had grown icy. She no longer felt the cold. Her hands were too busy. She was too joyful.

First she had fashioned a mound of mud and dirt, long and narrow like a heap of soil over a new grave. Then she'd begun to shape it, dimpled legs and a fat little body, a softly curved belly, chubby arms and a beautiful smooth head. She put bright shining river stones on the tiny face for eyes and gave it water-weed for hair and a smooth silky pebble for a sleeping mouth. She bent to kiss the cold lips and smiled.

Then she began to make another mound. One by one she raised the graves from the earth; again and again she pulled from them her own mud babies. They lay all around her cradled in the moss, three, four, five of them, and still she worked, making more graves and more babies. Light was fading so fast that she couldn't see their faces any more, but it didn't matter for she could feel their skins, soft and moist and slippery as a newborn. She gently squeezed their chubby limbs and stroked their damp hair. They were sleeping. They didn't cry, because they were glad to have her as their mother.

A great black bird fluttered on to the ragged roof of the cottage. It stared down at the woman, its head on one side. The harsh caw made her look up. Someone was standing in the door-way of the cottage. In the darkness she could just make out the faintest shimmer of pale bare limbs and flame-red hair. The woman smiled.

'There you are at last, my little Gudrun, where have you been? I've been searching for you everywhere.'

She'd known all along that the body they pulled out of the

pond wasn't her Gudrun dead. She knew her daughter would come home to her. Beatrice knelt on the ground and swept out her arms over the graves and the babies. They had all come back to her. And they would never leave her again.

The sun was almost gone now. Only a sliver of red rind still showed above the hills and darkness crowded hard upon its heels. A gangling lad with straw-coloured hair and a dark-haired little girl stumbled homeward from the forest, dragging bundles of dead wood behind them by ropes looped across their shoulders. The girl trailed behind, wailing to her brother to wait for her. He pretended not to hear, but every now and then he slowed down, not enough for her to fully catch up with him, for he didn't like to be seen walking with her, but just enough to close the distance between them.

Their hooks were tied to the bundles of the dry kindling twigs they carried on their backs. The boy's sling was ready in his hand just in case a complacent bird or hare should amble across his path. Their grubby cheeks were flushed with exertion.

The little girl glanced fearfully over her shoulder. Imagine if the Owlman chased you whilst you were so weighted down, the wood dragging you back so you couldn't run. Imagine feeling the breath of his wings at your back, hearing the snap of his beak. The darkness gathered about her and every bush along the path took on an animate form, a cut-throat with a murderous knife, Black Anu with her long talons, the faerie birch with white fingers long enough to strangle the throat of such a very small girl. In the forest a vixen screamed and both children started like rabbits. They should not have left it so late. The boy knew it was his fault, but he cuffed his little sister to make her hurry and to hide his own fear.

A hollow tapping, like fingers on a coffin lid, echoed through the gloom. The children stopped dead. It was coming towards them. In the witch-light you could just make out a shape, like a man, but not a man, wings dragging on the ground, hopping like some great bird. The little girl struggled to free herself from the tangle of wood and rope that was pinning her down between the forest and the nameless thing. Her brother clapped a sweaty hand across her squealing mouth and dragged her off the path.

The melancholy knell of the leper's clapper drew nearer. Now they could just make out a figure limping towards them on crutches. One knee was bent under him, resting on a stick to keep the weight from his foot. A leper's cloak was pulled down over his face and flapped behind him. He passed the children crouched in the bushes, but made no sign that he had seen them.

The leper saw much, but registered nothing any more. His mind was as numb as the stumps of his feet. He didn't even turn his head as the boy fired stones from his sling at his sticks, jeering and boasting to his sister that he could knock the old crow off his perch. It was the boy's revenge on the leper for making him hide as if he was scared, which, of course, he wasn't, not for a moment.

The stones struck Ralph's back, leaving small dark bruises, but he was almost grateful for the sting. He could at least feel that. He didn't know where he was going, but he would hobble through the night and the next day and the next until he dropped from exhaustion, and even that would not be far enough away from this accursed village. For he knew the smell of the burning would cling to him like a drunken whore until they tumbled into the grave together. Ralph was not afraid of the dark, or the wolves or the Owlman. What could any of them do to him now that would not be a blessing?

Behind him, the little village of Ulewic hunkered down for the night, wrapping itself in the ragged smoke of a hundred hearth fires. The ditches and middens farted their noxious odours into the night air, but the village was comforted by the smell. It was the smell of its own fart after all. It shuffled down into the damp earth and its wooden bones creaked. Under the cover of darkness, bedbugs crawled out to feed on its frowsty flesh and the rats fought for its shit. Ulewic moaned a little in its sleep, that's all, scratched, but otherwise it did not stir. It was complacent, senile, old, tired enough to sleep for a thousand years, and why not? Those troublesome women had gone and would not come again.

With outstretched wings the barn owl, silent and pale as a dead child, flapped slowly across Ralph's path and he lifted his head. The winged cat from the threshing barn was seeking a new home. He turned his face away. Better not to think, not to feel, not to remember. He slammed his crutch against his foot as if to reassure himself his body at least was dead. Fiercely, he dragged himself on, then turned, suddenly desperate for one last look at her, but the owl had vanished.

Historical Notes

In the first half of the fourteenth century, Europe was experiencing a period of change and unrest remarkably similar to the present day. There were significant and rapid climatic changes resulting in widespread droughts, flooding and crop failure. The changes were so noticeable and drastic that the Pope ordered special prayers to be said in every church five times a day.

The fertility of both animals and humans had fallen markedly and people and livestock were becoming prey to new diseases sweeping the countryside, which created a climate of fear and suspicion. Lay people began to ignore ecclesiastical authorities, even on some occasions throwing priests out of their own churches and engaging in bizarre cults. Despite the terrible punishments meted out for crimes, general lawlessness, especially among young male gangs, was widespread.

Against this background a remarkable movement emerged in Europe that became known as the Beguinage Communities. Thousands of women who did not want to marry or take the veil began to set themselves up in female collectives. The women farmed and supported themselves through the practice of different crafts, particularly weaving. They traded, established hospitals, educated girls and wrote many books. They preached openly on the streets, translated the Bible into the local vernacular, long before this was officially done by the Church, and when they were excommunicated, these Catholic women took on the priestly role of administering the sacraments to one another and to others who were barred by the Church. They took no vows except that of celibacy for as long as they chose to stay within the beguinage, and they were free to leave whenever they wished. A number of the hospitals and schools which were founded by beguines in the Middle Ages still flourish in the cities of Northern Europe today.

Beguines often broke the power of local male guilds by deliberately undercutting them through their ability to trade via the network of beguinages. Some beguinages were protected by powerful and wealthy patrons, but many beguines encountered violent opposition from Church and society. Beguinages were attacked, their books were burned and the beguines were arrested on charges of heresy and gross immorality.

A number of beguines were charged with the 'Heresy of the Free Spirit', a doctrine similar to that held by Quakers today, which declared that the physical sacraments were not necessary to Christian practice or salvation, and that Christians did not need the mediation of priests. A number of beguines were burned at the stake for this belief, including Marguerite Porete, author of *The Mirror of Simple Souls*, who, in 1310, was executed for heresy in Paris.

The beguinage in Bruges, known as the Vineyard, was founded in 1245 by the Countess of Flanders, Margareta of Constantinople. Despite attempts by both Church and Reformation to destroy it, it remained a beguinage until 1927, when it was taken over by Benedictine nuns. Though many of the houses and the gateway have been rebuilt over the years, it is still one of the most peaceful and enchanting corners of Bruges. It is now a UNESCO World Heritage site and visitors who pass over the bridge and under the word *Sauvegarde* may freely wander around its beautiful and timeless cobbled lanes.

Beguinages flourished for several centuries in Europe, especially in Belgium, Netherlands, France and Germany, but for years historians claimed that there were never any beguinages in Britain, although many women from England went to join beguinages in France and Belgium. But recent research has revealed a number of tantalizing hints that attempts were made to set them up in England during the Middle Ages, although they quickly disappeared within a few years for reasons which so far have not come to light. This novel is, of course, a fictional portrayal of an attempt to found one such beguinage on English soil.

Flanders was at this period ruled by the Counts of Flanders. By 1256 Bruges had already secured the English cloth monopoly, growing prosperous on the cloth it made from English wool, so much so that the city had gained an almost unique autonomy to govern its own affairs. Mathew of Westminster wrote, 'All the nations of the world are kept warm by the wool of England made into cloth by the men of Flanders.'

The Counts of Flanders were pledged to the French King, but the powerful Flemish Guilds supported the English throne in order to maintain their supplies of wool, and at the end of the thirteenth century they invited Edward I of England to send an army to help them repel the French. Ties between Flanders and England were further strengthened by Edward III, who lived in Ghent, where his fourth son, John of Gaunt, was born in 1340. John of Gaunt's son became Henry IV of England. Throughout the thirteenth and fourteenth centuries trade between the east coast of England and Flanders was so strong that it would appear that more goods and people travelled to and from Norfolk and Flanders than between Norfolk and London.

There were a number of famines which affected England from 1290 onwards due to the changing weather conditions. The year 1321–2 was particularly bad in the east of England where extreme suffering was caused by failed grain harvests, yields falling by as much as 60 per cent. This was compounded by flooding as well as an outbreak of liverfluke in sheep and cattle murrain.

The 1321 outbreak of cattle murrain was believed to have been Anthrax, of which there are three methods of infection. The most common is Cutaneous Anthrax, which enters through cuts or abrasions on the skin, resulting in painless ulcers with a black necrotic centre. This spoils hides, but is rarely lethal. Inhalation Anthrax, where the spores enter the lungs, results in a flu-like illness with severe breathing difficulties and was, in those days, often fatal. The third method of infection is Intestinal Anthrax, which the child Oliver dies from in the novel. It was contracted by eating infected meat, causing severe inflammation of the intestinal tract with bleeding and usually resulted in rapid death.

From the thirteenth century, even in official documents, people did not use numbers for dates. Instead, they referred to the nearest Saint's Day or festival to date documents or events.

Throughout the Middle Ages the old Julian calendar was in use in Britain and Europe. In 1582 Europe adopted the Gregorian calendar, but Britain, hostile to Rome, refused to follow suit until 1752. As had happened in Europe two centuries before, when Britain switched to the Gregorian calendar there were riots in the streets because the calendar suddenly jumped eleven days forward and people thought their lives had been shortened by eleven days. We now run approximately thirteen days ahead of the old medieval calendar, which means that fixed events such as the equinoxes and the longest and shortest days fall on different dates to those they would have done in the Middle Ages.

Although in Roman times Julius Caesar had officially moved New Year to 1 January, many places on the fringes of the Roman Empire still kept to the old practice of celebrating New Year from 25 March to 1 April. In England during the Middle Ages, the years continued to be numbered from 25 March (the Incarnation of Jesus) and not from 1 January.

Ulewic, which in Old English means *the place of the owl*, is a fictional village, but is based on villages found on the coast of West Norfolk. Many of these villages became depopulated and eventually abandoned over the centuries from the time of the Black Death onwards.

Churches and chapels dedicated to the Archangel St Michael

were often erected on former sacred Celtic sites where the gods of air and earth met. Such sites were also said to be the entrance to the underworld, which is perhaps why old churches with the name of St Michael have frequently been associated with both black magic and the disappearance of bodies from graves.

The old woman with the gaping vulva carved above the church door is typical of what in recent years have come to be known as a *Sheela Na Gig*. These are found on medieval churches all over Britain, although most villages have their own local names for the carving. In style, the Sheelas are unlike any of the other medieval grotesques carved on these churches.

Some people argue the origin of these carvings is pagan and that the figure represents a much older Celtic goddess which was later incorporated into the Christian building. Others claim they date from between the eleventh and twelfth centuries and are purely Christian in origin, put there as a warning against lust. The problem with this theory is that many of the figures are hidden on church roofs or places where the ordinary populace would be unable to see the warning. And although some of these carvings may have been moved in later centuries, when the church was altered or repaired, it doesn't account for all of these hidden carvings.

Black Anu or Black Annis stories are to be found all over England and Ireland. Anu was originally the 'mother' form of the triple Celtic goddess, but like Lilith, as Christianity spread, she was transformed into a monster who was said to snatch and eat children. Black Annis is still remembered in the Dane Hills near Leicester where she was said to inhabit a cave called Black Anna's Bower which is supposed be connected by a series of tunnels to Leicester Castle. Black Annis would scuttle back to her lair through these tunnels after prowling the town at night. Black Anna's Bower has since been destroyed in building work, but the tale lives on. Her name also survives in many landmarks across Britain, such as Black Anne Pool in the River Erne in Devon.

Right across Europe, the owl was in ancient times sacred to

the goddesses symbolizing wisdom, and many of the Celtic and tribal goddesses had the power to change themselves into owls; for this reason the owl was never harmed. But when the goddesses themselves were demonized by Christianity, so was their symbol the owl, which became hunted and persecuted as an evil omen, a harbinger of death.

The Owlman was a familiar monster of the Middle Ages, part of the pantheon of strange and dangerous beasts such as the griffin, which had the wings of an eagle and the body of a lion. Like the Basilisk, the Owlman was believed to inhabit old church towers.

But unlike the other medieval monsters which have been consigned to ancient myth, the Owlman lives on in the human psyche. In 1995, an American student of marine biology wrote to a newspaper saying that she had witnessed a 'vision from hell' near the church in Mawnan, Cornwall, England. 'It was the size of a man, with a ghastly face, a wide mouth, glowing eyes and pointed ears. It had huge clawed wings and was covered in feathers of silver-grey. The thing had long bird legs which terminated in black claws.'

This was not the first sighting in Cornwall, for in April 1976, two young girls staying on holiday with their family ran screaming to their father claiming they had seen a gigantic feathered bird-man hovering over the church tower. The Owlman was also seen in July of that year by two girls camping in the woods near Mawnan church and in a separate incident by three young French girls who reported their terrifying ordeal to their seaside landlady. The Owlman put in another appearance two years later when he was seen by a young woman, and was eventually seen by a man. However such sightings are explained – hoax, adolescent fantasy, too much cider or a trick of the light – such reports demonstrate that we today are not so very different from our medieval ancestors for we share with them the same lusts, ambitions and hopes. And, like them, we are still afraid of the dark.

Glossary

Bid – The old name for a 'familiar', that is, an animal or bird with magical powers kept to do the bidding of its owner. Women who owned a cat or even a chicken were often accused of having a *bid*, a sign of witchcraft, an association which has given rise to the derogatory term for elderly women – *biddie*.

Black bane – The deadly disease Anthrax. It was named Black bane because the sores on the animal or human skin develop a black necrotic centre.

Bough cake – A long stick was threaded with a mixture of dried fruits such as apricots, apples and plums. The fruit was coated in batter and spit-roasted over an open fire. More batter was spooned over the fruits as they cooked until they were covered in a thick layer. Once cooked, the bough cake was rolled in honey and spices before being served.

Bull oak – An ancient hollow oak tree. There were several names for different shapes of hollow oaks. A bull oak was one with a hollow reaching to the ground which was large enough for sheep or pigs or even bulls to take shelter in.

Commissarius – Within the Church, he was a man who was personally commissioned by a Bishop to exercise spiritual authority within the Bishop's diocese or see. The Commissarius could preside as a judge in court on behalf of the Bishop.

Demon star – Also known as Lilith's star or Algol, it is in the constellation Perseus. It was considered the most dangerous star in the heavens, bringing evil and death, for it seems to wink like a great eye. A girl born under its astrological influence was said to bring a curse upon her family and any man she married. The star appears to wane in brightness over four and a half hours, remaining dim for twenty minutes, then increases to its original intensity for sixty-nine hours. We now know this is caused by a dimmer star eclipsing a brighter one.

Drindle – East Anglian dialect word for a trickle of water or tiny stream.

Green sickness – Serious, often fatal, anaemia caused by what today would be labelled *Anorexia nervosa*. Common in the Middle Ages among pious teenagers and 'saints' who regularly starved themselves to mortify the flesh.

Harrow – In some places, the name derives from *Hearg*, which is Old English for a pagan site of worship.

Henbane – Botanical name, *Hyoscyamus niger*. 'The seed that breadth madness.' Known since AD 1000, the leaves, which are the most poisonous part, can cause giddiness, restlessness, hallucinations and, if ingested, death. It was used widely in medieval medicine, when the seeds were heated over charcoal and the fumes inhaled as an effective painkiller or anaesthetic.

Jack-in-the-green/Devil's prick – Botanical name, *Arum maculatum*. Also known as Lords and Ladies, because of its resemblance to male and female genitalia. This poisonous herb had many medicinal uses in the Middle Ages including inducing menstruation. It was also used by young men as a love charm. It was said to have grown at the foot of the cross where drops of Christ's blood fell on it, marking it from that time onwards.

Ka – A cry of affirmation, meaning 'so may it be', traditionally used in the Norfolk and Suffolk region to seal a spell.

Mould – When the high spring and autumn tides wash over a beach they leave behind salt water which is dried by sun and wind, forming a salty crust in the top layer of sand or silt. This layer is known as *mould*. In the Middle Ages the mould was scraped off by the salt-makers. It was then washed and filtered to extract the salt in the form of brine. This was the first step in the salt-making process. (See also *Weller*.)

Need-flame – On Samhain Night, what we now call Halloween, all fires in the village had to be extinguished and relit from a *need* or *neid* fire, that is, one that had been kindled by friction, usually by striking a flint. This was to drive away evil and encourage the sun to return. In some areas people made their own need-fires, in others a communal fire was lit, with every householder collecting a need-flame from the fire to kindle their own hearth fires. Where a communal need-fire was lit, debts or disputes had to be settled before the householder was allowed to take a flame from the fire.

Ordeal by water – Under King Athelstan (925–39) and later, Edward the Confessor (1042–66), trial by water (*iudicium aquae*) was enshrined in law as one of the tests of guilt or innocence for all crimes. The suspect was bound hand and foot, then thrown into water. If they sank, they were innocent. If they floated, they were guilty. This was based on the belief that water was used for baptism, therefore water would not receive anyone who was guilty and refused to confess it. Ordeal by water was officially abolished in 1219, under Henry III, but its use continued unofficially for many centuries, increasingly being reserved for those suspected of witchcraft.

Purefinding – Collecting dog dung to sell to leather tanners. Dog excrement was vital to purify skins and hides by breaking down the collagenous proteins prior to curing and tanning. Treating the skins with dog excrement was called *puering*. Dog dung was therefore a valuable commodity in the Middle Ages, with white dung being the most highly prized.

Reckling (Also written as *recklin*) – Lincolnshire and East Anglian dialect word for the smallest pig in the litter. A runt. Often applied to a weak and sickly child.

Rough music – Sometimes know as ran-tanning, it was a way of expressing social disapproval of such things as adultery or wife-beating. Neighbours would gather outside a wrongdoer's house for three successive nights, banging metal objects. If by the third night the victim hadn't taken the hint and left the neighbourhood, they would be dragged out of their home and beaten. It was erroneously believed that if a 'ran-tanning' was in progress and the victim was badly injured or died as a result of the beating, the assailants could not be punished by law. This custom, often used on those thought to be engaged in sexual immorality, continued well into the nineteenth century all over Britain and in one sense still continues today when local people surround houses of suspected paedophiles to try to force them out.

Soul-scot – As well as each household having to give tithes, a percentage of livestock, grain, candles, etc., to the Church on pain of minor excommunication, the Church also demanded scots, or sums of money to perform certain rites such as christenings and marriages, including a soul-scot, money paid to the priest to perform the burial rites, in addition to money which also had to be paid for a Mass to be said for the soul of the deceased. This scot was enshrined in law by King Alfred, AD 871–901, and was hated by the poor who saw it as a tax on death.

Toadsman – An East Anglian term for a horse whisperer. A man could gain extraordinary powers over horses, pigs and people, by killing a Natterjack toad and carrying the corpse against his chest until it rotted to bones. The bones were floated in a river at midnight. The bone which floated upstream was magic, and the person who took hold of it would be pulled across the river by it, after which they would possess the power.

Weller – Along the East Coast a common method of producing salt in the Middle Ages was by sand and silt washing. The brine washed from the sand would be boiled in lead pans over peat fires. This was done by the wellers, who had the most difficult job in the salt-making process. Brine contains six different salts, each crystallizing out at a different rate. Only the third, *sodium chloride*, was the one used for preservation and flavouring, so the weller had to be adept at collecting this particular salt at precisely the right time without it becoming contaminated by the others. The remaining salts, collectively known as the bittern, were usually discarded.